C. Dale Brittain

MAGE QUEST

A Baen Books Original

Baen Publishing Enterprises
P.O. Box 1403
Riverdale, NY 10471

ISBN: 0-671-72169-0

Cover art by Laurence Schwinger

Map by Eleanor Kostyk, from a sketch by the author

First Printing, May 1993

Distributed by Simon & Schuster
1230 Avenue of the Americas
New York, NY 10020

"WIZARD! TURN HIM INTO A FROG!"

"Wizard, could you release the bindings enough so that they can drink?"

I adjusted my spell to allow the bandits a little arm motion. The king put tin cups of scalding tea into their hands. They drank slowly, looking at us thoughtfully over the rims. In the lantern light and the beginning of dawn, they would have seen two white-bearded men, one very slightly built.

The leader of the bandits looked at King Haimeric shrewdly. "So you didn't find it either, eh?"

I had no idea what he was talking about and I doubted the king did either, but that didn't stop him. "Of course not. You seem to imagine that we ransacked the silk caravan after my wizard paralyzed you, but instead we sent it safely on its way. If you're looking for caravan loot, you won't find it in our camp. Do you employ a wizard?"

I was having trouble keeping up with the king's line of reasoning, and from the looks on their faces, so were the bandits.

"No," said the leader, eyeing me warily.

"I asked if you had a wizard," said King Haimeric, pulling his eyebrows into a frown, "because I wanted to be sure you understand the lesson that we will teach *you* if you follow us again. My own wizard will turn you all into frogs."

It had been ten years since the disastrous transformations practical and I had long since worked out where I had gone wrong with those frogs. I watched the king's face, knowing he was going to expect some spectacular display of magic at any moment.

"Don't pay any attention to him," said one of the bandits to the leader. "He's just bluffing."

That made it all very simple. I turned that one into a frog.

Baen Books By C. Dale Brittain

A Bad Spell in Yurt
The Wood Nymph and the Cranky Saint
Mage Quest

DEDICATION

To Bob, with thanks for all the story conferences

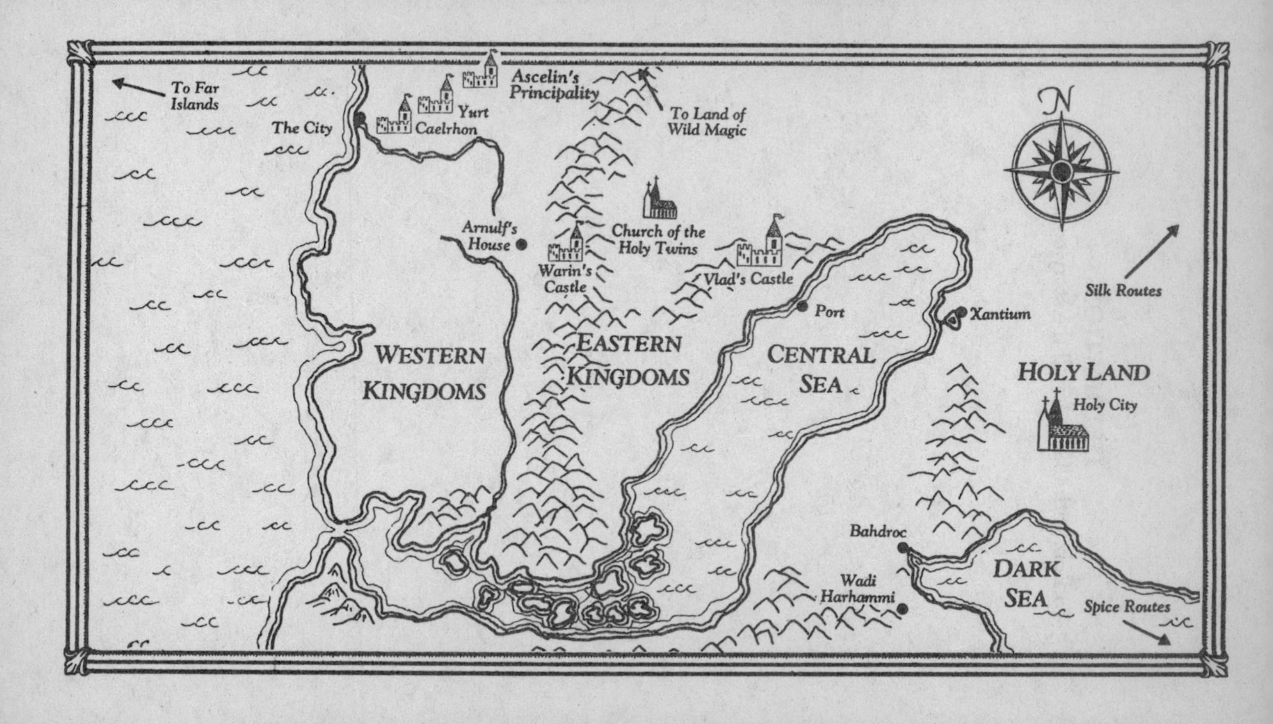
To Far Islands
The City
Caelrhon
Yurt
Ascelin's Principality
To Land of Wild Magic
N
Arnulf's House
Warin's Castle
Church of the Holy Twins
Vlad's Castle
Port
Xantium
Silk Routes
WESTERN KINGDOMS
EASTERN KINGDOMS
CENTRAL SEA
HOLY LAND
Holy City
Bahdroc
Wadi Harhammi
DARK SEA
Spice Routes

CONTENTS

PART ONE

Quest

1

Christmas was over, and everyone was grumpy — that is, everyone except the king.

King Haimeric of Yurt came back inside the castle from the courtyard. He had been seeing off the king and queen of the neighboring kingdom who, with their family, had spent Christmas with us. King Haimeric had a faint smile on his lips and a faraway look in his eyes, as though seeing well beyond the stone walls of the great hall. I noted irritably that many of the pine boughs hung on those walls had started losing their needles.

"Wizard!" he called to me as he settled himself on his throne before the roaring fire and arranged his lap robe. "I've just heard something wonderful."

I pulled up a chair to sit next to him. The royal castle of Yurt had once been a defensible castle, a center of wars, but for the last several generations the Christmas festivities were about as exciting as we got. Even the time we were all attacked by a dragon, just as we finished opening the presents, had been nine years ago. I really had eaten too much this last week or two, and the weather had been bad enough that none of us had gotten much exercise beyond walking to and from meals.

"So what have you heard?" I asked the king, feeling dull but trying my best to sound interested.

"The king of Caelrhon was just telling me very exciting news: someone has developed a blue rose!"

It was going to be even harder to sound interested than I thought. "But I can create a blue rose for you with magic any time you like. I haven't practiced wizardry on your rose garden in the past because I assumed you liked doing the crosses yourself, but a new color shouldn't be hard."

I hesitated inwardly even while I spoke. An illusory blue rose would certainly be easy enough, but the color would shortly fade. I didn't know offhand a spell to change something's color permanently, much less to pass that color on to the next generation of roses, but I might be able to improvise something.

"Not a magical blue rose," said the king with a wave of his hand, "but a real one."

I considered saying that, always assuming I could do the spells correctly, the color on my blue rose would be as "real" as the color on this rose he had heard about. But I hated to argue with my king. "I've never seen a blue rose," I said instead. It appeared I would be hearing quite a bit whether I wanted to or not and I might as well be agreeable about it. "Some of your deep red varieties shade into violet, but that's not very close."

"That's right," said King Haimeric, then fell silent, staring into the fire.

I went into a reverie of my own. Maybe I wouldn't have to hear about this rose after all. At Christmas one was supposed to feel congeniality and love for one's fellow man, but I was instead having to fight against feeling dissatisfied with life in such a quiet little kingdom. I was just wondering if there were any Christmas cookies left and, if so, if they had all become stale, when the king startled me so much that I forgot all about being grumpy.

"I'm an old man and I've never been on a quest," he said. "I think it's about time."

I was not an old man, in spite of the white beard which I kept hoping, against all evidence, gave me an air of wizardly wisdom. But I had never been on a quest, either. Perversely, when I had just been thinking Yurt was too dull, going away from it suddenly seemed too adventurous. The thought of leaving the royal castle, where we were comfortable and safe from the sleet, and starting off on some unknown but doubtless highly dangerous journey filled me with horror.

But the king said nothing more about a quest, and in the following weeks I decided it was just a momentary whim brought on by the mention of the blue rose. But the idea kept nagging at the back of my mind. In the nearly ten years I had been Royal Wizard of Yurt, King Haimeric had never been gone from the kingdom for more than a month or so at a time and, for that matter, neither had I.

I loved Yurt, but sometimes, unexpectedly, when sitting down to dinner with the same people I had sat down to dinner with for ten years or looking out across a snowy landscape, a vision came to me unbidden. Sometimes it was a complicated vision of exciting experiences and adventures never met at home, but usually it was just a scene: riotous red flowers spreading their blooms beneath an intense sun; a bazaar where bright colors, foreign voices, and complex spicy odors competed for attention; and palm trees swaying by an azure summer sea.

If the king was thinking of going on a quest, then the most horrifying thought was that he might go without me.

King Haimeric spent January as he usually spent January. His eyeglasses perched on his nose, he went through the rose catalogs that were shipped from the great City, studying the sketches of newly developed varieties and the extravagant descriptions of their colors and scents. Haimeric loved his rose garden second only to the queen and their son — and probably the kingdom of Yurt itself — and I suspected his own new varieties were superior to anything the

City growers could produce. But that had never kept him from studying the catalogs assiduously all winter or from sending off orders for new rootstocks as soon as the cold weather began to break.

"Now this horse," said Prince Paul.

I had been thinking about the king and his roses while standing in the stables, but the boy's voice brought me back quickly from my thoughts.

"All right," I said. "But remember not to kick or swing your feet. This gelding's bigger than the mares, and you don't want to startle it."

It was warm and dusty in the stables, and the snow falling outside seemed very far away. I lifted the royal heir slowly straight up with magic, then sideways over the wooden gate of the stall. He stretched out his legs, remembering not to kick, as I set him down on the gelding's broad back. The horse turned its head in some surprise to stare at him, but Paul stroked its mane and spoke soothingly. At age eight, the boy was already better with horses than I had ever been.

"Ready?" I said, then lifted him slowly up again, over the gate, and back beside me.

Paul grinned at me and I grinned back, with the schoolboy feeling of getting away with something naughty. Paul was perfectly safe, I knew, and would not fall off even the biggest horse as long as my magic held him, but I was still fairly sure that, if asked, the queen would not have approved.

"Now this horse," said Paul.

"Wait a minute," I said. "We're not going to proceed through the entire stable, putting you on the back of every horse in Yurt."

"Well, you did agree, Wizard," he said, looking at me with calculating green eyes, "that riding my pony wasn't going to prepare me for bigger horses."

"That still doesn't mean I'm going to lift you onto every horse here. Choose one more, then we'd better stop."

Paul walked down the row of stalls, considering. Gwennie, who had observed him silently so far, went after him.

They came back together. "The chestnut stallion at the far end," said Paul. "Then I promise not to ask any more."

"But that's your cousin Dominic's stallion. It's the biggest horse we have."

"I know," said Paul. "That's why I chose him. You promised!" he added when I hesitated.

Prince Dominic, I was quite sure, would not approve of his young cousin sitting, even for a minute and even if very quietly, on his favorite stallion. But if I was willing to go along with Paul's game in spite of what the queen might think, I was certainly not going to worry about Dominic.

"All right," I said. "But this really is the last one."

Paul, Gwennie, and I went down to the far end of the stables. Several cats came to rub against our ankles, and Gwennie picked up and stroked a kitten. Dominic's stallion gave us what I would have called a surly look, but when I lifted Paul up onto his back he made no movement, though the skin twitched all along his neck and side. The stables were very quiet with the only sound that of tearing hay as the horse in the adjoining stall pulled off a mouthful.

"Now me," said Gwennie.

"You want to get on the stallion, too?" I asked in surprise. Gwennie, the castle cook's daughter, was almost exactly the same age as Paul and would tag after him all day if her mother let her, but she had always seemed nervous around horses.

"Put her up behind me," said Paul. "We can pretend we're galloping across the high plains, trying to get there in time to win the treasure."

I hadn't heard the story of the treasure of the high plains before, but Paul was always coming up with something new. "Just be sure you sit very still while pretending," I said.

For a moment, I left Paul to stay on the stallion's back by himself and turned my magic to the girl. She was white-faced and sober, but when I hesitated, she said, "Come on!" as imperiously as the royal heir. I lifted her slowly and gradually, using the words of the Hidden Language to guide her over the stall gate and onto the stallion's broad back. I set her down with her legs sticking straight out and her face whiter than ever.

The horse shifted uneasily, feeling the sudden increase in weight. Paul kept his balance without even thinking about it. Gwennie took a firm grip around his waist.

"Don't be so frightened," said Paul, not unkindly. "Now, we have to make it to the fortress by sunset or it will be too late. The sun is setting fast! Come on, Whirlwind!"

This was not in fact the stallion's name. I wasn't even sure Prince Dominic had given it a name. Paul, riding across the high plains on Whirlwind, at least had the sense not to dig in his heels.

But Gwennie, wanting to show Paul she was not frightened, suddenly kicked the stallion in both flanks and let out a high whoop.

Dominic's stallion jerked hard against his headrope, trying to rear. When the rope held him down, he lashed out with his heels against the wall. The wall gave a hollow boom, and the stallion kicked again.

Even Paul looked frightened. I held the children tight with magic and lifted them together as rapidly as I dared without further startling the stallion. In a few seconds, they were out of the stall and back beside me.

I started to say something, to warn Gwennie that it was not a good idea to kick a high-strung stallion bred to carry someone who weighed well over two hundred pounds. But I looked at her face and realized any warning of my own would be superfluous.

"We can continue the story of the treasure of the high plains up in the nursery," Paul told her. His own color had come back almost immediately, but I was pleased that he showed no signs of wanting to continue the story on a horse's back — at least, not yet.

The children were starting toward the stable door hand in hand, and I was trying to decide if the stallion, who had stopped kicking and merely gave me another surly look, was indeed all right, when the outer door opened, letting in daylight, a whirl of snowy air, and the constable.

Paul and Gwennie darted out, Paul giving me a conspiratorial grin over his shoulder.

"There you are, Wizard," said the constable. "The queen said you were with Prince Paul. I should have known you'd all be in here with his pony."

We had, in fact, barely looked at Paul's shaggy little pony while in the stables. "What is it?"

"You have a telephone call."

II

A wizard looked at me from the base of the magic glass telephone. The call was from Zahlfast, the head of the transformations faculty at the wizards' school in the great City. Even the tiny image of his face looked both irritated and worried.

"Have you heard from Evrard?" he asked without preamble.

"Evrard?" I said in surprise. "I haven't talked to him in, what would it be, a year now. He was leaving on a trip."

"Well," said Zahlfast, "he hasn't been in touch with the wizards' school since he left, so I'd hoped you might know where he was."

Now that I thought about it, it was somewhat strange that I hadn't heard from Evrard in so long. Nearly eight years ago, he had briefly served as wizard to the duchess of Yurt and, although he had soon returned to the City, we had always stayed in at least intermittent contact. "I would have thought he'd be back months ago," I said.

"So would I," said Zahlfast. "A wizard can normally take care of himself, but on a long trip to distant lands anything can happen."

I had always been closer to Zahlfast than to any of my other former teachers at the wizards' school, in spite of all that embarrassment with the frogs in his transformations practical exam. If he was worried, it was with good reason.

"Evrard told us before he left that he'd try to keep in touch with Yurt. He's been serving as wizard for, who is it, your king's cousin?"

"My queen's uncle," I corrected. "Sir Hugo." I paused then, trying to remember if the City nobleman in whose elegant household Evrard had been employed for the last few years was indeed her uncle or, perhaps, a cousin once removed.

But Zahlfast did not give me time to try to work out the connection. "Well, your queen's uncle's wife — " He gave up and started over. "The lady whom Evrard served has just contacted us. She said that her husband, with a small retinue that included his wizard, have now been gone long enough that she's become very worried. He sent her messages fairly frequently when they first left, but for some months now she's heard nothing. And when she finally got a message from the East today, it wasn't from him but from the governor's office in Xantium. They said he'd signed in with them when he came through on his way east, but he's never gotten back."

I knew what he was about to say and, thus, why Zahlfast was irritated as well as worried. Everyone in the City knew that the school trained its wizards to serve mankind, and many people therefore felt that any favor they asked was a fair request.

"She asked us if we could find her husband. The

governor's office in Xantium had made it clear that they considered *their* duty done once they notified her he was missing, so she immediately thought of the school. Of course I told her we couldn't search for a person hundreds or even thousands of miles away, past all the western kingdoms and even the eastern kingdoms. The school doesn't even maintain contact with the wizards and mages east of the mountains. But we *are* worried about Evrard."

I was touched. Evrard had never been a particularly good wizard — not even as good as me, a comparison from which most wizards would have flinched — but it was nice to see that the school was concerned about all its graduates.

"So I'd hoped you might have heard something, that they were fine but had decided to stay in a warmer climate until winter was over or something of the sort," said Zahlfast. "But if you haven't heard — and I think you're the only person outside the household to whom any of them might have written — we may have to start trying to trace their movements from the Holy City, the last place from which they sent a message home." He snorted. "School-trained wizards usually stay in the western kingdoms, and I certainly would have hoped any wizard had enough sense not to go on a *pilgrimage*."

I had forgotten that until he mentioned it. It wasn't just an ordinary trip on which the queen's uncle had gone. It had been a pilgrimage to the Holy Land.

"A wizard has to go along wherever his employer needs him," I said.

"I know, I know," said Zahlfast. "Of course he had to go, but I still don't like it. Well, if by some chance you do get a message from Evrard, let us know immediately." And he rang off.

I stood by the silent phone for several minutes, tapping my fingers slowly. If Zahlfast had thought it worth calling me, he must be more concerned than he had wanted to suggest. I wondered if there was something specific he hoped I would do, and then began thinking that, regardless of the school's plans, I should initiate my own search. Neither Evrard nor I had ever had much respect for each other's magic, but I was still better friends with him than with any other wizard of my generation.

I could see him before me in my mind's eye. He had fox-colored hair, belied by guileless blue eyes and a large number of freckles, an excellent sense of humor, and a truly charming smile, especially when he had just gotten a spell wrong. I had the impression that the queen's uncle was very pleased to have him. I did hope he wasn't dead.

The phone abruptly rang and I jumped. The constable put his head around the corner, but I had already snatched up the receiver.

But it was not Zahlfast. Instead, it was a servant in livery I did not recognize, asking for the queen.

I found her in the great hall with the king, told her she had a call, and sat down to wonder what could have happened to Evrard and his employer. They could have been knifed for their purses or been left alive but had everything stolen so that they had no way to pay for their passage home. They could have been overtaken by an avalanche while crossing the high mountain passes or slipped from an icy track into a cleft hundreds of feet below. They could have been shipwrecked and drowned. They could have been killed by a lion in the desert. They could have died of thirst and heat while wandering lost. Or they could have been captured by anyone ranging from a bandit, greedy for ransom, to a bizarre magical creature.

By the time one reached the Holy Land, one was far beyond the western kingdoms, where generations of wizards had channeled magic into reasonably orderly and predictable pathways. Since magic is a natural force, part of the same forces that had shaped the earth, it should work wherever one was, but away from the western kingdoms it might be hard to control or might be channeled in unexpected ways. Pilgrims at the holy sites should probably be safe from dragons and nixies, but those sites were surrounded by cities, deserts, and seas unlike anything in the west. I wasn't sure I trusted Evrard to react well to unexpected new spells or magical creatures.

The queen came back into the hall. The smile that normally hovered on the edge of her lips was, surprisingly, not there.

She was still worth looking at. With the emerald eyes she had passed on to Prince Paul and her midnight hair, she was the most beautiful woman I had ever met. Even though she was only half the age of King Haimeric, she was so obviously in love with her husband that my intermittent dreams, that she would decide to love me too, had never progressed beyond dreams.

She sat down by the king. "That was my aunt in the City," she said. "She's worried about my uncle."

I sat up straighter, abruptly paying attention.

"It's been nearly a year since he left on pilgrimage, and months since she's heard anything from him. She's frightened and she wanted someone to reassure her that he must really be all right. She even said that their wizard told her before they left to get in contact with us if she hadn't heard anything for a while. I'm afraid I couldn't give her much reassurance. She said she'd already talked to the wizards at the school about searching for her husband, but they said they couldn't help."

I was watching the queen, not the king. Therefore I was startled when, after a brief pause, he suddenly spoke with decision.

"If he's disappeared and no one has heard from him, then the only solution is for someone to go after him. I myself shall go."

The queen took a short, sharp breath, but she did not raise the objections which I myself had to bite back.

"I told you earlier this winter about the blue rose," the king continued. "According to the rumors — and it was even mentioned in one of my rose catalogs — the rose has been successfully grown by an emir south of the Holy Land. I can try to find your uncle, try to find the rose, and make a pilgrimage myself. I've always wanted to go on a quest."

They had forgotten all about me. The shadows of a winter afternoon darkened the great hall, but they did not bother to turn on the lights. The fire on the great hearth flickered yellow, but its light reached only a short way into the room. I sat in semidarkness, feeling I should not listen to their conversation but shy to remind them of my presence by standing up and leaving.

"I'm afraid it's no use trying to talk you into letting me come with you," said the queen. It was not quite a question.

"No use at all, my dear. If I don't come back, you'll need to be here to act as regent, to make sure Paul grows up to be the excellent king we know he will be."

"I'll miss you. I don't like to hear you talk about not coming back."

"And I shall miss you." He chuckled quietly. "You visit your parents every summer, so I know what it's like to be left behind. But unless I'm dead, you know I'll be back."

"I know, but . . ."

"And I wouldn't go if it were only a quest for the blue rose. If your uncle is captured or lost, I may be the only one who can save him. Who else, after all, is there for your aunt to ask?"

The queen caught her breath in what just escaped being a sob. But her voice was steady. "You're right, as always. If even the wizards can't help her, we're her best chance to find him."

"Good," said the king. "I wouldn't have gone if you could not have borne it. But I shall tell the court this evening that I'm going."

"I shall miss you, Haimeric," the queen said again. She slipped out of her own chair and slid in next to the king on the throne. "I know, I really know, that you'll be safe and will come back. But people are changed by travel — they gain new perspectives, new ideas. I don't want to be left behind when you think new thoughts. I love you just as you are."

There was no chance now that either one would notice me. I rose and tiptoed quietly away.

III

Before the king could tell the court that evening that he was going on a quest, we heard a loud clatter of horses' hooves in the courtyard. The constable jumped up from the supper table and hurried out to see who could be arriving at this hour. When he returned a few minutes later, it was with the duchess and her tall husband.

I should have known. Duchess Diana had a way of turning up unexpectedly. We hadn't seen her in months; she had in fact not even been in the kingdom over Christmas, being instead with her husband in his principality two hundred miles away. I had the odd feeling that she had somehow known the king was about to announce his quest.

The duchess and Prince Ascelin pulled off their travel cloaks by the fire and stamped the snow from their boots. After they had bowed formally to the king and queen, the constable seated them at the main table; the rest of us moved our chairs to make them room, and the cook hurried in with extra plates.

King Haimeric seemed to have reached the same conclusion that I had, that their arrival was connected with his quest, but to him it seemed perfectly natural. "I'm glad you two are here," he said. "After you've had your supper, I'm going to make an announcement."

But Duchess Diana and Prince Ascelin did not seem immediately interested in the king's announcement. They ate heartily, asked what had happened recently in the kingdom of Yurt, and told us stories of their stay in Ascelin's principality.

It was impossible not to like the duchess. She was some ten years older than her cousin the queen, which made her five years older than me. She had probably the quickest mind in the kingdom and she enjoyed a good laugh at pretension and folly even better than I did.

"The twins are fine," she said in response to a question. "The weather was so bad today we left them in my castle when we decided to ride up to see you. They're growing so fast they may even catch up with you, Paul!" to the royal heir.

The king took no part in the conversation — nor did I. I watched him surreptitiously as I finished dessert without tasting it. He looked both excited and oddly contented. The queen, on the other hand, sparkled with wit, keeping the conversation going constantly, pressing the duchess for details on everything from the harvest carnival in Ascelin's principality to what Father Noel had brought the twins for Christmas. But I thought I saw a deep pain at the back of her emerald eyes and wondered if the king saw it, too.

At last the servants began clearing the tables, and the king gathered the knights and ladies around him before the great hearth. The members of the court, who had no idea what the king would announce, looked puzzled as he had them bring up chairs. I considered creating some magical illusions to help set the mood, perhaps palm trees by an azure sea, but decided to let King Haimeric make the announcement in his own way.

The fire snapped and flared orange. A king could not go off to face unknown dangers without his Royal Wizard, and if he did not realize it then I certainly did. He would have to take some knights with him, too, of course. I glanced at their faces, wondering which ones. Joachim, the Royal Chaplain, cocked a questioning eyebrow at me, but I just shook my head.

"As I said," said the king when he had everyone's attention, "I want to tell you all something. I've mentioned to several of you at different times that I would like to go on a quest before I die. And now something has happened that indeed makes such a quest imperative. The queen's uncle, Sir Hugo, who left on pilgrimage a year ago, has disappeared, and with him his wizard and two knights."

The court had not heard this. There was a murmur of concern and surprise.

"My quest, then," the king continued, "will be to find him if he is alive, to avenge him if he has been killed, to rescue him if he is in danger, and if possible to bring him home."

Again there was a surprised murmur. "How are you going to find him?" asked the queen's aunt, the Lady Maria.

"The only thing to do," said the king, "is to follow the route he took, through the western kingdoms, through the eastern kingdoms, to the Holy Land. He last sent a message to his wife from the pilgrimage sites."

Most of the court were still trying to assimilate the news that their king, who rarely left Yurt, was actually planning a long journey. But two people reacted at once.

One was Prince Paul, who had been sitting quietly beside his mother. He now leaped up with an eager shout. "Oh, please, Father, please, may I come along?"

The other person was the chaplain. At the mention of the Holy Land, Joachim's dark eyes caught fire and he started to rise from his chair. He stopped himself then, but I could tell that the king was no more going on pilgrimage without his Royal Chaplain than without his Royal Wizard.

Prince Paul's shout, even though he was immediately overcome with shyness when he found everyone looking at him, shook loose reactions from the rest.

"Ascelin and I will come with you, of course," said the duchess. "After all, Sir Hugo's wizard was once my own ducal wizard."

"And I'll come!" "And I'll come!" cried all the knights present.

King Haimeric waited until the hubbub died down a bit, then turned first to his son. "I would love to have you with me, Paul," he said solemnly. "But this quest is too dangerous to risk both the king of Yurt and the royal heir to Yurt. If I don't come back, you'll need to be here to take care of your mother and to succeed to the throne."

Paul nodded, as solemn as the king. "All right, Father," he said, swallowing disappointment with visible effort. "I'll try to be a king you can be proud of." He paused. "But when I grow up, *I'm* going on a quest and no one will stop me then!"

King Haimeric smiled at his son and turned to the rest of us. Behind him, I could see the queen quietly and thoroughly ripping a lace-trimmed handkerchief to pieces.

"I appreciate everyone's willingness to accompany me," said the king. "But I can't possibly take you all. We'll have a better chance of finding the queen's uncle if we can move quickly and unobtrusively. I'm not even going to travel as king of Yurt, but only as a simple pilgrim. I might take two or three of you, perhaps. . . ."

There was a new outbreak of voices as all the knights pleaded to be among the two or three. The servants had long since given up any pretense of clearing the tables and hovered at the edges of the group, listening.

The king looked genuinely troubled to have to disappoint so many people.

But he made his choices quickly. "You come with me, Dominic," he said. "We've been through a lot together over the years, and it seems right that we should share this quest."

Prince Dominic was the king's nephew and had been heir apparent until Paul was born. He had come to the royal castle of Yurt as a young boy, almost fifty years ago, and had been there nearly ever since. Since I planned to be along on this quest as well, I would not have picked Dominic. Like his stallion, he tended to be surly, and I had never been one of his favorites.

But he might be a good person to have along in a tight spot. There was still plenty of muscle on him, even if he now had to brush his sandy hair carefully to hide the thin spot.

"Thank you, sire," he said gravely, twisting the ruby ring on his second finger. "I probably know Sir Hugo better than anyone else here, from that year I lived with him in the City. And I am delighted to serve my king."

"And me?" said the duchess, irrepressible.

"No," said the king regretfully. "Not you. I can't take the queen because she needs to be here to bring up Prince Paul, and I can't take both you and your husband for the same reason. *Someone* has to bring up those twins of yours, and they're quite a handful from everything I hear. If I took the duchess of Yurt, then both my counts would hear about it and insist on coming, too. No, my lady, I'll take your husband if he's willing, but I can't take you."

The duchess started to frown but stopped herself in time. There was a brief pause while everyone remembered that, while the rest of the knights present were the king's liege men, Prince Ascelin, the duchess' husband, was prince of his own principality as well as duke of Yurt by marriage. He would accompany the king as an equal.

Ascelin rose to his feet. He was by far the tallest man in Yurt, being well over seven feet. Another man might have been overshadowed by the force of his wife's personality, but Ascelin had always been a formidable person in his own right. He bent into the formal bow, trying not to smile. "I shall follow you with pleasure, Haimeric," he said in his deep voice.

Good, I thought. Between his height and Dominic's bulk, our group should present an imposing enough appearance that no cutthroat would try to sneak up on the slightly built king.

King Haimeric looked around the room. "Two knights," he said thoughtfully, "especially warriors like you two princes, should be enough."

"You'll need servants with you, certainly," said the assistant constable quickly. "I'll gladly come with you, sire."

But the king smiled again and shook his head. "Thank you for the offer, but this *will* be a pilgrimage as well as a quest, and we will travel very simply, without servants." The assistant constable nodded reluctantly, but the cook, to whom he was married, positively beamed.

"I shall, of course, ask the Royal Wizard to accompany us," the king added.

That was a relief. When he turned down servants, I was afraid for a moment he was going to turn down everyone in his pay. "And the Royal Chaplain," I said quickly.

The king looked slightly surprised, then nodded. Years of my company had made him used to me speaking up without what the finicky might consider proper respect. "Since our trip will take us to the Holy Land, we should certainly have our chaplain with us."

The chaplain's eyes were still ablaze, but he replied calmly. "Thank you. I shall ask the bishop to send another priest to serve the castle while I am gone."

"If the chaplain's going," said Prince Paul, trying

desperately to salvage something, "does that mean I won't have to have any lessons until all of you come back?"

"No, you're old enough for a tutor now," said the queen, speaking for the first time since the end of dinner. She smiled as she spoke and seemed to have her voice well under control.

The king looked around slowly at the assembled court. "There are five of us, then," he said, "a good number for a dangerous mission. We'll start preparations at once, and I shall write to other royal courts in the western kingdoms to tell them to expect us. We'll leave right after Easter."

But we ended up with six people in our party, not five. Two weeks later, while the constable and assistant constable were still making lists of what we needed and pulling boxes out of the storeroom, a lone horseman rode up to the castle at sunset.

I had been out walking, trying to harden my body enough to be ready for a trip of hundreds, indeed thousands of miles. Even the best magic can only do a limited amount to compensate for physical weakness. As I walked, I ran through spells in my mind, deciding what magic I should review because it might be useful in a strange land.

It was so cold that the snow squeaked underfoot. I came back to the castle as shadows became deep blue and the sun tinted the western sky crimson.

I paused before the drawbridge, breathing hard and enjoying the view, then noticed a figure emerging from the woods below the castle hill. He had a long sword slung from the saddle, and his horse was lathered in spite of the cold day.

Yurt was so peaceful that normally I would have assumed that it was a friend coming to visit. But thinking about people captured by bandits had made me uneasy enough that I started putting a paralysis spell together just in case.

Halfway up the hill, the horseman noticed me. He was silhouetted against the sunset so he was only a shape, not a face, but he looked like a young man. He swept off his hat and waved with it. "Hello, Wizard!" he called as though he had known me all his life.

Even when he reached the top of the hill and pulled up next to me, I did not at once recognize him. He had jet-black hair, was dressed in black leather, and had a gold hoop in one ear in the latest fashion for young aristocrats. Were it not for the friendly smile, he would have appeared intimidating as well as strange. And yet there was something oddly familiar about him.

"Hugo!" I cried suddenly as recognition came.

"Glad you remember me," he said with another smile, swinging down from his horse and wringing my hand. "You didn't think you'd be able to leave on this trip without me, did you?"

Hugo had been a tall and rather gangly youth, learning knighthood in the royal court, when I first came to Yurt ten years earlier. He had returned home to his family a year or two later, but other than his beard, the earring and increased musculature, he looked very much as I remembered. He was related to the king or the queen in some way, I recalled. He was — he was the queen's cousin, the son of the man who had disappeared.

"I expect the Old Man is sitting on a warm beach somewhere," said Hugo, grinning, "surrounded by scantily clad dancing girls. He *said* he wanted to go on pilgrimage to contemplate the state of his soul, but I hear the East can be distracting! I can't approve, of course, I'm much too fond of Mother. It's high time he came home. But in case he's not all right" — and for a second his cheerful mask cracked a fraction — "I'd better do my best to find him."

I accompanied him into the castle, thinking that he would make a good addition to our company. As a youth, I remembered, Hugo had had an excellent sense of humor. The chaplain still didn't, in spite of years of my trying to teach him, and the king had a sweetness of temper that precluded many of my best jokes. I had never known Ascelin well enough to joke with him and Dominic was out of the question.

These cheerful thoughts reminded me of something much less cheerful. Evrard, lost on the same expedition as Hugo's father, had also had an excellent sense of humor. And somewhere along the miles of road between here and the Holy Land his bones might be lying, bleached white by the same sun that shone on the azure sea.

IV

Easter came early that year. Patches of snow still lingered in the woods, although buds on the trees gave their branches a slightly fuzzy look against the pale sky. On Easter Monday, the last preparations were finally made for our expedition to find the elder Sir Hugo, his wizard Evrard, and the knights who had accompanied them.

All of us had new gray cloaks with scarlet crosses embroidered on the shoulder. Tents, blankets, rope, clothing, food, pots, weapons, armor, maps, shovels, boots, water bottles, and the king's spare eyeglasses were all organized and packed, so systematically that I wondered if we would dare actually use anything. In the morning, all we would need to do would be to strap the packs onto our horses. The night before leaving, I asked the chaplain to my chambers after dinner for a last glass of wine.

He sat quietly by the fire, long legs stretched out before him. My study was so neat, tidied and straightened in preparation for my absence, that I hardly felt it was mine anymore. I wondered if I should put a magic lock on the door when I left and decided against it. It would open only to my own palm print and, if we didn't come back, the queen might want these chambers for her new wizard.

"It's strange, Joachim," I said as I poured out the wine. "I'm ready to go, I've been eager to go for more than six weeks, yet now that we're about to leave I feel a curious reluctance. We're going off into something so different from our life here in Yurt, so hard to imagine in advance, that it could almost be death. It's as though I won't exist after tomorrow."

He sipped from the glass I handed him and looked at me from deep-set eyes. "I will not drink again from the fruit of the vine until I drink it new in my father's kingdom," he said. "Is that it?"

That was the problem with having a priest as my best friend. He was always saying incomprehensible things. "Maybe," I answered cautiously.

Then I added, "But it's a good thing we're going, because I'm afraid I was on the point of going stale. A lot of wizards these days change posts after eight or ten years, going back to the school to serve as assistants and guest lecturers or moving up to a bigger kingdom that wants an experienced wizard."

"And are you going to move up then, Daimbert?"

The chaplain was the only person in Yurt who used my name rather than calling me Wizard; but then I was the only one who called him Joachim rather than Father.

"No, of course not. I like life here in Yurt, and besides, I'm not nearly a skillful enough wizard that a bigger kingdom would want me. And the school is unlikely to consider me a good person to guide the student wizards."

"I talked to the bishop on the telephone this afternoon," the chaplain said in an apparent change of subject. "You'll be pleased to hear that he finally agrees with you, that magic telephones use perfectly innocuous magic and involve no pacts with the devil."

"And what else did you and the bishop talk about?" I asked, deciding not to comment that the bishop was certainly slow enough to grasp the obvious, especially since it was almost a year since his own provost had had a telephone installed in the cathedral. I wasn't particularly interested in the bishop, but it was better to talk than to sit in silence, feeling the emptiness of the unknown voyage before us.

"It really has been easier communicating with the cathedral this last year, rather than having to rely on the carrier pigeons," said Joachim, not answering my question. I wondered if he and the bishop had discussed some spiritual issue which they thought was unsuitable for a wizard's ears.

But after a moment of staring into the fire, Joachim spoke again. "He confirmed that the new chaplain will arrive here within the week. It's always hard to get one on short notice, but he thought that this young priest would do very well here. I'm sorry I won't be able to help him settle into his duties."

The wizards' school would certainly not send out a substitute wizard to Yurt while I was gone. For one thing, unlike priests who claimed to show each other Christian charity, wizards were well known for fighting all the time and I would never have allowed it.

"I shall miss Yurt," added Joachim. His comment didn't seem to have anything to do with the bishop, but since it fitted in well with my own mood it seemed appropriate.

We sat in silence for a few minutes. The castle was quiet around us. My chambers opened directly onto the main courtyard, but no one came or went on this dark, damp night.

"The bishop once went to the Holy Land himself," said Joachim as though there had been no pause in the conversation. "It must be over forty years ago, when he was a young priest. He did the pilgrimage thoroughly, too, starting in the great City by the sea and visiting the holy sites there and then stopping at most of the shrines on the way. Last week he sent me the guidebook he'd used, with the shrines he visited all marked. It took him over a year to reach the Holy Land."

I had met the bishop only once. As a wizard, I was always a little skeptical of claims of great authority by members of the organized Church, and our brief meeting hadn't made me take to him personally. But I knew Joachim thought of the bishop almost as a father. I, on the other hand, had lost my parents when small and certainly didn't consider the masters of the wizards' school as substitute fathers — for one thing, I knew they would have resisted any suggestion that I was their son.

"Well, it would be silly for us to go west to the City to start our trip," I said absently. "We know Sir Hugo and his party were fine when they left home. By going southeast, we'll be able to pick up the pilgrimage route well along, without a lengthy detour." But then something the chaplain had said struck me. "Wait a minute. I lived all my life in the City before coming to Yurt. I don't remember it having holy sites."

Joachim looked up at me and smiled, something he didn't do very often. "Of course it has holy sites, even if a merchant's son and a young wizard never paid any attention to them. Christianity began in the Holy Land, but the City was the capital of an empire then, and early missionaries tried to establish the true faith there as well. Many of them were martyred in early years by imperial forces, and the places where their holy bones were laid to rest became shrines for the faithful."

"Oh, churches," I said with a shrug. "Of course the City has a lot of churches. We couldn't visit every holy shrine in the western and eastern kingdoms anyway. It would take much too long to get to the Holy Land and you'd never keep track of them all. Besides, Yurt has its own shrine, with the Holy Toe of Saint Eusebius the Cranky, if someone just wanted to see a holy site."

Joachim didn't answer. In the black linen of his

vestments, he almost merged into the shadows of the room. I wondered if he had something else on his mind but didn't like to press him. I turned on a few more magic lamps to brighten the dark corners and got up to pour more wine.

"It will be good to see my family," the chaplain said unexpectedly as I handed him his refilled glass.

"Your family?" Joachim rarely spoke of his family, although I knew he had at least one brother. I had the sense from something he had once said that he had been supposed to inherit the family business and a certain coolness had crept into his relations with his relatives when he decided to become a priest instead, but I had never had any details.

"Yes." He glanced at me briefly, then looked away. "My brother has been asking me to visit for close to a year now. He says I should really meet his children before they grow any bigger, which is true, but I did not feel I could take the time away from my duties here. He wrote again this week and asked me to stop and see them on our way to the East. They're only a short distance off our route, so when I talked to the king about it he said we would all go there. Now I'm trying to remember how long it's been since I've seen him."

So that was what had been on Joachim's mind, I thought. I was relieved that he had not been worrying about the bishop. The bishop intermittently imagined some undue influence on the chaplain from his friendship with a wizard, although as far as I could tell, I had never been able to influence Joachim in anything.

"You've seen your brother at least once since I became wizard here," I said. "You met him over in the cathedral city of Caelrhon."

"Six years ago," said Joachim with a nod. "But I haven't seen my brother's wife since I left home for the seminary, and I've never seen their children at all."

"Is there any particular reason why he wants to see you now?"

"He didn't say specifically," said Joachim, his dark eyes distant. "In his last letter he hinted at some problems coming out of the East and affecting the family business. For a moment, I even wondered if it might have something to do with Sir Hugo's disappearance, but that would be too much of a coincidence. After all, almost all luxury trade is connected to the East in some way."

I waited to give him a chance to say something more about his brother. When he didn't and silence again stretched long between us, I used his mention of Sir Hugo to bring the topic back to the major purpose of our coming quest.

"What do you think can have happened to Sir Hugo's party?" I asked. I myself had no good ideas in spite of six weeks of theorizing. Although Zahlfast and the other masters of the wizards' school seemed relieved that someone had volunteered to go look for Evrard, they also had no ideas.

"Death, illness, imprisonment, loss of money, loss of will to return," said Joachim, which seemed to sum up the possibilities. "If they are dead, I am glad they were first able to visit the holy sites where Christ's feet trod."

I decided not to respond to this last comment. Instead I said, "It *is* a perilous journey, even now."

"It must always be somewhat tense in the East," the chaplain agreed. "Politically, there are a few independent governors still left over from the fall of the Empire, then the emirs, and the royal Son of David — and that's only the beginning. It must be complicated on a religious level because the Children of Abraham and the People of the Prophet also have holy shrines in the Holy Land, as well of course, as the Christian shrines."

"Don't they all worship the same God?" I asked. If the organized Church had always lacked interest for me, comparative religion held even less.

"There *is* only one true God," said Joachim dryly.

"I've mostly been thinking about the glamor of the

East," I said, deciding that now was not the time to learn more comparative religion. "All the different peoples and cultures. The spices, the flowers, the bazaars — "

"How about the different magic?" the chaplain surprised me by asking.

"Well, there *certainly* is only one true magic," I said self-righteously. "But you've got a point. The mages there work their spells somewhat differently than we wizards and there are different magical creatures. The school doesn't even teach eastern magic now, although they used to have one wizard who taught it forty or fifty years ago. They sent me an old copy of his textbook to take along, *Melecherius on Eastern Magic.*" The thick book made a bulge in my neatly packed saddlebag.

"I've even heard that one can still see Ifriti east of the Central Sea," I added. "I hope we can see one. It would be enormously exciting, although it would probably be dangerous, too. It seems there may be a lot of dangers before us."

Joachim glanced at me from under his eyebrows. "Otherwise there would be less merit in the voyage."

I gave him up. Tomorrow we would be leaving for places I had never seen and experiences I could not imagine, and my best friend on the trip was filled with concerns I had no intention of sharing.

We left at dawn. Five of us were mounted, although Ascelin was too tall to ride a horse for more than short periods and would walk beside us. The king, the two princes, and Hugo all wore light armor under their cloaks. Joachim didn't because he said it would be inappropriate for a man of God; I didn't because I didn't want to be bothered by the extra weight. Three packhorses, heavily laden, were ready to follow us. I thought that even though King Haimeric said he was going as a simple pilgrim, not a king, no one who saw us would doubt that our group consisted of four aristocrats, a priest, and a wizard.

The horses' breath made frosty clouds around their noses, and a paper-thin layer of ice lay on the puddles among the courtyard's cobblestones. But the sun, rising pale orange in a cloudless sky, promised warming weather. Everyone in the castle turned out to see us off. Paul and Gwennie, hand in hand, watched from a doorway. Behind them stood the duchess' twin daughters, three years younger than the royal heir.

The queen smiled up at the king, her cheeks dry although her eyes seemed unnaturally bright. "I know it will be hard to send messages regularly," she said, "but if you're near a telephone, do call or if you meet someone coming this way, do write!"

I was going to miss the queen, too, but I couldn't tell her. For one thing, I was quite sure she would not miss me in the slightest. All I could do was watch her say good-bye to the king and imagine it was me.

But then my eye was distracted from the royal couple by the sight of the Duchess Diana and Prince Ascelin on the far side of the courtyard. She had climbed onto a mounting block so she could reach him, and they stood with their arms around each other, paying no attention to anyone else.

"Now, are you sure you know everything you'll need to do in the rose garden this summer?" asked the king, seeming more concerned with his garden than his family. "The entire blossoming season will be over by the time we're back. Remember what I told you to do if thrips start to infest the blooms again." But then he suddenly leaned down from the saddle and kissed his wife, something I had never seen him do publicly before.

"And we're off!" cried Hugo, taking this as a signal to depart. He blew a long blast on his horn and urged his horse forward. Ascelin looked up abruptly from his wife's embrace; the other horses all jumped and followed Hugo's. We dashed across the drawbridge and down the hill, followed by waves and cries of farewell.

We reined in our horses at the bottom and entered the woods more sedately. Ascelin, momentarily left behind, caught up again. "Warn me next time you're going to burst into a gallop like that," he said to Hugo with a grin.

"We *had* to start with a gallop," said Hugo. "It's the only appropriate way to start the Quest of King Haimeric and his Giant Henchmen." He made it sound like one of Paul's stories.

Dominic was having a little trouble calming his big chestnut stallion. The horse that had tried to buck off Paul and Gwennie seemed reluctant to obey the king's burly nephew, either.

"Come on, Whirlwind, come on," I heard Dominic say soothingly, holding the reins tight with one gloved hand and patting the stallion's neck with the other.

"I didn't know that was your horse's name," I said in surprise, once the stallion decided it was easiest to be quiet and walk with the rest of us.

Dominic turned to me with a sudden smile, which was another surprise; he normally smiled even less than Joachim. "It didn't use to be," he said. "But Prince Paul renamed him."

Paul might not be going to the Holy Land with us, I thought, but at least Whirlwind might get a chance to race in search of treasure across the high plains.

After feeling somewhat apprehensive about this trip, once we started I enjoyed it thoroughly. We went at an easy rate, letting the king set the pace. Ascelin, on foot, had no trouble keeping up. After a day and a half in which all the hills, streams, and woods we saw I knew by name, we passed out of the kingdom of Yurt and into new territory.

New scenes greeted us constantly as we rode: sunlit hills dappled with shadow, villages tucked into sheltering valleys, wheat fields where the new light green shoots burst from the dark earth, wild daffodils bright beneath leafless oaks, and birds tugging at last year's grass for nesting material. Any difficulty we met, a sudden cold shower of rain, a ford where the horses splashed mud on us, villagers who looked at our equipment and charged us outrageously for fresh bread, was quickly left behind and forgotten. And somewhere ahead of us was the sun-warmed Central Sea with palms and flowering lemon trees rustling in the sea breezes.

All of us, except perhaps Hugo, were sore and stiff the first few days. But then our muscles became used to the constant exercise and our legs to gripping a horse.

"I'm still not sure my old bones will make the whole journey to the East and back," said the king to me as we rode along, sounding remarkably cheerful about it. "But it's good to be off on a quest after decades of worrying about the governance of Yurt. Prince Paul will grow up to be an excellent king whether I return or not and, if by some chance I do, I may have the only blue rose in the western kingdoms!"

We spent the first few nights in the castles of lords the king knew; once we stayed in an inn, all squeezed together in one big bed in the only private room the inn afforded; but most of the time we camped. Hugo put a sign reading "Giant's Lair" on the tent he shared with Ascelin, until the prince ordered him rather sharply to take it down.

We took turns keeping watch at night. The king said that no one would attack a little group of pilgrims, but Ascelin insisted and I had to agree with him. Hugo had the final watch on the first night we camped, and he woke the rest of us at dawn. When we crawled reluctantly out of the tents, he already had water boiling for tea and bright pink ribbons braided into Dominic's stallion's mane and tail.

Ascelin also thought it was funny, from the imperfectly concealed laugh lines around his eyes and mouth, but the rest of us, who had lived for years with the royal nephew, knew enough to keep our faces perfectly sober.

"Are you responsible for these ribbons?" Dominic asked Hugo with steely calm.

"Of course," said the young man gaily. "Don't you think they add a certain spritely air?"

"I don't want my horse to have a spritely air," said Dominic, a hard twist to his mouth.

But Hugo, laughing and setting out the tin teacups, paid no attention. I didn't think it was quite as funny as he did, but I did have to admire his nerve in getting close enough to the stallion's heels to braid in the ribbons. It took Dominic nearly until we were ready to go to get them out again.

The next day when we stopped for lunch Dominic made some excuse to stand up and go over to the horses. He was gone for several minutes. When he came back, well wrapped up in his gray cloak against the cool air, he was frowning.

"Have you examined your sword recently, Hugo?" he asked gravely. "I just noticed it when I went to check on Whirlwind and it looked — well, I don't want to accuse our wizard of anything, but I would have to say it looked enchanted."

Hugo jumped up, and so did I. We hurried to where his horse stood grazing, a long sheath hanging from the saddle.

But something was wrong. Instead of a hilt protruding from the top, there was what looked like a big smoked sausage. I probed with magic. That was certainly what it was.

"My sword!" cried Hugo in dismay, reaching for it. "What's happened to it?"

There came a sound of a low chuckle from behind us, rough-edged as though it had not been used very often. When we spun around, Dominic tossed his cloak back to show that he held Hugo's sword concealed beneath it.

Hugo, incredulous, slowly drew the sausage from his sheath. Dominic was really laughing now. The sausage, three feet long, was wrapped its entire length in pink ribbons.

V

We came over a hilltop, buffeted by a damp wind. Dominic, riding in front, pulled up hard.

In the valley before us was a small merchant caravan, half a dozen mule-drawn carts accompanied by two mounted men. But the mounted men had their hands up and were trying to control their skittish mounts with their knees, for on the hillside just above them, their backs turned to us, were four helmeted horsemen holding drawn bows.

Hugo reacted at once. Not even taking time to pull on his helmet, he gave a yell and kicked his horse forward. Dominic and Ascelin were only a second behind him. I hadn't seen Dominic move that fast in years.

The startled bandits spun around, trying unsuccessfully to maintain their seats and keep their bows steady. Before they could aim again, our party was on them.

Hugo swung his sword in a great arc toward the bandit who seemed to be the leader. It slashed through his crimson cloak, but the steel bounced with a dull clang off the armor hidden underneath. The bandit's bow flew from his hands as Ascelin grabbed the momentarily-stunned leader and wrenched him from his horse. Dominic whirled his mace, and two well-aimed blows on two more bandits' arms made them drop their bows in anguish.

At this point, I had recovered from surprise enough to come forward and start putting paralysis spells on everyone. The two bandits Dominic had clubbed toppled from their horses and the leader went still in Ascelin's hands. But that left one more.

I looked up and saw him galloping desperately away down the valley. The other bandits' horses ran, riderless, behind him.

"Shall I fly after him?" I yelled to Dominic.

"Let him go," the prince answered with satisfaction. "They're bound to have friends and the friends ought to hear what happens to bandits."

The king and Joachim, who had been left behind, came up with our packhorses at the same time as the mounted men from the caravan seemed to decide we weren't a second group of bandits about to turn on them, having once despatched the first group.

We all came together by the wagons at the bottom of the hill, a group with varied emotions. Dominic, Ascelin, and Hugo were highly pleased with themselves, I thought all out of proportion. Although there were only three of them to the four bandits, they had had the advantage of surprise as well as Ascelin's size, plus the assistance of a supposedly competent wizard, me. I was angry that it had taken me so long to react; Hugo would have killed the leader if it hadn't been for his armor, whereas I should have been able to disarm him easily with magic. The king looked excited and a little apprehensive, Joachim concerned, and the knights who were supposed to be protecting the caravan, embarrassed.

A man in a rich purple cloak jumped off the first of the wagons. "Thank you!" he said heartily. "I don't know what we would have done if you hadn't come along," with a sharp glance at his knights. "We hadn't expected to meet bandits in this region — although I myself am only taking this road for the first time, since the lord in the next river valley over started charging tolls on his bridges. We have a lot of valuable silks on the way to market. Can I reward you with a few bolts? The color of your choice, for yourselves or your ladies?"

The king smiled. "We appreciate your offer, but we don't need a reward. I'm the king of Yurt." So much, I thought, for traveling anonymously. "Even when not at home, I feel it part of royal responsibility to keep the roads safe for honest men — and you can tell that my knights feel the same way!"

"What shall we do with them?" asked Ascelin, stirring the three paralyzed bandits with one toe. They were breathing, but they were stiff and immobile; I doubted they would remember much of this.

"We should kill them," said Hugo enthusiastically.

"No," said the king thoughtfully. "We may have caught them, but I have no rights of justice outside my kingdom."

"And you can't kill a defenseless man," said Ascelin to Hugo reprovingly.

"Look at this, Hugo," said Dominic pointedly. "The bandit leader has an earring just like yours."

"We passed a castle about an hour ago," said the merchant, pointing along the road in the direction that we were going. "You can just see the turrets beyond that hill. If the castellan there doesn't have rights of justice, he'll certainly have a dungeon where these malefactors can be kept until they're turned over to the proper authorities." He looked at their motionless forms quizzically, then at me. "What *did* you do with them?" he asked with what I hoped was awe.

"Just a little trick we wizards know," I said airily, fairly satisfied with my ultimate role in this.

As we continued south, the bandits tied onto the packhorses, I positioned my horse next to Hugo's so I could talk to him. Joachim seemed to have the same idea, for I discovered him on Hugo's other side.

I spoke up quickly, feeling that the young lord needed to hear good sense before he heard Christian morality. "Hugo," I said conversationally, "you could have gotten yourself killed back there."

"But I didn't," he said with a grin.

"You might have had an arrow in the eye if the bandits had been on foot rather than on horseback."

"That's why I yelled, to startle the horses." I was

quite sure he had not thought this through, but I couldn't very well contradict him. I had a sudden, very unpleasant vision of Sir Hugo's party starting happily home from the Holy Land and of bandits leaping out of ambush and putting an arrow through Evrard. But I couldn't mention this to Hugo because the next arrow would have been for his father.

I switched tactics. It was no use trying to make him realize the unnecessary danger he had put himself in if he was happy to have been in danger. "Why do you think the king brought his Royal Wizard along?"

Hugo shot me a quick look. "To deal with dragons or whatever magical creatures we run across."

"And also," I said, giving him a wizardly stare, "to deal with bandits. You saw me paralyze the three of them. If you'd given me fifteen seconds before you attacked, I could have had them all tied up neatly with magical spells."

"You wizards take all the fun out of everything," said Hugo grumpily. "I know perfectly well why there haven't been any decent wars in the western kingdoms for close to two centuries, not since the Black Wars. You don't want to let the aristocracy do what we're trained to do."

"We certainly don't want you killing each other," I said.

"Our own wizard would never scold me for saving us all from bandits."

I realized he meant Evrard. But if he had seen much more of Evrard in the last few years than I had, I thought I still knew the red-headed wizard better. "Didn't your wizard ever tell you that he'd decided to study wizardry in the first place because he was fascinated by the history of how wizards had stopped the Black Wars?"

Hugo didn't answer, which I took as an affirmative.

"I don't doubt your courage, Hugo," I continued. I thought, but decided it would be tactful not to say, that he was still young enough that his own death would not seem a real possibility to him. "And there will be ample opportunity on this trip for you to show it. But if you don't mind putting yourself in danger, you might at least think about the bandit leader. You would have killed him if he weren't wearing armor."

"It's nice armor, too," said Hugo thoughtfully, "much higher quality than you'd expect to see on a highwayman. It's even better than mine. I wonder if it would fit me."

I was not about to be distracted. "Doesn't death seem like a rather stiff penalty for trying to rob a silk caravan?"

"Don't go all moralistic!" Hugo cried. "The castellan to whom we're taking these bandits may well hang them all if they're multiple offenders. I know King Haimeric never hangs anybody, but justice is sharper a lot of places outside of Yurt."

"You still can't act as judge and executioner yourself," I said sternly. I was rapidly starting to feel out of my depth. Since I, unlike Evrard, had *not* become a wizard out of fascination with the end of the Black Wars, and because Yurt really was very peaceful, I tended not to think about the morality of judicial execution or, for that matter, much about deep moral issues at all.

"Even the Church recognizes killing in self-defense and the possibility of a just war," said Hugo.

"This was not self-defense," said Joachim.

I had been wondering when the chaplain was going to join this conversation. Priests were supposed to worry about morality. Wizards just try to keep as many people as possible alive and well.

"And killing someone," Joachim continued soberly, "even in self-defense or to save another innocent life, still leaves a stain on the soul."

Hugo, who had turned toward the chaplain, seemed abashed. I myself still found Joachim's burning dark eyes intimidating. "Well, I didn't kill him and I didn't mean to kill him."

I expected he was telling the perfect truth — at all the tournaments in which he had taken part, everyone would have been wearing armor and he would not have even thought about the effects of a razor-sharp sword on a man who did not have mail under his cloak.

But I was tired of worrying about morality. So when Hugo suddenly looked up and said, "What a castle!" in an entirely different voice, I was happy to change the subject.

And it *was* quite a castle. Among the tumbled hills before us rose a high ridge of red sandstone, at least a hundred feet tall. Cut into the sandstone were narrow windows; perched on top, staring sternly down at the fields surrounding it, was the castle itself. Pennants whipping in the wind from the tops of the towers looked tiny, making us realize how high the castle really was.

We all pulled up for a better look. The castle was so well situated for war that we were momentarily stunned. "It would be impregnable," said Ascelin. "There's no way to scale the sandstone cliffs, especially with men inside shooting out. And I expect the stairs inside, going up to the castle, are very narrow and could easily be blocked against an enemy."

"I'm sure the castellan does indeed have rights of high justice," commented the king with a chuckle.

The castle rose higher and higher above us as we approached. Encircling the base of the sandstone ridge was a tall curtain wall, also built of red stone, but the gate stood open. Two soldiers stepped forward menacingly as we approached.

"Greetings," said the king. "We would like to see the lord of this castle. We have captured some bandits."

The soldiers took a good look at us and our packhorses and then abruptly fled with startled cries. Giving each other surprised glances, we dismounted and came through the gate on foot.

"It's a good thing we caught these bandits," said the king, "if even the sight of them bound terrifies the people here."

"It's a good thing the castellan has such a fine castle if his soldiers are all cowards," replied Dominic.

Inside the walls were all the working parts of a castle that someone would not want to transport up narrow stairs cut inside a cliff: the stables, the kennels, the armor shop, the mews, the kitchens, and the big grain storage bins. Down at the far end stood a set of gibbets; this castellan did indeed practice high justice.

We waited politely for someone to come meet us, but for a few minutes there was only panicked shouting and scurrying. I even wondered momentarily if some bizarre spell had made everyone here think that we were dragons. But a quick probe found no spells other than my own.

After a while, one of the soldiers came back. "Are — are they dead?"

"Of course not," I said. "I paralyzed them with magic."

He hesitated. Something very odd indeed, I thought, was happening here. Did they think we were another band of ruffians ourselves? If so, why did they make no effort to resist us?

"You'd better go up to the castle," the soldier said at last, "and talk to the constable."

There was a brief pause while we tried to decide if it was possible to carry the bandits up the stairs. Finally I broke the spells that held them. They looked disoriented and confused as we untied them from the packhorses, then pulled them to their feet and tied their hands behind them. As we started toward the castle, Ascelin, Dominic, and Hugo each had a bandit in front of him, a dagger point resting against the back of his neck.

The first flight of stairs was wide enough to give us few problems, even though the steps were uneven and extremely dark. There were no windows and we had to feel our way. The sandstone walls were gritty on either hand, and I heard Dominic cursing quietly as he bumped his head.

We came out into what appeared to be a guard room cut into the stone. A single window gave a little light. On the far side, the stairs started up again, much narrower and even darker.

The soldier leading us glanced at Dominic and Ascelin. "We'd better take the outside stairs," he said.

The bandits, who had said nothing, turned toward a door set in the room's outer wall, next to the window. The soldier opened the door, which led to wooden stairs built on scaffolding on the outside of the cliff. These were much wider than the inner stairs though the gaps between steps made them potentially treacherous.

I glanced down as we came out into chilly daylight and saw that we were already forty feet up. This was indeed an admirable castle for war. Even if an enemy made it as far as the guard room, he would still have to climb either the narrow inner stairs, which could easily be blocked, or the outer wooden stairs, which could be set on fire.

But how had the bandits known that the doorway led to the stairs?

All of us except the bandits were breathing hard when we reached the top of the cliff and entered the castle itself through another door. We came into a great hall, well lit by tall windows looking out in all directions across the countryside.

"They can afford windows, being up so high," I heard Dominic say appreciatively to Ascelin. "In Yurt, all our windows open onto the courtyard."

But I was thinking about the bandits rather than castle architecture. Was it because they been captured and brought here for justice so many times that they had known where the stairs were and had been able to climb them so readily, even with daggers pressed against their necks? If so, why had they not yet been hung?

The constable of the castle came forward, looking at us with wide eyes. "What — what is it that you want?"

King Haimeric greeted him formally and told him what had happened. I was pleased to note that he did not say that he was king of Yurt; maybe he, like me, was starting to wonder if the castellan had made some nefarious pact with the bandits.

"And so," finished the king, "we are bringing these bandits to your lord for judgment." The three bandits, listening, all looked unaccountably amused.

"You caught these men," said the constable, "but you aren't trying to ransom them? You brought them here — you brought them so that the lord of this castle might exercise justice?"

"That's what I said," said the king patiently.

"But — "

The leader of the bandits answered for the constable. "But *I* am lord of this castle."

There was a short silence while we all struggled to keep our faces straight. "In that case," began King Haimeric sternly, "I must warn you, as an aristocrat and a giver of justice, to stop your wicked attacks on the defenseless."

It was no use. Dominic took the king firmly by the arm and we all got out the door and staggered down the stairs somehow. Even Joachim was laughing as we tumbled out into the courtyard.

But as we galloped away from the castle, I couldn't help glancing back. The castellan's initial reaction had been the same amusement that convulsed us all, but he must also have been horribly shamed to appear before his men a bound captive. For the first time this trip, we may have come across a difficulty we could not simply leave behind.

PART TWO

King Solomon's Pearl

1

I awoke all at once and lay perfectly still, waiting for whatever sound had wakened me to come again.

Inside the tent, it was pitch black and completely silent. I couldn't even hear Joachim's breathing. But then I heard the faintest creak from his side of the tent; he must have heard the sound as well and was leaning on his elbows, listening.

It came again, the sharp crack of a broken twig followed by muffled hushing sounds. Our tents were pitched in a little grove, and someone, or something, was creeping up on us.

I was out of the tent with a quick scramble and was hit by air so cold I immediately wished I had brought a blanket with me.

But there wasn't time to go back. Where was Dominic? It should be his watch. Shivering in my pajamas, I crept toward the edge of the grove, straining to see.

The moon, three days past the full, hung red and deformed-looking above me. In its pale light I could at last see Dominic, a dim and bulky form. He moved his head as though he too had heard something.

Before I could speak or move closer, there was a dull thunk as of leather hitting bone, a grunt, then Dominic pitched forward. Behind him stood a smaller figure, arm upraised.

I yelled, a magically amplified yell that shook the

trees, and I filled the grove with a great flash of light. The light was gone in two seconds — even the best magic light needs to be attached to something solid. But before it faded I had seen four startled and frozen figures, and Dominic's body facedown on the ground.

If they remained still for five seconds, I had them. I threw out coils of magic, shaped with the Hidden Language to make thin air into bindings as strong as cord. My binding spell wrapped around the four, imprisoning them. It was not as thorough as a paralysis spell, but I didn't have quite enough time for a paralysis spell.

I tried another flash of light and saw that I had all four. It must be, I realized, no more than a minute since I had scrambled out of the tent. In spite of the cold, I had to wipe my forehead with a pajama sleeve. Magic, especially rapid magic, is hard work.

But what had happened to Dominic? I groped toward him, then saw the rest of our party emerging. Hugo and Ascelin had swords in their hands, but the king, more usefully, had brought a lantern.

With the lantern's light, I found the royal nephew and bent over him. He was breathing loudly, eyes shut. As I watched, his eyes flickered, and his fists clenched. Not dead then, I thought gratefully, as I took the jacket Joachim handed me.

"Look at this!" called Hugo, who had gone back for a lantern of his own. "It's the same bandits!"

Indeed it was the same bandits, their faces distorted by the shadows cast by a lantern at their feet. Struggling unsuccessfully against the binding spell, they glared at us silently.

"What was your intention?" the king asked them sternly. "We let you go today out of courtesy to other aristocrats, but what sort of honorable and aristocratic behavior is this? Were you going to take vengeance on us for humiliating you by slitting our throats while we slept?"

Dominic abruptly sat up, rubbing the back of his head. He tried to lurch to his feet, but Ascelin kept him seated with a hand on his shoulder.

"We weren't going to slit anybody's throat," protested the leader.

I wasn't at all sure I believed him. I was coming close to Hugo's point of view, that the best thing to do might be to kill them.

"It's the middle of the night," said Ascelin. "Let's leave them to learn some sense by standing bound by the wizard's spells for a few hours. Then we can question them in the morning."

"It would have been my watch soon anyway," I said, "so I'll keep an eye on them while the rest of you get some sleep."

Hugo clearly would have preferred to do something spectacular and warlike, but he contented himself with rounding up the bandits' horses and tying them to a branch. In a moment our party returned to the tents, Dominic assisted by Ascelin.

Watching the two princes in the flickering light of the lantern the king held for them, I thought that it was good to see them managing to get along with each other on this trip. When they had first met, nearly eight years ago, they had detested each other. But then Dominic, always a snob, had not known at the time that Ascelin was a prince.

Our camp became quiet again, and I added a few details to the binding spells that held the bandits. It is possible to break out of an improperly made binding spell, and I had pulled the magic together very rapidly. I didn't want to paralyze them, however, even if that would have held them more securely, because I wanted them to remember this experience.

They soon stopped struggling and gave up cursing me a short time later when I did not answer. What was I going to do with them? The school made us swear enormously solemn oaths to help mankind, but it only taught us magic, when at the moment, what I felt I needed most to know was how to deal with people unlike any I knew in Yurt.

The moonlight made the stars pale in the center of the sky, but from where I was sitting, I could see the Hunter striding low over the horizon. Soon he would be gone from the sky for the summer.

We certainly couldn't kill the bandits in cold blood, even if they had crept up on our tents planning to kill us. We were still in the orderly western kingdoms, not much more than three weeks away from Yurt, and there were legal methods for dealing with such things. But I didn't like the idea of loading them onto the packhorses again, then trying to find a nearby castle that exercised high justice — other than the castle of the bandit leader himself.

The night dragged on. In a marginally successful attempt to stay warm, I rekindled the fire over which we had cooked supper. I kept yawning, but I was shivering too much to doze. It would have been Joachim's watch next, but I let him sleep, not wanting to leave him with the responsibility for guarding bandits restrained by magic. After a while, the eastern stars gradually faded as the horizon grew gray.

I heard a rustle from the tents and looked up to see the king and his lantern approaching. He sat down next to me, pulling his cloak around him.

"Go back to your tent, sire," I said. "I won't be making the morning tea for another hour."

"I couldn't sleep anyway," said King Haimeric with a shrug. "We have to decide what to do with the bandits."

I could see them faintly now, ten yards away, standing as stiffly as if they were tied to trees. The long cold night, I hoped, would have sobered them. "We can't very well have them following us all the way to the Holy Land," I said quietly. "But I don't understand it. Why would a castellan turn to banditry?"

"I don't know," said the king in a worried voice. "I realize we're not in Yurt anymore, but it's still very strange."

"Short of killing them, I don't see what we can do that won't make them feel even more humiliated and even more bent on vengeance."

"We can give them some tea," said the king. "They've had a cold night of it. Since you've got the fire going anyway, put on the kettle."

This made no sense at all. I stared at him a moment in the lantern light, then went to fill the kettle. He was, after all, my king.

In a few minutes, when the tea was brewed, we walked over to the bandits. "We weren't going to slit any of your throats," the leader growled. "I hope you realize we wouldn't rob a caravan for a few baubles or a few bolts of frippery, and we aren't murderers, either. We just wanted to teach you a lesson."

"That was my nephew you knocked on the head," said the king gravely. "He may look at all this differently. But at the moment he's asleep. Would you like some tea before he wakes up? It can't have been comfortable standing here all night. Wizard, could you release the bindings enough so that they can drink?"

I adjusted my spell to allow them a little arm motion. The king put tin cups of scalding tea into their hands. They drank slowly, looking at us thoughtfully over the rims. In the lantern light and the beginning of dawn, they would have seen two white-bearded men, one very slightly built.

"All right," said the king sternly, taking back the empty cups. "I believe you. I won't ask you what kind of lesson you planned to teach us, because I'm quite sure I won't like the answer. An aristocrat like you should know better. Your own fields and your rents should provide you plenty of income within the law — to say nothing of the proceeds of justice."

The leader of the bandits looked at King Haimeric shrewdly. "So you didn't find it either, eh?"

I had no idea what he was talking about and I doubted the king did either, but that didn't stop him. "Of course not. You seem to imagine that we ransacked the silk caravan after my wizard paralyzed you, but instead we sent it safely on its way. If you're looking for caravan loot, you won't find it in our camp. Do you employ a wizard?"

I was having trouble keeping up with the king's line of reasoning and, from the looks on their faces, so were the bandits.

"No," said the leader, eyeing me warily.

"If we let you leave with your lives," I said, hoping this fit in with whatever King Haimeric was doing, "and I say if, hire a wizard at once." The king gave me a quick look, and I realized it was probably not his intention after all to urge them to take on a new employee. But it was too late to stop now. "A real wizard," I continued, "one from the school in the great City."

A school-trained wizard would certainly be able to stop them from preying on any more merchant caravans — unless, of course, he ended up with his own throat slit. But he'd do much better than a magician, someone who had picked up a little of the Hidden Language here and there and might see nothing wrong with banditry.

"I asked if you had a wizard," said King Haimeric, pulling his eyebrows into a frown, "because I wanted to be sure you understand the lesson that we will teach you if you follow us again. My own wizard will turn you all into frogs."

It had been ten years since the disastrous transformations practical, and I had long since worked out where I had gone wrong with those frogs. I watched King Haimeric's face, knowing he was going to expect some spectacular display of magic in a moment.

"Don't pay any attention to him," said one of the bandits to the leader. "He's just bluffing."

That made it all very simple. I turned that one into a frog.

The king laughed, a quite genuine laugh. "Anyone else think the wizard is bluffing?" He picked up the bullfrog that had been a bandit a moment ago and held it out toward the rest with both hands.

The bullfrog looked up at them with wide, confused eyes, then gave a sudden booming croak. After a moment of stunned silence, the other three bandits began to look at each other with poorly suppressed smiles.

"Turn him back to himself, Wizard," said the king.

In a moment, I had him a person again, and I quickly restored the binding spells around him. His throat continued to pump like a frog's for a few seconds, which now set the other bandits laughing.

"Any tea left, Wizard?" asked the king. We gave them all another cup.

"Now," said the king when they had finished — two even thanked us — "it's almost day. My knights, the ones who overpowered you yesterday, will be up shortly. They may not look at this incident as tolerantly as we do — especially my nephew. But we're on a pilgrimage and it's important to return good for evil when one is on a pilgrimage. Therefore, I'm going to let you go."

I stopped myself just in time from objecting.

"But I want you to remember," said the king very seriously, "not to attack any more merchant caravans and," glancing toward me, "to hire yourself a competent wizard at the first opportunity. And certainly don't try to follow us again. If you do, not only will my wizard turn you into frogs, he will have a dragon attack you first."

This, I feared, really was a bluff. I certainly couldn't summon a dragon from the land of wild magic.

The bandits seemed to be taking no chances. They agreed readily, and when I broke the spells that held them, they went at once to their horses. As they mounted, I heard one call another "Froggie," with an accompanying slap on the shoulder. The sound of galloping hooves brought the rest of our party out into the dawn.

I didn't want to take any chances, either. Leaving the king to explain to the rest what he had done and letting them start breakfast, I tried to improvise an appropriate spell.

It would have to be an illusory dragon. The problem with most illusions is that they fade quickly, usually within a few minutes. I thought I might be able to manage something that lasted a little longer — my predecessor as Royal Wizard of Yurt used to make illusions that would last for hours. But the difficulty was to guess *how* long. It would need to be here when — or if — the bandits came back, but I didn't want it to hover all day and terrify anyone else who used this road.

I decided at last to create an illusory dragon, all but the final twist of the spell that would bring it together, and to attach the nearly finished spell to a pebble. When the pebble was moved, say, kicked by a bandit's horse, that would complete the spell.

I had never done anything like this before, or even heard of it, so it took me a while to work out the spells, and then I tried making a small practice dragon. It worked even better than I expected. I put the pebble on the ground, kicked it, and a one-foot-high blue dragon appeared and shot illusory smoke at me for a minute before fading.

In a few more minutes, I had put the spells together to create a thirty-foot scarlet dragon, one with three sets of bat wings and extra-long talons, and attached the spells to a small stone. I placed it very carefully on the road in the direction back toward the bandits' castle. Now, if they were the first ones along this road, it should work perfectly.

Before joining the others, I looked at my stone in assessment. The faintest outline of the dragon hovered around it, the almost-completed spell just on the edge of visibility, but I hoped the bandits, riding fast, wouldn't notice it until it was too late.

"Wizard!" called Hugo. "There's only a little tea left! Do you want some?" I hurried over to the fire, indeed wanting some.

Shortly afterwards, we packed up the tents and started south again. Dominic had a lump on the back of his head but insisted he was all right. I kept glancing over my shoulder, wondering when someone would follow us along the road.

We had climbed up the far side of the valley, perhaps a mile away, when the sound of distant voices was carried to us on the wind. I pulled up my horse and looked back.

There were several groves of trees in the valley, but I thought I could tell where we had camped last night. Just visible beyond was a splash of scarlet, though we were too far away to pick out any details. The distant voices, shouting and screaming, faded away. I laughed and hoped that it had indeed been the bandits.

11

Spring advanced rapidly as we moved south. The woodland flowers disappeared as we moved into kingdoms where the trees had already leafed out. Here, too, the hills were a different shape than the hills of home, the rooflines of the houses different, the very style of clothes worn by the people working in the fields different from those worn by the villagers of Yurt. To all of us and especially to Dominic, the newness and variety was a heady experience in itself.

After a month of traveling south on less-frequented roads, we finally picked up the main pilgrimage and commercial route that ran from the great City down toward the Central Sea. We stopped at our first pilgrimage church, a small dark structure that seemed little visited even though it stood close to a busy road. But it had vivid and complicated stone sculptures, about which Joachim read to us from the bishop's guidebook.

"The saint here miraculously cured thousands of a disease whose name is no longer remembered. It has been forgotten because the saint cured it out of existence."

Hugo lifted his eybrows ironically at me. From the sculptures, it looked as though the disease was thought to have rotated men's heads around backwards.

After two days of jostling with other travelers on the road and another night in an inn — we got two beds this time — we left the route for the detour to visit Joachim's family. We headed through fields and meadows swathed in fresh yellow-green toward the manor where his brother lived.

We looked at each other critically that morning. After a month of travel, we were all grubby, as well as leaner and browner than when we left home. That is, all except the chaplain himself: He had somehow managed to keep himself tidily shaved and his clothes relatively unwrinkled.

"Looking forward to someone else's cooking?" I asked Ascelin as we lowered ourselves delicately into a stream which, even under a sunny spring sky, felt cold enough to have ice in it. I tried without much success to work up some lather to wash the smell of woodsmoke out of my hair.

He plunged his head under water and came up snorting and laughing. His dark blue eyes contrasted sharply with his tanned face. I passed him the soap. "I should ask all of you that question." We had decided, the third day out, that Ascelin was by far the best camp cook and had made him prepare the suppers ever since. He could even make passable biscuits over the fire. "Anytime you want to take a turn — "

"I wanted to ask you something," I said as we dried ourselves off and tried to shake the wrinkles out of the only clean clothes we had left. "I've been wondering about this for a while. Why did you and the duchess show up at the royal castle just as the king was about to announce his quest?"

Ascelin pulled a shirt over his head. "Didn't Diana tell you? Sir Hugo's wife had called her that morning."

"Sir Hugo's wife — "

"He's Diana's relative as well as the queen's uncle — just a more distant relation. His wife was, of course, very worried about him. She was hoping, I think, that he might have been in contact with us, although I don't know why he would write us and not his own wife. But she did mention that she'd already talked to your queen. Diana guessed that at least some of you from the royal court would be planning to go look for Sir Hugo and she had no intention of being left behind." He chuckled. "In spite of racing up to the royal castle through a snowstorm — and me on foot! — she still couldn't go along."

Ascelin leaned his back against a tree to pull his boots on. "Looks as though I need new soles," he said to himself, then gave a quick smile. "I must be in the best condition of my life, keeping up on foot with five mounted men.

"My lady Diana was very disappointed, as I'm sure you can guess," he went on. "But Haimeric was right: we couldn't have both gone and left the twins behind. You might have done better with her than with me, however — even if I am a better camp cook."

He fell silent for a moment, looking out across the stream. "She is a remarkable woman, Wizard. I wouldn't tell this to anybody but you, but after all you did help bring us together. I miss her terribly — before this we'd never been separated for more than a day or two since we were first married."

I pulled a few words of the Hidden Language

together to create an illusion, just a tiny illusion, a dark-haired woman about a foot high wearing a leather tunic and wide gold bracelets. I liked to do at least a little magic every day. Wizardry is hard enough that I was always afraid of going rusty. It wasn't very difficult to create illusory images of people I knew, though I didn't do it often.

Ascelin saw what I was doing and caught his breath. "That's Diana!"

"Don't try to touch it," I said. "Your hand would go straight through her."

I had expected him to be pleased, but he turned his back sharply on me. I looked at his wide shoulders thoughtfully. I didn't even miss the queen that much. I shrugged, said the two words to end the illusion, and stood up to stamp my heels down into my own boots.

It was with neatly trimmed beards and clean — if badly creased — clothes that we rode up to the manor house. We had telephoned from the inn two days ago and were expected.

Since I knew Joachim's brother Arnulf was involved in commerce in some way, I had expected, without really thinking about it, that his house would be something like the cramped urban house I myself had grown up in. Instead, it was a gracious, two-story edifice, built of stone the color of mellow gold. Long wings encircled a courtyard and wide lawns led down to the river. A cherry orchard bloomed beyond the house. It was big enough that it probably could shelter nearly as many people as the royal castle of Yurt. Either built after the Black Wars, I thought, looking at the tall windows, or else built by someone who could afford very good protection.

Liveried servants hurried to meet us as we clattered into the courtyard. A few guards loitered conspicuously near the house doors. I glanced at Joachim, wondering how it felt to be back in his childhood home after more than fifteen years away. But his face, often hard to read, now seemed to have no expression at all.

The main door swung open and Arnulf, the lord of the manor, appeared, holding out both hands in greeting. "Joachim!" he cried. "This is delightful! I'm so glad you were able to come. And King Haimeric of Yurt, I presume? You honor us!"

Joachim's brother was a shock. He looked like the chaplain and yet not like the chaplain. He had the same hair, the same height, the same deep-set dark eyes over high cheekbones, even if he did not have the chaplain's gauntness. But the effect was as if Joachim had been taken out of his own body and someone else put in his place.

The chaplain tossed his reins to me and went to meet him. The brothers started to shake hands and embraced instead.

"Well, Joachim, at least you don't make me kiss your ring," said Arnulf with a laugh. "Does that wait until you're made bishop?"

Joachim neither laughed nor answered the comment. "It's good to see you," he said instead and turned to introduce his brother to the rest of us.

"Claudia's eager to see you, too," said Arnulf, "and of course the children can't wait to meet their Uncle Joachim."

Joachim took a deep breath. "And I them."

We were shown to the guest rooms and told that lunch would be served in half an hour. The rooms seemed sybaritic after our weeks on the road, feather beds covered with clean white sheets, long windows curtained in blue, and plenty of hot water. An efficient serving maid unpacked our bags and took our clothes away to the laundry.

We had been given five rooms in the guest wing, all next to each other, while the chaplain was taken off to the family wing of the house. I took the opportunity to shave my cheeks more thoroughly than I had been able to do with cold water that morning. The soap was delicately scented with lily of the valley.

I stood by the window to dry my face, enjoying the light breeze coming through the open casements and the sight of birds hopping purposefully across the lawn. I was distracted from a pleasant reverie by the sound of voices.

Joachim and his brother were strolling along the outside of the house. Arnulf spoke as they came under my window. "It's as though they'd disappeared into thin air. And nothing left — except the sign."

They continued out of my earshot without speaking again. I looked soberly after them. Sir Hugo's party had also disappeared into thin air.

There came a sharp knock, making me jump. "Come in!" I called and Ascelin entered, ducking his head as he came through the doorway.

He closed the door behind him and motioned me away from the window. "What's going on here?" he asked in a low voice. "Is everyone here under a spell?"

Startled, I probed at once for magic and found none. As my mind slid lightly along the surface of magic's four dimensions, I could sense the presence inside the house of all our party except Joachim, as well as many minds I did not know, but none of them was a wizard. I found Joachim and his brother down by the front door, the house guards in the courtyard and, in the stables, minds I assumed belonged to the stable boys, but that was all. I came back to myself and looked up into the prince's worried eyes. "No one's under a spell here. Why did you think so?"

He shook his head. "It must be hunter's instincts. This whole house feels as though something has just happened or is about to happen and I don't know what it is."

I had felt nothing of the sort, but then I was no hunter. Ascelin, I knew, had many years of experience in guessing or sensing where animals were hiding and when they would break into the open. I shook my shoulders to dispel a sudden chill that could have been prescience and could have been my imagination.

"We should all stay close together," said Ascelin, "and leave here as soon as we can."

"But we just got here," I protested, "and Joachim hasn't seen his family in years!" All of us had been in high good humor this entire trip. An onset of unprecedented caution, just when we reached such a comfortable house, seemed entirely uncalled for.

"And why did his brother want him to visit *now*?" demanded Ascelin.

I was suddenly reminded of the bandits who had thought that there was something specific hidden in the silk caravan and that we, too, were looking for it. Arnulf, I knew, was involved in some way in the luxury trade with the East. Could there be, here in this house, something valuable enough to make a castellan turn outlaw?

"I don't know if you overheard," said Ascelin, "the other day when we were at that inn, but several of the merchants were talking about very strange rumors coming out of the East, and I thought I heard one of them say that they involved the kingdom of Yurt. . . ."

Before I could respond to this startling information, there were brisk steps in the hall outside and another knock. "My lords?" It was Arnulf's constable, come to tell us that lunch was ready. A few minutes ago, I would have gone to the dining room with pleasant anticipation. Now, as we walked down the wide carpeted stairs, I felt instead a stir of misgiving.

But nothing about lunch seemed ominous. The dining room was carpeted and curtained in green; the view from the window was of bright flowerbeds with the river beyond. The table glistened with silver and crystal. Arnulf and Joachim were already there when we came in.

"Claudia said she and the children would be right down," said Arnulf. "Ah, here they are." In the hall we heard children shouting excitedly, and the door swung open with a bang. But there was immediately an abashed silence as they spotted us. For a second I saw our group as the children must see us, six strange men standing looking toward the door, three of them rather formidable warriors. Even clean and well-dressed, we felt like a wild and woodsy group in this delicate and gracious setting.

"Go on in, it's all right, don't you want to meet your Uncle Joachim and his friends?" came a laughing woman's voice. Claudia, the lady of the manor, came through the doorway herding two boys and a girl before her.

Claudia was another shock. She was the only woman I had ever met who came close to being as beautiful as the queen.

She did not look at all like the queen, having curly russet hair, already escaping from the coiffure into which I was sure she had just combed it, and a skin so fair it was almost transluscent. She had a merry sweetness of expression and yet an air of tender concern in her eyes that made someone who saw her — or at least me — feel she must be protected at all costs from anything troublesome or sad.

She came immediately across to Joachim, wearing the tiniest firm line around her mouth as though determined not to be as shy as her children. She took his hands, looked into his eyes, and gave an almost tentative smile. I would have felt her expression, both sweet and vulnerable, was devastating if it had been turned on me. "You haven't changed at all," she said softly.

"Nor have you," said Joachim. "It's been too long. So, these are my nephews and my niece."

Claudia brought the children forward to meet their uncle, then all of us were introduced to her and she invited us to sit down at the table. Servants came in with steaming platters.

She was the perfect hostess, serving the king first,

making sure each of us had what he wanted, asking about our trip and listening attentively to our answers and, at the same time, somehow keeping her children quiet and orderly and their meat cut up in bite-size pieces.

But twice, as her husband sat beaming genially at the other end of the table, I thought I saw her shoot a worried look toward him.

III

"I understand your family is also in commercial imports?" said the Lady Claudia to me.

"Was. My parents died when I was little and my grandmother kept the warehouse going, but she died while I was still in the wizards' school. We imported wool from the Far Islands and wholesaled it to the cloth manufacturers."

"How interesting," said Claudia with a bright smile. In fact it wasn't interesting at all, which was part of the reason I had become a wizard instead of a merchant. I would probably have done an even worse job of running a wool wholesale business than my grandmother had; there hadn't been much left over when she died and I had to sell the warehouse to pay the firm's debts.

"And now you're a wizard," said Arnulf genially. "I gather the wizards' school keeps a fairly close eye on all of you — even tries to establish your routes when you travel."

"Not really," I said in surprise. "Of course the school tries to coordinate the practice of wizardry throughout the western kingdoms, but wizards argue with each other too much to allow close oversight." Arnulf nodded but said nothing more.

The chaplain seemed much more sober during lunch than I would have expected from someone home to see his family after a long absence. "You know, Joachim," said Claudia when dessert was served, "I still can't get used to seeing you in priest's vestments."

Dessert was lemon pie, and one of the dishes served earlier had been rice with almonds. We didn't have rice in the royal castle of Yurt very often, lemons even less frequently. Although I had always assumed that coming to Yurt had been the move into luxury for Joachim that it had been for me, perhaps I was wrong.

"Did he use to wear an earring when you first knew him?" Hugo asked Claudia with a wink for Dominic.

The chaplain did smile at that and brought both earlobes forward with his forefingers to show they had never been pierced.

"No," said Claudia, also with a smile. "He always dressed very soberly, even when he was still expected to take over the family business."

"It's just as well I didn't," said Joachim. "My ideas of fair business practice would have lost our firm everything we had in two years. You and Arnulf would be lucky to have a cottage of your own, much less this house."

He spoke lightly — or at least lightly for him — but Arnulf gave him a look that just managed not to be a scowl. There had been an argument here, I thought, perhaps accusations of immorality on one side and accusations of being hopelessly unworldly on the other, that still festered after more than fifteen years.

"He's been such an excellent Royal Chaplain," put in King Haimeric, "that we in Yurt, at any rate, are very glad he *did* become a priest."

"You wouldn't want to try your hand at the family trade one more time, Joachim," asked Arnulf breezily, "perhaps arrange a trade for me while all of you are in Xantium?"

He spoke as though it were a joke, but Joachim took it seriously. "No." He shot his brother an intense look. "I gave up all worldly commerce when I entered the seminary."

The topic was dropped there, and Claudia asked Ascelin about his principality as she poured us all tea. The prince shook off the air of watchfulness that had hung about him for the last hour and answered graciously. She seemed very well informed about everyone in our party. The chaplain must have written his brother about all the people in Yurt, I thought, and I felt at a disadvantage that he had never told us nearly as much about the people here.

After lunch, Claudia went off with the children, and Arnulf took us on a tour of his grounds. As we came through the flowering orchard, I thought that we would be many miles away when the cherries were ripe.

Arnulf's foreman came up to him with a question as we were being shown a pasture where fine horses grazed beyond a white fence. The lord of the manor excused himself and went, taking Joachim with them.

"Listen carefully," said Ascelin as soon as they were out of earshot. "We have to get out of here as soon as we can."

This was the same surprise to the others that it had been to me.

"Don't you think everyone here is just a little nervous, having the chaplain home again after so long?" asked the king when Ascelin tried to explain his instinctive feeling that something was about to happen. "You heard them at lunch; he must have left after some sort of quarrel that they're all trying hard to forget."

"And if something here *is* about to explode," said Dominic, "we'd be cowards to run away."

"I think Ascelin's right," said Hugo with a frown. "It could be any number of dreadful things. Arnulf, after all, trades with the East, where the women grow fur on their bodies down to their knees and have two-foot tails, and where enormous horned snakes guard the pepper groves."

"What are you talking about?" demanded Ascelin.

But Dominic nodded soberly. "The boy has a point.

It's one thing to flee a human enemy, another a monster."

I, too, was about to protest, to tell Hugo that he knew perfectly well that the women of the East were not furry, that he himself had suggested to me that his father was surrounded by dancing girls. But then he gave me a broad wink and I stopped in time.

"We couldn't leave anyway," said King Haimeric. "The servants have our bags and, down in the stables, they're reshoeing our horses. Why don't we just ask Arnulf if he has any problems on which he'd like our help?"

"All right," said Ascelin, "but I still want to leave as soon as our horses are ready. We should all stay close together. That means you, too, Hugo. I wish the chaplain hadn't gone off with him."

We moved in a group in the direction that Arnulf and his foreman had gone. I thought irrelevantly that anyone seeing us would assume we had become so accustomed to each other's company while traveling together that we could not now bear to be separated.

But we did not find the lord of the manor. "Sire," I said to the king, "tell the others about the bandits, about how they were apparently expecting to find something in that silk caravan. I can search more quickly by using magic."

I left them sitting on a pasture fence and hurried back toward the house. Enormous horned snakes or not, I wished the chaplain had not gone off with Arnulf.

I found him, unexpectedly, not with the lord of the manor but with the lady. Claudia sat on a bench under a tree in the garden, singing and playing a lute, while Joachim sat at her feet, his dark eyes fixed on her face.

Surrounded by the colors and scents of a spring garden, dappled with the sunlight that made its way through the young leaves overhead, they seemed caught in a song of heart-wrenching beauty, where the afternoons were endless and the dailiness of ordinary life was so far away to be non-existent.

And then I listened to the words. "So kiss me as you

say good-bye," sang Claudia. "Kiss me and ask not the reason why. But my heart shall take an eagle's wing, away to fly."

I froze, caught between feeling I should slip away without disturbing them and feeling that I must stop this at once.

But Joachim smiled and motioned me to join them. Claudia looked up from her lute, saw me, and stopped in the middle of a word.

"Please go on," said Joachim. "I'd forgotten how well you sing."

Flustered, Claudia started again, but a completely different song. This was a seafaring tune about courage and shipwreck.

I let the melody wash over me while I probed with magio for Arnulf. I found him in the stables — either supervising the reshoeing of our horses, I thought with Ascelin's suspicions, or else making sure we could not leave.

"Excuse me, my lady," I said abruptly when Claudia came to the end of the song. "We've all been wondering, perhaps you can tell me. Why did you and your husband ask our chaplain to come visit you now?"

Joachim frowned at my rudeness. But Claudia seemed too delighted that I had not asked her what she meant by singing love songs to a priest — and her husband's brother at that — to mind. "It's something to do with our trade caravans," she said lightly. "We have, of course, hoped for years that Joachim would come home to visit, but there's some business matter that made it especially urgent now. Arnulf can explain it to you, I'm sure; I never pay much attention to business myself."

"Maybe you should," said Joachim, but looking at me rather than her.

"You never did," she said softly.

"But you never had any intention of becoming a priest," he said with a smile, scrambling to his feet, "or, in your case, a nun."

As he and I walked back toward the others, I wondered uneasily if Arnulf knew all the time what his wife was doing.

If he meant harm to us, he certainly treated us well in the meantime. Our horses were still not ready at the end of the day, but the first of our clothes came back clean from the laundry. Ascelin went white when we returned to our rooms and found our armor and weapons gone, but Arnulf's constable reassured him that they had just been taken away to have the rust polished off and the edges sharpened. Even our boots were gone to be resoled.

After another luxurious meal, Arnulf invited us into his study while Claudia supervised preparing the children for bed. Candlelight gleamed on polished wood and brass. I scanned the shelves quickly, looking for books of magic, but saw mostly account books, books of history and geography, and some literature. A bright fire took the chill from the spring evening.

"Joachim tells me you're wondering why I asked him to come home now after all these years," said Arnulf, stretching out his long legs. In the candlelight, the brothers looked more alike than ever. "I hadn't meant to worry the rest of you with this, but maybe I could use your help."

"What's disappearing into thin air?" asked Ascelin intensely. He had gotten this from me.

"Wait, wait," said Arnulf cheerfully. At least he and Joachim sounded different. "If I'm going to tell you about this, I'd better start at the beginning."

"And what's that?"

Arnulf was more than willing to answer. He had in fact, I thought, brought us to his study specifically to tell us. I wondered abruptly if anything he said was his real concern or if he had created a story to distract us from something else.

"It's believed," began Arnulf, "and this, I must stress, is only a rumor, that King Solomon's Pearl has been found again."

IV

If the story was created for our benefit, at least the Pearl had not been, for King Haimeric seemed to have heard of it. "But I didn't think it could be found," the king said slowly. "I'd always heard that it had been hidden inside a golden box, inside a sealed amphora, inside a locked cabinet, inside a sunken ship, in the deepest rift of the Outer Sea."

"That's right," said Arnulf, "hidden by the Ifriti a thousand years ago. But if an Ifrit had hidden it in the sea, he might be able to find it again. And the story I have heard is that it is now somewhere in the East and that someone has located its hiding place."

"And what is this Pearl?" asked Hugo.

"Since no one has seen it for a thousand years," said Arnulf slowly, "we have only story and legend. But the legend is that it is an enormous, flawless black pearl, permeated from its creation with the forces that shaped the earth, and which the Queen of Sheba brought to King Solomon as a wedding gift. Something of such perfection, something of such historical significance, would always be beyond price.

"But there is more. King Solomon, it is said, imbued this Pearl with all his wisdom and magic. It gives power to those who hold it, so that they will always prosper, that their setbacks will be only temporary, and they will in the end find their hearts' desire."

The room was silent for a moment except for the crackling of the fire. The candle flames were reflected in the absolute black of the windows.

"But if it's so priceless," said Hugo at last, "why doesn't the royal Son of David still have it?"

"The Captivity of Babylon," said Joachim. I wondered how much of this he had already heard.

Arnulf nodded. "Exactly. The Sons of David after Solomon long had the Pearl, but when their city was sacked and the Children of Abraham were taken as slaves to Babylon, the Pearl was lost to them."

"This doesn't sound like a very reliable magical object to me," I said, "if it let them all be enslaved."

"It's years since I heard about it," said King Haimeric slowly. "But my impression was that the Pearl was stolen from the royal treasury and that Babylon attacked shortly thereafter."

"The Bible tells us," commented Joachim, "that King Zedekiah had broken his covenant with the Lord."

"Others have also suggested," said Arnulf, "that the Pearl would only aid its owner as long as that owner acted from the purest of motives. We have so little information. But the story one hears most often is that this flawless pearl *did* have a flaw. It would always aid the people who held it, sometimes for a year, sometimes for five centuries. But sooner or later its powers would fail, only to be revived in the hands of someone new."

I leaned back in my chair and shivered in spite of the fire's warmth. Something out of the old magic created long, long before modern wizardry had begun to shape and channel the forces of magic with reliable and reproducible spells, something carrying both enormous powers and a fatal flaw. . . .

"Solomon himself," Arnulf continued, "in all his wisdom, is said to have locked up the Pearl late in his life and refused to touch it again. For centuries after it was first stolen, the story goes, it kept appearing and disappearing around the East. From Babylon, it was taken deep into the inner desert by nomads. It was stolen and stolen again a hundred times and every time it was stolen its flaw was revealed sooner. For a century, the governor of the imperial city of Xantium held it and his city flourished beyond all others in power and in wealth. But then it was lost again, until it reappeared in the hands of the Prophet's nephew — brought to him, I have heard, by an Ifrit. And the People of the Prophet flourished in might, and the caliphs held the Pearl for two hundred years.

"But after two centuries, either the Pearl began again to reveal its flaw or the very desire for its power drove men mad, for fratricidal wars broke out among all the People of the Prophet. And it was then that the last of the caliphs renounced both its power and its perils by sending the Ifriti to hide it deep in the sea."

Arnulf fell silent. For several minutes we thought our own thoughts until a log settled in the fireplace with a sharp crack. I looked toward Ascelin. I was still wondering if any of the magic I knew would be at all useful, but he looked as though he had reached some sort of decision.

Hugo spoke first. "But what is the connection of the Pearl with you and Father Joachim and things disappearing into thin air?"

Arnulf looked uncomfortable. I wondered if what he was about to tell us was a lie. "It's the caravans," he said after a brief pause, "not just mine, but many of the luxury merchants'. Stories are running wild throughout the East that whoever found the Black Pearl is trying to smuggle it into the western kingdoms. All of us, therefore, have had to put on extra guards."

The story was not just running through the East, I thought. It had already reached the lord of the red sandstone castle.

"We could understand it if our caravans were just being attacked by bandits — bandits have been a feature of the luxury trade as long as it has existed. Silks, spices, saints' relics from Xantium — we all have to deal with them. Why, just last fall, when I wasn't more than a week's ride from here, I was set upon by bandits, though the knights with me fought them off successfully.

"But my caravans, at any rate, haven't merely been attacked. I've had repeated messages from my agents in the East and there seems no obvious answer. Several of my caravans, four of them as of last month, have simply disappeared."

He paused again; when he continued it was so quietly we had to lean forward to hear him. "Men and animals were left standing, but the wagons and goods were gone. They said there was an abrupt rush of air and then my caravans were gone without a scrap remaining. Only," and his voice dropped even lower, "only there was always a sign dug into the hard sand and stone of the road. The sign of the cross."

"Ifriti," said Ascelin into the ensuing silence.

Arnulf shook his head. "I don't think so. Ifriti could certainly carry off a caravan without a trace, but they would not mark where they had been with a Christian cross. I'm not sure the Ifriti recognize the power of God at all and, if so, they probably follow the Prophet. That's why," flicking his eyes toward Joachim, "I'd hoped my brother the priest would have some ideas."

None of us had any ideas, or any ideas we wanted to tell Arnulf. But Ascelin, back in our chambers later that evening, seemed convinced he knew what had happened.

"He's got Solomon's Pearl here in this house," he said, low and intense. We were all gathered together in his room — all of us except, again, Joachim.

"Can you sense it, Wizard?" asked King Haimeric.

I tried for a moment, then shook my head. "I don't find any indication of a magical object here in the house, but that might not mean anything. Any natural object with a spell attached to it is still a natural object and the spell itself is hard to recognize unless it's actually active."

"If he's got it," said Dominic, who had been very

quiet all evening, "then he's hoping to get the might of the Church to help him keep it."

Ascelin nodded, a quick motion with his chin. "That's why they suddenly asked back the brother they virtually threw out all those years before."

"Wait a minute," I protested. "I don't think they threw him out. They may have quarreled over business ethics, but Joachim decided he wanted to be a priest. He and his brother write each other fairly regularly, even if he hasn't been here since he went off to seminary."

"They disagreed on more than the ethics of the luxury trade," said the king slowly, "but our chaplain still left of his own will."

"What do you mean?" I asked. Joachim had still not said anything to me to explain his long absence from home.

"It's the Lady Claudia, of course," said the king with a smile. "Didn't any of the rest of you notice it?"

I looked at him in amazement. I had certainly not mentioned finding her singing to the chaplain.

"Notice what?" asked Dominic.

The king looked at him affectionately. "You've lived almost all your life in the royal castle of Yurt, since you were four years old, and I don't think you ever noticed anything there, either."

"What are you talking about, sire?" said the royal nephew, just avoiding sounding rude.

"Well, I've never told the queen, either," said the king with a distant look, "and I must say it hasn't been much on my mind in the years since I married her, but you might as well know. Dominic, I spent most of my life in love with your mother."

This was the same shock to Dominic it was to everyone else. "But — she never suggested — "

"I don't think she ever knew," said Haimeric with a reminiscent smile. "It won't hurt to tell you now. But didn't you ever wonder why the king of Yurt grew to be an old man without marrying?"

"I was your heir," said Dominic warily, as though awaiting much worse revelations.

"Of course, and a good heir you were. You were my own dear brother's boy, as well as hers, and I loved you as though you were my own. But I couldn't bear to marry anyone else while your mother was still alive. After your father was killed fighting in the eastern kingdoms — saying he had to make his own fortune, which I never have understood, when he knew he always had a home in Yurt — and you and she came to live in the royal castle, I couldn't think of loving someone else. Your father sent all those jewels back to Yurt when he died, of course, but all she wanted was *him*."

He paused briefly and smiled. "I'm not surprised at that. I'm sure you've heard since you were little, Dominic, about your father: that he was the handsomest man in three kingdoms, the bravest warrior, the staunchest friend. All of it's true."

He then hesitated again, while Dominic uneasily twisted the ruby ring on his finger. "You probably didn't realize this," King Haimeric went on, "but your mother was a lovely woman. Not as beautiful as the queen, of course, but lovely and vibrant all the same. Even after she died, I don't think I would have considered marrying if I hadn't met the queen."

And I thought I had known my king. I felt as though a piece of ordinary flooring had been pulled up to reveal a whole busy world beneath. But I felt reticent to ask him more and, if we were all in danger from King Solomon's Pearl, we didn't have time. "What does this have to do with Arnulf and his caravans?"

"It explains," said the king, with the same reminiscent look, "that Ascelin and his hunting instincts may be picking up something quite different from imminent peril. He may only be picking up unrequited love."

I felt a sudden conviction that King Haimeric had known all along that I was in love with the queen. If so, he had never said anything and I was certainly not going to be the first to mention it. *She*, at any rate, I was quite sure had never had any idea.

"You're good friends with the chaplain, Wizard," the king said. "Hasn't he ever mentioned the Lady Claudia to you?"

"Not even once," I said slowly. "But — but I think you may have it backwards. He didn't go into the seminary loving her and he didn't come back here still in love with her. If anything, she was in love with him."

"Come on," said Ascelin impatiently. "It doesn't matter who's in love with whom." Quite a comment, I thought, for someone who missed his own wife so badly. "We have to plan how to get away from here before we're seized by the fatal spell of the Pearl."

"Wait a minute," interrupted Hugo. "I doubt he has it here. But don't you think this Pearl must have something to do with the disappearance of my father?"

"It must," I said, thinking rapidly. "Sir Hugo and all his party vanished abruptly, as abruptly as those caravans. Unless they were all killed by bandits — and I shouldn't think they would be, so close to the Holy Land and accompanied by a competent wizard — this sounds like the same sort of disappearance. Somebody in the East has mastered an Ifrit and is using it to capture anyone or anything he thinks may have the Black Pearl."

"So if Arnulf does have the Pearl here already," said Hugo, "no one else realizes it. And whoever's got the Ifrit is continuing to look for it."

"How do you master an Ifrit, Wizard?" asked Dominic.

I was certainly not the person to ask, but I didn't want to say so. "It's very hard," I said, "and requires spells very unlike anything we normally use in the western kingdoms." Fortunately Dominic did not press me for details.

"Whether Arnulf already has the Pearl here and wants us to help him keep it," put in the king, "or whether he, like probably every other merchant in the East, is wondering who *does* have it and how he can stop his caravans from being attacked in the meantime, he certainly wants us as his friends. I don't think we need fear him, Ascelin."

The tall prince looked dubious but nodded. "I still think we should stay watchful."

We all jumped when a sharp rap came on the door. It opened to reveal Arnulf and Joachim.

"I just wanted to make sure you were all set for the evening," said the lord of the manor with a smile. "All having a last bedtime conversation, eh?" He must have suspected we were discussing his affairs, but he was too polite to say so. He did have more tact, I thought, than the chaplain — probably good for business. "There's a bell in the hall you can ring if you need anything. Sleep well!"

As the brothers left, I wondered, as I had this afternoon, if Arnulf had sent his wife to attempt to seduce Joachim. So far I didn't think it was working, but I very much wanted to know if he had.

V

In the morning, while Ascelin went to the stables to see if he could speed up the reshoeing of our horses, I went in search of the chaplain. I found him near the garden, playing volleyball with Arnulf's children.

I had never seen Joachim play volleyball before; for that matter, though he often talked with Prince Paul and Gwennie on topics beyond their lessons and took them on walks through the countryside, I couldn't recall him doing *anything* I would have called playing. But now he and his niece were matched against the two boys, using a low, child-sized net over which he towered.

"All right, we're all tied evenly," he said to them,

laughing, when I came up. He straightened out his vestments. "Let's stop there and give your uncle a chance to catch his breath. Yes, yes, we can play again this afternoon."

As he and I walked into the garden and sat down on the bench where Claudia had played the lute the afternoon before, he said, "I'm glad we were able to come. I wouldn't want to miss my niece and nephews."

I looked at him sideways. Any worry or concern he might have had about coming home after so long seemed gone. He looked only happy and relaxed. He also made no attempt to explain or justify the Lady Claudia's singing, which I would have felt compelled to do in the circumstances.

"Why did your brother really want to see you?" I asked. The flower-scented air was warm and a bird sang from a nearby branch.

"He told you last night," said Joachim, looking out across the landscape. He didn't sound very concerned. "He'd hoped I'd have an idea of who or what might be responsible for his disappearing caravans, and of course, he hadn't dared say anything specific to me in a message that might be intercepted. I'm afraid I have no ideas that could help him. Now he's asked me to keep alert for any clues while we're in the East."

"Has the Lady Claudia asked you again to transact business for the firm while we're in Xantium?"

"No," said Joachim in surprise. He turned his dark eyes on me. "This whole situation seems, I must say, more like a problem for a wizard than a priest."

"I don't understand it, either," I said, shaking my head slowly. "It sounds as though two separate people, at least one of them Christian, have mastered Ifriti: one whose Ifrit recovered the Black Pearl for him from the deepest rift of the sea, and the other who's using his Ifrit to seize merchant caravans in search of it."

"How *do* you master an Ifrit?" asked Joachim, just as Dominic had.

Joachim I trusted. "I haven't the slightest idea."

The chaplain did not pursue the topic. In a moment he began humming softly the same tune, I realized, that Claudia had sung the day before.

"Ascelin thinks your brother has the Pearl here," I said abruptly.

Joachim smiled. "That seems unlikely. If it really does have the power to make its owner prosper, he wouldn't be losing all those caravans."

I didn't like the thought of our going into an East where at least one, if not two, Ifriti were making travelers disappear; I also didn't have much faith in Joachim's brother, but I couldn't say either of these things — or ask the chaplain if Claudia really was trying to seduce him. Instead I asked, "If Arnulf just wanted a priest's opinion, didn't he have a closer one to ask?"

This made Joachim look distressed as none of my other questions had. "Not one he knows and trusts. He hasn't kept a chaplain since he's been married."

"Well, most merchants don't," I said, speaking from my own experience.

"Maybe not, but merchant families who live like aristocrats — which we certainly always did — have households like aristocrats and that includes chaplains. My father always employed a chaplain and, of course, Claudia herself is from an aristocratic background. But the chapel in the house is now closed up and they have to go to town for church service — if they go at all."

"They don't keep a wizard, either," I said. "Even some of the smaller City merchants employ wizards." The sharp business practices which Joachim had felt he could not follow at least did not include using illusion to improve the quality of the merchandise.

But Joachim wasn't interested in wizards. "It was not Arnulf's idea to dismiss his chaplain," he said. "It was the Lady Claudia's." He abruptly stopped looking concerned. "You know, Daimbert, if I *had* decided to stay here, it would have been because of Claudia. But service to God took precedence, of course. It may not be a very humble thought, but I have wondered once or twice if the reason why she dismissed their chaplain, when they got married five years later, was some sort of oblique attack on the priesthood that had taken me."

His eyes looked slightly ashamed but still highly amused at his own thoughts. The queen had worried that the king might come back changed from his experiences in the Holy Land. We weren't more than six weeks out of Yurt, but so far, so many new sides of people's personalities were being revealed that the royal court might not even recognize us — assuming, of course, we reached home again.

If Joachim thought that the Lady Claudia was trying to make up for lost time now that he was here again, he didn't say so. I wondered if her singing had all been quite innocent and if I had an impure mind to imagine otherwise.

Hugo had asked Arnulf to let him look at some of the books in his study. He found the full story of King Solomon's Pearl there, and he entertained us all at lunch with other accounts he had found of creatures who lived in distant countries.

I wondered, listening to him, how much of it he really believed or to what extent he was teasing Dominic, who took it all very seriously. "And did you know," said Hugo, his eyes bright with excitement, "that if you go around to the far side of the world the people there all have enormous feet and toes so that they can cling to the earth and not fall off?"

"Don't be silly," said Ascelin, but as though he was thinking of something else. "You can't fall off the earth. Besides, there's nothing but the Outer Sea on the far side of the globe."

It was hard to tell how many of the travelers' tales Hugo had picked up were real and how much imagination. Much worse monsters than anything he described could and did live in the northern continent of wild magic, even though I did not think they frequently visited the East — or at least hoped not. Ifriti were real, but I was not nearly as sure about the people whose faces were in their bellies. Arnulf, who must have had excellent information about the East, made no attempt to contradict Hugo on anything.

But this thought gave me another. I had been assuming that Arnulf must make the journey east regularly, but maybe if one were a very wealthy merchant one did not, relying instead on one's agents. If he had been personally attacked and his caravans were beginning to disappear, he might well prefer to send someone else — such as us — than to go himself.

The next morning, our horses were finally ready, our clothes all clean, our boots resoled, our armor and harnesses polished. The air seemed sultry for this early in the summer as we mounted our horses in the wide courtyard.

"We were delighted to have you all," said Arnulf genially. "Be sure to stop here again on your way home."

The Lady Claudia came out of the house at the last minute, carrying a small foil-wrapped parcel that looked, from the way she held it, heavy for its size. Paying no attention to anyone else, she walked up to Joachim's horse.

"I want you to have this," she said in a low voice, not meeting his eyes.

"What is it?" he asked with a smile.

"It's a present. But don't open it yet. Wait to open it until you're far from here."

I had a sudden dreadful suspicion of what that small package contained.

Joachim shrugged and unbuckled his saddlebag to slide it in on top of his Bible. He took Claudia's hand affectionately for a moment, but I did not see him look back as we all rode out a moment later.

I, however, glanced back over my shoulder to see the Lady Claudia, looking quite small in the spacious court of her manor house, waving her handkerchief after us.

There were rumblings of thunder in the distance as we headed back toward the great eastern route. "Do you have your weather spells ready, Wizard?" Dominic asked.

Normally, I didn't like to use weather spells. Any magic, no matter how trivial, has far-ranging effects and to change the weather for any reason less than protecting the crop from hail had never seemed very responsible. But I didn't want to get soaked to the skin any more than Dominic did. I pulled up my horse and shaped a few spells in the Hidden Language to move the densest of the clouds a little further away from us.

The sun came out above us though the air stayed damp, and the darkness over much of the landscape gave the sunlight an artificial quality. I was about to hurry to catch up to the others when I realized that Ascelin was standing beside me.

"What do you think, Wizard," he asked, his blue eyes intent. "Are we carrying the Black Pearl now?"

We both looked toward Joachim, riding with the others a few hundred yards ahead. It seemed horribly likely.

"But why would Claudia give it to us to take back to the East?" I asked.

"Maybe she wanted to get it out of their house before its curse affected her family. Or, maybe, knowing its powers for good were so strong, she wanted to give it to a man she loved more than her husband."

I thought that Ascelin would have to tell Prince Paul some of the stories of his vivid imagination — assuming we made it home to Yurt. "If so," I said, "why didn't Arnulf object?"

"He may not have realized what it was."

If Ascelin could guess, Arnulf would certainly have guessed — unless he had deliberately had his wife try to renew her earlier friendship with Joachim for the express purpose of getting that package into his saddlebag. I immediately thought of several other "presents" Claudia might have given the chaplain, including a love potion to make him return to her or a deadly viper sealed in a ceramic vase ready to leap out and bite him when he broke the seal. More prosaically, the package could have held a miniature portrait of her in a marble frame or even a new Bible. But I did not think so.

"We have to make him open it right away," said Ascelin.

"We can't 'make' the chaplain do anything," I said. "But I'll certainly ask him about it."

The others had stopped and were waiting for us. As Ascelin and I hurried to catch up, I wondered how I should ask to see a present I was sure was highly significant and highly dangerous.

PART THREE

Bandits

1

"She said to wait to open it until we were far from there," Joachim told me. "We aren't far away yet."

His comment was quite reasonable if Claudia had given him a portrait of herself, quite unreasonable if it was actually the Black Pearl — or some other dangerous magic object that Arnulf wanted us to take into the East for reasons of his own.

I tried probing with magic to see inside Joachim's saddlebag. A variation on the far-seeing spell would allow me — or so I hoped — to peek inside the foil-wrapped parcel. Unfortunately, it was completely dark inside. Delicate magical probing from the outside wasn't going to tell me much, other than that whatever was in there was not alive. Not a viper then, I tried to reassure myself, and certainly not an Ifrit.

By evening, the thunderstorm had moved off, though the air stayed damp. We sat around our fire eating Ascelin's cooking again. Joachim's brother had sent along a bag of rice as well as replenishing our other supplies, and Ascelin had made a fairly successful stab at cooking it. I wondered how rude it would actually be to open Joachim's present behind his back. Unfortunately, the answer seemed to be very rude.

But the more I thought about it, no matter what Ascelin believed, the more I doubted it was King Solomon's Pearl. In fact, I wasn't even sure there really were rumors that the Pearl had been found again or if Arnulf had dragged up some old story to distract us from whatever real rumors might be running through the East. In that case, he might indeed have found whatever the bandits had been looking for in the silk caravan and have had his wife try to renew the flames of old passion with Joachim so that the chaplain would take a package from her without any suspicion of what it really contained.

But here I came back to the original problem, that we were carrying an unknown magical object, and the wizard, me, who should have been able to deal with it, was held back by friendship and politeness from doing so.

I looked off toward the east. We were in an area of low, rolling hills, but in the rain-washed evening air a line of distant mountains marched along the horizon. Ascelin and the king had the maps out and were discussing the route.

"The main road cuts south toward the Central Sea," said Ascelin, "but it really is shorter to cross the mountains into the eastern kingdoms and come down to the sea on the far side. That way we also avoid the most dangerous part of the sea voyage. Arnulf recommended we come this way, and I probably would have anyway. I've hunted in these mountains and know the passes."

"But will the passes be open yet or will they still be snow-bound?"

"They should all be open except for the highest, and we won't need to take the highest. The lowest pass, in fact, is also the shortest route — it's directly east of here. It's not used very much, but that's only because the road is so narrow at points."

The king contemplated the map a moment. "I know Warin, the king of this kingdom. I wrote him this winter to say that I was going on a quest to the East and he wrote back to be sure to stop and see him. He, too, had heard the rumors about the blue rose. He agrees with you about the mountain passes, by the way."

"My father telephoned us from King Warin's castle on his way to the Holy Land," put in Hugo.

"Since everyone seems to agree we should go that way," said the king, "it sounds as though we must!"

"I know King Warin, too," said Ascelin.

I came over to look at the map myself, suddenly realizing that I knew the Royal Wizard of this kingdom. Elerius, three years ahead of me at the wizards' school and, it was rumored, the best student the school had ever had, had become Royal Wizard here when he graduated. I hadn't been in contact with him in several years, but I assumed he was still here. In spite of its somewhat isolated location, the kingdom was reputed to be enormously wealthy, with gold and jewels from mountain mines.

Elerius might well have heard of the Black Pearl, I thought. And I could use the castle telephone to call the wizards' school. Magic telephones were still scarce over in this part of the western kingdoms, and although Arnulf had one, I had felt highly reluctant to call the school to check on his story with him right there.

We rode east for three days, the snow-capped mountain peaks coming closer each day. The landscape around us became uneven, cut with unexpected ravines. The hills were flinty with little topsoil and the few villages we passed seemed to live entirely from grape-growing. The men working among the vines gave us sharp looks but did not wave. Joachim still showed no indication of opening his present, and I didn't like to press him.

We stopped at our second pilgrimage church, one listed in the appendix of Joachim's book because it was not on the main pilgrimage route, although apparently it had been highly regarded for fifteen hundred years.

As we came over a rise, we saw before us a small, octagonal church made of white marble, with the fluted columns of a structure built in the later days of the Empire. But as we came closer, we saw that what I had first thought was the entire church was, in fact, only the upper storey; and below it was another structure, this one made of rough, dark stone with tiny windows in the style of churches built in the chaotic years that followed the breakup of the Empire.

"This can't be right," said Hugo. "How could they have built the earlier building second?"

"Wait until you see the whole thing," said Joachim with a smile.

"You mean we haven't yet?"

As we rode closer, we saw that the dark stone structure we had thought was the church's lower storey was, in fact, built on top of another church, this one highly decorated with elaborate carvings; that under this was another level where the stonework was smooth and polished, the stained-glass windows tall and pointed; and that at the very bottom was a fifth church built in the modern assymetrical style where, even though the walls had to be very thick to support the levels above, there were still broad expanses of glass, and dark red stones had been set into the white walls to make abstract designs. The whole five-storey church was sunk into a wide hole in the ground.

"It used to be on a little hill," said Joachim, enjoying our surprise. "The hill was made mostly of small stones and the stones became popular among pilgrims, as souvenirs of their visit — and even, for those of simple faith, holy relics in their own right. Soon the hill disappeared, leaving the original church standing well above the new ground level. So the priests here decided to add a new church, under the old one." He swung down from his horse and picked up a loose stone himself. "The process was repeated three more times."

We visited all five levels and Joachim talked to the priests there. I tried to contemplate how many pilgrims it must have taken to wear away a hole as big as the one in which the church now sat. "There's a major pilgrimage here every Midsummer," said Joachim, consulting his book, "and two other smaller religious festivals. The hills are covered with the tents of the pious at Midsummer as far as two miles away."

I had also not really appreciated before how relatively scarce wizards were in the western kingdoms compared to priests. The latter would be found in every village, in isolated churches like this one, and in every — or nearly every — aristocratic court, whereas even a large kingdom might have only a handful of wizards. The king, too, took a stone when we left.

Toward the end of our third day of riding east, we saw an enormous castle rising before us at the very base of the mountains. Dozens of towers and turrets rose above high walls that encircled not just the castle itself but all the hilltops around it. Those walls, pierced with arrowslits and guarded by towers at every corner, must have been at least a mile long. I had once assumed the royal castle of Yurt was a good example of an impregnable castle built for war, but this journey was showing me I was mistaken.

We zigzagged up a steep approach beneath those walls, but the gates before us stood wide and welcoming. "Tell your king that King Haimeric of Yurt is here to visit him," the king told the armed guardsman who met us. Although a second guardsman immediately stepped up to take his place as the first went off with the message, he showed no sign of attacking us and instead gave us an interested look.

King Warin, word came back almost immediately, would be happy to receive us. We passed through the wall, up another zigzag stretch so steep we had to lead the horses, then across a bridge over a deep and narrow ditch and through another set of gates into the castle itself. We were then led through the courtyard, where servants took the horses, and into the great hall.

The hall was about the same size as the great hall in Yurt, but there the comparison stopped. The outer castle walls may have been dark granite, but the interior walls of this room were green marble, set with semi-precious stones that flashed in the light of the magic lamps. Even the flooring was marble. It seemed very cold, I told myself in loyalty to Yurt.

King Warin was seated on his throne on the far side, surrounded by liveried attendants. They backed away, bowing, as we approached, but six liveried knights remained close to the throne. Talking to the king was a man dressed in black and silver whom I took to be the Royal Chancellor. The king lifted his grizzled head as we came up. He had an enormous ring on his forefinger, and the cloak thrown across his shoulder was made of wolfskin.

I expected him to frown at us in august majesty, but instead he rose to meet us with a smile. The knights stepped forward with him. "Haimeric! It's been years. I should have known the rumors about a blue rose would bring you out of that little kingdom of yours. And you," with a pleased look at Ascelin, "I know as well. You helped me when those undead creatures invaded my kingdom many years ago. Prince Ascelin, that's it."

I glanced around surreptitiously as we were introduced, wondering where his wizard might be. But when I asked, King Warin told me what I should have expected. "We don't have a wizard right now, I'm afraid."

"What happened to Elerius?"

"He left nearly a year ago," King Warin said regretfully. "Another kingdom closer to the City needed a new Royal Wizard, and the teachers of your school recommended him. We were terribly sorry to lose him, but I don't think my kingdom held many challenges for him any more. You knew him, I gather?"

"I knew him when we were in school together," I said, thinking that Yurt still seemed to have plenty of challenges for me.

"He really was extremely good," Warin continued reminiscently. "I think that's why we haven't been satisfied with any of the other young wizards the school has tried sending out. Did you know, Haimeric, he installed our telephone system within three days of taking up his post? And then," with a laugh, "he apologized for taking so long, saying that if he had taken more courses in the technical division it would have taken only two!"

It had taken me six months, not three days, to get the telephone system working in Yurt and then we had ended up with telephones unlike anyone else's. Fortunately, King Haimeric did not mention this.

"Maybe you can help us, Wizard," added Warin thoughtfully.

For a second I felt again the cold majesty I thought I had sensed when we first came in, but which his friendly manner had belied. As a wizard, I was highly sensitive to mood and partially concealed thoughts, but I was also highly sensitive to my own imagination.

"Just after Elerius left, a group of pilgrims stopped here. They had a wizard with them. He left something he said was a special message for another wizard. So far, none of the new wizards whom the school has tried sending us has been able to read it — part of the reason we decided not to keep any of them. Maybe you can; I'm sure Haimeric wouldn't keep an incompetent wizard!"

This was clearly meant to be a joke, but I took it seriously. "I'll have a look," I said as casually as I could.

King Warin lifted one hand in a lazy gesture and his dour chancellor, who had been hovering just at the edge of our circle, hurried away. I was immediately convinced that the group of pilgrims had been Sir

Hugo's party and that the wizard who had left the magic message was Evrard.

11

The chancellor returned with a box so black it seemed to absorb the light from the magic lamps. "I'll need a little privacy for my spells," I said with what I hoped was calm dignity. If it actually was a message from Evrard, I wanted to read it before anyone else. And if it took a while to figure out the spells, no matter what wizard had left it, I didn't want an attentive audience.

The chancellor led me to a small parlor opening off the great hall. I probed carefully, trying to find what kind of spell permeated this box. No way to open it, not even a seam, was visible.

I had over the years grown to distrust my sudden convictions, which tended to be wrong most of the time. Evrard, I told myself, still wasn't a good enough wizard to have created a message that several highly qualified graduates from the school couldn't read. Of course, the alternative was that some truly incompetent wizard had tried to leave a message and had only made something unreadable.

Abruptly, I caught a glimpse of a spell I understood. It was a very simple spell, so simple, in fact, that I had almost overlooked it while probing for something more complicated. I said a handful of words in the Hidden Language and a seam suddenly appeared all around the box. The lid slowly opened. Inside was a parchment scroll, written on both sides in incomprehensible symbols and combinations of letters. But when I said a few more words, they scurried across the page and shaped themselves into a clear message.

It was from Evrard after all.

"Beware, any wizard who reads this," it began.

I glanced quickly toward the great hall. Our party was still standing there, talking to King Warin and his chancellor.

"You are in danger of your life." Could this be one of Evrard's jokes? "King Warin, I think, is a sorcerer. Last night I saw unmistakeable evidence that he is dabbling in the black arts."

I looked toward the hall again and met King Warin's eyes across a space of twenty yards. They were almost unbearably cold and seemed to bore straight through to my bones.

I tore my eyes back to the message. "We have also just heard some very strange rumors coming out of the East. King Warin, I think, knows more about them than he wishes to say. This is not a good place for a young wizard."

That was it except for Evrard's signature. I said a few quick words in the Hidden Language, the letters of the message rescrambled themselves, the lid of the box slammed shut, and even the seam that marked the opening disappeared.

I took two deep breaths and squared my shoulders, then walked back into the great hall.

"I'm afraid it really is an unreadable message," I said, handing the box to the chancellor. "No wonder none of the young wizards from the school had any luck with it. The wizard who created it seems to have gotten his spells wrong. The one thing I could determine from it, sire," turning to King Haimeric, "was it was left here by Sir Hugo's wizard."

"That's right," he said in high good humor. "We were just hearing how his party had stopped here."

"You all remember Evrard," I said, "from when he served as ducal wizard of Yurt that one summer. I think he's developed into a fairly good wizard, but he always used to like improvising new spells and not all of them worked." I apologized silently to Evrard for impugning his abilities. He would understand.

Ascelin, who had spent our whole visit to Arnulf deeply suspicious, now laughed reminiscently. In this castle he appeared to find nothing to fear. "Well, his rather unorthodox magic gave me the excuse I needed to woo my lady the duchess," he said.

I looked at King Warin from the corner of my eye. Could he really be a sorcerer? He was certainly no wizard and, as far as I could tell from a few delicate spells that I hoped he wouldn't notice, he didn't even have as much magical training as most carnival magicians. But there was something about him, a latent power, a suggestion that he might be appreciably older than his grizzled hair would indicate, that could mean that here was someone who knew just enough of the Hidden Language to take himself and those around him into deadly danger.

Although he was talking animatedly with Hugo about his father's visit, he seemed to feel my eyes on him for he turned his head just enough to meet my glance. His smile reached nowhere near his eyes.

His chancellor slipped away to arrange accommodations for us. A whole maze of chambers, passages and stairs led off the great hall. This castle, I thought, had been built and added to for centuries. We ended up in a large chamber with more than a dozen beds intended, I expected, to put up the knights of a visiting dignitary.

I was relieved to see that our saddlebags had already been brought into the room and that the corner of Claudia's foil-wrapped present was just visible under the flap of Joachim's bag. At this point, whatever it contained, I did not want to lose it.

In spite of the marble floor and the heavy, silk-worked tapestries on the walls, the wide room felt grim. The fire burning at one side seemed to cast no heat. King Warin was wealthier than Joachim's family could ever imagine being, but there was nothing here of the sybaritic feel of the Lady Claudia's guest chambers.

"I think Warin's as old as I am," said the king, "but he looks at least twenty years younger. The air must be healthy this close to the mountains!"

I had another explanation, but I didn't want to voice it here. And if King Warin was a sorcerer who dabbled in black magic, what did that say about the man who had been his Royal Wizard for twelve years?

We were served dinner in the middle of the great hall, with no other members of Warin's court there except his ever-present chancellor and the stony-faced knights ranged behind the king. The platters and even the bowls by our places for bits of rind and bone were made of heavily worked silver. Not only did Warin not have a Royal Wizard, he didn't seem to have a Royal Chaplain, either. King Haimeric talked as we ate about the blue rose, which I had been surprised to hear Warin knew about, as nothing about this castle suggested a rose fancier. Then the king moved on to the topic of the Black Pearl.

"King Solomon's Pearl?" said Warin, with that same good humor and openness floating on top of a bitter cold which only I seemed to feel. "I certainly haven't heard anything about it, although since the main trade routes all run west of here, rumors from the East wouldn't reach me quickly. After all, the mountains are full of bandits so the luxury caravans stay well clear if they can."

Evrard, I thought, had heard here "very strange" rumors coming out of the East.

"In fact, I'm not sure I ever knew anything about the Pearl, beyond that old legend that the caliph had had it hidden in the sea, what would it be, a good millennium ago."

"Well, we've heard enough stories that it's been found again," I put in, "that I'd like to call the wizards' school to see if they have any more accurate information. Would it be possible, sir, to use your telephone this evening?"

"Of course, of course," said Warin, the perfect host. "Ask them, too, when that new wizard they promised me is likely to arrive!"

Several young wizards sent back as unsuitable — especially since one or all of them would have told the school about Evrard's message — would be good enough reason for the Master of the school not to send Warin any more. That is, I thought, unless Elerius had told them the king was not a sorcerer, just someone with very high standards for his employees.

I would very much have liked to ask the school about Elerius, but when the dour chancellor led me to the telephone room, he showed no sign of leaving. He leaned against the wall, his arms folded and his eyes on me, as I waited for someone to answer. I could see the telephone in the wizards' school, a tiny image in the view screen. Elerius might have installed the phone here in three days, I reminded myself, but I had been the first wizard to invent a far-seeing attachment for telephones.

A young wizard answered, and in a few more minutes I was talking to the school's librarian. "I need all the information you have about King Solomon's Pearl," I told him. "How soon do you think I could get it?"

He seemed surprised. "Is that the Pearl that was hidden in the sea all those centuries ago? I'm not sure we have very much on it."

"I need whatever you have, especially information about its powers and attributes."

I had hoped the librarian could give me the information immediately, or at least by tomorrow morning, and my heart sank when he said he hoped to have something for me within twenty-four hours. "Oh, yes, that will be fine," I said as unconcernedly as I could. I should have realized that it would take a while to find references to an old story that had come to an end a thousand years ago. I didn't like spending another day in this castle, but once we crossed the mountains into the eastern kingdoms we might not have access to any more telephones at all. "Let me talk to Zahlfast."

"So you're in Elerius's former kingdom?" my old teacher asked me a minute later. "Evrard and his party got there, too, we hear."

"That's right," I said, glancing at the chancellor. I hoped Zahlfast could see him in his own view screen. "He even tried to leave some sort of magical message here, but it's all garbled."

Zahlfast opened his mouth and closed it again. "I gather the king there has been spoiled by Elerius for any other young wizard," he said after a very short pause. "He still wants a Royal Wizard, so we'll have to see if there's an experienced wizard somewhere who'd jump at the chance of serving in such a wealthy kingdom, even if it is somewhat isolated."

There was no way to speak directly, mind to mind, over the telephone. I tried to read in Zahlfast's face whether he thought the king here might really be a sorcerer or if it was all Evrard's imagination, but such information was too complicated to be conveyed by facial expressions.

"The librarian tells me you've been asking him about some of the old stories," Zahlfast continued. "If Evrard has disappeared due to old stories coming to life, we'll have to reconsider the efficacy of modern, organized magic."

As a joke, it was a fairly weak attempt. Zahlfast, I thought, must really be worried. I wondered if he had any information about the Pearl that he didn't dare tell me.

"Give my greetings to the Master," I said inanely and rang off.

The rest of our party had already gone to our wide, cold room. "Did the telephone work well, Wizard?" the king asked. "I'll ask Warin tomorrow if I can call the queen."

I nodded and drew Ascelin to one side. I had not yet told anyone my suspicions. "You knew the king here, years ago," I said quietly. "Tell me: do you trust him?"

"I don't trust very many people in this kingdom," said Ascelin with a glance toward the others, "and all of them are in this room."

I took a deep breath. So his ease in the great hall had been a façade for King Warin's benefit — it had certainly been good enough to fool *me*. "When you hunted here, you helped track down undead creatures made of hair and bone. Did you have any suspicion that King Warin helped make them?"

Ascelin's eyes narrowed, but he slowly shook his head. "Those were made by an old magician and he got away. The king was just delighted to have the creatures out of his kingdom."

Ascelin's distrust was general, then, not tied to any specific knowledge of King Warin. "Just curious," I said and told him no more. Unfortunately, I knew Evrard was capable of making jokes in highly dubious taste.

King Haimeric was pleased to have an excuse to visit with his old friend Warin for another day, especially since we had been dodging rain ever since Arnulf's house. This time, Ascelin did not let the weapons out of our room, and he polished off the few rusty spots that had appeared in the last four days himself — but then King Warin's staff showed no sign of being as helpful as Arnulf's.

The phone call from the wizards' school came while we were at dinner. The king had been talking again about the Black Pearl, discussing our visit with Arnulf much more openly than I would have preferred, but I didn't dare leave the school waiting while I tried to shift the conversation. This time, the chancellor did not accompany me but stayed at the table.

"I don't have a lot," the librarian said apologetically. "It is a fascinating story, but there's very little to it." I listened as he told the story of King Solomon's Pearl, essentially as we had already heard it from Joachim's brother and as Hugo had found it in Arnulf's books. "The accounts stress that it would become enormously dangerous if used from base motives. I've asked around the school," he finished, "and no one here has heard that it's been found."

"Has anyone talked to the merchants down in the City to see if they've heard such rumors?"

"I haven't," he said in surprise. "Why would merchants have information on magical objects not known to the wizards' school?"

Though set in the middle of the great City, the white-spired wizards' school had always held itself somewhat aloof from the City's concerns. "All right," I said. "Thank you." So Arnulf was, as I had thought, trying to distract us from something else and I couldn't even imagine what that might be.

"Well, it's always interesting to be asked about something different for a change," said the librarian. He looked down at the heavy volume he held in his hands. "This is one of the books that used to belong to Melecherius, and I expect I'm the first person to have it off the shelf since he died. . . ." He flipped to the sign-out slip tucked in the back and then said in surprise, "No, I'm wrong. It was checked out five years ago by Elerius."

I didn't have time to wonder, in the brief moments I might still have to speak without being overheard, why Elerius had been interested in the Black Pearl. "Is Zahlfast available?" I asked instead.

While waiting impatiently for him to come to the phone, I kept listening for a step in the corridor, for King Warin's chancellor to overhear my conversation.

"You should know by now that we don't like wizards calling us up all the time for advice," Zahlfast began irritably when I finally saw him in the view screen.

But I interrupted. "Quick. Do you know what was in the message that Evrard left here?"

"Of course I do," he said in surprise. I saw his eyes

flick past my shoulder and I looked back involuntarily myself, but there was no one else in the room. "Three extremely promising young wizards in a row have come back to the City in disgrace and told us about it. You'd think that *someone* would have had the sense to change the spells so that the message was something innocuous, rather than making the lame excuse that they couldn't read it and then getting themselves dismissed for incompetence."

I hadn't thought of changing the spells either, being too startled by the content of the message.

"We don't like to tell young wizards very much about their new posts," he continued, "because it's better if they can work everything out on their own, but this time it looks like we'd better. That kingdom is much too critically placed, just below the passes into the eastern kingdoms, not to have had a Royal Wizard for a year."

"Did you ask Elerius about it?" I hoped my end of the conversation was bland enough that, even if the chancellor was lurking just outside the door, he would find nothing in it to pass on to his master.

"Of course we did, the first time a young wizard returned to the school with a wild story of sorcerers." Zahlfast unexpectedly smiled. "So you're wondering yourself whether to believe it? Don't worry about it. Elerius told us it was a complete fabrication. I thought you knew Evrard well enough yourself to realize that he has a rather odd sense of humor sometimes."

Yesterday, I had thought Zahlfast worried. Today, he did not seem worried at all. I was also irritated with him for having sent me in search of Evrard and yet not telling me the one solid piece of information they had, that Evrard had felt his party was in danger long before they reached the Holy Land.

But they *had* reached the Holy Land safely. King Warin was a dead end for the purposes of our quest.

"The librarian's told me about this Black Pearl,"

Zahlfast continued with another smile. "Keep your eyes open in the East. I must say it all sounds rather farfetched, but if it is real and has been found, the school will need to acquire it. A highly charged magical object like that would be very dangerous except in the hands of skilled and thoroughly trained wizards."

I heard at last the step I had been straining for. The dour-faced chancellor looked around the corner. "Excuse me, but the others are ready for dessert and wondered if you were going to eat any more of the main dish."

I quickly said good-bye to Zahlfast and returned to the great hall, wondering why I should believe in my bones a message which both Zahlfast and Elerius had dismissed. All I had against the word of a wizard who had lived here twelve years was the strange contrast I kept feeling between Warin's surface politeness and something underneath, and the fact that King Haimeric had thought he had aged rather slowly.

Well, King Haimeric had been sick for several years, a decade ago, so he might not be a good basis for comparison himself. And Warin had certainly put his youthful years behind him. If one were going to make a pact with the devil, I thought, it would be more sensible to ask for youth than for middle age.

Conversation at the table had shifted in my absence to Dominic's father, who had apparently spent a few weeks in this kingdom fifty years ago, on his way east. King Warin looked at me as I pulled out my chair.

"The school doesn't know much about the Black Pearl, either," I said with my best attempt at cheerful normalcy. From what Warin had said earlier, Elerius did not seem to have passed along whatever he had learned about the Pearl to his employer. I therefore did not mention that he had read the school's books on the topic several years earlier. "Thanks for waiting dessert for me."

"Your father was a remarkable man," Warin said to

Dominic, picking up the conversation where I had interrupted. "You look a little like him. Prince Dominic could outwrestle any man living, won the heart of every woman between the ages of twelve and eighty, and feared nothing, either in this world or the next."

"I didn't know your father was named Dominic too," said Hugo.

"You're named for your father," said Dominic. "Why shouldn't I be named for mine?"

Dessert was iced lemon pudding, not what I would have chosen for a chilly evening even if I had been hungry. As I ate slowly, taking no part in the conversation, I wondered again how Elerius could have lived here for years and never felt what I now sensed about his king. There had been, I remembered, rather strange and contradictory stories about Elerius's background and parentage. Could he perhaps have been a sorcerer's son, this particular sorcerer's son?

I licked my spoon and pushed the thought determinedly away. I was getting as bad as Ascelin.

III

We prepared to leave King Warin's castle the next morning, but just as we were saddling our horses, the chancellor came into the courtyard to tell me I had another telephone call. As I followed him inside, I wondered if the school had found some further information, but the face in the view-screen was that of Elerius.

I was so surprised to see him it took me a moment to find my voice. But he spoke briskly and cheerfully. "So, you're in my old kingdom, I hear! I gather King Warin is still waiting for a new wizard from the school. Like to change kingdoms, Daimbert?"

He said it as a joke, which I hoped was not intended as an insult. He looked at me from tawny hazel eyes under rather disconcerting sharply peaked black eyebrows. I took a breath and started to ask him what he knew about the Black Pearl, but he interrupted me.

"I heard you're looking for young Evrard," he said, "and I realized I have some information that may help. I was in the East last year on private business and I spotted him across a crowd although I don't think he saw me — a red-headed wizard is hard to miss!"

"Where was this?"

"In the Holy City. There were rumors flying throughout the city that Noah's Ark had been found after all these centuries, somewhere far to the south, near the emirate of Bahdroc. They must have heard the rumors. Maybe the emirate was where Evrard and his employer have gone." An expression I could not define flitted across Elerius's face as he spoke; I decided it must be embarrassment to admit that he himself had been in the Holy Land.

"We know they reached the Holy City," I said in excitement, "and their last message was that they were going south. That must be why. What do you think? Could there be any truth in the rumor? And have you heard the stories that King Solomon's Pearl has been found?"

"Delightful stories but, I'm afraid, highly unlikely," said Elerius lightly. "Give my regards to King Warin." He rang off.

East of King Warin's castle, the road along which his chancellor directed us became narrow and much rougher. We found ourselves climbing slowly but steadily in great arcs across a slope where a few scattered sheep grazed, but there was no sign of human habitation. At one point two rangy dogs came racing after us, but they slunk off when Whirlwind leveled a kick at them.

I decided to try again to persuade Joachim to open his present from Claudia — that is, if his saddlebag still contained that present, if Warin had not stolen it and substituted something else. I had had enough time to imagine several more things it might be, such as the money to pay Arnulf's agents, which he did not dare send any other way now that bandits were becoming more frequent, or a special magic bottle designed to capture an Ifrit.

But I had voiced none of my fears to the chaplain. In fact, I realized I had spoken to him very little since we left his brother's house. I wanted to know why Claudia had been singing love songs to him and if he really thought it all as innocuous as he appeared to. Since I didn't know how to ask this, I had said nothing else, either.

"When we're a week away," Joachim told me when I finally broached the question again, "then I'll open it. Why are you so interested anyway?"

I hesitated a minute, then decided he had the right to know. "Ascelin thinks she gave you King Solomon's Pearl."

We were riding two abreast on the narrow road, our saddles creaking and my harness bells jingling. Joachim looked at me incredulously, then came very close to laughing. "No wonder you're so curious," he said. "But I already told you: if Arnulf had something that would grant his heart's desire, he wouldn't be losing his caravans. And he would certainly not allow his wife to give it to someone else."

"Well, I don't think it's the Pearl, either," I said. "But what could it be? Maybe Arnulf has some complicated and dangerous transaction he needs to have taken care of in the East and he's sent the materials to do it along with us. Since you refused categorically to transact any business for him, maybe he's hoping that this way you'll be tricked into doing so. Or maybe," I paused for a second, then pushed on, "Claudia has given you a love potion."

Joachim smiled. "That would make no sense. She's known since I left for seminary that I didn't love her. And she's a married woman, my own sister-in-law."

It was a good thing, I thought and not for the first time, that he was a priest. "But it has to be *something*!"

"All right, Daimbert," said the chaplain indulgently. "Four days' ride may be far enough away. I'll open it this evening and you can help me in case it's something dangerous and magical."

I was now immediately convinced that it was something completely prosaic, but I didn't say so. I would find out for certain soon enough.

What had looked like the top of the slope as we climbed upwards turned out to be, when we finally paused to rest the horses, only a short level area before stony crags began to rise again. The road before us disappeared into a defile overhung with forested cliffs.

But Dominic was looking back in the direction we had come, not forward. "What a view!" he said.

It was, indeed, quite a view of the western kingdoms, out across green hills and patches of woodland to wide pastures far beyond. The air was clear and we could see for countless miles. The land was scattered with compact villages in the blue distance. Far below us, finally looking small, was Warin's royal castle.

"This is it," said Dominic cheerfully. "The next castles we see will be in the eastern kingdoms."

I realized with a start that, somehow without my noticing it, Dominic had changed. I had always thought of him as a rather hard and surly person, but I could remember no signs of surliness for the last few weeks. Maybe being in motion, rather than sitting around a royal castle where he wasn't even royal heir anymore, was what he had needed, in which case we should have sent him off on a quest years ago. Or maybe being clubbed on the back of the head by a bandit had knocked some good humor into him.

This thought, however, gave me another. I looked ahead with concern. The narrow road looked like an excellent place for bandits.

We continued onward, on a road so rough and

pocked with holes that clearly no one had worked on it this spring. "King Warin has been neglecting his responsibilities," commented Ascelin darkly. "His kingdom goes all the way up to the pass."

In some places we had to go single file as the road swung sharply around a corner or climbed so steeply that a lather broke out along our mounts' withers. But it was beautiful in a wild way, the rocks around us shaped by water and wind into grotesque formations, dark evergreens clinging to the slope with roots like giant, deformed fingers. Repeatedly, it seemed that we must have reached a dead end at last, and repeatedly the road slipped around a rock and continued on and up.

For two hours I kept alert for bandits, probing constantly with magic but finding no other human minds. I checked behind us as well as ahead, not trusting King Warin not to send his own knights after us.

But after two hours, worn out from constant spells, I stopped. One couldn't live like this, on the jagged edge of suspicion. We had come out above the first, steepest area and Ascelin told us we were making good progress toward the pass. A desolate meadow stretched relatively level for a half mile in front of us. With the road temporarily wide enough to ride abreast, I pulled my mare even with Whirlwind.

I was tired of thinking about the Black Pearl and the Lady Claudia. "Have you ever been in the eastern kingdoms before?" I asked Dominic. "I never have; the school's sphere of influence really stops at these mountains."

"I've meant to come here for years but, somehow, I never have either," said Dominic. "Ever since you wizards stopped all the wars in the western kingdoms, young aristocrats have had to cross the mountains if we want to see any fighting. You know, of course, that's how my father was killed. I grew up with my mother warning me about the horrible dangers of looking for honor that way; by the time I was old enough to make my own decisions, I started feeling too responsible as royal heir of Yurt to follow his footsteps."

"Well, I certainly hope we don't run into any wars," I said. "We're on pilgrimage."

"And that's part of the reason I'm glad we're coming this way," continued Dominic. "You heard King Warin talking about how everyone always admired my father. Well, I've been hearing some variation of that story all my life. Maybe it was partly fear that I wouldn't measure up to him that kept me at home, but now that I'm traveling east at last I don't feel jealous of him so much as I want to learn more about him. My father is buried in a pilgrimage church east of the mountains. Neither Mother nor I ever visited his grave."

We *definitely* should have sent Dominic on a quest years ago.

"I don't think, even if we run into a war, they'll bother some harmless pilgrims," he said. "But I must admit it gives our trip a little excitement, a little spice even, which I'm afraid Yurt misses most of the time."

"I'm interested in meeting the wizards east of the mountains," I said. "I assume they practice essentially the same magic as in the western kingdoms, rather than what the mages of the real East use. The book I brought along on eastern magic doesn't include anything west of Xantium. But the magic of the eastern kingdoms may be closer to the old magic of earth and herbs than to modern school magic."

At this point, the road narrowed once more; again evergreens and rocky cliffs hung above us. I dropped in behind Dominic, keeping my mare's nose well back from Whirlwind's heels.

I was thinking about the eastern kingdoms, wondering why the wizards' school had never tried to influence them, when I heard a sudden grunt before me. I looked up in disbelief as Whirlwind reared, screaming. There were not one but two men on his back.

Someone had Dominic around the throat and was trying to wrestle him off and keep his own seat. This must be what he meant by excitement and spice.

Hugo and Ascelin turned sharply around and raced back to Dominic's aid, their swords out. I madly tried to shape a spell that would bind only one of the wildly thrashing men before me — if Dominic fell off, his own stallion would trample him.

"Hang on, Dominic!" bellowed Ascelin. "I've got the scum now!" He had the bandit by one leg and was tugging. Hugo had seized Whirlwind's reins and tried to hold him down.

The men before me had sorted themselves out enough that, in two more seconds, I would have had a binding spell working, when I heard another grunt and thump.

"Stop!" came a ringing voice. We all stopped and looked, even the bandit trying to choke Dominic. A second man was behind Joachim on the chaplain's horse, an arm across his chest and a knife at his throat. "Drop your swords or the priest dies."

Ascelin and Hugo turned very slowly and dropped their swords. The bandit behind Dominic jerked the prince's sword from the sheath and sent it clattering to the ground.

"All of you!" yelled the bandit at King Haimeric. "And you, Wizard, don't even think of starting one of your spells."

"I am unarmed," said the king. "I am on pilgrimage."

I doubted this would make much impact. I sat my horse as though paralyzed while a third bandit appeared out of the trees and yanked the king's and my cloaks back to look for weapons. I tried to give Joachim a look of encouragement, but his eyes were cast down and his lips moving. His horse kept shifting and he was having trouble controlling it without moving his head even slightly.

I didn't dare try any spells. Bound or paralyzed, the

bandit behind Joachim might cut his throat as he fell from the horse; a flash of light or a clap of thunder could make him jerk the blade. I didn't dare try turning him into a frog for the same reason.

I should have known at once that the lord of the red sandstone castle was not a real bandit. These men were ragged, weather-worn, filthy, and one of them was missing an eye.

"Get down, all of you!" said the first bandit. Dominic was now sitting slack before him, and the bandit had managed to gather up the reins. "We're taking your horses. Move!"

There didn't seem to be any alternative. We all dismounted, Dominic managing to slide down on his own though rubbing his neck.

"Where's your money?" yelled the bandit leader.

"In my saddlebag," said King Haimeric. The bandit jerked the bag open and pulled out a small jingling pouch with satisfaction. The king didn't mention that that was only a fraction of the money we had, as all of us had other pouches tucked into our belts.

The third bandit, who had collected everyone's swords, now gathered up all the reins and tied the horses together single file. He mounted my mare. "Don't try to follow us!"

The leader kicked Whirlwind into motion. All the horses surged forward, Joachim still mounted and still held hostage.

With a great clatter of hooves, they disappeared up the road ahead of us and around an outcropping of rock. I flew after them, not daring to let them get away while they still had Joachim.

As I rounded the outcropping, I saw a dark figure lying stretched across the road. Paying no attention to our horses disappearing again around the next rock, I dropped to the ground beside the chaplain.

"Joachim! Say something! Are you all right? Did they hurt you?"

The chaplain, to my intense relief, started to sit up. "I've had all the breath knocked out of me. The bandit said something about me not being the one they wanted after all and tossed me off."

"Thank God you're alive," I started to say, then stopped short. Joachim hesitated when almost sitting, then slumped again to the ground. A crimson stain spread rapidly across the collar of his vestments.

IV

The others ran up behind me. Ascelin dropped to his knees, pulled the knife from his boot, and sliced the cloth away from Joachim's neck. A jagged cut was oozing blood.

"It's a vein, not an artery," he said over his shoulder. "But he's losing blood fast." He held the edges of the wound together and tried to apply pressure.

"A good thing it's not an artery," commented Hugo. "You can't very well put a tourniquet around someone's neck."

I found the remark distinctly unamusing and so did Ascelin. "Start a fire," he told Hugo, "and go find some water. You'll have to boil it. Well, I don't care! Use your armor if you have to."

Joachim lay perfectly still, his eyes closed and face white. Blood kept oozing from his neck as fast as Ascelin wiped it away. In a few minutes, though it seemed like hours, Hugo returned from having found a spring among the rocks, carrying water in his breastplate. He lit a fire with the flint and steel at his belt and, without a word but with a loud sigh, balanced the breastplate over it to have all the shiny finish scorched and darkened.

"I'm supposed to be a hunter," said Ascelin bitterly. "I should have known better than to lead us straight into ambush. Trust bandits to grab the one man who couldn't protect himself."

"I think they wanted Arnulf, not the chaplain,"

commented Hugo, adding twigs to his fire. "These must be the same bandits who attacked him last fall."

"Shall we try to get him back down the mountain?" said Dominic when the water had boiled and Ascelin carefully cleaned the chaplain's wound. "I could carry him." The blood had finally stopped flowing, but Joachim had not opened his eyes again.

"It's too late in the day," said Ascelin. "It would take us hours to get to the castle, and I hate to move him at all."

"And I don't trust King Warin," I said. "He must have told those bandits we were coming. This road's used little enough that it wouldn't be worth their while waiting for stray travelers." I thought but didn't say that if Elerius had wanted more challenges here he should have tried getting rid of the bandits — unless Warin liked them.

King Haimeric looked at me in real distress, but Ascelin nodded. "We'll spend the night here. The chaplain's in shock from loss of blood and must have something to eat. Try to keep him warm and give him water if he wakes up. I'm going hunting."

He had lost his sword but still had his bow, slung over his shoulder. He strung it and strode away, leaving the rest of us looking at each other wide-eyed.

The air was warmer than the ground. I used a lifting spell to raise Joachim about a foot and then we wrapped our cloaks around him while the sun sank toward the western horizon below us. Dominic and Hugo gathered more wood to keep our fire blazing hot. With what little attention I had left from keeping my lifting spell going, I kept probing to see if the bandits were coming back. We would be helpless, except for my magic, if they did.

But the first mind I sensed approaching was Ascelin: he had shot three rabbits. Joachim opened his eyes at last and said something so softly I couldn't hear. I bent over to listen, then realized he was apologizing for giving us so much trouble.

I adjusted my spell to sit him up at an angle so that he could eat a little rabbit once Ascelin had skinned and roasted them. Everyone on the mountain, I thought, would see our light and know we were here.

But, with our horses and all our baggage, the bandits might well have all they wanted of us. I took a bite of rabbit myself, so hot it scorched both my fingers and my tongue, and was surprised to discover how hungry I was.

It was now full dark. "I'm going for a doctor," said Ascelin, rising to his feet. "All my ointments are gone with our baggage and I don't like the looks of that wound." We started to object that it was too late, but he shook his head. "I've got eyes like a cat. There has to be a village somewhere on this mountain with a competent doctor. Don't expect me before morning." He was gone with a rattle of loose gravel under his boots before anyone could speak again.

It was a long night. Maintaining the lifting spell required all my concentration, especially as I became more and more tired. The others took turns watching and feeding the fire. At one point Joachim woke up again and started to speak very softly. I tried to respond but found it too difficult to talk and work magic at the same time. Then it became clear that he didn't really need a response, that he was telling of events that had happened long, long ago, when he was still the oldest son of a merchant in the luxury trade, before he had even thought of becoming a priest. I hoped he would tell me these stories again some time when I could listen properly.

In the darkest, stillest part of the night he suddenly said, much more clearly than he had said anything for some time, "You can let me down, Daimbert. I'm very grateful for your help, but you're exhausted, and man is not sustained by magic alone."

I was too tired to argue. I set him down with cloaks both under and over him, got him some water, and fell immediately into sleep so deep as to be untroubled by visions or dreams.

Several hours later I was awakened by the sound of his voice. It was still soft, but it had changed indescribably.

I pushed myself to a sitting position. It was shortly before dawn and, although I could see our campsite clearly, everything looked unreal and slightly ill. On the far side of the fire, Dominic nodded at me, but the king and Hugo were huddled together under a single cloak.

"It's no use, Claudia," said Joachim, very quietly. His eyes were closed; his chest was rising and falling rapidly. "I wish you wouldn't cry. This is hard enough for me as it is. You'll always be in my prayers."

I jerked around, fully awake. Yellowish blood was seeping from under the bandage on Joachim's neck and his face was flushed. I put my hand on his; he patted it with his other hand. "There, I knew you'd understand. I've been called to the service of God. It is a great and terrible calling, and there is only one way to answer."

"He's becoming delirious," I said to Dominic. "I wish Ascelin and the doctor would hurry."

Dominic brought me some water in the belt buckle we were using for a cup. Joachim managed to drink it, though he gave me a puzzled look. He might not even recognize me.

Ascelin finally returned in mid-morning, haggard and accompanied by a shriveled little man on horseback. "All right, you promised me the second half of my fee as soon as we arrived," he said even before dismounting. Ascelin scowled but paid him.

"All right," said the doctor somewhat less reluctantly. "Is this the patient? What have you all been doing, fighting with other ruffians? You'd think a priest would know better than to get involved with the likes of you."

Ascelin shook his head at us behind the doctor's

back. This looked like a conversation they had already had several times on the way up the mountain.

"All right, let's see this wound." The doctor peeled away the bandage with practiced fingers. Joachim winced as he touched the spot but kept his eyes closed. "Infected, as I feared. And I don't need to tell you about infection this close to the brain. The knife was certainly dirty, possibly even poisoned, though I doubt it." He seemed almost to be enjoying himself as he poked around in his saddlebag for various ointments. "A good thing you thought to clean the wound right away or he might be dead already."

I stared at him. "He's not — he's not going to die, is he?"

The doctor glanced up at me from smearing something out of a jar into the wound. "You're a wizard, aren't you? All right, maybe you should try some of your magic. I think I've done all that medicine can do." He rose briskly, rebuckled his saddlebag, and mounted.

"Thank you for coming," said Ascelin somewhat tardily as the doctor rode away.

I grabbed the tall prince by the arm. "He's not going to die, is he?" I asked again, more desperately.

"I hope not," said Ascelin in a low voice. "I just wish those bandits hadn't gotten everything. What I don't know is whether they intended to kill him as well as steal the Black Pearl from him, or whether they sliced his throat essentially by accident. I did manage to buy a few things in the village." I realized then that he was holding a kettle, packed with blankets and food. "You can have your breastplate back, Hugo."

I sat down again by Joachim and took his hand. He did not respond. "Please don't die," I told him. The doctor might speak brightly of using wizardry, but magic had never had much effect over the earth's natural cycles, over sickness and health, birth and death.

Ascelin rolled up in one of the new blankets and fell asleep at once. "I'm sorry, sire," said Dominic to the king. "I should have kept a better eye out for bandits. This is my own fault."

It was, in fact, mine for giving up on my spells too soon. For that matter, if I had marked all our possessions with some sort of magic mark, I might be able to track them now — that is, if I dared leave Joachim.

"It's not your fault," said King Haimeric, "but it may be mine for allowing the chaplain to accompany us without even a breastplate to protect him. But in a day or two, when he's better, we'll continue, either forward over the mountains or back into the western kingdoms. And then we'll get some new supplies. You remember I insisted we bring along four times as much money as you and Ascelin seem to have thought we'd need, so we still have plenty. We weren't going to want our heavy clothes much longer anyway."

If Warin had sent the bandits after us, I thought, they might have been looking specifically for Claudia's present. They were welcome to it. I was now convinced that it was something carrying a great curse, something that she had understandably wanted to get away from her children and which had then called down an attack on us.

I watched Joachim's face, wondering if his were a healthy or unhealthy sleep and how long it would take for the doctor's ointments to take effect. I could keep the rain away with weather spells, but I wasn't sure what else I could do. The herbal spells known to be reliable against disease had all been turned over to the doctors generations ago.

Dominic scrambled to his feet. "I'm going to try to find Whirlwind."

"But you'll be walking into deadly danger!" protested the king.

"If they can ambush me, I can ambush them," said

the prince with a grim smile. "Come on, Hugo. We'll track them together."

The king shot me a worried look but said nothing further. He and I watched them disappear; then everything was again quiet, except for a bird singing cheerfully far down the hill.

V

An hour went by, two hours. Ascelin was still asleep. I didn't know if it was good or bad for Dominic and Hugo to have been gone this long.

"Daimbert." I heard a faint voice behind me.

I swung back around to the chaplain, between fear and hope. His dark eyes looked nearly normal.

"Daimbert, do you know any of the psalms?"

"Well, not really," I stammered. "But — there's the one you often read at Sunday service in chapel, the one with 'Thou shalt not be afraid' in the middle."

"That's the one," he said, his eyes shut again. "Please say it for me."

I said it slowly, trying to remember all the words correctly. "He that dwelleth in the secret place of the most High shall abide under the shadow of the Almighty. I will say of the Lord, He is my refuge and my fortress, my God; in Him will I trust. . . . Thou shalt not be afraid for the terror by night; nor for the arrow that flieth by day; nor for the pestilence that walketh in darkness; nor for the destruction that wasteth at noonday."

The chaplain smiled a little when I had finished, but he did not open his eyes. "That's better. I should not be afraid to meet God."

"But Joachim! You're not dying. The doctor was here and put some ointment on your wound to heal the infection."

He nodded, a very slight motion of his head. "My

mind had been wandering a little, but I remember now. Tell the others not to go after the bandits; I have forgiven them. It is good to have my mind clear again, to be able to repent of my sins while there is still time. I assume there is no priest on this mountain to say the rites, but you can pray for me."

Jesus Christ. I put my face in my hands. If he truly thought he was dying, I couldn't argue with him. I tried praying, but the saints do not normally listen to wizards, especially those filled not with purity and contrition but with fury and despair.

My thoughts were broken by the clatter of hooves and the long blast of a horn. I leaped up, ready to defend the chaplain with every spell I had or my bare hands if necessary.

But it was not the bandits. It was Dominic and Hugo.

"We found the horses, sire!" cried Hugo excitedly, lowering his horn. "We kept on following the tracks and, after a few miles, Dominic tried whistling and his stallion whinnied back!"

"I don't think they know much about horses," added Dominic with a chuckle. "Look at the condition they're in!" The horses' hair was dark and caked with sweat. "They hadn't even unsaddled them, just turned them loose after rifling the luggage. We saw no sign of the bandits themselves. Come on, Whirlwind, come on," rubbing his stallion good-naturedly between the eyes. "You probably taught them a thing or two about high-strung horses, didn't you?"

Even the packhorses were there. Ascelin was awake now; the rest of us pulled the saddles and packs from the horses to see what might be left, while Dominic began rubbing them down. Though he was not as excited as Hugo, from the way he held his shoulders he was even more pleased and proud.

There was a surprising amount still in the luggage. Most of the food was gone, as were some of the cooking pots and spare clothes. But as well as *Melecherius on Eastern Magic*, the bandits had left the tents, the rice, the maps, the lanterns, the ropes and supplies for the horses, the king's spare eyeglasses, some of the blankets, and virtually everything in the chaplain's saddlebag. The foil-wrapped present was gone, but his Bible and crucifix and the pilgrim's guide were still there.

"Those were real bandits, all right," said Ascelin, "but it certainly seems as though they were looking for something specific. They've taken the food and money, of course, but beyond that they didn't really care."

I slipped the crucifix into Joachim's still hands. He was asleep, having apparently not heard the horses. I leafed through his Bible and found the right psalm. I didn't seem to have gotten more than a few of the words wrong.

"Did you try cooking the chicken I brought up from the village?" asked Ascelin. "You didn't?" He shook his head, smiling. "Since I have to do everything on this quest myself, I'm not sure why I even bothered to bring the rest of you along. I'm going to make the chaplain some soup. I think I'll put rice in it."

Everyone but me seemed in a surprisingly good mood. Hugo whistled as he got out his bag of polishing sand and started trying to get the black off his armor.

"I wonder if these men were looking for the same thing those first bandits were looking for," said the king. But I no longer cared. Joachim was still breathing steadily. I read him several psalms in case he could hear me.

"I guess we'd better wake him," said Ascelin at last. "He needs nourishment to get his strength back, and the soup's ready."

I touched him gently on the cheek. His skin was burning hot. "Come on, Joachim, wake up. You know how good Ascelin's soup is. Wake up."

He continued to breathe, but there was no other response. I tried moving his hand, with no better luck.

"Ascelin," I said, hearing the panic in my own voice, "he won't wake up."

The prince had found his own wound ointments in the luggage. He eased the bandage off again and frowned at the wound. The edges of the cut skin were turned back and black; between them, the flesh was green.

"Well, the doctor already tried this ointment," Ascelin said, "but, perhaps, if we used this other one —"

But I was gone, flying down the hillside. My only thought was that I must find herbs, must find them at once. Thanks to what I had learned from my predecessor, the old retired Royal Wizard of Yurt, I knew more herbal magic than most school-trained wizards. Modern magic was a magic of air and light, but the old natural magic of earth and herbs, magic that relied on the innate properties of objects, was the only magic short of pacts with the devil that could break through the cycle of life and death.

I realized I had no idea where I was going and stopped, hovering in midair. I could see King Warin's castle far below, but I certainly wasn't going there. Off to one side, partly hidden by the slope of the hill, were the closely packed roofs of a village that must be where Ascelin had found the doctor. Well, his medicine had already proven ineffective.

Beyond the village on a little rise were the scattered white crosses of a cemetery. Joachim would not even have a pilgrimage church like Dominic's father. Tomorrow we would bury him there on that hill.

This was such a terrible thought that it started me flying again, though I stopped when I realized I was still flying madly, without direction. I dropped down into a meadow, where the sheep gave me somewhat puzzled looks, and forced myself to look calmly and rationally at plants.

I saw no plants that I recognized as having medicinal

qualities, but there were plenty here that did not grow on the hills of Yurt. I tried to remember my wizardly predecessor, dead almost eight years now, and the lessons he had taught me in recognizing a plant's properties.

I closed my eyes and hovered on the edge of magic's four dimensions, slowly turning the flow of magic with the powerful syllables of the Hidden Language. I opened my eyes and picked a plant at random to probe with magic. This one seemed to have no useful properties at all. I tried another, this with a yellow flower. As near as I could tell, it might be useful in cases of muscle strain. A third would sicken chickens, and the fourth sicken cows.

It was late in the afternoon when I flew back up the mountain carrying a double handful of a blue-flowered plant. If I remembered the old wizard's lessons correctly, it should be good against fever and infection. But the sheep seemed to like it, for I could find very few specimens and those were eaten almost down to the ground. The search for whole plants had seemed interminable. As I hurried back to our campsite, I feared I was already too late.

The others looked at me soberly as I dropped into their midst. "He's still alive," said Ascelin, "but he's still unconscious."

I already knew he was alive; the first thing I had looked for was whether they had covered his face.

"We've been taking turns reading the Bible," said the king.

"Boil these up," I said to Ascelin, pushing my precious plants into his hands. "It's the last thing I can think of to do."

In a few minutes, I packed the hot, wet plants onto Joachim's throat. They steamed and he twitched a little, but I could see no immediate change. Not wanting to lose any of their efficacy, assuming they had any, I propped Joachim up and slowly dripped into his mouth the water in which the plants were boiled.

The rest of us ate Ascelin's chicken soup, leaving a little simmering at the edge of the fire in case the chaplain woke up. It felt depressing and demeaning that we, as humans, were so bound by our physical bodies that in the middle of crises of life and death we still had to eat.

We pitched the tents, and I lifted Joachim gently with magic to carry him in out of the wind and cool air. His skin was not as hot as it had been earlier, but I did not dare guess whether this was due to the fever breaking or the chill of death setting in.

I sat next to him, listening to his breathing, while it slowly grew dark outside. Joachim had saved my life my first year in Yurt. If I couldn't save his, all my wizardry was worthless, of no more value than a handful of brass coins. For the first time, I thought I understood why a wizard might plunge into black magic, mix the supernatural into his own spells with all of black magic's powers to reverse natural laws, even if it meant the loss of his soul.

Hugo put his head into the tent. "I'll watch with him for a while. Why don't you get some sleep?"

"I can't sleep anyway. But come in if you want." I mentally forgave him for his remark about the tourniquet.

Hugo came in, dropping the tent flap behind him, and settled down next to me. "I'm sorry he's sick," he said after a moment.

"Yes," I said because there didn't seem to be anything else to say. We sat quietly for several minutes.

"You and the chaplain have been good friends," said Hugo at last. There was a curious intimacy of sitting near him in the dark, hearing his breath but not able to see him. "I didn't think wizards and priests were friends very often."

"They're not," I said. When the silence began to stretch out again, I forced myself to say more. Hugo, without his normal bravado and bantering manner, seemed very young and vulnerable; I did not want to dismiss him with monosyllabic answers. "Wizards and priests follow different sets of laws and gain power from very different sources. But Joachim and I have been friends since a short time after I became Royal Wizard of Yurt — even though I started our acquaintance by suspecting him of evil."

"I think Father Joachim was always different from most priests." I didn't like the way Hugo put it in the past tense but made a sound of assent. "He was already Royal Chaplain of Yurt back when I was being trained in knighthood," he went on, "but at the time I didn't pay much attention. I think I've always assumed someone would become a priest only if he didn't have the courage or the manhood to become anything else. My own father's chaplain is well-meaning and fussy. But the Royal Chaplain is different. He always thinks he's right, like all priests, and wants everyone else to have the same opinion he does, but it's still not the same."

I said nothing but let him continue.

"He doesn't just preach about morality but acts as though he takes it very seriously himself. And he's stayed brave even while dying. Do you know why he decided to become a priest in the first place?"

I made myself answer. "I don't think he felt he could do anything else. You met the Lady Claudia. She may be too old for you, but she's a stunningly beautiful woman, and Joachim rejected her love because he felt God had called him."

Hugo thought this over. "Ascelin said he thinks she gave him King Solomon's Pearl. What do you think? Do you think she still loves him? Do you think the bandits tried to kill him on purpose because he had it?"

"I have no idea," I said, not caring this time if I sounded dismissive.

After a few more minutes, Hugo spoke again. Our sleeves brushed as we shifted, but most of the time we could have been disembodied minds, close together in the night with death very near.

"I realize," said Hugo, "that in spite of all my knighthood training I've never before actually seen anyone dying from wounds suffered in battle or in ambush. Have you?"

"I've watched someone die before," I said slowly, not liking the way he'd phrased the question.

"What do you think?" he persisted. "Is it really true, what the priests tell us, that we go to heaven when we die?"

"That is what they tell us. Joachim, at any rate, seems fairly sure of it."

This time Hugo did not answer. We sat in silence for hours. At any rate, I assumed it was hours; I quickly lost all track of time and it began to feel that this night had already lasted as long as most weeks. From the sound of his breathing Hugo had dozed off, and I myself had to fight increasingly powerful waves of drowsiness. Bodies needed sleep, too, no matter who might live or die.

My mind had wandered far away, halfway between waking and dream, when a soft sound brought me abruptly back to full consciousness. That sound was my own name.

"Hugo?" I said, but Hugo was asleep. It was Joachim who had spoken.

"Daimbert, I must apologize," he said quietly. "I'm afraid I have given you a great deal of trouble and worry."

I put my face down next to his. "I don't care. It would be worth any amount of trouble and worry if I could save you from death."

"But I'm afraid it's all for nothing," he continued. I was weak enough that, against my will, tears began leaking down my cheeks. I was so unhappy that it took me five seconds to understand what he said next. "Because it looks like I'm not going to die after all."

I shook Hugo awake, crying hard now for no reason at all. "Light the lantern," I told him and "Keep your eyes shut," to Joachim. Hugo and I carefully lifted my herbs away from the wound. The cut was clean, pink, no longer infected.

Hugo scrambled out of the tent to tell the others. I broke the wad of herbs open, because while it was still damp in the center the outside had dried, and reapplied it. "Thank God," I managed to say, although my voice no longer seemed to be working correctly.

"I'm afraid my mind may have wandered again for a while," said Joachim, "but I have a vague recollection that, somewhere through the evil dreams, I heard talk of chicken soup. Do you think there might still be some?"

PART FOUR

The Eastern Kingdoms

1

We stayed at our mountain campsite among the rocks and evergreens a week, by which time the cut on Joachim's throat was little more than a scab and the horses were getting restive. I used the time to read *Melecherius on Eastern Magic* thoroughly. Ascelin hunted and made two more trips down into the village to buy bread and other supplies.

The fact that no one came by in all that time, not the bandits, not the king's chancellor to check on stories of travelers ambushed less than a day's ride from the royal castle, not any other traveler, made me even more convinced than I had been that King Warin was behind the attack on us. King Haimeric still refused to distrust his old friend, but he had discovered during the week that he was outnumbered, four to one, with the chaplain abstaining.

I thought grimly that if they were the same bandits who had tried to attack Arnulf last fall, then this was why Arnulf had sent whatever was in the package with Joachim rather than going anywhere himself, but I did not mention this to the chaplain.

Ascelin and King Haimeric looked again at the maps. "With spring another week along, we should have even less trouble with the passes," said Ascelin.

"Dominic's not the only one who wants to go to the eastern kingdoms to visit his father's grave," the king said. "I've never been there, either."

When we started eastward again, Ascelin went first, his bow strung and ready, looking around with hunter's eyes at anything that could be an ambush. I rode at the rear, probing with magic. No one would be able to attack us by surprise this time.

In spite of the tension, all of us found our spirits rising just to be on the road again. We passed a number of narrow tracks branching off from the main road, which could have gone to the royal mines and could have gone to the bandits' hideout. The road quickly grew so steep that in several places we had to dismount and lead the horses.

As we climbed, I kept glancing surreptitiously at the chaplain out of the corner of my eye, fearing that he would find the ride too exhausting. If he did, he gave no sign, and in fact several times he appeared to be singing, half under his breath. This was the man, I reminded myself, who had thought that peril gave additional merit to the journey.

When the road finally leveled out, it clung halfway up the side of a gorge, with peaks high above us blocking out the sky and a rushing river far below. The stonework looked ancient, as though dating from the Empire, but the road appeared sound. A cold wind blew steadily through the gorge. In several places, waterfalls shot from the cliffs above toward the river below and the road went under them. As we passed beneath a solid, roaring mass of water, damp dripped onto our hair and gave life to vividly green ferns clinging to the rock wall, though on either side the cliffs were barren.

"Aren't we up to the pass *yet*?" Hugo asked as the road emerged at last from the gorge but immediately started to zigzag upward across a dry mountain slope.

"We won't be up to the pass for two more days," said Ascelin. "And it certainly won't be a smooth road from then on, either."

When we stopped for the night in a hollow sheltered by evergreens, Joachim asked me, "Why have you been watching me all day? Afraid your wizardry might not have healed me fully?" There was an amused glint in the back of his dark eyes.

"I didn't heal you with wizardry," I said patiently. "Let me explain it again. The words of the Hidden Language by themselves have little power either to sicken or to heal. Certainly there are herbs, potions, compounds and the like, products of the earth, that will do both, and some wizards in the old days used to do as much with such compounds as with the real forces of magic. But nowadays most wizards avoid such messiness. All I did was what my predecessor in Yurt used to do: use the spells of wizardry to discover and, at most, augment the powers of growing things. Herbs' attributes can provide a shortcut or even go where spells do not go, but they are inherently unpredictable. I can't be nearly as confident about a healing herb as I could be about a modern spell."

I stopped in the middle of this academic discourse and smiled at him. "I think you know me well enough to realize that even my modern spells don't always work quite the way they're supposed to."

"I'll take my chances on the quality of your spells," he replied, with the same almost amused look. But then he became more sober. "I'm sorry, Daimbert, that I waited so long to open Claudia's present. Now you'll never know what was in it."

"It's not worth worrying about," I said. I didn't want to think any more about a woman who had hypocritically tried to remind her brother-in-law of her former love for him, just so she could give him an object so accursed it would nearly kill him.

But Joachim had more to say. "I hope you don't think me foolish, Daimbert, but in a way I was testing myself during our visit. I realized that, at some level, I had stayed away from my old home for so long because

I was afraid that I might regret my decision to become a priest."

"And did you?" I asked in trepidation.

"Of course not, and that was one of the best parts of the visit. I deliberately spent time talking to Claudia and was pleased to find that I felt brotherly affection for her as my brother's wife and my niece's and nephews' mother, but nothing more."

"Is that why you let her sing love songs to you?"

The chaplain stretched out his long legs in front of him. I was relieved that he took my question with new amusement, rather than as an insult. "The songs she was singing had nothing to do with me. She's very happily married to my brother. I'm sure any particular affection she may have had for me vanished many years ago."

I looked at the chaplain thoughtfully. Joachim always assumed that everyone was a sinner, without letting it bother him, but it occurred to me that he also resisted thinking real evil of someone whom he liked and trusted. I had always hoped that the fact that he was willing to be friends with me was an indication that I was really virtuous the whole time. But that he would not even consider the possibility that Claudia had been trying to seduce him — or at least persuade him with seductive hints to take a "gift" from her unquestioningly — now made me wonder how deep my own virtue might actually go.

"The next time we reach a place with a telephone or a pigeon loft," said Joachim, "I will send her a message and apologize for losing her present. I just hope it wasn't anything very valuable."

It grew slowly colder as we climbed during the next two days; several times there were patches of snow in the ditches at the side of the road as well as on the towering peaks above us. But late in the afternoon of the second day we finally reached the pass and looked out eastward, a stinging wind in our faces.

Before us stretched broad green meadows, scattered with low wooden buildings and clumps of stunted trees. Cows grazed in the meadows and smoke rose from several chimneys. But we were not looking at the meadows. Instead, our eyes were drawn to the mountain to our left, which rose at least a mile higher than the high saddle on which we stood. We had caught glimpses of it as we climbed, but the mountain we were on had hidden its true size from us.

"The Snow Giant," said Ascelin, "and to our right is Diamond Mountain." This more southerly peak was scarcely lower. Storms swirled around their upper reaches, covering them with white mist, but suddenly a gust of wind a mile above us cleared the clouds away. The peaks seemed to glare down at us with the same unbearable cold which I had felt, on a much reduced level, in the eyes of King Warin.

We turned our attention then to the scene before us. The meadows, bright with flowers, sloped slowly down from where we stood, but several miles away the land started to rise sharply again, and grass gave way first to a line of dark evergreens and then to ice. The tips of the icy peaks were touched by pink from the sun behind us.

"I hope we're not going up those mountains," said the king. "I'm not sure my old bones would make it."

Ascelin laughed. "Don't worry, Haimeric. We're out of the western kingdoms now and over the pass. Our road will swing around the bases of the rest of the mountains we meet."

"Does the king of this kingdom have a telephone?" asked Joachim.

"We're not in a kingdom," said Ascelin. "Up here in the mountains most of the countries are very small — even smaller than Yurt — and are run by elected councils. And I'd be surprised if anyone east of the pass had a phone. They're a little old-fashioned here."

"Come on," said Dominic. "Let's get down out of the wind."

For the next week we traveled through scenery so glorious that it would have been worth the journey by itself, yet so overwhelming that I felt exhausted from more than riding at the end of the day. I was constantly reminded that, while magic might draw on the powers that had shaped the earth, those powers were so immense that all the wizards who had ever lived could only move them very slightly.

Ascelin was right that the worst of our climbing was behind us. Our road stayed in the valleys, narrow or broad, beneath the peaks, or at worst worked its way across the grassy lower slope of a mountain. With a view that often stretched for miles in all directions, we worried less about a surprise attack. We passed a number of tiny, jade-green lakes caught in folds of the landscape, reflecting the peaks above them.

The first two nights we asked hospitality from farmers near the road. In return for a few coins, they cheerfully put us up in the haylofts in the back of their houses, warm with the breath of the cows beneath, and gave us cheese and pancakes with honey and wild strawberries for supper. At night, listening to the dull clang of bells as the cows moved below us, I began to relax for the first time since we had seen King Warin's castle rising against the sky.

At the second farm there were two little girls in starched white aprons and tight braids, who kept creeping up to see us and then dashing away in giggling excitement. Ascelin looked after them in what I considered inexplicable melancholy until I realized that they must remind him of his own twins.

By the third day, our road joined the first of the much more heavily used roads that crossed the passes further south, carrying trade and travelers between the eastern and western kingdoms, even though the main routes to the East were still to the west of the mountains. Now there were regular inns; their rooms, though small, were scrupulously clean and the featherbeds were nearly as soft as the ones in the Lady Claudia's guest rooms. Cheese seemed to be featured at every meal.

The second inn had a pigeon loft. The innkeeper was a little dubious about trying to send a pigeon message any distance, especially over the high passes. He warned us darkly about the difficulties of messages that had to be transferred several times. But Joachim sent Claudia a letter, Hugo wrote his mother, and both the king and Ascelin sent letters to their wives. None of them told me what they put on the tiny rectangles which were all the pigeons could carry.

After a week in the mountains, our route began, almost imperceptibly at first, to lead us lower and away from the highest peaks. Then we rounded the base of a mountain and saw before us not another mountain but a glimpse of a distant blue plain. Ascelin, who had been striding in the lead, stopped short.

"This is as far east as I've ever gone," he said. "We're leaving the little mountain republics here; once we reach the plain we'll be in the eastern kingdoms."

"Then we'll be leaving peaceful territory," said Hugo, "to go into a land of war."

"Well, almost," said Ascelin. "You have to realize that these mountains are so peaceful in part because all the restless young men go down to fight in the pay of the eastern kings."

There was a tiny church in the bend of the road. Although from the outside it was dark and undistinguished looking, the inside blazed with candle light on luxurious silk hangings and golden reliquaries. "Both those thankful to be coming down out of the mountains," read Joachim from his guide, "and those starting the hard and perilous climb up into them, have traditionally left a small offering here."

I would have been happy to stay in the mountains. As we wound down toward the distant plain, I once again began worrying about how to protect our party. I had been brought along as a wizard to do so, but so far was rather short on success. In odd moments I tried to work out new variations of spells, wondering which ones might stop an army. Back when the wizards in the west had stopped the Black Wars, I thought, they had either been much more proficient at magic than I or else they had not had their best friends held hostage by the enemy.

As we came down the final steep slope into the eastern kingdoms, the rocky outcroppings on either hand yellow with gorse, we saw that the road ahead of us went through a massive stone gate. It was, I thought, rather useless as a gate because there was no wall, but as a symbol of a boundary it was very dramatic. It was at least twenty feet high and sprouting from the top were the carved stone heads of wolves.

As we approached the gate from one side I saw a dusty cloud rapidly approaching from the other. With a little quick magical probing, I discovered it was three mounted knights.

In a moment, the others saw them, too. Hugo, Dominic, and Ascelin glanced at each other and drew out the swords they had bought, at what they all said were highly inflated prices, up in the mountains.

But I said, "Wait a minute," and rode forward, shielding myself and my mare with what I hoped was a suitably strong protective spell. When the riders were thirty yards away, I acted.

I pulled out a pebble to which I had earlier attached an almost fully completed illusion and threw it as hard as I could. It bounced under the arch of the gate and turned into a dragon.

My dragon reared up, shooting fire, though the

dramatic impact was somewhat lessened when its head passed directly through the stonework of the gate. The riders pulled up hard, as well they might, desperately circling their horses as they tried to stay on. But showing surprisingly good discipline, in a few seconds they dropped back and raised their spears.

I was ready for those, too. I used magic to jerk their spears in quick succession from their hands and sent the weapons arching harmlessly away. They reached for their swords, with a presence of mind I admired, but I bellowed, "Stop!" in a voice amplified by magic.

Dissolving my dragon into a shower of sparks, I rode slowly forward, one empty hand raised before me. They had certainly stopped. Following King Warin's example, I tried to pierce them with my eyes, at the same time adding a few strengthening details to the spell that surrounded me.

"What do you mean, Wizard, trying to enter this kingdom with an act of undeclared war?" demanded the leader of the knights before me.

"I am not at war with anyone," I said with dignity. "We are peaceful pilgrims. But when I saw armed men galloping to attack my party, I felt I must act at once to protect us."

The knights looked at my cloak, embroidered with the cross, then past me to the others. "You're armed men yourselves, in spite of your pilgrim's tokens."

"Only in self-defense," I said. "We were recently set upon by bandits who nearly killed our chaplain."

The leader looked at me thoughtfully. I decided not to try to look honest and trustworthy for fear it would appear an unconvincing mask. "If you mean no harm," he then yelled to the rest of the party from Yurt, "put up your swords and approach slowly."

King Haimeric, I was pleased to see, kicked his horse forward immediately and the others were forced to follow. We all met under the arch of the gate where my dragon had stood a moment before.

"We are, as my wizard told you, simply pilgrims," said the king. "You can see I'm not even wearing a sword myself. At the moment we're making for the Church of the Holy Twins."

"The Holy Twins?" asked one of the knights facing us. He hesitated for a moment then said slowly, "They don't get very many pilgrims there any more."

"Why not?" said Dominic, quickly and brusquely.

The leader eyed him for a moment. "It's probably just a foolish story," he said, "but hardly anyone's been buried there for a good fifty years."

"What's a story?" Dominic persisted. I, like him, had the chilling impression that there was something terribly wrong about the church, and these knights knew it.

"Just a tale of the sort told to frighten children. Supposedly a long, long time ago, in the darkest part of the night, an evil wizard steeped in the black arts brought the dead body of a magnificent warrior there for burial. There was something about the wizard, a sense that he might even be able to communicate with the dead, that made other people much less willing to see their relatives lying there. . . . but I told you it was just a silly story," he finished briskly.

"Our wizard practices only white magic and we wish no evil to anyone," said King Haimeric. "Are you going to let us proceed?"

"All right," said the leader in sudden decision. "But I warn you, Wizard, that you're going to get your group into trouble if you go through the eastern kingdoms attacking border guards without provocation. At least in this kingdom, we're not at war right now, and we don't intend to be." He wrote us out a pass which he said we should show to any patrols we met.

"I admired your dragon," King Haimeric said to me as we rode on. "And I know Dominic and Ascelin think it necessary to carry weapons. But shouldn't you have told the knights we were pilgrims right away, rather than threatening them?"

Given another chance, I would do exactly the same thing. I started attaching a new spell to a new pebble and thought complacently that if I had lived during the Black Wars and the other wizards had needed me, I would not have embarrassed myself.

11

The church where Dominic's father was buried was in the center of a small town. Both Ascelin and I kept glancing suspiciously to either side as we rode through the noisy, twisting streets, but it was impossible to pick out potential enemies from so many people.

A final twist of the street led us to a covered passage and then to an open square, with the church in the center. Here, unlike the rest of town, it was quiet and peaceful. I had expected something sinister, but we found nothing of the kind. The church was built entirely of cobblestones, with alternating layers of darker and lighter stone. What should have been the main entrance, under the front porch, was bricked up, but Hugo found a small, unlocked door at the far end.

"The twin saints to which this church is dedicated," read Joachim from his guidebook, "were soldiers in their youth, until Christ appeared to them in a fiery vision in the middle of battle and they repented of their sinful ways. But soldiers in battle still call on their aid in time of peril and many are buried in their church."

The Holy Twins, I thought, must not have listened to Dominic's father — or, for that matter, to a number of other soldiers, either. It was an enormous though rather dusty church. Virtually all the stones with which the floor was paved and many of the lower blocks in the side walls were inscribed with the names of warriors buried over the centuries near their saintly patrons.

"The guidebook suggests this was a very busy

pilgrimage church," said Joachim, "but it must have been written before the incident the border guards mentioned."

"This end is all old graves," said King Haimeric. "The inscriptions are almost worn away. Let's try the other end."

Hugo, who had gone ahead, suddenly called back to us, his voice echoing under the high stone roof. "I think I've found him!"

Set into the wall about halfway down was a stone with newer carving than most in the church. The king fumbled with his eyeglasses and bent closer. Even in the dim afternoon light, we could read the inscription easily. *"Hic iacet Dominicus princeps Yurtiae,"* it said in the old imperial language: "Here lies Prince Dominic of Yurt."

King Haimeric stood with his hands folded, silently contemplating the grave of his younger brother.

"We should have come here years ago," said Dominic after a moment.

The king nodded. "But I always felt more responsible for the living than for the dead. If I had come when your father first died, your mother would have wanted to come too and brought you with her, even though you were a child. And then somehow the years passed and I never made the voyage."

"What's this?" asked Hugo suddenly, bending closer. "It looks like the carving of a snake."

It certainly did. In the corner of the stone slab was cut a tiny picture of a coiled snake, with what looked like a jewel resting on its coils. The image was strangely familiar.

"Take off your gloves, Dominic," said the king. His nephew slowly pulled off his riding gloves. Gleaming on his second finger, his ruby ring had as its setting a gold snake that matched the carving. "I thought at the time," said King Haimeric, "that those bandits were too hasty. They took our horses and our luggage, but they missed the single most valuable object we had with us."

Excluding whatever Claudia might have given Joachim, I thought.

"This ring was among the jewels my father sent back to Yurt with a faithful servant when he died," said Dominic. "Why would its image be carved on his tomb?"

"Let me see it," I said.

Dominic gave me an odd look but started tugging at the ring. He had not had it off for years, during which time he had grown quite a bit heavier, and it took a minute.

As I took it in my hand, Hugo, who was still examining the stone behind which Dominic's father was buried, spoke again. "I think this stone is loose."

We all bent down again to look. As the sun moved, a stray beam found its way from the high windows down to near floor level. The stone was not completely flush with the wall around it but protruded ever so slightly on one side. Hugo wrapped his gloved fingers around it and began to tug.

"What are you doing?" demanded Dominic, pushing him away.

But the king put a hand on his arm. "If the stone is loose anyway, perhaps we are meant to open the tomb. I have felt badly all these years that it was impossible to bring my brother's body back to Yurt to be buried with our parents and ancestors. Perhaps we should take his bones with us now."

"Excuse me, sire," said Hugo, "but are you really planning to cross the eastern kingdoms, go to the Holy Land, and then travel all the way home again with bones in your luggage?" But he was again tugging at the stone.

It came loose all at once and he fell back. The tombstone hit the paving with a bang that echoed through the church. I anticipated a waft of foul air, but there was nothing of the sort. All of us gave each other quick, uneasy looks, then went down on our knees to look in. Since I was holding Dominic's ring anyway, I lit it up with magic and held it out at arm's length, reaching into the tomb.

I was not sure what I expected to see, but it was not an untidy pile of tumbled bones. "What have they done to him?" asked King Haimeric in distress. Dominic said nothing, but his color slowly darkened to brick red.

In the tiny glow of the ring, we could see bare bones lying among the scraps of what had once been clothing. A belt buckle and a brooch lay at one side. The skull was at the back, a thin gold circlet loose around it and turned to an incongruously jaunty angle. The empty eye sockets glared at us balefully.

"Someone's opened the tomb, looking for something," said Ascelin.

"This ring," I said in sudden conviction. "And they didn't find it."

"By the way," said Joachim, who had not spoken since Hugo started pulling at the stone, "I wonder where the priests of this church are."

Ascelin leaped to his feet and reached for his sword. "A trap. I should have known it. We'll have to fight our way out."

Joachim put his hand on the prince's hilt to push the sword back into its sheath. "Don't forget that this is a house of God and no place for weapons of violence."

"Stay back," I said. "There's only one way they can come in. I don't want any more of you held hostage before I can disarm them." I flew the length of the church, wishing for the calm courage to match my words and hoping Joachim would not call after me that God's house was also no place for violent magic.

I stopped short of the door and probed with magic, expecting to find a mass of armed knights on the far side. But I found nothing. Just to be sure, I pushed the door open a crack and peeked out. The square in which the church sat was empty except for our horses, swishing their tails peacefully.

"There's no one there, Ascelin," I said and flew back. "Your hunter's instincts have failed you this time, I'm afraid."

"Let's get out of here before I'm proven right."

"Just a moment," said King Haimeric. He crawled partially into the tomb; when he backed out a moment later his gray cloak was filthy, and he looked grim but satisfied. "You're right, Hugo, that it doesn't make sense to take his bones with us now. But at least I've straightened them out."

"Come *on*," said Ascelin. He helped ease the tombstone back into place, pushing it in tight this time, then we all hurried toward the door. Realizing I was still holding Dominic's ring, I slid it onto my thumb, since it was too big for any of my fingers, and pulled my glove on over it.

I stopped the others short of the entrance, in case armed men had come up during the last minute, but my probing still found nothing. We hurried out and I caught brief glimpses of faces in windows high up around the little square. The faces looked frightened rather than hostile and disappeared immediately.

In a moment we were onto our horses and riding recklessly fast through the city streets. But the worst danger we encountered was a cart of vegetables pushed out of a side street almost directly into our path, which Whirlwind vaulted and the rest of our horses scrambled around. Outside the city gates, we covered two miles as fast as Ascelin, who ran holding onto Dominic's stirrup leather, could go.

"All right," he said at last, throwing himself to the ground under a tree. "We got away safely this time. Now I'd like to know what's actually happening."

"So would I," I said, dismounting and carefully removing my gloves. "And I think it starts with this ring."

I had always coveted Dominic's ring. The coiled gold

snake and the ruby made it just the thing to suggest wizardly wisdom and mystery. I had inherited a ring shaped like an eagle in flight from my predecessor as Royal Wizard of Yurt, but it wasn't the same.

Slowly I turned the ring in my hands, watching the ruby catch the light. "There might," I said, "just might, be a spell attached to this, something like the message spell Sir Hugo's wizard left for us in Warin's castle. I'll have to see if it's still working after fifty years. Sire, did your brother take a wizard with him?"

"No," said King Haimeric in surprise. "I only ever had the one Royal Wizard before you. I don't believe my brother's household ever kept one."

"Then the spell, if there is a spell," I said, "was put together by a wizard of the eastern kingdoms, someone trained differently than I. This may take a while."

I said that in the hopes that it would not take very long at all and that I could impress the others with my abilities, but this ring was not nearly as ready to yield its secrets as Evrard's black box.

"Then the carving of the snake on the tomb *was* a message," said Hugo to Dominic, "your father's way of telling you, only you, that the ring he had sent back to Yurt was somehow special. He just didn't think it would take you this long to get here."

Dominic ignored the second half of this comment. "Do you know if my father acquired all his jewels together," he asked the king, "or a few at a time?"

"As I remember," said King Haimeric thoughtfully, "it was a hoard he discovered or picked up somewhere — or perhaps captured in battle. His servant who brought the jewels back to Yurt told me at the time, but I'm afraid I didn't pay very much attention to that part of his account."

And that servant was long dead. Any secrets from beyond the grave would be revealed through wizardry or not at all.

I sat down under the tree, my back to the rest, and

murmured likely seeming spells under my breath. Behind me, Ascelin asked the chaplain, "Did your bishop visit the Church of the Holy Twins?"

"He never got into this part of the eastern kingdoms," said Joachim. "He took the main pilgrimage and trade route down along the rivers, west of the mountains."

"Ha!" I said aloud suddenly. The ruby on Dominic's ring was held in place not just by the goldsmith's art, but by magic and by a spell I recognized. With a few quick words of the Hidden Language, I loosened the spell. In three twists, the stone came loose; something tiny, scarcely bigger than a pin head, dropped into my hand.

I had an audience now. With no time to search carefully for the best spell, I improvised, trying a variation of a transformations spell to transform whatever tiny object I held into something bigger without, I hoped, changing any of its other properties.

And that turned out, almost to my surprise, to be the right spell. I was suddenly holding a piece of parchment in my hand with a message written out clearly. I looked first at the formal signature, *"Dominicus princeps Yurtiae,"* and then at the heading, *"To my dearest wife and son."*

I handed it to Dominic. "I think this is for you."

III

He read it out loud. "By the time you read this I will be dead." Dominic stopped, looked at the king, cleared his throat, and continued reading. "The servant by whom you will have received this ring will also have given you a more open letter of farewell. I hope the Royal Wizard will quickly discover this ring's secret, but if not, the snake I asked to have carved on my tombstone will be a clue for you."

"I was right," said Hugo. Dominic ignored him.

"The wizard I have taken into my employ, who will hide this message magically in the ring for me, is one I trust thoroughly, totally, and explicitly."

"That means he didn't trust him at all," interrupted the king.

"What?" said Dominic and I together.

"Didn't I ever teach you that code, Dominic?" asked King Haimeric. "Your father and I worked it out when we were boys. Because normally you say that you trust someone implicitly, trust them completely without having to say anything, to say that you trust them explicitly is to say just the opposite, that you express your trust only with your lips."

I tried to remember any occasions when the king might have said he trusted me explicitly. Fortunately I couldn't think of any.

"Is it possible," asked Ascelin, "if Prince Dominic employed a wizard after all, that he might have been the 'magnificent warrior' of the border guards' story?"

King Haimeric shook his head. "I don't think so. He was certainly a magnificent knight, but there was nothing about him that should inspire frightening stories."

Dominic read another sentence. "My wizard and I are both gravely wounded and ill from the same fever." He stopped again and looked up. "I thought my father was killed in battle."

"Wounded in battle," said the king soberly, "so badly he might not have recovered anyway, but his servant said it was the fever that finished him."

I glanced at Joachim out of the corner of my eye and said nothing.

"But we have learned of something wonderful," Dominic continued, "something marvelous, so special that I dare not mention it even in this secret letter."

"So we're still not getting any answers," said Ascelin, half under his breath.

"It is hidden far to the south of the Holy Land, in

the Wadi Harhammi. I can't even tell you how we found out, but you will know it when you find it."

Dominic lifted his eyes. "That's the entire message. Does it make any sense?"

"What's a wadi?" asked the king.

"It's a dry watercourse," answered Ascelin.

"The Wadi Harhammi," said Hugo, "south of the Holy Land. This message is fifty years old. Other people must have learned about it by now. I'm sure it's what my father was looking for when he disappeared."

"We have to go there," said Dominic. He spoke slowly, with dignity and determination. "Wherever this Wadi Harhammi may be, whether or not the marvelous object is still there, we must go in search of it. I cannot ask the rest of you to accompany me against your wills, but I have no choice. My father wished me to go."

We all looked toward King Haimeric. This was still his quest, no matter what messages from the dead we might receive. The king nodded thoughtfully. "After fifty years, whatever he'd found or heard of is unlikely still to be there. But you're quite right: we have to look. Besides, the stories of the blue rose say it's being cultivated south of the Holy Land."

Dominic handed me the parchment. "Since this is a magical message, Wizard, you should carry it."

Ascelin stood up. "Whatever your brother had heard of, Haimeric, someone thought it important enough to break into the tomb to try to find the secret. If they're looking for the snake ring, and they know we have it, we could be in constant danger."

King Haimeric smiled. "I appreciate your concern, Ascelin, but this enemy of which you speak must already know the secret's not in the tomb and will think we don't have it either or we wouldn't have come here to look for it."

"Could I have my ring back?" Dominic asked me.

I had almost forgotten I was holding it. Even if all of

us still seemed more willing to follow the king in search of his brother than Dominic in search of his father, the burly prince certainly had a right to his own ring. I reattached the ruby, reapplied the binding spell to keep it in place, and handed him the ring, but the piece of parchment I slipped inside my jacket.

We traveled southeast through the eastern kingdoms while summer advanced rapidly around us. The king had been right, back in the mountains, that we soon wouldn't need our heavy clothes. Ascelin kept us to back roads and away from the cities. If we were being followed, neither his hunter's instincts nor my magic could find anyone behind us. But we became lost ourselves on the narrow roads at least once a day, so someone else might have had even more trouble.

Although the border guards of the first kingdom beneath the mountains had said their kingdom was not at war, the other countries apparently all were. We became lost most commonly when trying to dodge the lines of soldiers we saw approaching in the distance, or to get away from the main road when a long line of carts, carrying heavily guarded supplies, appeared before us.

"I wouldn't have wanted to miss the eastern kingdoms for anything," said Hugo in my ear, as he and I lay in the underbrush near the main road, watching horses pass by, waiting until the road was clear so we could get the others and follow it ourselves. Harnesses jingled and dust rose from hundreds of shod feet. Spear points glinted in the sun, but the faces of the riders were hidden by their helmets. "It's like the hiding games I used to play when I was little, but it's deadly earnest," he added cheerfully.

Hugo might think it an exciting game and Joachim might think there would be great merit in dying on this pilgrimage. But if we ended up as six fresh heads on poles, like the ones we had seen last night, I doubted we would appreciate it.

I felt a new respect for the wizards of the eastern kingdoms, who I kept hoping to meet at some point, although about the only people we had met so far were frightened farmers from whom we bought food. Ending war in the western kingdoms, it appeared, had not made the western aristocracy any less interested in fighting, only more likely to go help the wars continue east of the mountains.

"That's the end of the troops," I said, rising cautiously to my feet. "Let's get the others."

We followed the main road a short distance, back in the direction from which the troops had come, and were just looking for a good place to leave the road again when Hugo, in the lead, reined in abruptly. "Look at this! They aren't — they're not real, are they?"

"I'm afraid they are," said Ascelin grimly.

Before us rose a pyramid made entirely of human skulls. An inscription carved in stone at the base told us proudly that these were the enemies that the local king had had killed within a single year. Amazed, I tried to calculate how many skulls might be in the pyramid and gave up. It towered at least twenty feet above the road. The skulls, all clean of flesh and hair or any identifying mark, were very neatly arranged to stare at us.

Hugo made no more comments about games; indeed, he said nothing more for the rest of the day. For that matter, the rest of us scarcely spoke, either. We hurried on, but the shadow of that pyramid seemed still to fall between us and the sun.

"I have to apologize, Haimeric," said Ascelin as we sat around our fire that evening. We had taken lately to making very small fires. "I had no idea the eastern kingdoms would be this dangerous. Even though the main pilgrimage route is at least half again as long, we should have stayed with it. Although I'd never been east of the mountains myself, I know a number of men who have. They've spoken of battles, of course, but nothing this widespread. I don't know if it's the season of the year — I realize that they've mostly been here in the fall and winter — or if whatever 'strange' stories are coming out of the East are stirring up trouble here."

"The Bible tells us," commented the chaplain, "that in spring kings ride to war."

"Sir Hugo and his party came this way in the spring a year ago," said Ascelin, "and I'm sure they didn't have anyone with them as good as I am in finding the way and hiding tracks. And yet, from everything we know, they had no problems until they left the Holy Land. If I didn't know better, I'd think something we ourselves had done was responsible for all this."

In the next few days, however, we saw fewer troops; slowly we began to hope that we had put the worst of the wars behind us. Ascelin still spoke darkly of how everything from the bandits to these wars seemed to be managed for our maximum peril, but he couldn't decide if Arnulf was behind it, King Warin, or perhaps someone else we did not even know.

One afternoon, tired from weeks of travel and from a long day's ride under a sun which had grown more and more intense, we came around a corner and found our path barred by a wall of flame.

Whirlwind reared up, but the rest of our horses, as tired as we, only stopped. I dismounted and approached cautiously. This was magic, but I wasn't yet sure what kind.

But just as I started probing with magic, the flames disappeared. The ground was not scorched, not even warm. Illusion, then, but those illusory flames had had a solidity my best dragons always lacked.

A powerful eastern wizard would notice immediately that another wizard had tried to probe his spells. In this war-torn land, where safety was always transitory, I did not view meeting him with eager anticipation, but it was better to face him than to have him at our backs. I squared my shoulders. "There's a wizard up ahead. He means for us to stop, so it's no use trying to dodge around. I'm going to go talk to him."

"I'll come with you," said Hugo.

"Not you, Hugo," said Ascelin at once. "It had better be me."

I shook my head at both. "Courage and swordsmanship won't be any use against magic." I hurried forward without giving Hugo a chance to say he wasn't concerned about his personal safety — or myself a chance to start contemplating whatever dangers lay ahead.

A few yards past where the wall of flames had burned, a paved track turned off from the road. The stones were cracked and uneven, heavily worn in the center as though from a millennium of feet. I had somehow not noticed the track before. I paused for a minute, wondering what else might appear that had, a moment ago, been invisible. But then I turned to follow the track, for dancing twenty yards ahead of me along it were pale, inhuman shapes that still somehow suggested something human.

The ground began almost immediately to rise and the sky darkened overhead. I seemed to have stepped out of the visible world I had been in and into a world lying just beyond.

I stopped and looked back. My five companions were only thirty yards behind me. I could see them clearly as they all dismounted and sat down in the shade of a tree, but they were separated from me as if by a wall of glass. The sun still shone brightly on them, though storm clouds now hovered a short distance above my head. I wondered if they could even see the clouds from where they were — or, for that matter, if I really was on a hillside, for a minute earlier I would have sworn the land beyond the wall of flames continued level and smooth.

The air, hot all day, now became sultry as well from the lowering clouds as the track twisted and crept between jagged boulders. I gave up walking and lifted myself six inches above the ground to fly up the hill. Before me, although I had oddly not seen it until this minute, was the massive bulk of a castle. The sky beyond it darkened rapidly toward night. There were no windows or even slits looking out from the lower levels of the castle, but near the top were two large windows, lit from within by reddish light, that could have been eyes.

Beyond the castle I could hear wolves howling and I was briefly reminded of the wolfskin King Warin wore across his shoulder. A bolt of lightning, then another, struck the top of the castle before me, with a sharp crack and a lingering acrid smell but no following thunder. The sky was virtually black; I could no longer see the bottom of the hill behind me. I stopped and probed for the supernatural. It was one thing to go to meet a wizard, another to walk into a demon's lair.

But I found no evidence of black magic. I tried to reassure myself that school magic, even my own occasionally less than perfect grasp of it, should be at least as strong as the magic the wizards of the eastern kingdom learned under their apprenticeship system, but this thought did nothing to dispel the cold prickles moving up and down my back.

I crossed a bridge, glancing over the side to see a deep ditch disappear beyond sight, and reached the entrance to the castle. The broad, nail-studded doors were thirty feet high. They could have been a mouth to go with the glowing eyes of the windows, and the portcullis suspended above them the teeth. The castle was built, I could now see, of obsidian, dead black, as smooth as glass and with the edges of the stones as sharp as knives. Another bolt of lightning struck just as I raised my hand to knock.

With an ominous, high-pitched shriek, the double

doors swung open. I looked in, not wanting to enter until I knew what was there, but saw no one. Then, far down the black corridor, I saw a flicker of movement, disappearing away. It was not quite substantial, a ghoul or a ghost, and gone before I could probe with magic to see if it was illusion or real.

I waited. I was not entirely sure the castle itself was real, but if someone had created it for my benefit then he would certainly show himself. The air coming through the open doors was as cold as if it emerged from a hundred yards underground.

Then, echoing down the dark corridor, I heard a sharp click of heels. In the distance I picked out a pinpoint of light that quickly grew larger. A man was approaching, carrying a candle. And not just a man, I realized at once, but a wizard. As he neared the door I could see that he was immaculately dressed in a suit of black satin and that his face was as white as if it had been painted.

"Good evening, Wizard," he said with a smile that showed quite a few teeth but contained no good humor. "I've been expecting you."

I was about to protest that it was not evening, that it was only the middle of the afternoon, but an upward glance showed me that here, at any rate, it was night.

"You're from Yurt, aren't you," said the wizard before me. He had very strange eyes, expressionless even though they flicked constantly from side to side, almost as if they had been made of stone rather than living flesh.

"What do you know of Yurt?" I demanded.

"Princeps Yurtiae" it said on Dominic's father's tomb. But there were hundreds of other tombs in the Church of the Holy Twins, and we were a great many miles from there. Yurt itself at the moment seemed a hundred thousand miles away, a place as peaceful and brightly lit as though it were Paradise.

"Come in and I shall tell you a number of interesting

things," the wizard said, again with the tooth-filled smile. "I do not, however, know your name."

"Daimbert," I said cautiously.

"Come in, Daimbert. My name is Vlad. You may call me Prince."

I had wanted to meet the wizards of the eastern kingdoms, I reminded myself. By offering to tell me interesting things, by knowing already that I was from Yurt, this wizard had tempted me to enter his castle in a way that offers of wealth and dancing girls never would have. I wrapped a protective spell around me, although I did not know what I was trying to protect myself from, and stepped inside.

IV

The corridor was lit only by the wizard's candle. "Is this your principality?" I asked, standing between him and the doorway so that he could not close the doors before I was sure what I was getting into.

"It certainly is," he said with a slow blink. His eyelids, I noted, were translucent, like the eyelids of a snake, and did not hide the stone eyes behind them.

"And yet you're a wizard," I said unevenly, holding onto the door frame. I was suddenly swept with a terror so profound that for a moment I wasn't even sure I could stand unaided. This was either irrational fear of something outside my previous experience or good sense telling me to escape while I was still alive.

"Of course. I know over in the western kingdoms you wizards serve the kings and the aristocracy, but here we prefer to be our own masters."

In the shadows behind him I thought I saw — although it could have been the shadows from his candle — a viper moving slowly across the floor.

And then I knew the source of my terror. It had nothing to do with this wizard, strange though he might be. It was memories of another long corridor down which I had groped nearly ten years ago, the closest I had ever been to death and damnation. And that corridor had been in Yurt. If I was going to find safety, I would have to create it for myself, wherever I was.

I pushed myself forcibly away from the door. "I'm curious, Prince," I said. "Is this castle real?" The door frame, at any rate, was solid under my hand.

"It depends on what you mean by real," he answered ambiguously and turned his back to *me*. He certainly seemed unafraid of me. "Come with me, and I think you'll find out several things about which you've been wondering."

As soon as his back was turned, I tried another quick magic probe to reassure myself that he was human and no demon. But then I followed, watching the floor for snakes. The door stayed open behind me, but beyond it was only night and wolves.

Candles held by invisible hands preceded us down the corridor. Prince Vlad led me into a room off the corridor where I had hoped there would be more light, but it was windowless. Heavy hangings covered the wall, worked black on black, with brief shots of white in a design confused and disconcerting enough that I tried not to look.

"I've been waiting for you ever since my old friend, King Warin's chancellor, said you were coming this way," he said, sitting down in one black leather chair and motioning me into another.

"Warin? You know him?" The terror I had tried to dismiss by the doorway was back again in full strength.

"I already told you I know a number of interesting things, including the answers to many questions I'm sure you've asked yourself."

"And what do you want in return for this information, Prince?" I asked, trying to make his eyes meet mine.

"Very good, Daimbert," he said as though pleased. "I knew you would not disappoint me. Of course I want something. What I want is knowledge from you."

"I don't think I have any knowledge that you would want," I said slowly.

"Of course you do," he said with another smile. I wondered briefly how many teeth he actually had. "You're a school-trained wizard and know the wizards' secret of perpetual youth. It's obvious — you've got a white beard and hair, and yet you're still youthful and vigorous. What age are you really? A hundred? A hundred and fifty?"

"I'm not yet forty." I had no intention of telling him about the incident that had turned my hair white overnight. "School magic has no secret of youth. Wizards in the west may live well past two hundred, but if we do it's because of the same spells that wizards used for generations, even before the school was founded — the same spells, I expect, available to you."

His stone eyes managed to convey disappointment. He pursed his thin lips, then smiled again. "We'll return to this in a moment. But you in the west know how to see and to hear someone over a great distance, I understand."

"Telephones," I agreed. "But don't ask me, Prince. I've never been any good at technical magic." I was not going to explain that the far-seeing attachment, while my own invention, had been discovered essentially by accident. "The wizard you probably should ask is Elerius, who used to work for King Warin. By the way, does the king know that you consider his chancellor your friend?" I leaned forward and then wished I hadn't, because the wizard's white face up close was like a mask. For a moment I felt irrationally convinced that beneath that mask was the face of a corpse. "You said you had information for me. The first information I want is how you knew we were coming."

"Warin's chancellor sent me a message as soon as you left his kingdom."

I was about to interrupt and ask how that message

was sent, since pigeon messages between the eastern and western kingdoms were notoriously unreliable, and this wizard had no telephone, but I reminded myself that there were certainly other ways — a fast-riding messenger, even a spell-captured eagle of the high peaks. My guess was that Warin, even if he were a sorcerer, had no idea that his trusted chancellor was also in this wizard's pay — which thought made me wonder briefly if there had also been activities of Elerius's which he had not known about.

"My friend knew that I'd been waiting a long time for visitors from Yurt," Prince Vlad added.

"I know who you are," I said suddenly. The king's younger brother might not be someone to produce terrifying stories, but this man certainly was. "You're the wizard who was employed, fifty years ago, by Prince Dominic of Yurt."

"It was difficult tracking you across all those miles between the mountains and here," Prince Vlad continued without denying my guess. "Someone in your party is extremely good." I would have to tell Ascelin if I lived to see him again.

He motioned toward a black marble table on the far side of the room. "That is how I knew where you were." I went over to look. On the table was a three-dimensional map of what appeared to be this part of the eastern kingdoms. "Try the skull."

By the map was the face of a skull, with crystals set in the eye sockets. When I put it in front of my own face to look through the crystals, the model of the eastern kingdoms became enormous, as though I were an eagle flying over it. I could see armed men on the roads, houses tucked into clearings, castles at the river crossings. The tiniest movement of the head, even of the eyes, took one's line of vision miles. It would be hard to find people who were deliberately hiding, even with this magic, but my hands trembled as I slowly set the skull down again.

"It was only because so many of the other wizards of the eastern kingdoms owe me favors — either princes and counts in their own right or allied with kings — that I was able to keep track of you at all. Troop movements are a rather awkward way of easing people you can't quite see in the direction you want, but it was eventually effective. After all, you're here now."

"Wait," I said, without enough time to wonder how many of the soldiers we had seen and hidden from were actually being moved for our benefit. "You died of wounds and the fever fifty years ago."

"There are many versions of death," he said vaguely, pulling his translucent lids down over his eyes.

"But you are that wizard?" I demanded, determined to find out at least one clear piece of information.

"That's what you want most to know?" he said, opening his eyes again. He seemed to be able to see with them, but I was more and more convinced they were something artificial. "Yes, I might as well tell you that I am. If you're as young as you claim, you won't have known Prince Dominic, but I never trusted him. He told me he could fight a dozen men at once, but it took only ten to overcome him when we were both struck down. Even after his manservant and I buried the prince, I feigned a much worse fever than I actually had."

"He didn't trust you, either," I said. I paused, pushing back terror, and continued, "So you didn't actually die?" More than anything else, at the moment I wanted reassurance that, whatever he might have done with his body, his dead soul had not been sent back to earth from hell.

But he did not give me that reassurance. "Because I did not trust Prince Dominic, I didn't tell him that part of the magic necessary to uncover the Wadi's secret was an opening spell I attached to the ruby ring itself."

"What a shame," I lied. "We left the ruby ring home in Yurt."

To my surprise, he seemed to believe me. The living map of the eastern kingdoms, I realized, would not give him enough detail to be able to see for himself. I presumed he didn't trust King Warin's chancellor either and had therefore not questioned him closely about the jewelry worn by the visitors from Yurt. I spread out my own hand ostentatiously, to show my eagle ring set with a tiny diamond.

"It's probably gone from the Wadi by now anyway," he said regretfully. "When that servant left for Yurt, he took the ring with him, and I was — well, too weak to stop him or follow him. And I certainly have never liked the idea of wandering the western kingdoms, threatened by school-trained wizards. So I have waited a long time for someone from Yurt to come east and have never even bothered going to the Wadi."

"What was hidden there?"

My question came out much louder than I expected and hung in the air between us. The wizard half turned away, then smiled slowly. "Maybe I don't trust you, either, Daimbert. If you want to know that, you'll have to teach me much more of the magic of glass and steel."

"Glass and steel?" I said cautiously.

"That's what we call school magic here in the eastern kingdoms, your technical magic that can keep working even without an active mind saying the spells. *Our* magic is a magic of bone and blood."

I had assumed that the wizards of the eastern kingdoms, without anything comparable to the organization of the wizards' school in the west, would be hard pressed to restrain warfare. Instead, it sounded as though war and death were their normal occupations.

"What did you give King Warin's chancellor in return for the information that we were coming?"

"You have so many questions, Daimbert!" he said, showing his teeth again. "And you've given me no information yet. Before I tell you anything else, I want to know that spell of yours that allows western wizards to live well past two hundred."

I considered this for a moment, keeping my eyes on my companion's black satin suit because I didn't want to look at his face. The powerful spell that would slow down — though never reverse — natural aging was not taught until near the end of the eight-year program, and the teachers always impressed on us that our oaths to help humanity did not include meddling with nature's cycle to give all our friends an extra century or two of life

But a wizard, even one here, surely knew that spell anyway. By showing him the spell I might be able to convince him that I had no secret knowledge he wanted. "Give me some paper," I said. "I'll write it out."

It was a long spell and took a while. While I wrote, I thought over what little information I had from him so far. If King Warin, via his chancellor, had some sort of connection with the wizards of the eastern kingdoms, then that might explain why Evrard had called him a sorcerer. The strange form of magic that had shaped this castle and maybe even the physical being of the man across from me might look like the black arts, at least to someone like Evrard who had never actually met a demon.

This would mean that Elerius had not lived for twelve years in the castle of a man who had sold his soul to the devil, which was a relief, though I continued to suspect he might have picked up some form of magic he would prefer not to share with the masters of the school.

I still didn't know what connection there might be, if any, between Joachim's brother on the one hand, with his talk of King Solomon's Pearl, disappearing caravans, and the very real present his wife had tried to send with us and, on the other, the mysterious object of which Prince Dominic had learned shortly before his death. The only person who might understand the connection was King Warin. And I doubted Warin would trust this wizard either.

I passed the pieces of paper across to Prince Vlad. "Here it is, but I'm sure you already know this spell."

He seized the paper avidly, but I thought I could again see disappointment in his features as he scanned the spell. "But this will do nothing to make someone younger!"

"That's what I told you." I hesitated, then pushed on. "For that you need the supernatural."

He shot me a sudden glance from his stone eyes. "Or to know something that apparently even you don't know."

How to give motion to inanimate objects, I thought, how to prop up a sagging and decaying body with the dead flesh and blood of others or even with wood and stone. If he had had to rebuild a badly wounded body with incredibly complex magic, no wonder he had not been able to restrain Prince Dominic's servant from returning to Yurt. "I don't know anything about it," I agreed.

"Then it may prove less useful stopping you than I thought," he said slowly, "unless — unless you actually *did* bring the ruby ring with you from Yurt."

Caught in my lie, I tried to brazen my way out. "We had no idea there was anything magical about that ring itself," I said, which was true. "You must know that we stopped at Prince Dominic's tomb to see if it might have any secrets to yield, which we wouldn't have bothered doing if we'd known the secret was back in the treasury of Yurt." I paused, then tried to give him an intimidating glare. "If you say you have information for me, why not prove it by telling me who opened that tomb? Was it you?"

This surprised him. "Why would anyone open Dominic's tomb?"

"You're lying," I said, to conceal the fact that I had been myself. "You said we would exchange knowledge, but you opened the prince's tomb to get something you hid there when he was buried."

He didn't take the bait. Instead he shook his head. "Maybe that servant — he always was a fool — let some information drop on his way home. Or our source of information on the Wadi Harhammi may have regretted letting that information out — and, before you ask, I'm *not* going to tell you what that source was."

"But you know the opening spell," I said suddenly, not admitting that we had the ring with us but not bothering to deny it any more, either. "That must be more than anyone else has — except, possibly, this 'source' of yours. At least one other person is searching desperately for that information but doesn't have it. Maybe what Prince Dominic called something wonderful, something marvelous, is still there! Do you want to come with us to the East to look for it?"

I jumped to my feet as I spoke. This wizard with the artificial eyes was the last person I would normally have chosen for a traveling companion, but if he was with us where I could watch him, I would not have to worry what he was doing behind our backs.

"I do not leave my castle," he said slowly. "I had hoped that in return for the information you need, you would find it for me and bring it here."

Something that even such a powerful wizard could covet for fifty years must be marvelous indeed. "You clearly don't have any knowledge I need or want," I said. "You've been bluffing, Prince."

"I could tell you what's concealed in the Wadi. I think you would prefer to know before, rather than after, you use that opening spell."

"Come with us, then, and tell us as we go," I said, "or we'll find out for ourselves anyway. I'm offering to take you along, but if you stay here you know I won't be back."

"You won't know what to do with it, even with the opening spell, even with the ruby. Swear to me by all the forces of magic that you will bring it back and I will reveal its powers to you when you arrive."

"And once you have it, you'll get rid of us? Not likely, Prince."

His eyes came fully open as he pushed his face close to mine. "If you try to rush out of here now, even if your magic can fight past the powers that guard me, I think you'll find that armies will pursue you all across the eastern kingdoms —until they catch you and kill you."

I grabbed his arm. It felt almost like a normal human arm. "Then our only safety is having you with us. I don't *care* if you don't want to leave this castle. You're going to now!"

With force and magic I dragged him from the room. He struggled against me, but I was stronger. The corridor, unlit by any candle, was completely black. I yelled out a spell and, for an instant, it was lit up as bright as day, and I could see the corridor's end and the studded nail doors, opening onto night.

V

I started to rush down the corridor, then heard a gasp from the wizard that sounded like genuine pain. I paused, unsure if this was a trap, and turned on the moon and stars on my belt buckle. They cast a pale glow, no brighter than a candle, but I could see his eyes squeezed shut and a strange, almost melting quality to one cheek.

"Why did you shine that light?" he said in a low, nearly indistinct voice.

"To see to get out of here and to scare back your ghouls!"

"You will not escape from here. You think those doors are safety, but outside it's midnight and my wolves will meet you. Let me go and I shall let *you* live."

My heart was pounding too hard to make any sort of rational decision possible. "I don't know how long I've been in your castle, but it must still be sometime in the afternoon. Come with me and I'll let you live!"

In the glow of my belt buckle, I hurried on, still dragging him with me. He was putting up very little resistance now.

But as we reached the door I heard him chuckle. Just outside the door, wolves were howling.

"It is not midnight," I said between clenched teeth. A flash of lightning hit just below us on the hill; for a second I could see the wolf pack, enormous furry beasts, nearly as tall at the shoulder as I, their eyes and teeth glowing phosphorescent.

The natural world, I told myself, was much more powerful than any wizardry. Prince Vlad could make it appear night, but it would not actually be night until the earth had turned. Even his storm clouds, brought with the magic he called the magic of blood and bone, could be blown away by the wind.

Especially if that wind was aided by weather spells. Standing just inside the door, still holding onto him, I shouted the spells that should drive a storm higher, further away, that will bring the sunshine back out over a threatened crop.

And the sky split open. If I saw the Last Judgment with living eyes, I thought irrelevantly, I would know what to expect.

Black, tattered clouds pulled back, letting the late afternoon sun pour its light onto the wizard's hill. The wolves, even bigger and closer than I had thought, gave me a startled look, then turned and trotted away.

But everything else lay revealed with the sickening, partially decayed look of something rediscovered after long burial. Only the obsidian castle, with its window eyes and gaping mouth, stayed solid and untorn.

The wizard shrieked. I released his arm involuntarily, then stared at him in horror. He had his face in his hands, but two round stones dropped from between his fingers and rolled away.

I went down on my knees beside him. "My God! Have I killed you?"

"Don't — mention — God — to — a — wizard," he said very slowly, as though having to force out each word. Several other parts of his body now seemed loose, only held in place by his clothes. He dropped his hands and turned his eyeless face toward me. One cheek was nearly gone. "I told you I never left my castle," he said, slightly more strongly. "You haven't killed me, you'll be disappointed to discover. But it will take me years to rebuild this body. Curse you, Daimbert!"

He tried to make it a resounding shout, but it came out as a half-stifled rattle. I didn't wait to see what particular curses he might call down on me. I fled down the hill, pausing just once to look back and see him crawling in through the door of his obsidian castle.

"He's not dead," I said, lying stetched out on the ground with my face on my arms, trembling all over. "But I don't think he'll be able to come after us."

Joachim put a hand on my shoulder, but no one said anything for a moment. "I think you should have killed him," said Hugo. "After all, he wanted to kill you."

"That was a threat," I said. "He didn't want me dead so much as he wanted information — information which in fact does not exist."

"He betrayed my father by withholding information," said Dominic darkly. "Even after fifty years, that betrayal must be avenged."

"I avenged your father without meaning to," I said. "I never even imagined that the wizard's physical body was only held together by spells that would dissolve in daylight. At least I know why he's never come to Yurt after the ruby ring."

"I should have avenged my father myself," Dominic muttered. "The one useful thing we've learned is that whatever he wanted us to find in the Wadi is probably still there — and involves my ring. All the business with Arnulf and Warin and the bandits must be something entirely separate."

"Unless King Solomon's Pearl is real," I said in a low voice, "and that's what's in the Wadi. If it really will give someone his heart's desire, that wizard is hoping it will give him the ability to rebuild his body properly."

There was another long pause. "You realize," said Hugo to me at last, "that we never saw anything — not the hill, not the castle, not even the wolves."

"It's all real," I said, making myself roll around and sit up. "It's concealed by magic, but it's still there. That's why I know he's still alive — the spells are much too complicated to be maintained without an active mind behind them. Keeping those spells going will take all his energy for a long, long time."

"Then let's go," said Ascelin. "The further we are from real wolves the better." He offered me a hand to pull me up. "So he admired my ability to leave no tracks, you say?" he added with a grin.

We sat on the terrace outside an inn, eating grilled fish and salad with dark-cured olives and drinking white wine. A trellis covered with climbing flowers shaded us from the afternoon sun. Off in one direction we could see sage-covered hills, scattered with gray-green olive trees and, in the other, sunlight flashing on the Central Sea. Red sails leaned in the wind as ships large and small headed in or out of harbor. We didn't recognize the kind of fish we were eating or most of the herbs in the salad and none of us cared.

Joachim came back to the table and sat down. I lifted my eyebrows interrogatively. "I was finally able to talk to Claudia on the telephone," he said. "It was hard to hear her; I don't think the telephone's spells were working very well. She never did say what had been in the package. She just said she was sorry it had been stolen, but that it didn't really matter."

"Did you say that bandits had nearly killed you in order to steal it?" asked Hugo.

"Of course not," said the chaplain in surprise. "I've already told you, I'm sure they wounded me by accident. At any rate, I wouldn't want to worry Claudia."

"I'll try to telephone the queen after dinner," said the king.

"And I'll try Diana," said Ascelin.

"I hate to tell you this, Ascelin," said Hugo, his mouth full and motioning to the waiter, "but this is a lot better than your cooking."

"Are you ready for the roast lamb?" asked the waiter. "It will be out in just a moment. Let me refill your wine glasses."

We hadn't had any wine since we left King Warin's castle. The local vintage had a flinty undertone and tasted wonderful.

"Success," said Ascelin, lifting his glass as though in salute. "All the way down through the eastern kingdoms to the sea, without being killed, without being captured, without even being in battle. Next time, Haimeric, I *will* stick with the main routes, but even with all the delays, we're as far along as we would have been if we'd stayed west of the mountains."

"Isn't our slow progress due in part to the rest of you having to wait for me?" asked the king.

"No, having to wait for me on foot," said Ascelin with a smile. "If you all had stallions like Dominic's, you'd have been in the Holy Land weeks ago."

"So how do you think we should go from here?" asked Dominic. "Along the coast or out to sea?" He finished the last of his salad and poked Ascelin with his elbow. "I ask, of course, knowing that whatever you suggest, we should do just the opposite."

The waiter came out at this point with a steaming platter, lamb scented with garlic and rosemary. I felt my capacity to keep eating was unlimited.

"Pilgrims normally follow the coast road," said Ascelin. "It's a safe route and it goes by a number of pilgrimage churches, including all those dedicated to the martyrs killed back in the days of the wars between Christians and the People of the Prophet. Those were the wars which drove most Christians, except those of Xantium, into the west. Even pilgrims with no intention of going as far as the Holy Land often follow part of that route."

"That's the way my bishop went," put in Joachim.

"But traders stick to the sea," Ascelin continued. "It's certainly faster and a lot easier for anyone with heavy goods. The most dangerous part of the sea voyage is west of here, through the shoals and islands, and we've already skipped that part."

"Even if we are on pilgrimage ourselves," said Hugo, "our principal goal is still to find my father and his party. I think we should try to get to the Holy Land as quickly as possible and start searching for them from there."

"We'll be able to book sea passage to Xantium from here," said Ascelin. "All routes in and around the Central Sea pass through Xantium. That's where your brother's agents will have their offices," with a glance at Joachim, "and that's where the last overland route to the Holy Land begins."

The king nodded. "You've taken us safely so far, Ascelin. I'll trust you to continue to guide us. Tomorrow we'll book our passage."

There were three couples at the next table, talking and eating and apparently enjoying themselves nearly as much as we were. The women wore yellow or blue cotton dresses, printed all over with flowers. "We never get fabric like that at home," commented the king. "Maybe I should buy some to take home for the queen."

"I've already told you, sire," said Hugo with a grin, "don't load up the luggage now. Wait until we're on our way home."

I had been too busy eating to join in the conversation, although, to my surprise, I found myself slowing down on my third helping of lamb. I dipped a piece of bread in the juices on my plate and wondered where the palm trees I had expected might be.

The terrace where we were sitting was high above the harbor; off in the distance I could see marshy land bordering the sea, but no palm trees swayed anywhere in sight. I swallowed my bread and asked about them.

"Don't worry," said Ascelin. "You'll see plenty of palms when we get to the East." I wondered if we would also see the dancing girls that Hugo had imagined with his father. "There are even some in the marshy areas near here. It will probably be a few days before we sail, so we can look for them if you like."

The waiter, carrying a tray filled with strawberry tarts, interrupted us at this point. But palm trees became our goal for the next two days. Ascelin was able to find a ship going to Xantium that was willing to take us. While it was loading its cargo, we followed steep, rocky paths down to the harbor and from the harbor, along sandy beaches that led for miles in either direction. Here at last were the palms I had imagined during the winter in Yurt, their old fronds lying dry and close to the trunk, their new fronds branching out from the top, reminding me oddly of the way that young Prince Paul drew pictures of trees.

"So is this it, Wizard?" Hugo asked me with a chuckle. "Everyone is searching for something on this trip. The chaplain wants pilgrimage churches; the king wants a blue rose; I want to find my father; Dominic, having found *his* father, is now looking for whatever's in the Wadi; and Ascelin wants the chance to boss everyone around that I'm sure the duchess doesn't give him at home. And you're on a quest for trees?"

I laughed, but his comment started me thinking. I had thought that I was on this quest to find Evrard, as well as to assist my king however I could, but I might well be searching for something else. There was an old saying I had first heard as a boy in the City, "What ye seek, and what ye find, will oft-times be of different kind."

As we and our highly dubious horses boarded the ship at last, and the sails creaked up the mast to catch the dawn wind and take us out of the sage-scented harbor, I wondered again what I was seeking. Once out of harbor, the sails filled and the lines tightened, and the bright waves began slapping against our ship's hull as we started east along the coast. Whatever it was, or whatever I would find, we seemed to be heading toward it.

PART FIVE

Xantium

1

The great City by the western sea, the city where I had grown up, did not have a name. For official purposes it was called the Urbs, but that was only City in the old language of the empire that had once been centered in it. Those who lived there merely called it the City, as though there were no other or, at least, no other that mattered.

As our ship, with its cargo of furs, leather, and six pilgrims, rounded the headland and entered the great basin of Xantium harbor, I realized what a hopelessly provincial attitude that was.

"The duchess and I should travel more," said Ascelin, leaning on the railing next to me. "She would love to see this city. Maybe when the girls are bigger we can all come."

But I wasn't listening. Above us, on top of a sheer cliff, an enormous tower glowered down on us and I could sense that we were being watched with magic as well as eyes. Massive iron rings protruded from the cliff at water level. Another tower stood on another promontory a quarter mile away. The only way into the harbor was through the narrow, black-watered channel between them.

"In times of war," commented Ascelin, "I understand they chain the harbor shut."

The harbor itself was as large as a lake and jammed

with hundreds of ships and boats, from tiny dinghies to massive vessels that dwarfed our own ship. Many were trading vessels of the sort I had been accustomed to seeing in the City docks, but many others seemed to be pleasure barges; even among the ones I assumed were traders were a great number with riggings I had never before seen.

A long ship came up behind us and shot by into the harbor, its banks of oars dipping and pulling smoothly. "Probably rowed by slaves," said Ascelin.

The others had come up to stand by us at the railing. "I thought Xantium was a Christian city," I said to the chaplain.

"It is, or at least its governors are Christian," he said gravely. "But God is worshipped in many ways. And they interpret Christianity somewhat differently here than do the bishops of the west. After all, the Bible does not specifically forbid slavery, although all right thinkers must realize that as men and women are brothers and sisters together under God, slavery cannot be tolerated."

The sailors hurried back and forth, and some swarmed up the mast to release the booms as the captain negotiated through the shipping. We tried to stay out of the way, looking at the city that covered the hillside beyond the harbor.

It reached most of the way around the basin. Directly above the docks rose gray walls, pierced by open gates. Behind the walls the city strode up the hill, a jumble of towers, minarets, and spires. The high walls followed the edge of the water for several miles on either side before turning inland, but the city continued beyond the walls, an incoherent mass of buildings large and small, some painted brilliant colors and some dark. A complex of smells, flowers, spice, and garbage, mingled with the salt tang of the harbor.

"We're entering the East at last," said the king.

"In fact, sire," said Joachim, "it depends on how you

define the East. Xantium is indeed called the East's gateway, but we're still west of the Holy Land, and everyone knows that the Holy City is in the exact center of the inhabited earth, so that there are still thousands of miles of the true East beyond."

And I had thought when we entered the eastern kingdoms that we were already somewhere in the East.

"I wonder how difficult it would be to travel deep into the East," said Ascelin thoughtfully. "It would be worth it to see which of the tales are really true, to see the bushes that produce tea and spices, the stones from which silk is spun."

"I've heard," put in Hugo, "that silk isn't really spun from a stone at all but rather made by some kind of worm. How about it, Wizard? What do they teach in your school?"

If they taught about silk manufacture in the wizards' school, they had certainly not taught it to me. "It's a secret known only to the wise," I replied airily, then groped for something I could say with certainty. "But I can assure you that silk is *not* made by worms."

Our ship now moved very slowly on just one sail, little more than drifting among the moored vessels. The captain steered us carefully past the moorings and then along the tangle of wooden docks that protruded from the city gates. At last we slid smoothly up next to a dock and stopped with only the slightest bump.

The sailors all cheered and busied themselves tying down the sails and the lines. The gangplank went over the railing with a clatter. Already a group of burly men were moving out along the docks toward us, members of the dockhands' guild I assumed, though the dockhands in the City at home had never worn cobalt blue tunics and shoes with long, curled toes.

We went off first, before the real cargo, leading our horses. The king spoke briefly with the captain about finding a good place to stay. I heard the captain add, "I've picked up from a few things your party has said that you're *missing* something. Missing objects from all around the Central Sea have a way of ending up in Xantium. You might try the Thieves' Market."

Our horses were stiff and restless from the voyage, especially Whirlwind. He sniffed the air as though in disgust and decided to treat every person, every bale on the docks, and every piece of trash blown by the wind as a potential threat, an excuse for whinnying and rearing. Dominic clung grimly to the bridle, using his own weight to hold the stallion down, and stayed close behind Ascelin.

I stopped to stare at a tall pole from which three dead men dangled limp over the water. A dockhand saw my stare and smiled.

"Don't you hang thieves in the west?" he asked. "The governor allows no one to violate the integrity of Xantium harbor, not the thieves' guild, not amateurs. Of course, the old governor was rather soft and let things get out of hand, but the new one's really cracked down the last few years."

We picked our way along the docks to shore where we were stopped by black-robed officials before we could enter the gates.

"Governor's orders," said one crisply. "Xantium is finally being run efficiently. He's the last Christian governor as one heads east, so all pilgrims have to sign in here. Then if you're not back in a few months, we can send word to your relatives in the west. Be sure to remember to sign back in when you return from the Holy Land."

I remembered that the governor's office had given Sir Hugo's wife the news that he and his party had never returned to Xantium. The book we had to sign asked for a relative or friend and then for a second person to notify in case the first could not be reached.

We all put Yurt's queen in the first column, then I wrote down the wizard's school, Joachim his bishop, Hugo his mother, Ascelin the duchess, and King

Haimeric and Dominic the king of Caelrhon, the kingdom that bordered Yurt. The king wanted to put King Warin, but the rest of us wouldn't let him.

I wondered briefly if Sir Hugo and his party — or at least Evrard — had put down the royal court of Yurt as the party to be notified if the governor's office could not reach Sir Hugo's wife.

We continued through the city gates and into the narrow streets beyond. The buildings leaned so closely over the streets that these were very dim. The ground floors were jammed with shops and businesses. Loud voices greeted us on every side, offering us accommodations, young girls fresh from the country, hot baths, exquisite jewels, spicy dishes, purple silks, fine weapons and maps of the city. King Haimeric ignored them all, walking with Ascelin beside him, following the directions the captain had scrawled on a piece of paper.

In a few minutes we emerged from the noisiest streets into what appeared to be a residential area. Dark-haired children who had been playing in the gutters raced up to beg for pennies. Halfway down a dead-end street a silver-plated bush protruding from a housefront marked the inn to which the captain had directed us.

"Do you think we dare stay here, Haimeric?" asked Ascelin in a low voice. "If anyone followed us through the eastern kingdoms, it would have been easy enough for them to find out which ship we'd taken and they'd quickly discover the inn the ship's captain recommended. And thanks to an officious governor, we've told anyone in Xantium with enough money to bribe his clerks that a party from Yurt has arrived."

Ascelin had already been worried about our safety back when we visited Joachim's brother. Arnulf's manor house, surrounded by rich green, seemed as alien from Xantium as though it had been on the moon. In retrospect, I thought, it must seem safe and secure to him.

"We'll only be here a few days," said King Haimeric. "I doubt this enemy you imagine is anywhere near as good at tracking as you are."

"I just hope they aren't still planning to kill the chaplain," said Ascelin darkly as we turned through an elaborate doorway into the inn's flowering courtyard.

But we stayed at the inn for only half an hour. Once we had booked our rooms and stabled our horses, we started out again toward the Church of the Wisdom of Solomon.

"It's Xantium's most famous sight," said Joachim, "even if we didn't need to give thanks to God for our safe sea voyage."

"Solomon's the only man, I think," said Ascelin thoughtfully, "ever to combine the functions of priest, of king, and of magic-worker."

"According to Arnulf's books," put in Hugo, "the last of the caliphs, the one who renounced Solomon's Pearl, was both a mage and a secular leader, though I guess he wasn't a priest."

"This church," said Joachim, "is dedicated to Solomon's *Holy* Wisdom."

The innkeeper had given us a map over which the chaplain and Ascelin bent their heads to find the best route. Without a map we would have been hopelessly lost in under ten minutes. The maze of streets was jammed with people who all, unlike us, seemed to know exactly where they were going. We spotted a few who also appeared to be pilgrims, but most were very different from anyone ever seen in the west. Dark-skinned men in striped robes and headdresses; women so heavily veiled that only their eyes were visible; men at whom Dominic frowned, whose cheeks were rouged and eyes outlined in black; long-legged warriors, some nearly as tall as Ascelin, wearing turbans and wide, curved swords; half-naked children; black-robed clerks talking seriously to each other; sumptuously dressed dandies who moved in the center of a group of bodyguards; and grumpy-looking women, dressed drably and carrying net bags full of vegetables, all jostled together in the streets.

Once or twice I thought I saw someone following us, but it was impossible to keep track of anyone behind us in such a crowd, even with magic.

"I'd looked forward to seeing the East," I said to the chaplain, "but it's even more, well, *different* from Yurt than I'd expected."

"That's why one travels," he commented. "At home, you're always looking in a mirror. Everything you see becomes so familiar it is almost an extension of the self. Elsewhere, you see everything *except* yourself." He paused, then added thoughtfully, "I think we need them both: the contemplation of our inner souls and the jostling out of ourselves, the reminder that we are not the entire world and shall meet even God face to face."

Most of the housefronts along the streets were blank, but whenever we passed one whose gate was open we caught a glimpse of a passage leading to a cool-looking courtyard, bright with flowers and often with a fountain.

It was hot and steamy even if the mid-afternoon sun was blocked before it reached our level. For the two weeks we had coasted along the north edge of the Central Sea, the sea breezes had kept us cool, but it was now indubitably high summer and a much hotter summer than anything known in Yurt.

We moved with Joachim and the king in the center of a square formed by the rest of us, even if it meant that we sometimes jostled the people we met against the housefronts. Ascelin was as alert as I, and Hugo seemed wound up almost to the breaking point. When the chaplain stopped abruptly, we all stopped.

We had come around a corner. One side of this street was lined not with buildings but with a fence, and a shadowy courtyard lay beyond. A bell, with the same tone as the chapel's bell in the royal castle of home, began to sound. Its note was sweet and restful, as though the noises of the street were a thousand miles, rather than just a few feet, away.

Looking through the fence, we saw a group of men in dark vestments walk through the courtyard in procession, carrying candles and singing. Their expressions were rapt; anything on our side of the fence might as well have not existed. For a moment I thought they were priests, but the shaved crowns of their heads made them unlike any priests I knew. They disappeared through an archway on the far side of the courtyard and the bell's ringing came to an end.

Joachim turned and started walking again. "Monks," he said to me. "We don't have them in the west and I'd never seen them before. They're somewhat like hermits, except that they live together, under the fatherly direction of a leader."

"More like nuns?" I asked.

Before the chaplain could answer, we heard another sound, a piercing, modulated wail coming from a minaret under which we were passing.

"It's the priests of the Prophet," said Ascelin, "calling the faithful to afternoon prayer."

Considering that I was supposed to be a well-educated wizard, I didn't seem to have had any idea all trip what we would see. Maybe when we met some eastern mages I'd have a chance to show off my own knowledge out of *Melecherius on Eastern Magic*.

But we reached the Church of Holy Wisdom without meeting any mages. There was a tiny square in front of the great doors where a peddlar was selling little bottles of purportedly holy water. We pushed by him without listening to his pitch and went up the steps and inside.

From the outside, it was impossible to tell the size of the church, but from the inside it was enormous. We all stopped in amazement to look around.

Candles gleamed from golden candelabra, lighting

up a forest of porphyry columns and green marble arches. The floor beneath our feet was onyx veined with gold. Windows through which the sunlight poured pierced the dome high above us. The air was thick with incense. Mosaics made of a hundred thousand glittering tiles illustrated Bible stories.

As we walked slowly into the church we saw the biggest mosaic of all. The saved and the damned rose in alarm from their coffins to see the sky split open above them. I approved of the artist's rendering of the scene. Christ in majesty, thirty feet high, dressed in brilliant blue and rimmed in gold, greeted us and them with a raised hand.

There were a large number of other people in the church, pilgrims, men who appeared to be priests even though their vestments were purple instead of black, women who seemed to have stopped in for a quick prayer on their way home from the market, and even some of the tall, turbaned men we had noticed earlier. But the size of the church swallowed us all up without even seeming to notice.

As we reached the main altar and Joachim went to his knees, I thought I saw a flicker of motion behind us, as though one of the other people in the church did not want us to see him.

I probed quickly with magic. Someone was there, all right. I rose two inches above the floor to be able to move silently and darted around the base of a column. A black-haired boy squatted there, looking around the far side. He turned and saw me just too late.

I had him by the back of the shirt as he jumped up to run. "I'm a mage," I said. "I don't want to hurt you, but if you try to get away you're going to become a frog."

He was apparently willing to believe me for he went limp. I pulled him from behind the column and to the others without letting down my guard.

"Good work, Wizard," said Ascelin. "Is this the person who's been following us?"

"I think so. He doesn't seem armed."

"It's a boy," said the king. "Surely he can't mean us any harm."

"What did you mean, boy?" asked Ascelin.

He ducked his head, but he did not strike me as at all afraid of us, which I certainly would have been under the circumstances. His black eyes flashed and he gave me a grin before answering Ascelin.

"In the name of God, the All Merciful," he said, "I wish you peace. I only want to help you. Perhaps you need a guide through the city streets? Perhaps you need to hire someone to take you where you're going? Perhaps you'd be willing to pay someone to take you safely to the Thieves' Market?"

Ascelin and King Haimeric looked at each other. "It's certainly not shown on the city map," said the king.

"I trust this boy explicitly," said Ascelin pointedly. "How does he know what we might be looking for?"

"Many pilgrims who come to Xantium are looking for more than the route to the Holy Land," said the boy.

"What's your name?" asked the king.

"Maffi, revered lord," said the boy, giving me another grin. At this rate, I really would have to turn him into a frog just to prove that I was a wizard.

"If we hired you as our guide," said the king, bending down to the boy's level and ignoring Ascelin's warning glare, "we'd have to wait until you'd taken us where we were going before we paid you. With the streets so crowded, you do realize that we'd worry you'd just dart away with our money and leave us stranded."

"Of course, revered lord," said Maffi. "And I'm so sure you'll be pleased with me as a guide that I'll be happy to take whatever you want to pay me, once we get there."

"That's settled, then," said the king. "Shall we go?"

"As soon as we finish giving thanks for our safe voyage," said Joachim.

Maffi, in spite of starting his conversation with us by praising God, remained standing while the rest of us obediently knelt in front of the altar. I looked at him sideways and wondered if he followed the Prophet rather than being a Christian. I had never known any of the People of the Prophet before.

11

Back out in the streets Maffi took the lead, slipping easily through the crowds while we tried to keep up with him.

"Do you think that wizard in the eastern kingdoms, the one who wanted to betray my father, has telephoned here?" Dominic asked me in a low voice. He seemed to have picked up Ascelin's suspicions.

"He didn't have a telephone," I said. "And even if he had access to one, I don't think there are any telephones in Xantium. It's school magic; school-trained wizards tend to stay in the western kingdoms."

"But a renegade wizard might have installed one," said Dominic darkly.

Ascelin kept track on the map as well as he could of where we were. Maffi led us first to an enormous plaza where an open-air market was being held, voices and odors rising from booths jammed close together. But this did not seem to be the market to which we were going for he only cut through one corner and again hurried down narrow streets. He next led us through what seemed to be the city's main governmental center. We had to step back abruptly as a curtained palanquin came straight toward us. Burly slaves carried the poles on their shoulders and peacock feathers fluttered from the corners. The edge of the curtain lifted as the palanquin came even with us, but it dropped back into place before we could see the face within.

Here the streets temporarily grew broad and there were even open, sunny squares with fountains playing in the center. For a moment we caught a glimpse of a white, domed palace. But then we plunged back into narrow streets and started downhill. As near as I could tell, we were on the far side of the main city hill from the harbor.

As we approached the outer walls, lower and looking less well maintained than those where we had first entered the city, the crowds became less dense. Some of the people we passed in doorways looked at us curiously, as though surprised to see pilgrims here.

Maffi, who had stayed almost but not quite far enough ahead that we would lose him, darted around a corner and was lost to sight. When we turned the corner a few seconds later, we found two tall, turbaned men blocking our path.

Hugo had his sword out in a second and elbowed the rest of us back behind him in the narrow street. "Come on!" he shouted. "Whichever one of you wants to attack first! But the other one had better run for a priest because there won't be any use going for a doctor!"

But the men smiled and presented empty hands. "In the name of all-seeing God," said one, "we do not intend to attack you. We have been waiting for you. We knew that sooner or later we'd see you at the Thieves' Market, Arnulf."

Ascelin pulled Hugo back and frowned. "Arnulf?"

The men looked past him to Joachim. "Even after all these years, and even disguised as a priest, you're entirely recognizable, sir."

"I'm afraid you're mistaken," said the chaplain. "You've taken me for my brother. Are you his agents?"

One of the men glanced around and lowered his voice. "You're quite right, sir. It's better to maintain the disguise. We'll accompany you to the Market."

Joachim hesitated for a second, sliding a finger

inside his collar and along the scar, but then stepped confidently forward, forcing the rest of us to follow. I looked again for Maffi and didn't see him.

The shortcoming of even the best magic is that it cannot tell you what someone else is planning. These men, whom Joachim seemed ready to trust, could be leading us to our deaths. But beyond freezing their curved swords into their sheaths, which I did at once, I could think of nothing else to do but stay very close to the chaplain.

It had never been clear from Joachim's account of his telephone conversation with Claudia — and it might not even have been clear to him — whether she had ever gotten the pigeon message he sent her from the mountains. If she had not heard until that phone call that whatever she had given him had been stolen, then Arnulf probably had not had time to get word to his agents here before we arrived. They should know, then, what King Warin's bandits had stolen from us and expect us to have it.

"We'll have to hope it is still for sale," said one of the men. "I assume you've brought what he wanted, Arnulf."

"I already told you," said Joachim, too honest to maintain a deception that could have been very informative, "you've mistaken me for my brother."

"But you did bring it with you?" The turbaned men seemed disturbed for the first time. They stopped and looked at Joachim fully. Ascelin and I tried unsuccessfully to ease between them and the chaplain.

"Bring what?" he asked.

"The magic ring, of course," said one of the men in an undertone, with a quick glance around. "Hidden in a bag of money as you said you would bring it to us."

Dominic jammed his hand with the ruby ring into his pocket.

"My brother's wife gave me a gift before we left," said Joachim, in a voice clear enough that the turbaned men tried to shush him. "I never saw what was in it.

But it was stolen as we crossed the mountains into the eastern kingdoms. The captain of the ship we took here suggested — obliquely, it's true — that something stolen from us might itself end up in the Thieves' Market."

"We're here now," said one of the men cautiously. "Don't you trust us either? At least we can find out if he's sold it to anyone else."

Ascelin looked at me with raised eyebrows. Short of seizing the chaplain bodily and carrying him away, we didn't have much choice but to follow. The narrow street we had followed debouched into a broad square, just inside the city's outer walls.

The sparse population of the last few streets was again replaced by noisy crowds. The square was full of booths, striped awnings protecting the people and goods from the harsh sun. Beneath the awnings was piled everything from clothing to weapons and the spaces between were jammed with people. "I wonder if any of them sell rootstocks for roses," said the king.

For a second, as our street sloped down into the market, we could see the crowds from above, but then we were down among them. There was the same wild mix of people we had seen in the city streets. "Watch out for pickpockets," said Ascelin in a low voice.

But the turbaned men smiled. "In fact, the Thieves' Market is probably one of the few places in Xantium where you *don't* have to beware of pickpockets. The thieves patrol themselves. Of course, you do have to beware of everything else. . . ."

Including you, I thought. My mind raced, trying desperately but unsuccessfully to think why Claudia would have sent a magic ring with us, assuming that was indeed what had been in her package.

We were now pushed on every side by sweating bodies so that it was hard to pick our way, and almost immediately I lost any sense of direction. The tiny alleys between the stalls were even more of a maze than the city streets. Voices on every side urged us to buy spices, armor, shoes only slightly used, silken robes, snacks, mirrors, and jeweled pendants. I caught glimpses of glittering brocade, of peacock feathers, of knives whose blades were inset with enamel, of tooled leather, and of bales of uncarded wool such as used to arrive in our warehouse in the City. On the far side of the market, I thought I saw a carpet rising above the heads of the crowd with two men seated on it, but when I rubbed my eyes it was gone.

I tried probing with magic and found layers and cross-layers of spells so dense and so strange that I immediately gave up any attempt to understand them. I doubted Melecherius had understood them either. Even aside from a carpet that could fly, the colors and the quality of much of the merchandise must be heightened by illusion.

"Was everything here stolen?" Hugo asked Ascelin in an undertone.

One of Arnulf's agents answered for him. "Not necessarily. Some of the merchants here just prefer a more, well, informal setting than the government-regulated market. But a lot of the merchandise *is* stolen and the market is run by the thieves' guild."

"Why does the government allow it?" protested Hugo.

"Do you think the governor has a choice? Didn't you know what he had to offer the guild in return for the safety and integrity of the harbor?"

I looked again for Maffi, but it was hopeless. The turbaned men found their way without hesitation through the dense crowd, taking advantage of every momentary gap in the press of humanity to move forward while we struggled behind them. Abruptly the crowd opened up, so unexpectedly I almost pitched onto my face.

We had reached a final booth on the very edge of the market. Its awning was closed, but a chess puzzle was set out on a board next to it. Unlike every other booth, this one was surrounded by a clear space ten feet wide. It was as though no one wanted to come too near.

One of the turbaned men let out his breath in a hiss. "I'd feared to hope, but it is still here. I can see the feet. Arnulf, or whoever you claim to be, you will remember, won't you, all we have done to inform you and all we have done to bring you safely here?"

The striped awning hung to the ground, but in a second I saw an eye through a slit, and with a sharp whirl the awning was wound up. We were abruptly confronted by an enormous black stallion.

It was big enough even for Ascelin, so still and so uniformly dark that it could have been ebony. After an amazed second, I realized it *was* ebony. It was a magnificent work of art, but it wasn't real.

And then my eye was caught by something far more fascinating. Standing behind the ebony stallion was a mage.

Ascelin bit off a warning as I stepped forward into the space where no one else dared go. But I was too fascinated to care. A man bulging with fat, almost as dark as his horse, decked with odd bits of colored silk as though he made up for not being able to fit into ordinary clothes by wearing a lot of different small ones — all I saw was someone bristling with magic.

This was completely different from meeting the self-styled prince in the eastern kingdoms. His magic had been recognizable, even if dark and twisted with inturned evil. The magic I felt from this man was almost as novel as meeting magic itself for the first time.

"A mage who dares step up boldly," boomed the mage in a voice between a bellow and a laugh. His smile showed a gold tooth as his dark eyes scanned the rest of our party from Yurt, apparently liking what he saw. "And not a local magic-worker, I would guess, but one from the western kingdoms!"

I met his eyes, a voice in the back of my brain telling me insistently that I ought to be wary and afraid, and feeling not at all afraid. Instead I felt fascinated, as well as both amused and disgusted with Melecherius, whose book had never prepared me for this. The mage's eyes were pitch black and the pupils completely filled the sockets, as though he did not have any whites. "Yes," I heard myself say, "I am Daimbert, Royal Wizard of Yurt."

The eyes widened, but still no white showed. The mage lifted his belly off the counter and came around his horse and out to meet me. "And I am Kaz-alrhun, the most powerful mage in Xantium. I have long hoped that someone from Yurt would visit me!"

I coveted the beautiful dark color of his skin and wondered briefly if he might be from Sheba.

"You've heard of Yurt?" I asked politely. The voice inside my head was now screaming that my absence of fear was a clear sign that he had put a spell on me, that he must be connected with the eastern wizard who had tried to betray Dominic's father, but somehow the message didn't get through.

He didn't say anything more about Yurt. "Western wizards come here but rarely," he said instead, apparently as interested in me as I was in him. Magic hung about him, crackling the air until it seemed it must be visible. If any mage could master an Ifrit, I thought, this one could. "The last western wizard I saw was red-haired, but that was a great many months ago."

"Evrard," I said aloud. Maybe, at last, we were on the trail.

"I hear, in the west, interest in my magic horse is high," he said.

I wrenched my attention from him to the ebony animal. "Does it move by magic?"

"Of course! Even you of the west must know that on Judgment Day all of us who have made lifelike images will be asked to set them in motion. Unless we can make them move by themselves, we will be denied heaven."

This was news to me, but then I had never made any lifelike images. "How does it work?"

"Mount, and I shall demonstrate it to you!"

The stirrup was too high for me and there was no mounting block, so I flew straight up to land on the horse's hard wooden back, as I had lifted Prince Paul up on Whirlwind's back on a wintry day that could have been a lifetime ago. For a second I saw my companions and Arnulf's agents, clustered together a few yards away and looking highly concerned, but I had no time to spare for them.

"Do you observe that little pin on the side of the neck?" asked Kaz-alrhun. "Give it a turn to the left, and hold on tightly!"

I thrust my feet into the stirrups, took a firm grip on the reins with one hand, and twisted the little pin.

The response was immediate. The horse was instantly alive, still ebony-hard but moving, muscles rippling. It tossed its head, pranced for a second, gave a whinny that resounded throughout the Thieves' Market, and launched itself into the sky.

All the fear I should have been feeling the last ten minutes abruptly made itself felt. The stirrups held my feet in immovable bands of steel; the reins felt welded to my left hand. Wind rushed past my ears and clouds rapidly approached my startled eyes. I was flying straight up on a magic horse into the sky above Xantium, with no way to stop it and no way to get off.

III

"You knew all along he was putting a spell on you," my brain told me accusingly. "Now the horse will toss you off at some likely spot and fly back to its master. Didn't you wonder why no else wanted to get near?"

At least, I answered myself grimly, if I got tossed off

I knew how to fly. The thought gave me the strength to try to find some way to control this animal.

Melecherius was no use here. I had already determined that turning the little pin to the right had no effect and giving it further turns to the left only made the animal rise faster. But then, on the opposite side of its neck, I spotted a second pin.

A hard twist here and the magic horse slowed its ascent and leveled off. In a moment I thought I knew how to master it. The process was a little tricky because the reins still kept my left hand imprisoned but, by reaching from the pin on one side of its neck to the pin on the other, from the one that made it rise to the one that made it fall, I was able to control our flight.

Once the fear drained away, it was unexpectedly exhilarating. My hat was long gone and the wind blew back the hair from my hot forehead. The land below, the city, Xantium harbor, the Central Sea, could have been a highly detailed and contoured map — the magic map of Prince Vlad. I flew far higher than I had ever dared go on my own, with none of the hard work that comes with flying and yet with an ease of motion and a quickness never found in the school's air cart. It was only because I knew my friends from Yurt would be worried that I made myself turn the horse around and aim it, as well as I could, toward the Thieves' Market.

I wondered how hard it would be to maneuver the last bit, but here the ebony horse's own spells seemed to take over, for it landed lightly and exactly where it had begun, at Kaz-alrhun's stall. He had been standing at the chess board and looked up with a wide smile, having apparently just solved his puzzle.

The horse went instantly as still as wood again and my feet and hands were released. I scrambled down and the crowd that had slowly moved up around the mage in my absence surged back again.

I flashed a reassuring smile toward my companions.

"Well," I said to Kaz-alrhun, "I'm enormously impressed. A horse like this could command any price you asked from King Solomon himself. And its motion won't keep you from heaven on Judgment Day!"

"Do you think your master will wish to buy it?" he answered with a proud chuckle.

He'd been testing me, I thought, and so far I hadn't failed too badly. And I had been thinking fast during the five minutes while the ebony horse brought me back down again. "Your price is a bag of money, I believe?" I said cautiously. "And, oh yes," as though I'd almost forgotten, "some sort of ring." I tugged on my eagle ring. "Will this one do?"

The mage threw his head back and burst into a great laugh. "No, it will not, Daimbert!" A flash of light touched my hand and I yanked at the ring in good earnest as it instantly became scorching hot.

I had it off after what seemed an hour, though it was probably only a few seconds. In my other hand, the ring was again its normal cool self. I sucked at the back of my finger while glaring at Kaz-alrhun. "And what was that supposed to prove?"

"That that is not the ring I desire," he said with another laugh.

I slid the ring back on, as though nonchalantly, watching for any sign of returning heat. "Does the name Arnulf mean anything to you?" I asked cautiously.

"That is the name of your master?" replied Kaz-alrhun. "To me it is a mere name. Do you intend to tell me he is a mage whose magic will outmatch mine?"

This sent him into a new round of laughter, leaving me a few seconds for rapid thought. Arnulf had heard of this magic horse from his agents and coveted it fiercely. But the price Kaz-alrhun had put on it was something he did not have. The price was a ring from Yurt.

For a second, I almost thought I understood it all.

Arnulf had not dared to go to Xantium himself. Therefore he had sent Joachim in his place, knowing that his agents would mistake the chaplain for him, at least at first, and lead him to Kaz-alrhun's magic horse. Even though the chaplain had refused to conduct any business deals for his brother's firm, Arnulf assumed that once here Joachim would bargain honestly, buying the horse for his brother — the only person, in fact, whom he could trust not to keep the ebony horse for himself. And Joachim would have the price with him. Claudia had not been successful in wheedling him into agreeing to conduct the transaction, which made it more risky. But he was still supposed to have the "gift" which Claudia had given him on parting, since he would accept something from her with far less suspicion than from Arnulf himself.

But here my reasoning broke down. Arnulf certainly had no ring from Yurt to send to Xantium — or, if so, I couldn't imagine where he had gotten it. Dominic stood only a short distance from the booth, his father's ruby ring winking on his finger, the magic ring which I would have thought the mage really wanted, except that he seemed to show no interest in it.

"Tell me about this ring you claim I was supposed to bring you," I said casually, as though negotiating myself.

"You know well this ring and its properties," the mage said, holding me with his eyes. "You have received a free ride, but do not anticipate any more until you can deliver it."

"Perhaps I could obtain this ring for you," I suggested, "if I knew what powers it was supposed to have."

"If you are from Yurt," said Kaz-alrhun, abruptly not smiling at all, "you already know. And you already know its relation to the Wadi Harhammi." He watched me closely for my reaction to his mention of the Wadi; I did my best not to show how surprised I was. "You have amused me mightily, Daimbert," the mage continued, "not least because I see so few western wizards, but I do not like dissimulation."

Neither did I, and Arnulf had lied to us thoroughly. "Maybe I'll be back tomorrow," I said lightly. "Perhaps by then you'll have decided you'd be willing to take something other than this ring."

"Or perhaps by then you will have decided to produce it," growled Kaz-alrhun.

I turned without any sort of farewell. This would be a dangerous mage to have angry with me and, at the moment, I had no way to placate him. My companions were still waiting a short distance away, but Arnulf's agents were gone.

Joachim gripped me by the arm before I could speak. "Are you all right? Does that horse move with the supernatural power of evil?"

"Come on," I said to all of them with a jerk of my head. "It moves by magic alone, but let's get back to the inn while we're still alive."

It took us ten minutes to find our way to the edge of the Market and another ten to find the street on which we had come in, but then Ascelin was able to locate our position on the map and we retraced our steps hastily.

We had only gone a quarter mile when I saw a boy's ragged form waiting for us ahead. Maffi stood with a fist on one cocked hip, looking pleased with himself. "So, did you do your business in the Thieves' Market, my masters?"

The king objected as Ascelin started to yank him off the ground by the front of his shirt. The prince set him down but shifted his grip at once to the boy's arm. "Were you hired to bring us there?"

"Of course!" he said saucily. "In the sight of all-knowing God, you hired me yourself! Now, you promised to pay me what my guidance was worth. Did I not bring you there safely, just as I promised?"

"Those men in turbans didn't hire you?" Ascelin persisted.

"Of course not," said Maffi agreeably. "And I was very pleased to see that they had not harmed you."

Ascelin let him go, disgusted. "I'm not going to get any clear story out of him, that's certain."

But King Haimeric took a coin from his belt. "You did bring us safely to the Thieves' Market, just as you promised, and you deserve your fee." Maffi took the coin and examined it with interest.

Ascelin started to speak and instead turned away. But I stepped forward quickly.

"Maffi, maybe you can help us some more."

He smiled broadly up at me. His face was streaked with dirt, but his eyes were bright. For a second, I wondered if he had any home or family to take care of him, or if he had to live on Xantium's streets by his wits. If so, I would pay him even if he was lying to us. But he might also be very useful.

"As you guessed, we are indeed looking for something, something stolen from us earlier. It's a ring."

Dominic started to say something and thought better of it.

"Westerners like us would become hopelessly lost and cheated in the Thieves' Market. That's why I need *you* to look for it for us. Meet me — " I hesitated, not wanting to tell him the address of our inn if he didn't already know it. "Meet me tomorrow at noon on the steps of the Church of Holy Wisdom. Then you can tell me if you've located it and, if so, we'll go together to buy it."

"Will any ring do?"

This was a problem because I wasn't sure what I was looking for myself. "No, this is a special one." I wasn't about to tell him I'd never seen it. "It's had a magic spell put on it and it's clearly identifiable as being from Yurt. Don't ask for a magic ring specifically, because then they may try to cheat you with a plain one, but — "

Maffi interrupted with a laugh. "You need not teach

me how to bargain. I was born in the Thieves' Market! Same payment schedule as today?"

"Same as today," I said, and he raced back toward the Market.

Ascelin frowned deeply. "Would you like to tell us, Wizard, what you're doing?"

"Of course. But let's get back to the inn and have dinner. The magic flying horse made me hungry."

The inn served us fried eggplant for dinner. King Haimeric had never had eggplant before; even in the City, it was uncommon outside a few eastern restaurants. He ate his slowly, telling us one minute that he liked it tremendously and the next that he didn't, trying to decide if the queen would like it or if the royal cook could find a better way to prepare it.

"What's this ring you're trying to find?" asked Ascelin as the waiter brought us pastries sticky with honey and cups of spiced tea.

"I think it's what the chaplain's sister-in-law gave him, what the bandits stole from us," I said slowly. I went on to explain my theory that Joachim's brother had intended using him as his representative in buying the ebony horse from the mage, while concealing from him that that was what he was doing.

The chaplain shook his head. "I cannot believe in such a deception. Claudia gave me a present, I presume in memory of our old friendship, but it wasn't anything important or valuable. She told me so herself when I apologized for losing it."

But no one paid attention to this. "Why do you think the ring will have traveled from the mountains across the eastern kingdoms to Xantium?" asked Hugo.

"It shouldn't have," I agreed. "But I think it's worth looking for. After all, if Arnulf had heard there was a flying horse for sale here, with the price a magic ring, Warin may have heard it too. Kaz-alrhun seems fairly determined to have it. The real flaw in my theory," I added, "is that Kaz-alrhun was expecting something *Yurt*. He'd heard of the kingdom and thought it important, even if he'd only heard of it from Evrard — by the way, did you hear him saying he'd met Evrard?"

"We already knew Sir Hugo's party passed through Xantium," said the king. "Since everyone here wants to guide us to the Thieves' Market, the same thing must have happened to them."

"He said he wanted a ring from Yurt only in order to mislead you," said Dominic. "It's my ruby ring he's after and he must have seen it on my hand today. That wizard in the eastern kingdoms certainly wanted it. Somehow the story got out that the spell to reveal the, the — whatever my father had found in the Wadi — was hidden in his snake ring. That's why someone had opened his tomb."

"But neither the mage nor Arnulf made any attempt to get your ring away from you," I said. "Maybe Arnulf had gotten hold of a different magic ring, with different properties, to swap to Kaz-alrhun for the ebony horse, yet for some reason it's important for it to be from Yurt."

"I still don't understand," said Joachim, "even if my brother did send a magic ring with us, why he could possibly want a flying horse. I would not believe it even now if his agents had not been so sure. He does not even employ a wizard. My father and grandfather never had wizards either — I wouldn't have thought anyone in our family was interested in magic."

"It's not the horse itself," I said suddenly. "He wants the horse for transportation. Since he thinks King Solomon's Pearl has been located, he wants some way to get very quickly to where it's hidden, and then to get safely away just as fast."

Hugo and Ascelin both shot me unexpected smiles, and Hugo said, "That's it! Especially if it's guarded by an Ifrit, he can't possibly get to it by normal transportation."

"I hope for Arnulf's sake," said Ascelin, "that this

ring he supposedly sent with us isn't *also* supposed to reveal the Black Pearl. Otherwise he and the mage could have a very unpleasant meeting at the Pearl's hiding place, he with the horse and the mage with the ring."

"If by some chance, Joachim," I said, "your brother ever does buy that magic horse, tell him not to worry about staying on. Instead, tell him to be sure to look for the second pin to help guide it."

IV

I found my way through the narrow streets to the Church of the Holy Wisdom at noon, as a wailing from the minarets again called the faithful People of the Prophet to prayer. I did not expect to see Maffi or, if so, assumed I would find him ready with some woeful story why he couldn't find the ring I wanted. It was because I doubted he would even be there that I had refused Ascelin's offer to accompany me. But the way Maffi leaned against the door frame of the great church, waiting, exuded confidence.

"You found it?" I asked in amazement.

But he just gave me a mysterious smile. "Maybe. Come and look for yourself."

As I hurried after him, I wondered how many powerful magic rings were circulating through the east, in search of how many significant magic objects. There was Dominic's ruby ring for starters, then the ring Arnulf had sent with us, the ebony flying horse, then the Black Pearl, whatever Dominic's father had found in the Wadi Harhammi, and now whatever Kaz-alrhun hoped to discover with the ring from Arnulf.

I looked at the boy darting down the street in front of me, sandals slapping on the paving, and felt foolish to have pitied him. Whether he had a family or not he did not need anyone to look after him. He seemed without any difficulty to have found a ring I had not been completely sure even existed.

I was beginning to recognize the narrow streets that led down the far side of Xantium's hill toward the Thieves' Market, but the sounds and smells of the Market struck me afresh as we came out among the striped awnings. "Over this way," said Maffi confidently. He slipped easily around booths, under tables, through knots of men who looked at me impassively from under folded headdresses that hid most of their faces. I caught up with the boy in the far corner of the Market.

It was slightly quieter here. I felt a prickle of unease. An ebony chess piece, a rook, was lying on the ground and it looked strangely familiar. "Wait," I said, "before we go any further. Who is this person who has the ring? Did he tell you how he obtained it or how much he wants for it?"

"It's the right ring, all right," said Maffi with a grin. "He'll tell you how much he wants himself." He gestured toward a booth whose striped awning was drawn shut, though a sandaled foot showed beneath it. "Go ahead!"

I still hesitated, but he turned at once and disappeared into the crowd. Oh well, I thought. If he didn't even wait to be paid, it wasn't my fault. I could always find my own way back by flying high enough to see the harbor and then locating the inn from there. I stepped resolutely up to the booth.

I expected the awning to be pulled back, but instead the foot disappeared. I pushed the fabric aside myself and looked into shadows so dark that it was impossible to make out any detail, although I thought I saw a pair of shining dark eyes.

"Hello? I heard you have a ring for sale?"

"Come in, come further in," said a muffled voice. "I have it here at the back."

I entered slowly, letting the awning drop behind me.

"I can't see anything," I protested. "If you've really got a ring I'd be interested in, let's look at it in daylight."

The air crackled, giving me half a second's warning: not nearly enough to resist the binding spell that abruptly held me tight. I toppled over with a painful thump.

"Push back the awning," said the muffled voice. "Let us see what he has brought."

I lay, paralyzed from the collar bone down, on the filthy paving stones of the Market with several men bent over me. Someone let in a little daylight, and in a moment my eyes grew accustomed enough to the dim light so that I could make them out. As I should have expected, one of them was the enormous black shape of Kaz-alrhun.

"Let him keep that eagle ring," he said, "but see what else he has."

Hands reached into my pockets. They pulled the knife from my belt and the piece of parchment from inside my jacket.

"A piece of paper with an eggplant recipe, a smooth stone, and what looks like a buckle off a harness," said one of the other men, examining what had come from my pockets.

But Kaz-alrhun was looking at the piece of parchment, reading Prince Dominic's letter to his family, and his black eyes grew round. "Well, Daimbert, I knew you had brought more with you to Xantium than you cared to say. Your party is dressed as pilgrims, but I see that your goal lies far beyond the Holy Land. If you had told me you had this at once, all this trouble might have been unnecessary! Tell me, where did you obtain the parchment?"

"It was magically concealed inside a ring," I said in resignation.

"Well, since you cooperated at the last, Daimbert," Kaz-alrhun said with a chuckle, "even if not entirely voluntarily!" he paused for another laugh, "I have a mind to let you live. What do you think?"

"I think it's a fine idea," I said cautiously. Even though I could not move, I could feel all sorts of damp things soaking through my clothes, and my shoulders were sore and stiff. I tried a spell to lift myself off the ground and found that this binding spell not only held me physically, but also blocked my access to all but a few words of the Hidden Language. The only bright spot was imagining turning Maffi into a frog the next time I saw him, preferably a frog about to be eaten by a water snake.

"But you attempted to mock me, Daimbert," the mage said, "coming to the Thieves' Market with the ruby ring and then trying to buy my horse with a different ring entirely." His laughter was gone now. "I do not like to be mocked."

It sounded as though he thought I knew far more than I in fact did. I wondered resignedly what it was.

"And I do not wish you to cause me any more problems at once," Kaz-alrhun added thoughtfully. "I think you will just leave town, immediately. Perhaps in a few days you shall have determined, even with your western magic, how to break my binding spell!"

"What do you mean, leave town?" I said, trying to keep panic out of my voice.

"On a trade caravan, of course. Laugh at your fate, Daimbert! No man can in dread change the day of his death, but he can with laughter chase dire dread away."

One of the men with Kaz-alrhun scooped me up and tossed me over his shoulder. I didn't feel like laughing, even to chase dire dread away.

"You'll never get away with this," I said. "My friends knew I was coming here today." This was not strictly true, but Ascelin would certainly come to the Thieves' Market if I didn't return to the inn. "They'll be very cautious when I don't return. You'll never be able to steal the ruby ring."

"But you and I know that none of them is a mage," said Kaz-alrhun in a good-natured bellow. "You do not have the pieces to win this phase of the game, Daimbert. When your tall swordsman friend seeks you here, there will be nothing to see." He nodded to the man who held me. "There should be a caravan leaving from the north gate within the half hour."

The man darted out of the dimness of the booth into the brilliant sun, with me slung over his shoulder. He turned quickly from side to side for a moment, then set off at a trot.

I opened my mouth to say something, to try to negotiate with him, and found my vocal chords frozen. I was hanging upside down on his back and a glance at my upper body showed that I had been covered with illusion to look like some sort of paper-wrapped parcel.

And what would the mage do to Dominic? While we hurried along the less crowded streets through the back of Xantium, I tried probing the spell that held me. I had new sympathy for the castellan and knights I had made stand in binding spells all night. Parts of my body felt numb and others itched almost unbearably, but there was nothing I could do about it.

I lost track of where we were long before I had any idea how this spell worked. We came suddenly under the arch of a stone gate, and by stretching my neck around, the only part of my body not held motionless, I could see a small collection of mule-drawn carts.

Turbaned men were tying down the loads and shouting to each other. The man carrying me stepped up to the last cart and said something I didn't catch, though I heard a clink of coins. The next moment, I had been dumped amidst bales of what felt like cloth and had a tarpaulin pulled across me. I was still struggling unsuccessfully to find a way to unravel Kaz-alrhun's spell when I heard a shout, the cart beneath me creaked, and the caravan began to move.

There wasn't much air beneath the tarpaulin; in the sun, it almost immediately grew extremely hot. I breathed shallowly, sweat running down my face, trying to imagine what my companions would do when I didn't return — and when the mage appeared among them with a flash of light and demanded Dominic's ring.

Kaz-alrhun's spell twisted and turned beneath my probing almost as if it were alive. I recognized the shape of the spell from Melecherius's book, but I still could not unravel it. Several times I thought I had it and each time it eluded me. I reminded myself grimly that I had wanted to see eastern magic.

I soon felt as though I was caught not just by a spell but by a nightmare. As breathing took more and more effort, I gave up even trying to undo the spell that held me. I hovered on the edge of consciousness, between dreaming and hallucinating. It seemed like an eternity, though it was probably closer to three hours, when the cart beneath me stopped moving.

"Well," said a voice, "shall we look at what Kaz-alrhun sent with us?"

The tarpaulin was jerked off, letting in sun-baked air that tasted deliciously refreshing as I sucked it desperately into my lungs.

I blinked my eyes then and looked up at the two men bending over me. They were Arnulf's agents.

I tried to speak and discovered my voice had returned. A glance downward showed that the illusion that made me into a parcel had also worn off. "I've been put in a binding spell," I croaked. "Help me up and give me something to drink."

"It's — it's a man!" said one of them. Maybe the sun was slowing his reasoning powers as badly as it affected me.

They pulled me into a sitting position and offered me water out of a leather bag. It was lukewarm and absolutely delicious, even if it did dribble down my chin. I was too grateful to accuse them of taking part in a plot to kill innocent wizards. By now, I thought, the mage must have seized Dominic's ring — and maybe even Dominic. I would have to formulate a plan of action as soon as I could act — or, for that matter, think clearly again.

"It is — are you not the mage who was with Arnulf?" asked one of the turbaned men.

"Yes," I said, giving up the effort of persuading them that Joachim was not his brother. I glanced at the long, curved swords at their sides, but they showed no sign of drawing them. "Your friend Kaz-alrhun wanted to get rid of me."

"But why?" they said in what appeared to be real distress. "Has he broken his agreement?"

I shook my head and made a new effort to understand the magic that held me. "We didn't give him the ring he demanded in return for his ebony horse."

"But Arnulf told us before he came that he would have it!"

For a moment, I had thought I understood at last, that Kaz-alrhun wanted the ruby ring to get into the Wadi himself, but this ring Arnulf had sent with us to buy the flying horse seemed to be something entirely different.

"I was carrying a magical parchment," I said, "which seemed to please Kaz-alrhun, though I certainly hadn't meant to give it to him. This binding spell appears to be his punishment for riding his horse without any intention of giving him what he wanted."

"But if he has the parchment, now," said one of the agents, "and if he thinks it will do just as well as the ring, then Arnulf should be able to take the horse! Kaz-alrhun may work out of the Thieves' Market, but we have found that he honors his bargains."

I couldn't even begin to agree, but it was too complicated for an argument. I glanced up while struggling anew with the spell and saw a dark shape, not quite a cloud, scuttling low through the sky. "An Ifrit!" I cried involuntarily, panicked because of my helplessness.

Back in Yurt, I had said I wanted to see an Ifrit — all my wishes were coming true with a vengeance.

V

The two men whirled, but then they relaxed and laughed. "That is not an Ifrit. It's just a bit of a sandstorm. The wind will pick up sand and dust and carry it some distance. Sand demons, they are sometimes called."

I didn't like this talk of demons, but if we were, at least momentarily, safe from Ifriti, I wanted to get free of the binding spell before the next danger appeared. Suddenly I saw how it went together, with an ingenious twist I had never seen before, though Melechcrius hinted at it. In a few more seconds I was able to dissolve the spell and finally stretch my cramped arms.

Arnulf's agents stepped back abruptly as I moved and I realized they might be as frightened of my anger as I was irritated with them. If Arnulf's negotiations had all gone amiss, then both he and and "his" wizard would have good reason to be furious with the agents who had sent him word that everything was ready.

I took another pull of water and massaged my temples. I looked around, at the mule-drawn carts whose drivers were now sitting off the road in the shade, at the dusty and empty road itself, and at the sage-covered hillside leading down to the sun-flecked Central Sea. Xantium was a dark mass in the distance.

"So, do you normally transport Kaz-alrhun's victims out of Xantium when you're not plotting to betray your employer?" I asked conversationally. If the mage had attacked Dominic to get his ruby ring, the prince might be on the next caravan. But if Kaz-alrhun had wanted a different ring, Arnulf's ring, badly enough to give his flying horse for it, then Dominic's ring might not have any real interest for him after all.

"No, no!" the agents said together. "We have never done anything against Arnulf's interests!" When I frowned, one added, "We did not realize the mage's parcel was a man."

I stood up slowly. "Perhaps Arnulf will appreciate that, in Xantium, you have to put a powerful mage's interests ahead of his," I said with deliberate sarcasm. "Are you heading north now?"

"No," said one of the agents. "We were about to return to Xantium. Whichever market Arnulf's caravans make for, we always travel with them the first ten miles or so out of the city, until they are out of easy range of city-based thieves. Certainly if Kaz-alrhun pays us to add an occasional parcel to the load, we are willing to accommodate him, but that does not mean we're working against Arnulf's interests!" He paused for a moment, then added, "You will explain to him, will you not, that we never meant any harm to you?"

"We'll see," I said gravely. At least they hadn't asked me yet to pay them for their trouble. The drivers took my standing up as the signal to start again. They remounted the wagons and snapped their whips over the mules' backs. With shouts and creaks, the caravan started off along the dusty road.

By this time, Dominic's ring would be gone beyond easy recovery. I felt too tired for the concentration flying required, so I started walking with Arnulf's agents. They were eager now to be helpful and pleasant.

"I've heard that a number of Arnulf's caravans had been captured by an Ifrit," I said. "Is that part of the reason you don't accompany them very far?"

They looked at each other in surprise. "I do not know where you could have heard such a story," said one. "Only one caravan has disappeared completely, off to the east of here. And we cannot be absolutely sure its disappearance was due to an Ifrit because no one saw it. The drivers described a whoosh of air, then they and their mules were left standing and the carts were gone. If caravans really were disappearing in large numbers, all the mages in Xantium would bend their magic to prevent it."

I wondered if there was any truth at all in Arnulf's story. "It did seem fairly unlikely to me. And wouldn't it be odd for an Ifrit to leave the sign of the cross?"

The agents looked at each other again. "We had not heard anything about the sign of the cross," said one in distaste.

Then the entire account of Ifriti capturing caravans, I thought, was Arnulf's invention, an excuse to bring Joachim into his affairs. I still had no firm sense whether his story of the Black Pearl reappearing was real or an additional invention, but I tended toward the latter. I was distracted from this speculation by another thought. "You aren't Christian?"

"Of course not," with dignity. "We follow the teachings of the Prophet."

Since Xantium was, at least in its government, a Christian city, I was intrigued that Arnulf should employ non-Christians as his agents here. Maybe that was why he had no chaplain: he didn't want someone piously trying to introduce religion into sound business decisions. "I know almost nothing about the Prophet," I said. "Could you tell me a little as we walk?"

By the time the walls of Xantium rose before us at the end of the day, I had learned much more comparative religion than I had ever imagined. I had not realized before that the People of the Prophet had been pagans before the Prophet came to them, nor that he had incorporated what he considered the best elements of the rather inadequate religions — as he saw it — of Abraham and of Christ. I had to be fairly noncommittal in my responses to conceal the fact that these men also knew much more about Christianity than I did.

But as we talked, I was also thinking. The bit of

sandstorm, the sand demon, might in fact have been Kaz-alrhun on his magic ebony horse, off to the Wadi Harhammi. I remembered Ascelin commenting, back in the eastern kingdoms, that a number of events seemed to have been managed for our benefit. Could the mage have been behind them all?

Or was the shadowy and rather ominous figure I thought I sensed, manipulating and maneuvering us, King Warin, or Arnulf, or someone else entirely? Whatever we had stumbled onto must be something much more complicated than the disappearance of Sir Hugo's party.

Even though the school had heard nothing of the Pearl's reappearance, the lord of the red sandstone castle was ready to turn bandit for something hidden in a shipment of luxury silks, perhaps one of the "parcels" Arnulf's agents had been willing to transport for Kaz-alrhun. Our arrival in King Warin's kingdom had been intriguing enough for him to set real bandits on us, and our passage through the eastern kingdoms had led Prince Vlad to set in motion extensive troop movements, even wars, for the purpose of bringing us to his castle. We had heard of very strange rumors coming out of the East, but it seemed instead that everyone else, except for us, felt that something very strange was coming out of Yurt.

"Tell Arnulf to go himself to talk to Kaz-alrhun," said one of the agents as we reached the north gate of the city. "We certainly tried to negotiate fairly for the horse."

"And reassure Arnulf that we had nothing to do with your kidnapping," added the other. "Kaz-alrhun likes to have a little fun sometimes, but he means no real harm."

I didn't like to think what the mage did when he actually meant real harm, but I was footsore and hungry, with painful ribs and a bad headache.

But then my eye was caught by a small form under the

gate. As I spotted him, he saw me and turned to run.

With new energy I flew under the gate after him. A frog was too good for him. I started putting together the first words of the Hidden Language to transmogrify him into a deformed cockroach.

"I found him, my masters, I found him!" I heard Maffi shouting.

And suddenly Ascelin stood before me, his sword out and a grim expression on his face. Maffi hid behind him, peeking at me past his leg.

I dropped to the ground in surprise as Hugo stepped out of a side street. Both his and Ascelin's expressions changed at once, to relief tempered with exasperation. "There you are, Wizard!"

"Where are the others? Has Dominic been attacked?"

"Everyone's looking for you," said Hugo, "and no one has been attacked." That was a real relief. "Where have you *been* all day? Didn't you realize we'd be afraid that now our party, too, was going to start disappearing?"

I glanced behind me and saw no sign of Arnulf's agents. "I was kidnapped," I said, "thanks to that boy there."

"I told you I'd find him!" cried Maffi, still not coming out from behind Ascelin.

The prince sheathed his sword, reached down, and dragged him forward by the collar. "You didn't tell us you'd led the wizard into ambush," he said coldly.

"But I didn't!" the boy protested. It was his absence of fear or even respect that was perhaps the most irritating. "I led him to the Thieves' Market, just as he asked, to someone who had the ring he wanted to buy."

"He led me to Kaz-alrhun, who took the parchment I'd found in Dominic's father's ring," I said. "Don't tell me the boy then offered to help you find me."

"At least we didn't pay him yet," said Hugo.

"And *you* didn't pay me yet, either, Mage!" said Maffi, turning his bright eyes toward me.

Ascelin shook his head, lifted the boy off the ground, and tossed him away. Maffi landed in a heap but sprang up at once. "I'll be around if you want to hire me again!" he called and scampered off.

I sighed. "I'd been about to turn him into a cockroach, but it's too much effort."

"Since we're leaving Xantium tomorrow," said Ascelin, "we shouldn't have to see him again."

"The king and Dominic have been trying to get in to see the governor," said Hugo as we started walking through the narrow city streets, "and the chaplain's gone to talk to the bishop, but none of them thought they'd have much success. We were all going to meet back at the inn in a little while. Ascelin and I had been trying — without any luck — to get some sense out of the people in the Thieves' Market when Maffi found us."

I was touched that they had all been concerned for me. But if the king was having trouble getting to see the city's governor to tell him about the very real disappearance of a wizard, then there was no hope for the vague plan I had made on the way back to Xantium, of enlisting the governor's help to deal with what might be a political plot so vague I couldn't even explain it to myself. "We may — though probably not — now own the ebony horse. I'll tell you about it once I have something to eat."

VI

The sun-drenched road from Xantium to the Holy Land led southeast across a tawny landscape. I could see I would have to revise upwards my ideas of far, dry, and hot. Away to our left, we could see the trade route along which silk from the Far East came after a journey of thousands of miles to this end of the Central Sea, after being transferred to several or even dozens of different caravans.

Hugo pushed back the hood of his cloak to let the wind ruffle his hair. "It's good to be on the road again!" he said. "Once we find my father, let's keep on going, right across the desert, down to the jungles of the ultimate south, or else off to the Far East where they eat nothing but spices!"

Whirlwind was nervous and restless after two days in the stables of the inn and two weeks before that on board ship. After trying unsuccessfully to hold his chestnut stallion in, Dominic finally said, "I'll be back!" and took off at a gallop.

Ascelin, being on foot, did not need to keep to the road. For the first mile he was almost as full of restless energy as the stallion, ranging ahead, climbing up on the rocks on either hand for a better look into the distance, stooping to examine an odd print. But then he came back to the pace the king had set with his mare and strode beside me.

"I'm wondering about something," I said to him, looking off toward the trade route. "Arnulf's agents suggested that an Ifrit had attacked a silk caravan *east* of Xantium, but Arnulf himself told us that it was specifically *his* caravans that were attacked. I would have thought they weren't his caravans until his agents in the city had bought the silk from whoever transported it from the east."

"I haven't believed anything Arnulf told us yet," said Ascelin.

"But the agents did confirm his story about a caravan's disappearance," I objected, "even if they did say it was only one caravan."

Before I could pursue this further, Hugo called out. "Wizard, come look! I think there's something very strange in here!"

He had stopped abruptly, looking back at the packhorse he was leading. I swung down from my mare and approached slowly, probing with magic. There was certainly something alive in one of the packs.

And I thought it was human. Ascelin and I carefully

unbuckled the straps that held the tents, then abruptly let them drop to the ground. A startled cry came from within their folds. Ascelin poked at the canvas with his foot. It unrolled further and a shaggy black head emerged.

"Greetings, my masters!" said Maffi, looking at us with shining eyes. "May God be praised, it is good to be out in the air again."

"I thought we'd seen the last of you," said Ascelin in disgust.

"I didn't have a chance to tell you when we met yesterday evening," said Maffi to me, ignoring the prince, "but I found the ring you wanted!"

"Liar," muttered Ascelin.

But I said, "Wait," as he reached for the boy. "Maffi, are you trying to say that the ring Kaz-alrhun told me he wanted for his flying horse actually exists?"

"Of course it does," he said with a bright smile, putting his hand into his pocket. "And here it is!"

I took the ring from him slowly. It was an onyx in a plain gold setting. Most startling of all, carved into the stone in tiny but clear letters was the word "Yurt."

I probed it with magic. There was certainly some kind of spell attached to the onyx. It seemed virtually new, even its tiny crevices free of dust. I held the ring carefully on my palm and looked across it to Maffi.

"So did I do well, my masters? Will you reward me handsomely?"

"Tell me where you got this," I said evenly. All my previous assumptions were crumbling. It had seemed unlikely all along that the bandits who had stolen Claudia's package from us would sell it to someone who would bring it to the Thieves' Market in Xantium. It now seemed more unlikely than ever.

"I stole it from Kaz-alrhun last night," said Maffi with a grin.

"Kaz-alrhun told me he wanted a ring which, in fact, he already had," I replied, "and which, completely by coincidence, he had acquired through the thieves' network. And you stole it after leading me to him so he could ship me out of the city. Is that what you're trying to tell me?"

Dominic came galloping back at this point, his stallion damp with sweat but not breathing particularly hard. He started to speak but stopped when he saw the boy. "Good," said Maffi, glancing up at him. "I was afraid you'd decided to leave one of your party behind in Xantium. That would not have been a good idea. Nice horse, by the way."

"You haven't answered my question," I persisted.

"You're from Yurt, aren't you? That's why I thought you'd want this ring. Give me something to drink and I'll tell you the whole story."

While Ascelin gave him a waterskin, I probed the ring again. Because magic is a natural force, a spell is often hard to recognize unless it is actually in action. But the onyx seemed imbued, unexpectedly, with school magic. It was powerful magic, too, the work of a master wizard.

"If you stole this ring from Kaz-alrhun," I tried again, "do you know when he acquired it?"

Maffi gave me a mischievous look. He was enjoying this. But for a change he gave me a straight answer. "He acquired it yesterday morning, about an hour before I met you at the church of the Holy Wisdom."

I wondered if this could possibly be true. "Yet when you took me to buy the ring, you didn't tell me that I'd be buying it from Kaz-alrhun. . . ." I didn't have time to pursue the issue of how thoroughly Maffi had deceived me. Apparently, I was not alone. "Who did he acquire the ring from?"

"I don't know his name," said the boy, taking another pull of water and looking troubled for the first time. "I'd never seen him before. He was richly dressed in the western style, even though he wore a dark cloak that he probably thought would mislead thieves. He had iron gray hair and a look about him that somehow, well, suggested a mage. Not like you, my master!" he added brightly.

I didn't have time to wonder if this last comment was meant as an insult. "King Warin," I said.

"You can't mean that!" said King Haimeric unhappily. "That would mean he really did set those bandits on us."

But this was not news to any of the rest of us, even if Warin did feel more comfortable preserving some of his prestige among his fellow kings by hiring out his dirty work. "So Arnulf did send a ring with us to buy the magic horse," said Ascelin, "and King Warin, wanting the horse himself and knowing the price was the ring, stole it from us. This seems to be a ring destined to be stolen, if this boy stole it from Kaz-alrhun after Warin gave it to the mage."

"Then if the mage was still in Xantium when he lost the ring last night," I said, "it could not have been him, leaving Xantium on a flying horse, that I thought I saw yesterday afternoon in the sandstorm. It must have been Warin."

"But how would Warin have heard about the flying horse?" asked Dominic.

"That wouldn't be difficult," said Hugo. "If Arnulf's agents here heard about it, then King Warin's agents must have as well."

"Why would Warin have agents in Xantium?" protested the king, but no one was listening.

"Did Arnulf's agents tell Warin's agents to steal the ring from us?" suggested Dominic darkly.

"So Warin followed us East," said Ascelin, "and arrived just after we did. Does he have the flying horse now, boy?"

"Kaz-alrhun does not have it any more," said Maffi cryptically and gave another grin. "How about some food? When I realized Kaz-alrhun wasn't going to take the loss of his ring with his usual good humor, I had to come to your inn so quickly I didn't have time for dinner — or for breakfast!"

Dominic gave him bread and dried fruit. "Does

King Warin have the ebony horse?" Ascelin demanded again.

"I already told you he did," said Maffi ingenuously.

I hoped briefly but improbably that Kaz-alrhun had not told Warin the secret of the different pins and that the king had been unable to work it out for himself. Instead I tried to concentrate on the question of how King Warin had learned there was a flying horse for sale, and that the price was a magic ring from Yurt — or, at least, a ring carved with the kingdom's name. The onyx ring was heavy in my hand.

"I think I understand," said Dominic suddenly. "Arnulf had somehow heard about my ruby snake ring. Because he knew he had no way of getting it, he had this ring made by a goldsmith and hoped to pass it off to the mage instead of mine."

"But the onyx ring can't have the same magic properties yours does," objected Hugo.

"Perhaps you all are right," the chaplain said slowly, "and my brother did send that ring with me, by way of his wife, because he was ashamed to tell me openly what he wanted. I shall forgive him the deception, but I now find myself less eager to stop and visit him again on the journey home."

"Wait," said Ascelin, flicking his eyes sideways toward Maffi, who was peacefully finishing off his dried fruit. "Are you sure we should be discussing this, when . . ."

But Dominic shrugged. "It doesn't matter what the boy hears or what he guesses, because he's going with us. He won't dare go back to Xantium after his latest theft, and we need to keep him under our eyes ourselves."

Ascelin immediately objected, but I did not listen. I was rather thinking about the chaplain's brother, Arnulf.

Someone — the mage, King Warin, Elerius, perhaps Arnulf himself — had started the search for a magic ring from Yurt by looking among the disordered bones in Dominic's father's tomb. But when it became clear that the real magic-imbued ring was not readily available, Arnulf had had the nearest wizard cast the spells for a substitute magic ring.

He and his family had never kept a wizard. Therefore, when Arnulf heard that an ebony flying horse was for sale, one that would allow him to fly to wherever the Black Pearl was concealed and get away again, and that the price was a magic ring, he had had to go in search of a wizard — perhaps the same wizard he had already hired a decade earlier to install his magical telephone system.

The wizard he found was the royal wizard of a kingdom not very far away, a kingdom located in the foothills of the eastern mountains. Arnulf had had the onyx ring made for him by Elerius.

I stared at the ring in my hand, not liking this at all. There was nothing unusual in a royal wizard performing such a task for someone without a wizard in his service, as long as it did not interfere with his own responsibilities. It had been a piece of luck for Arnulf that the nearest wizard just happened to be the one who was probably the finest graduate the school had ever produced. Arnulf must have offered him something quite extraordinary in return. I wondered uneasily what.

And Elerius would certainly have told his master, King Warin, what he had done. At the time, the king might not have found it significant. By the time he realized he wanted a magic ring himself, Elerius had moved on. So Warin had waited, knowing that sooner or later the onyx ring would make its way toward the east. He had, I remembered, written to King Haimeric about the blue rose and urged the king to stop and visit him on his trip. He had known there was something special about Yurt, that it had something to do with the ring Arnulf had requested from his wizard. It must have seemed an answer to a prayer when we stopped by directly from Arnulf's house.

Or perhaps not a prayer, I said to myself, remembering Evrard's veiled warning that he had seen the king engaged in the black arts, but something much more ominous.

I mentally shook off this thought. Elerius had taken the same oaths to help mankind as did all wizards; the best pupil the school had ever had was not going to dabble with demons or assist his master in crime. After all, I reminded myself, he had been off to a new post many kingdoms away by the time Warin set his bandits on us. I did not feel as reassured by this as I would have liked.

Ascelin stood up, breaking my train of thought. "Then if the boy's coming with us, we'd better start on our way again."

"First," said Dominic, "I want to show you something I found, just a little way down the road."

We followed him for a half mile, then he pulled up his stallion and pointed. Cut deeply into the stone by the side of the road was a sign, that could have been an X and could have been a cross.

"This then must be where my brother's caravan disappeared!" said Joachim.

"And look at this," said Dominic, pointing. Cut below the cross, rather shakily, was something much smaller that might have been the letter Y. "Is this for Yurt?"

Ascelin stood with his hands on his hips, looking back toward Xantium. "Whatever it is, we'd better move on quickly. Kaz-alrhun will soon guess what happened to his ring if he doesn't already know. Hugo, take the boy up behind you on your horse."

"I'm sure if the mage pursues us," said the king, "our wizard will be able to protect us, but it would be better not to give him the trouble."

"Of course, of course, good thinking," I said, sliding the onyx ring onto my finger and glancing back toward the city. I very much doubted I could protect anyone from Kaz-alrhun.

PART SIX

Holy City and Emir's City

1

"The Church of the Sepulchre is the most holy spot in Christendom," read Joachim from his guidebook. "Every year on Good Friday all the lamps and candles here and, indeed, in all the Christian churches of the Holy City are extinguished. On Easter morning fire from heaven kindles the lamps. Then all the bells in the churches of the city are rung, and the holy flame is used to relight the lamps in all those churches."

I looked around, impressed in spite of myself. Normally I would have doubted a story of fire from heaven as a tale for the credulous or else the work of an unacknowledged wizard. But in this small circular church, whose porter had waited to let our group in until the previous group of pilgrims had gone, it was impossible to doubt. Between the columns that ringed the church were mosaic depictions of the crucifixion and resurrection; written all the way around at the top of the wall, in the old imperial language, was the message, "GRAVE, WHERE IS THY VICTORY? DEATH, WHERE IS THY STING? FOR AS IN ADAM ALL SHALL DIE, EVEN SO IN CHRIST SHALL ALL BE MADE ALIVE."

The church with its mosaics, altars dedicated by the various eastern and western groups of Christians, and silken hangings was not the rough cave I had expected. In the center there was no roof, only a wide, circular opening through which the chaplain told us the fire from heaven descended. The hot air from the opening made the flames of the silver lamps sway, their light dancing on the precious stones of the altars.

"This way," said Joachim quietly. He led us out not the way we had come but to a door on the opposite side which opened onto a dark, cramped stairway cut into the rock. Dominic and Ascelin kept their heads well down as we eased ourselves around the spiral. We emerged into the cave I had expected to find in the church above, the Sepulchre itself.

Candles burned at either end of a stone slab, two feet across and as long as a man. The slab, of course, was empty. It struck us, or at least me, even more powerfully than the decorations and the lamps of the church above. We did not speak but knelt by the slab until another porter came over and told Joachim in a low voice that the next group of pilgrims was waiting to enter.

We left by a narrow door at the far end, not quite looking at each other. But I, at any rate, and I thought the rest, felt that we had truly reached the goal of our pilgrimage.

"The duchess and I should try to be here at Easter," said Ascelin a little louder than necessary as we came up a flight of steps into bright daylight.

"We haven't been to the Mount of Olives yet," said Joachim, his solemnity falling away in the sunshine. For the last week or more he had been as eager and enthusiastic as a boy, as all the towns we passed began to be places mentioned in the Bible.

On the long overland trip from Xantium to the Holy Land, in spite of watching constantly for mages, Ifriti, and bandits, we had seen very little except an increasingly dense number of pilgrimage churches, all of which the chaplain insisted on visiting. Once we had entered David's Kingdom, and especially the last few days here in the Holy City, we had done little *besides* visit churches.

"And we still need to see Solomon's Temple," said King Haimeric, "although I understand it is not actually the temple Solomon built himself but one rebuilt after the return of the Children of Abraham from the captivity in Babylon."

"Of course," said the chaplain. "It was to the Temple that the child Jesus was brought by his parents on the fortieth day after his birth."

"And while you've been looking at all these churches," said Maffi unexpectedly, "you still haven't gone to look at the Rock."

"The Rock?" asked the chaplain.

"Of course. The rock on which God told Abraham to sacrifice Isaac."

Maffi stood next to Ascelin, the tall prince's hand resting on his shoulder. Even though, in the month since he had joined us, the boy had shown no sign of trying to escape, Ascelin, Dominic, and Hugo had tacitly agreed to take turns in keeping close to him. Ascelin seemed to be growing oddly fond of him.

"The Rock isn't in my guidebook," said Joachim, leafing through, "but it certainly sounds as though we should visit it. Maybe after we see the Mount of Olives."

I had already noticed this. For three days he had led us through the Holy City, a bustling, modern capital, much cleaner and better laid out than Xantium although also much smaller. The entire time it appeared that to him nothing built in the last fifteen hundred years, since the later days of the Empire when Christianity had become fully established, even existed. The city was sacred to three religions, but the chaplain had looked only glancingly at the sites holy to the Children of Abraham, taking us by the spired castle of the royal Son of David without a real look, and had not even slowed down when passing those sites holy to the People of the Prophet.

I wondered briefly if Maffi, too, considered this a pilgrimage, then remembered Arnulf's agents telling me that the true pilgrimage goal for those who followed the Prophet was somewhere deep in the desert, very far to the south. I was afraid I had not paid very close attention.

"I realize what struck me as strange about this place," said Hugo to me as we stood on the Mount of Olives, looking across the Valley of Josaphat at the tangle of city roofs on the steep slopes across from us. We had already seen the little church on the Mount which sheltered the stone from which Christ had ascended into heaven. "This city isn't built on the water."

He was right. The City back home and Xantium were both major ports; even the small cities that dotted the western kingdoms tended to be built on rivers. "It's probably because it's never been a trading center," I suggested. "It's been a place for kings and priests, but never for merchants."

"It also seems," continued Hugo in a low voice, "too, well, *wholesome* a city for you to expect someone to disappear. If there really were rumors here last year about Noah's Ark — and no one seems to have heard anything about it — then that, too, should be exciting but not perilous. Yet the last message my mother had from my father was the one he sent from here back to the City by another pilgrim, that he would go south a little way and then start for home."

"Then we'll go south as well," I said, squinting into the distance. "The Wadi that Dominic's looking for should be off in that direction somewhere."

"I've tried drawing that boy out," added Hugo, "and he won't say anything definite, but I keep getting the impression he met my father's party when they came through Xantium last year."

"The mage Kaz-alrhun had also met Evrard," I said, glancing toward Maffi. He stood beside Dominic now, quietly listening as the chaplain pointed out all the churches one could see from here, churches built on the sites of important events in the life of Christ and the apostles or of the martyrdoms of early saints, most of which we had already visited. "I don't know about you, Hugo, but I keep feeling there are too many coincidences here. Everyone, except of course us, seems to know what's been happening and what it has to do with Dominic's ring and with your father."

"Are you ready for the Temple of Solomon?" called the chaplain to us happily.

But that evening when we went to the room we shared in the pilgrims' hospice, he seemed oddly subdued. The white-painted halls were full of other travelers with crosses sewn to their shoulders. The hospice itself was very austere, the rooms small and undecorated, the beds hard, and the dining room serving only flat bread stuffed with lentils and cucumbers.

I tried to read more of *Melecherius on Eastern Magic*, but in the dim light of a single candle it was difficult to follow. More and more I had the feeling Melecherius had profoundly misunderstood what the mages had tried to teach him. I closed the book and glanced over at the chaplain. He sat on the opposite bed, leafing through his guidebook with even less light than I had, but then he did not seem to be reading.

"So have we seen all the pilgrimage sites, Joachim?" I asked, kicking off my shoes and stretching out, hands behind my head. There were no chairs.

"I'm not sure," he said slowly. "I don't like to admit this, but there are two or three churches in here, which I myself marked that we visited yesterday, but which I now have trouble remembering."

"They do all tend to run together after a while," I agreed.

"But they shouldn't!" he said with a flash of his dark eyes. "I've longed to visit the Holy Land all my life, to walk with living feet on the streets where Christ trod. Now that I'm here at last I can't have the holy sites all 'run together'!"

I pushed myself up on one elbow and looked at him. "Read the descriptions again," I suggested. "I know you won't have forgotten the Holy Sepulchre, so just concentrate on the smaller churches. Think about each one individually. It must say in your guidebook which ones have monks and that will help differentiate them. You should be able to pick out the one where the porter didn't want to admit Maffi and the one where Dominic banged his head. If you can picture all of us standing inside and think about whatever we saw first — mosaics, altar, candelabra — you'll then be able to get the rest of the details."

Joachim closed the book and flopped down. "I'm not an overly ambitious tourist," he replied gloomily, "getting different picturesque sites confused. I'm a priest who has visited the places where Christ lived and died to bring us salvation, yet who still finds himself thinking about supper at the end of the day, gets sore feet from walking and standing, and needs to consult a guidebook when the experience should be burned into my soul."

I thought about this in silence for a moment, knowing better than to offer any more of the memory tricks that had allowed me to squeak through the wizards' school without ever being properly studious. I had, just barely, managed to save the chaplain's life, but it was going to be difficult if he now expected me to save his soul as well.

"Maybe it's the overall experience that's important," I offered, "not the details of the individual pilgrimage churches."

He turned to look toward me, a long, intense stare that suddenly turned into a smile. "Thank you, Daimbert," he said, stretching out again. "You're absolutely right."

"Right about what?" I said, startled.

"I should have realized this from the beginning," he said with surprisingly good humor. "Now I know why

I've been having to fight against spiritual dissatisfaction this entire journey. I'd assumed it was only the temptings of the devil and, of course, in part it was, but I now realize it also came from my own misdirected attentions."

It was no use asking him to explain what he meant. I wouldn't understand even if he did.

"I had thought that to come on pilgrimage to the Holy Land would be the culminating experience of my life, the opportunity for my soul to rise above mundane concerns at last and reach toward God. In part it certainly has been, but I was constantly irritated in finding myself still on and of the earth, worried by earthly things.

"Now you've made it evident, with your clear insight, that I'd been missing the point all along. 'The kingdom of God cometh not with observation, neither shall they say, Lo here! or, lo there! For behold, the kingdom of God is within you.' It is not my body that needed to go where Jesus lived nearly two millennia ago, but my spirit that needed to rise to meet the living Christ." He gave me a quick glance. "God can use even a wizard for His purposes."

"Glad to be of service," I mumbled.

Ascelin and Dominic found the Wadi Harhammi on an old, yellowed map they came across in the bottom of the map drawer of a dark bookstore in the oldest part of the city. None of the newer maps, even the most detailed, included it.

It seemed, from the rather confused symbols the mapmaker had used, to be up in the stony hills a few days' journey south of the emirate of Bahdroc. But the map showed no road leading to the Wadi.

"Do you still want to go there?" asked Ascelin. We all sat on the floor, crowded into the king's room in the pilgrims' hospice. "That mage certainly knew about the Wadi. I'm afraid we don't have much hope of being the first there — even if no one else had reached there already in the last fifty years."

"We may have to face the mage wherever we go," said Dominic. "I'm beginning to wonder if he's been toying with us, to let us travel all the way unmolested from Xantium to the Holy City."

"And don't forget King Warin," said Hugo. "He stole Arnulf's onyx ring from us on purpose to buy the flying horse, which by now has certainly taken him to the Wadi if that's where he was going."

"That is," I put in, "unless Arnulf's agents somehow managed to get the horse away from Kaz-alrhun first — after all, when I last saw them they seemed to think the horse was now legally Arnulf's."

"We should go south in any event," said the king, "because that is the direction Sir Hugo's party took. As the mage mentioned the Wadi Harhammi to us, he may also have mentioned it to them. We can ask after them in the oases along the way and, if we reach the emir's city without word, perhaps we can enlist his aid."

Maffi sat in the corner, following the discussion with bright eyes but saying nothing. I wondered uneasily if he was acting as Kaz-alrhun's agent. If so, I couldn't see how even a mage could get information from him while he stayed as close to us as Ascelin made sure he did.

Dominic looked at his hands, where the ruby of his ring shone in the candle light. "I shall travel to the Wadi whether the rest of you wish to accompany me past the emir's city or not. My father died with it in his thoughts. We were too foolish for fifty years to realize there was a message hidden in this ring, but even if I'm far too late I must get there at last."

Dominic glanced toward the king for confirmation as he finished, but the rest of us were already slowly nodding. This had been King Haimeric's pilgrimage, but we had now completed that aspect of the journey. Somewhere between Dominic's father's grave and the

Holy City, his quest and the search for Sir Hugo had become fused.

"I agree with you, Dominic," said King Haimeric. "We should carry out my brother's last wishes and at least try to find whatever he and his wizard thought was hidden there. Tomorrow morning we can send a message to the queen, by those pilgrims who said they were heading straight back to the City, so that she'll know we've been delayed."

"Whether we find anything in the Wadi or not," said Hugo, "the emir's city will be the best place to look for my father's tracks."

"It should also be the best place to find the blue rose," commented the king, brightening.

Ascelin rose to his feet and stretched, his hands brushing the ceiling. "Then tomorrow we'd better buy provisions," he said, "including more waterskins. It's going to be a dry journey."

II

The Holy City was at the southern end of David's Kingdom. Beyond the city, once we left behind the irrigated vineyards and olive trees, a land I had thought was already dry became even drier. The sky stretched for a thousand miles above us, cloudless and pale. The last remains of western civilization were left behind.

Ascelin had bought us all, including Maffi, densely woven white robes to replace our badly worn pilgrimage cloaks. I examined mine critically and decided it was made of goat's hair. I had been afraid the long robes would make us even hotter, but instead they reflected away the sunlight. The deep folds of the headdresses shaded our eyes; as long as we moved no more than necessary and stopped to rest in whatever shade we could find in the middle of the day, the dryness was more of a problem than the heat.

I had expected the desert to be completely barren, but even here plants grew, scrubby gray-green bushes spaced far apart, though the soil between them was bare and stony. The low, steady wind kept up a continuous murmur in the bushes. It sounded like someone speaking, just too softly to hear, a commentary in the background that we could not understand and never quite ignore. In the early morning and late afternoon, lizards scampered across the open spots, but in the middle of the day the only living creature we saw, other than ourselves, was the occasional snake or high, soaring bird.

Fortunately the road we followed led from oasis to oasis, spaced a day's journey apart, so that we could drink deeply of the alkaline water and refill the containers for ourselves and our horses. Sometimes the water merely seeped into a shallow depression scraped out between the palm trees, but usually there was a round basin, surprisingly deep, in which the water looked black though it ran clear when we ladeled it out. Ascelin warned us to be sure to shake out our boots every morning in case scorpions had crawled in during the night.

At the oases we exchanged a few words with other travelers, but there were not a lot of them, for the major trade routes between Xantium and the emir's city toward which we were heading did not detour through the Holy City. A line of jagged mountains, like teeth two thousand feet high, lay to our right, separating us from the main north-south roads.

For the most part the other travelers kept to their tents and we kept to ours. But always when Dominic was rubbing down Whirlwind at least one man wandered over, as though casually, to look the stallion over and remark on his size and strength. Whirlwind snorted both at them and at their own horses.

As the long, dry days succeeded each other, I kept looking for Kaz-alrhun, with or without the ebony horse, to swoop down on us from the sky, but he did not appear. I found myself hoping that if he did attack us he would do so soon, before we spent any more days crawling through this enormous and rocky landscape.

In the cool of the long desert evenings I tried without success to find the secret of the spell of the onyx ring. Maffi sat next to me, silent while I concentrated, his bony knees drawn up.

All I could be sure of was what I had discovered immediately, that it was a school spell, which meant technical and complicated. If it had indeed been cast by Elerius, the best wizard the school had ever produced, I was afraid that meant it was too powerful for my resources. Maybe I would have done better my whole career if I'd tried learning eastern magic.

I teased at the edges of the spell and suddenly thought I had caught a loose, revealing thread of its magic construction, but when I tried to follow it up I only discovered a large black spot before my eyes, as though I were somehow looking into the center of the onyx.

I put the ring back on my finger without learning any more of its secrets and took out *Melecherius on Eastern Magic*. I still hoped that somewhere in its pages was something that I could use against an Ifrit, if we met one guarding the secret of the Wadi Harhammi.

Melecherius was no more helpful this evening than he had been the evening before. Ifriti, the book told me with what I was increasingly sure was not first-hand knowledge, were essentially immortal, as full of unchanneled magic as dragons and as dangerous. "Have you ever seen an Ifrit?" I asked Maffi.

"No," he said thoughtfully, "but I know how to deal with them!"

"You do?" I asked in surprise.

"Of course. The tales tell all about it. Ifriti are cunning, but they're also stupid — a bad combination.

If you accidentally let one out of a bottle where it's been imprisoned by some great spell in the past, you can always get it to go back in by taunting it. Tell it you can't believe it ever fit in a space so small and, when it crawls back in to show you, quickly slap in the binding stopper!"

This didn't sound as though it would work unless Ifriti were even stupider than he suggested.

"Do you think I could learn to be a mage?" Maffi asked.

I looked over at his smile and bright eyes. "You probably could. I'm sure you're intelligent enough. But I don't know where you'd go to learn magic here in the East. I assume you'll have to apprentice yourself to someone — do you think you'll ever dare face Kaz-alrhun again?"

He laughed at that. "How about teaching me some of your school magic?"

"Well," I said slowly, "magic is really the same force throughout the world. What makes western magic distinctive is its organization and some of its technical discoveries — like telephones."

"I've heard about telephones," said Maffi, who never admitted *not* to have heard of something. "But when we in the East need to communicate long distances, we find a deep, dark pool, say certain secret words, and then we see the face we've been looking for!"

"Well, I don't know any communications spells that involve deep pools, but I could try teaching you something else. How about an illusion?"

There were surprisingly few people in Yurt interested in magic beyond asking me to produce whatever effect they needed at the moment. Even the king's brief interest in learning to fly was years in the past. I taught Maffi the elementary spell that would allow him to put an illusory spot of color on his arm or leg. He couldn't get the words to work for the full range of colors and the illusion faded, of course, after a few moments. But for most of the rest of our trip to the emir's city, he had a pink or purple spot on him somewhere.

"This land has been civilized for ten thousand years," Joachim said to me. "There were cities and temples and emperors and trade here while the men and women of what are now the western kingdoms were still dressed in skins and grubbing around in the woods after roots."

"Then it must not have always been as dry as it is now," I replied.

"The heat of summer may not be the best time to judge," he said, "but I do think the climate must be drier now." Among the broken stones that littered the side of the road were some that had clearly once been carved, as well as shards of pottery, the same tawny color as the stone but painted with dark concentric circles. Once I pulled up my mare to dismount and scoop up a silver coin from among the shards, its inscription so worn as to be illegible.

In the center of the day, when we sought out the narrow shadows of boulders and the heat beat on us like something solid, we sometimes saw mirages in the distance. A city, white-spired, lay just a few more miles down the road, flickering in welcome, though it always disappeared before we reached the place where it seemed to lie. It seemed as though the voice of that unreal city must be the voice in the wind talking to us.

"But it *is* a real city," said Maffi. He had been experimenting with the spell I had taught him and today had pink spots with purple centers on both hands. "Some people say that an Ifrit captured an entire city centuries ago, in the days of Solomon, and moved it around from place to place. But others say that cities are reflected from the desert sky as though from a mirror and appear and disappear before travelers. I think it's all right to see a city. It's when you start seeing lakes that you know you will soon die of thirst."

I wasn't sure whether to worry more about thirst, Ifriti, or bandits. The other travelers on the road, all of whom moved more swiftly than we did on their lithe, sure-footed horses, often gave us long looks from within the shadows of their headdresses, but none so far attempted to attack us, either by day or at night at the oases, under the dry and ominously rattling fronds of the palms. None of them seemed to be Kaz-alrhun or King Warin.

One morning Ascelin, whose watch it was, woke me shortly before dawn. "Could you watch for me, Wizard?" he asked quietly. "I'll be back very soon."

I crawled out under a sky brightening from gray to pink; he was gone before I could ask where. I relit our fire and started the water boiling for tea. As the sun's orange rim slid up over the horizon, he reappeared, looking pleased.

"It was a desert fox," he said, getting out the tin cups. "I saw her just at the edge of the oasis. I think she'd slipped down for a drink and had hoped to get away without being spotted. But I managed to track her — and it's hard tracking, too, on this rocky soil! I'd show you, but I don't want to frighten her. She's got a den with three kits a half mile from here."

The others were now stirring and coming to join us. "A desert fox has wonderful ears, very long," Ascelin added. "She must need them to listen for mice — or for men trying to follow her!"

During the second week of our journey south I began to worry about the king. He dismissed my concerns with a smile, but during the day I kept a surreptitious eye on him. He really was an old man, though he worked to make us forget that, and he was certainly the most frail of us in this searing and unforgiving land. He was very quiet, not talking even when Ascelin called a halt to rest and to water our horses, sometimes forgetting to take a drink himself unless Dominic reminded him.

Hugo, on the other hand, became as active in the heat as a lizard. He began strolling over to the black tents of the other travelers during our evenings in the oases and striking up conversations about his father. A small group of aristocratic western pilgrims and a red-headed mage should have been fairly conspicuous, but no one would acknowledge ever having seen them.

"We may have to appeal to the emir," Hugo said at last. "I can't tell if no one's really seen them or if these people just distrust us. What they need is a command from an important political leader. I wonder if there's the slightest chance the emir would even be willing to see a band of westerners."

We came down out of the stony desert hills among which we had spent three weeks and saw before us a white-walled city, the city of the mirages. It was surrounded by irrigated fields colored a fresh green we had almost forgotten existed, and orchards where both fruit and flowers grew together. Palm trees rustled in the wind along the fringes of the fields. To our right we could see a broad road coiling away to the northwest, the main route to Xantium.

"This is the fabled emirate of Bahdroc," said Ascelin, unrolling the map to show us. "We're well out of the Holy Land here, into a place where few westerners ever go. The last of the caliphs had his capital here a millennium ago and the current emir continues his rule, though on a much narrower scale."

I shaded my eyes to look at the city. In the center rose a sharp outcropping crowned with more white towers. On the far side of the city stretched a glassy lake or arm of the ocean, disappearing into the distance, the color of weathered jade.

"This city faces east, not west," Ascelin continued, "onto the landlocked Dark Sea, but if one crosses over the Sea one comes to the edges of the true outer ocean and to the harbors where spices and tea come in from the Far East."

"It's not a real trading center like Xantium," said Maffi somewhat smugly. "It's not much more than a way station. Here, pilgrims every year start the last stage of their journey to the most holy sites of the Prophet, and here the spices of the East are transferred from ships to land transport."

"Do they also import silk?" I asked.

Ascelin shook his head. "Silk comes overland from the northern part of the East and spices by water from the far southern parts. I don't know of anyone who's actually been there, but the true East must be larger than all the western kingdoms put together."

"I know someone who'd been to the East," put in Maffi. "He said that the men there can grow no beards, even if they try their entire lives."

"That seems unlikely," Hugo began, as though feeling the boy was interfering with his monopoly on specious travelers' tales.

But he did not get a chance to finish. The king startled us all by speaking for the first time that day. "Rosebushes!"

He had his face turned up, testing the wind. We all sniffed as well and caught it, a scent completely unlike the sharp smell of desert sage that had accompanied us the last three weeks: It was the smell of roses.

King Haimeric kicked his mare forward and the rest of us scrambled to catch up. We followed the steep stony track down to where it abruptly became a broad, smoothly paved road, between fields where swarthy men worked. The king galloped another quarter mile, then pulled up abruptly by a low fence. Beyond was a tangle of rosebushes.

Ascelin grabbed the mare's reins as the king leaped off. Haimeric vaulted the fence in a show of energy I had not seen in him in years and plunged between the bushes. "They may have the blue ones here!" he called back over his shoulder. "I see maroon and lavender, even a red darker than anything I've ever been able to grow, and — " He broke off as a man rose slowly from the middle of the bushes.

The man had Kaz-alrhun's bulk but was not as dark. It was *not* Kaz-alrhun himself, I told my wildly beating heart. He scowled down at the king, whose headdress had fallen back in his excitement. "Are you a westerner?"

"And a fellow rose grower," said the king with enthusiasm. "I've never seen colors like some of yours. We've heard, in the west, that someone here has been able to breed a blue rose. Might it be you?"

The chaplain and I exchanged glances and both shook our heads. King Haimeric was as excited to see an eastern rose garden as Joachim had been to see the churches of the Holy City. The king's age and frailty had all dropped away. His naked interest in roses was a much more powerful protection against harm than any spell I could have cast.

The huge rose grower's scowl turned into a wide smile. "Come and I shall show you what I have. I work for the emir, of course. He has roses of his own inside the palace, but there are several of us outside the city who also cultivate cuttings and do crosses for him. For two years now, he has announced to rose growers throughout the East that he has a blue rose. And the rose he has is mine!"

Maffi tugged at my arm. "If this man really is a grower for the emir of Bahdroc," he said in a low voice, "then he is a powerful man indeed."

The rest of us tied our horses to the fence and made our way cautiously amidst the roses' spiny branches. The king and the grower chattered away on topics ranging from soil acidity to aphids to crosses that just wouldn't breed true as they slipped between the bushes, far more easily than we did.

"Now this section is what I call my blues," the man continued from the far end of the garden. He and the king had pushed past glorious reds and yellows without slowing down. The bushes at this end seemed rather spindly to me and the blossoms drooped in spite of a soil watered so heavily it was spongy underfoot. "This was my first attempt."

The flowers in question were more green than anything, a rather sickly shade and with an unpleasant odor.

"But then I decided to try to approach blue from the direction of the deep reds instead," the man continued. He showed us several maroon blooms of the same color as ones the king had already spotted. "But we come now to the best of all."

I don't know what I expected, something enormous and showy probably, a sapphire blue that would take our breaths away. What we were shown instead was a rose with few and rather tattered petals, of a violet that could only be called blue if one overlooked the rather pinkish cast.

"I see," said King Haimeric, fighting disappointment with what I considered remarkably good grace. "And this is the blue which is exciting rose growers throughout the East?"

The huge man's smile split his face. "It is of a certainty! But I remain unsatisfied, as does the emir. We may have the first blue rose ever grown, but we want to make it better yet! You may notice it has but little scent. . . ."

That was the least of its problems, I thought, but said nothing.

"I wonder if it would be possible to meet the emir," said the king, his enthusiasm back as if it had never gone. "Did I mention I'm a king myself, back in the western kingdoms?" I froze, but he did not mention Yurt directly. "It would be a great honor to meet such a renowned leader and grower."

"You are a king, are you?" said the grower with an incredulous chuckle. "Well, they do have some odd customs, I hear, out in the west. You might interest the emir at that; he says that he likes to hear or see at least one new thing each day, but it is sometimes hard for him now that he is too old to travel. This time of day he generally holds open court for plaintiffs, so I am sure he would be happy to hear you and, I assume, your party." He looked Ascelin up and down, gave the rest of us a glance, shrugged, paused to lock the little gate in his low wall, then led us along the palm-lined road toward the city.

III

In the fields closer to the city, a tangle of rather sickly trees was being uprooted. We all stopped to stare in amazement at the creature doing the uprooting. It looked roughly like a horse with enormous, sail-like ears, but was far bigger. A very small man, or at least small by comparison, armed only with a stick, seemed to be directing it. Most surprising of all, the appendage like an arm with which the creature seized the tree trunks appeared to be its nose.

"What mage could have made — " I started to say and stopped. This wasn't the product of magic. An aura of spells sparkled in a rather unfocused manner over the emir's city, but this was an ordinary, living animal.

"Do you not recognize an elephant?" said Maffi loftily. "They are extremely strong and indeed enjoy work like this, but you can't keep them alive in the depths of the desert, because it's too dry."

"Don't try to pretend you know more about such creatures than we do," said Hugo reprovingly. "You know you've never been out of Xantium before."

"But I saw one once in Xantium," the boy protested, "near the governor's palace. I think someone sent it to him as a gift."

Just outside the emir's city we had to retreat to the edge of the road as a great mass of armed men emerged through the gates. The one in the lead carried, unsheathed, the most enormous sword I had even seen. In the center of a crush of turbaned heads, I saw one man who walked bareheaded. His eyes passed over us, but he did not see us. Hugo stared at him as though fearing it might be his father, realized what he was doing, and looked away.

"A condemned criminal, of course," said the rose grower in response to a question from the king. "He will be beheaded out at the edge of the desert, where the desert wind will come, cleanse away the blood with blown sand, and repurify. Do you not have a similar custom in the west?"

The king didn't answer, and we followed our guide on through the city gates. Our route took us past the spice warehouses where sharp mixed smells, both savory and sweet, struck us on every side. The iron doors were guarded both by armed men and by shadowy forms that reeked of magic, but the grower led us at too rapid a pace for me to probe properly. At a small open-air market, set between unwindowed bulks of warehouses, a ragged, dark-haired woman was buying for a single coin a bag of peppercorns that would have cost her a year's wages back in the west. The cooking smells that greeted us when we emerged into the residential part of town indicated that all cooks here used spices enthusiastically.

The emir's palace was in the very center of the city, built on a steep rocky pinnacle that rose above the crowded streets. We had to leave our horses at the bottom, in what appeared to be stables reserved for those visiting the emir, and climb narrow, white-washed stairs built half into the rock itself. Maffi gave Hugo a low, running commentary on the history of Bahdroc as we climbed, but I missed most of it.

At the top, a vizier gorgeously robed in satin met us and started to demand our business, but after a few words with the grower he motioned us through open gates. The grower led us without hesitation down a maze of airy arcades. Men with curved swords eyed but did not challenge us. I tried without success to keep track of the turnings and glanced back at Ascelin who, from the concentration on his face, was trying to do the same thing.

We emerged at last into a sunny courtyard with a fish pond in the center. A campaign chair, empty, stood in the center. Both floor and pool were paved with gleaming white marble. Swords, spears, and shields hung from white marble walls. No one was there, and the grower kept walking. "This is the courtyard of the emir's youth," he said over his shoulder.

But when he noticed that I had stopped, he stopped as well. I stood staring into the pond where brilliant red, blue, and gold fish, unlike anything I had ever seen before, swam about. They looked at me almost imploringly — maybe they wanted to be fed. But I was not particularly interested in the fish. I stared instead at a shadowy figure at the bottom of the pool, something low and flat with a number of legs. The legs were scrubbing busily at the marble, getting off the algae.

"It's a magic creature," I said to no one in particular, "but I've never seen anything like it before. What is it? It moves as though it was alive, but a mage must have created it."

The creature finished cleaning the marble and crawled out. It was a uniform gray and no more recognizable in full sunlight than it was in the depth of the pool. It went, dripping, across the courtyard and settled itself into the corner.

"It's an automaton, of course," said Maffi. "Don't you have them where you come from? You saw Kaz-alrhun's ebony horse."

"But I didn't realize a mage could make something that didn't even *look* like a living creature."

"Well, it's modern magic, of course," said Maffi good-naturedly. "I know you're a little old-fashioned in the west."

And I had thought the east old-fashioned! The rose grower led us on through another series of arcades to a second courtyard.

Here stood an enormous throne, sheltered by striped awnings. I expected to see the emir at last, but this courtyard too was empty. As we watched, a white peacock hopped onto the throne's stone seat and gave a shriek. Trees and bushes with flowers the color of blood grew all around. I saw birds hopping in the branches, and was caught by the metallic gleam from the feathers. One fixed me with a jewel eye.

"More automatons?" I asked as casually as I could.

"Of course," said the grower. "This is the courtyard of the emir's maturity where he commanded great armies and reveled in great luxury." As we headed out the far side, the automaton birds behind us began to sing, a song of such intense sweetness that I stumbled.

But the grower kept on walking. I had completely lost track of the turnings. Finally we reached a third courtyard, also open to the sky but lined on three sides with shady arcades. More flowers bloomed riotously in the center. In the distance beyond the lower fourth wall, we could see sunlight glinting on the Dark Sea. Here fountains played, and an old man, turbaned and dressed in dazzling white, sat on a bench by the fountains, watching us approach.

It was not precisely the image of the East I had had back in Yurt, but it was close. Another of the strange automaton shapes, radiating magic, stood behind the old man. The rose grower knelt before him and kissed the pavement between his hands. "Oh, glorious one, live forever! I have brought you something new and strange, a great wonder, travelers from a distant land who say that they have heard of your blue roses! One of them is a normal boy, but the rest claim to be westerners. Their skin may be pale and their accents strange, but their enthusiasm for roses is unfeigned."

I had thought that our skin had become quite dark

after months of travel, but we still could not match the swarthiness of the men here. The emir motioned with one hand. When he moved I could see that his white robes were sewn all over with pearls.

I got a better look at the automaton behind him, shadowed by an arcade. As I watched, and indeed the entire time we were in the courtyard, it spun about very slowly and deliberately, without a sound. It had five sides, five eyes and five arms, and each of its five hands clutched a long knife to protect the emir. Two enormous spotted cats on leashes, real animals these, reclined beside him. They gave us bored looks and turned away.

"These do, indeed, appear to be something new and strange," said the emir, although I would have thought we rather paled in comparison. "Approach, then, travelers from afar!"

There were rosebushes growing in the courtyard, but a surreptitious glance found no blue flowers. The king stepped forward at once, but Ascelin gripped my arm. "Something's wrong," he hissed into my ear.

The others were following the king forward. "You've been doing this ever since we reached Arnulf's house," I hissed back. "If you don't want to be here, fine, go back to the horses, but we can't let the king miss his opportunity to find his rose or, probably, for Hugo to find his father."

Ascelin bit his lip and flashed me a look from blue eyes that I had to admit looked surprisingly strange when the eyes of everyone around us were black. But he took a long, slow breath and stepped forward as well, without enough hesitation to provoke comment.

Since King Haimeric knelt before the emir, the rest of us did, too. "This one says he is a western king," commented the rose grower.

"But I come to you not as someone claiming equality," said the king, sitting back carefully on his heels, his first movement in the last hour that looked as though it might pain him. "Rather, I come as a suppliant. I have dreamed all my life of a blue rose, a true blue, one that would rival sapphires in color and the most expensive perfumes in scent." So my expectations were also his. "And we have heard in the west that you have grown such a thing."

The emir made a slight motion of his hand, and a man stepped out of the shadows at the edge of the courtyard to bring the king a pillow on which he settled himself gratefully.

"You then ask to see such a rose?" asked the emir. One of his spotted cats gave a long yawn, full of teeth, as though in disdain. I looked toward the grower, worrying that he might be offended by the king's implied insult to his best blue, but he only beamed as though proud to have brought the emir such an amusing guest.

"I seek even more, glorious one," said King Haimeric. "Even we in the west know that an emir's power, to help or to harm, to raise up and to cast down, is unlimited. I would like the rootstock of such a rose for my own."

At this, the emir began to laugh in what looked to me genuine amusement. "And this is your only request?"

"I do have other requests, glorious one," the king continued, undaunted. "We would like to inquire if you have perhaps seen friends of ours, a group of four westerners including a wizard. The wizard has red hair." The emir's smile disappeared abruptly.

There was a brief, very tense moment in which I could have sworn the air crackled. Ascelin nudged me with his foot and let his hand rest, as though casually, on his hilt. I kept my eyes on the silent automaton behind the emir and put together the first words of a lifting spell, to transport the king up and out of here.

But then the emir smiled again. It did not look to me like the same smile. "I am delighted to help such amusing guests. And you will be my guests, won't you?

I have rooms where you shall stay. Refreshment will be brought to you at once." For some reason, I could feel Ascelin start to relax. "We can talk more in the cool of the evening."

IV

The emir clapped his hands once and half a dozen young women darted into the courtyard. Their faces were veiled so that only their eyes showed, but the rest of their clothing was very brief and their loose, silken trousers did nothing to hide their legs. They whisked us to our feet with gentle touches under the elbow and escorted us, wordless but giggling, out of the courtyard, down more passageways, and into a low-ceilinged outer room whose single window led to a balcony looking down over the sun-drenched city and the Dark Sea. An open doorway led to a white-tiled room where hot water was already beginning to steam. The women left us for a moment but were back almost immediately with a tray of fresh fruit, a hot pitcher of what I assumed was tea, bread, and salt.

Ascelin plunged his finger into the salt and licked it off. Maffi joined him. "It's all right now," Ascelin said in a low voice when King Haimeric opened his mouth to reprove him. "They wouldn't share salt with us if they meant to kill us."

"But why should they want to kill us?" asked the king.

"The emir has seen my father," said Hugo in a tight voice.

"We were greeted as something to amuse a bored old man," said Ascelin, "but everything changed as soon as you mentioned Sir Hugo."

Maffi nudged Ascelin. "Not in front of the slave girls, my masters," he murmured.

The slave girls stood across the room, watching and whispering to each other. "Thank you," said the king to them. "We'll call if we need anything else." They trooped out, giggling again, and one winked over her shoulder at Hugo.

"They are slaves?" said Joachim to Maffi. "I fear I did not recognize them as such. I wonder what sort of 'duties,' degrading and debilitating to the soul, they are expected to perform in a place like this."

Ascelin closed the door carefully behind them. I poured a cup from the pitcher. It neither looked nor smelled like tea.

I hesitated, but Maffi took the cup out of my hand. "It's coffee, my masters," he said with a grin. "We of the desert were drinking coffee long before traders to the Far East began bringing back tea. Tea is such an insipid brew in comparison; I'm not sure why you westerners ever took it up."

He began an explanation of where coffee came from, somewhere far to the south of the desert where dry sand gave way to wet jungles, but I was not listening. Instead I stood quietly to one side, probing with magic. Even though I had snapped at Ascelin, I trusted his hunter's instincts more than I trusted anyone in the emir's employ.

I could find no one actively working magic in the palace, though the presence of the automatons made it hard to make sense of all the magical currents. But outside, either in the city or perhaps even beyond the city, I sensed a disturbance in the forces of magic, suggesting someone — or something — of enormous power. I came back to myself with a start, not wanting to let whoever or whatever was there knew I had spotted them. Either Kaz-alrhun, I thought, or an Ifrit.

"Is my father here?" asked Hugo in a low voice at my shoulder.

Since I had never met his father, I would not recognize his mind even if I touched it, but I knew his wizard. I let myself slide along the surface of the forces of magic, slipping past the minds of all those in the palace, a long process as there seemed to be a remarkable number of people here. But I did not find Evrard. "Not here," I said at last.

Hugo nodded glumly. "I hadn't expected it would be that easy. At first I hoped that if the emir liked King Haimeric he'd be willing to assist us, to command his dependents to help us investigate their disappearance. But as soon as the king mentioned the red-haired wizard and I saw the emir's face change, I knew he *did* know who they were, but there was no chance he was going to help us find them. If they'd just been held prisoner here, at least we could have tried to rescue them. . . ."

The king sampled the coffee and declared it strong, quite unlike tea, and much better than he expected. I tried some as well and agreed with his assessment. The aroma slipped into the consciousness as delicately as a distant melody, and a long, hot swallow made one feel rather abruptly awake. I wondered if King Haimeric was planning to take home to the queen some of the leaves or berries or whatever it was brewed from.

The sun had set, touching the Dark Sea with fingers of gold, when the emir sent for us. I had spent the afternoon making further desultory and unsuccessful attempts to unravel the spell on the onyx ring. Back in the emir's courtyard of old age, candles had been lit inside paper lanterns, giving everything a fairy glow. The air was no longer hot, but still warm, and lay on our arms like a sensuous touch.

Freshly bathed, dressed not in our goat's-hair desert robes but in the cleanest clothes from the bottom of our packs, we reclined on padded benches while the slave girls brought us iced sherbet and almonds. The last place we had had an iced dish had been at King Warin's castle, tucked into the foothills below icy peaks. I tried to calculate the nearest place from which the emir could obtain ice and how expensive the transportation would be, and gave it up.

A tune then arose from within the arcaded shadows

beyond the light of the lanterns. The girls began to dance, swaying back and forth, twirling around each other in a complicated pattern that I couldn't quite follow. Their bare feet moved quickly and surely; dark eyes flashed at us from above their veils. Then the music paused and again they served us, this time with diced lamb and pickled eggplant.

"If the old man is a prisoner somewhere," commented Hugo to me with a grin in his voice, "I hope he's got entertainment like this."

At last the emir spoke. "So you have come all this way in search of a blue rose, western travelers? I would have thought it would have been simpler to send a message to your agents in Xantium than to make such a difficult journey yourselves."

If any of the western kings kept agents in Xantium, the royal court of Yurt certainly never had. But King Haimeric did not respond to this part of the emir's remark. "Agents and messages are no use when one wants to see a blue rose oneself. It was messages and rumors that told me there might be such a thing here, but if you have really developed a blue rose I thought it unlikely that you would be willing to sell the rootstock, or even if the rootstock would survive transportation."

"And are you satisfied, now that you have seen my roses?"

In spite of the emir's friendly manner, I would have been very careful to be as flattering and diplomatic as possible. Someone accustomed to having people kiss the ground at his feet might not like to be reminded that his best blue rose was rather inadequate.

But King Haimeric surprised me. "No, I am not satisfied, glorious one," he said in a good-natured tone, "as I'm sure you would have guessed even if I lied to you. The roses your grower showed us out at the edge of the city are an excellent start toward blue, closer than anything I've seen in the west, but they are not the true, sapphire blue which I had heard rumored you'd grown. I expect you have something much better hidden away in the palace and have that rose garden at the entrance to town, where anyone can find it easily, to distract all but the most knowledgeable rose fanciers."

The emir was silent for a moment, either considering his reply or deeply insulted. There might in the morning be six more headless bodies on the edge of town, waiting for the desert to purify them. On either side of me, I could hear Ascelin and Hugo take determined breaths, though neither had worn his sword to the emir's dinner.

But the emir said in a mild tone, "You can see all the roses I have in my palace here in the courtyard. Do any of them seem finer to you?"

In the dancing shadows of the lanterns all the roses looked gray to me. "These are fine roses but they are not your true blues, either, glorious one," said the king. "If you have blue roses in the palace, you have concealed them well."

"But what good would a blue rose be if no one but I could see it?"

"You would know you had succeeded where no one had ever succeeded before," said the king. "Is the personal satisfaction enough?"

The emir did not answer. The girls now brought us a salad of lentils, onions, and olives, and when the melody struck up again from back in the shadows they resumed their dance. I would have enjoyed it more if I had been able to give it proper attention.

Since so many of my sudden convictions turned out to be wrong, I didn't know whether to doubt myself, but I now felt suddenly convinced that I knew what the older Prince Dominic had found in the Wadi Harhammi. "Something wonderful, something marvelous," he had called it. Ever since the eastern kingdoms, I had wondered if it was the Black Pearl. Now, I felt sure that it was a blue rose.

When the slave girls paused in their dancing, King Haimeric spoke again. "You are not sure whether to trust me with your secret, glorious one, and doubtless with good reason. I would not trust foreigners with the secret of a blue rose myself." In fact, King Haimeric would have told anyone interested in his roses anything they wanted to know, but I let this pass. "Perhaps, instead, I can ask again what I asked before. Did a group of pilgrims come through here, four men, one of them a wizard with red hair? Their leader, Sir Hugo, is a cousin of my wife."

The emir did not answer for a moment; the only sound was the quiet chirping of a bird somewhere along the eaves — a real bird, this time.

"Very few Christian pilgrims come down to Bahdroc from the Holy Land," the emir said at last from out of the shadows. "And I presume that most of those who reach my city never come to the palace. No, I cannot say that I have ever seen your friends." He paused for a moment, then added, "Perhaps my vizier may know more." He clapped once and a slave girl darted away.

In a few minutes the vizier we had seen briefly before came into the courtyard, panting and arranging his satin robes as though he had been summoned from the bath or from bed. I wondered how this man, who I presumed wielded enormous power of his own within the city, reconciled himself to being virtually the slave of the quiet old man in the pearl-embroidered raiment.

He stood stiffly before the emir, his hands at his sides. "No, of course I have seen no pilgrims such as you describe. If any such people did come to Bahdroc, I would most certainly have been informed. Two months ago several western women were here looking, they said, for the bones of some holy saint who had lived as a recluse in the desert even before the days of the Prophet. I found it all quite unlikely. They would not be the pilgrims you were seeking? I thought not."

The emir dismissed his vizier with a slight movement of one hand. The slave girls brought us bowls of yogurt and cucumber and little cups of strong coffee.

"Then if our friends did not come to your city," said King Haimeric, "I must apologize for troubling you about them. But let me ask you something else." The king was nothing if not persistent. "Have you heard the rumors that King Solomon's Pearl has been found again?"

The emir was silent again. But when he spoke it was as though there had been no pause. "I am surprised, travelers from the West, that you have heard the old legends. I have not heard anyone speak of the Black Pearl for many years. It was sunk beneath the Outer Sea centuries ago and could scarcely have been found again."

"Then I have one final request," said the king. "We believe that our friends were on their way to the Wadi Harhammi."

We believed no such thing, but I kept quiet.

"Tomorrow could you have someone direct us on the right road toward it?"

This time, the emir's pause was much longer. For a second the courtyard was dead still, then I heard a low growl from one of his big spotted cats. "Again, you seem to have been listening to the old legends," the emir said at last. "If you had listened better, however, then you would have realized there really is no such Wadi, that even in the legends its position is constantly shifting. The old slave women tuck the children into bed with stories of the fairies who live in the Wadi Harhammi, but that is all. By the way, I am not sure you ever mentioned it, but what is the name of your kingdom in the west?"

"Yurt," said King Haimeric.

The emir did not answer but clapped again at once. "Show our guests to their quarters," he said to the slave girls. "They will be staying with us all this week."

They helped us up from the couches with light

hands and giggles. Hugo held the hand of his slightly longer than necessary. "I wonder if we're going to find out more about these degrading and debilitating duties the slaves have to perform," he whispered to me. "I notice there's a girl for each of us, not counting Maffi, but he's too young anyway."

But the king dismissed the girls as soon as we reached our room. I rather hoped the look of disappointment they gave us was not feigned.

"I am afraid the emir lied to us," said King Haimeric as soon as the door shut behind them. "Perhaps he didn't have his wife join us for dinner because he didn't want her involved in this or because he was afraid of what she might let slip. It was clear he and his vizier knew perfectly well whom I meant when I asked about Sir Hugo's party."

"And he recognized the name Yurt," I said. "I wish you hadn't mentioned it, sire. It seems to have meaning here in the east. There has to be a reason it was carved on the onyx of Arnulf's ring."

King Haimeric dismissed this. "No one east of the mountains has heard of Yurt; even a lot of the other western kings don't recognize the name."

"That may be," I persisted, "but it was when he heard us mention Yurt that he told us we'd be staying. I wonder now if Sir Hugo's party might not have been captured specifically as bait for us, because they knew he and his party had a connection to Yurt."

"I didn't have a slave woman to raise me," put in Maffi, "but I certainly never heard fairy stories about the Wadi Harhammi. I would guess the emir knows exactly where it is."

"The mapmaker knew where it was," said Ascelin, "even if he didn't mark the road. But the emir doesn't want us leaving the city to find it. He calls us his guests, but if we tried to leave we'd find the doors barred against us."

"And what is he planning to do with us?" said Hugo. "The wizard says that if my father's party was ever here, they aren't here now." He paused for a long moment. When he continued his voice was low and rough-edged. "Does that mean they're all dead?"

V

The slave girls woke us in the morning with flat, chewy bread and more coffee. After they had checked to make sure we had enough clean towels and the king had told them politely that we could dress ourselves, they opened the door to slip away.

But one girl stayed behind. Her black eyes darted back and forth between us. "Be careful, westerners," she murmured, more to Hugo than to anyone else. I realized I had not heard any of the slave girls actually speak before. "This is not a good place for men of pale skin. The desert has been known to eat those who displease the emir."

"But how can we get out of here?" asked Ascelin. "The emir has said — you must have heard him — that we will be staying a week, which means whether we want to or not."

She glanced quickly toward the closed door through which the other girls had gone. "Just past noon, everyone will be asleep. The palace gate is guarded at all times, but I think I can distract the guard today. Once you reach the city streets, if you move quickly you should have no problems."

I saw Ascelin struggle successfully not to ask, "But why should we trust you?" Instead he said, "We are deeply grateful for your warning, but what can we, men you've barely seen, offer you in return for this aid?"

"It is not you," she said, still in that very low voice that made me wonder who might be listening at our window. "It's the mage in that other group of westerners, the friends you mentioned. The mage with the strange orange-colored hair."

Hugo bit off a shout. "Then my father's here after all!"

She shook her head at the delight and excitement in his face. "They were here for a week, close to a year ago. The mage—he was good to me. But they are not here now." She looked at both the palms and the backs of her hands. "I never told them what I have just told you, to try to make their way out during the noon period of slumber. And now—now the desert has eaten them."

Hugo froze, his eyes wide open. The girl darted away without saying more. The door closed almost soundlessly behind her.

"Then they *are* dead," said Hugo in a very strained voice.

King Haimeric looked at him worriedly. "She didn't say that," he said, "and we don't know anyway whether to believe her."

"I believe her enough to want to escape today," said Ascelin. "I never knew your friend that well, Wizard, but if a slave girl still remembers him fondly a year later, I must have missed a lot."

"It may all be a trap," said Dominic.

"If she was sent to us as a trap," replied Ascelin, "so that the emir could set all his guards on us as we tried to leave his palace, then we'll see what western steel can do against them."

Hugo, sitting with his head in his hands, looked up and almost smiled. "If they did kill my father, then I'd be happy to help send the whole lot of them to hell."

The palace was quiet all morning. No one sent for us or came to our room. Several times Ascelin and Dominic went out strolling, as though casually; Hugo, at Ascelin's orders, stayed behind. Slaves — men this time — turned the princes back from the emir's courtyard and from the main palace gate where armed guards also stood. But for the most part they were allowed to wander freely.

The third time they went out, shortly before noon,

they came back grinning. "I think we found where the emir keeps his wife — or rather his wives," said Ascelin. "There's a separate wing of the palace with only one corridor leading to it. The air — somehow it *smelled* different. And I heard voices, including a number of women's voices and the voices of children, such as I have not heard anywhere else here."

"But they certainly didn't let us in for a better look," said Dominic. "I just hope the front gate isn't guarded by men like that when we try to escape! That's why we think it must be the emir's wives in there. The first row of guards, all of them with those curved swords, never even let us get close to the second row. And *they* were even bigger, almost Ascelin's size," with a punch for the tall prince's shoulder. "But they looked somehow — I don't know, not soft, because they had plenty of muscle, but effeminate. I wonder how many women the emir actually has!"

The chaplain looked shocked, Hugo intrigued in spite of his misery. "We don't have time to worry about why the emir would want more than one wife," said King Haimeric. "If we trust that slave girl, it is time for us to go."

Dressed again in our desert robes, we slipped out into the hallway. The whole palace was still except for the sound of our own breathing. As quietly as we could, we followed the network of passages which Ascelin and Dominic had determined led to the main gate. I went first, probing with magic. Twice I waved those behind me to a stop, but the person I had sensed turned another way. Most of the minds in the palace around us were dozing or asleep.

"There's the main palace gate up ahead," whispered Ascelin. We all peered carefully around the corner. The last passage led straight for a hundred yards to an open gateway. No one blocked our way. "Now's the time to find out," the prince added grimly, "how much that slave girl really liked Sir Hugo's wizard."

We went on soundless feet down a passage which seemed suddenly to have grown to five times its original length. I would have lifted myself from the floor for even quieter flight except that I needed my attention to watch for the approach of hostile minds. The doorways on either hand were all shut, except for the last one.

It was, I guessed, a guard room. In it were two minds, not asleep, a man and a woman. I cautiously peeked around the door frame. The room was dark, its window shuttered, but I could hear on the far side soft voices and a sudden giggling.

We went past the doorway one at a time on tiptoe. The king was the lightest on his feet of all. The open gate was just beyond and then brilliant midday sunshine beat on our suddenly freed heads. We descended the steep stairs from the pinnacle on which the palace was built, first slowly and quietly, then more and more quickly, as final escape seemed less and less likely as it came closer and closer.

The stables at the bottom of the stairs stood open. The stable boys were stretched out asleep on bales of hay. We saddled our horses with fingers made clumsy by haste and stilled inquisitive whinnies with hands across the horses' nostrils. The sound of hooves on the flagstone floor as we led them out sounded as though it should wake the dead.

It did wake the stable boys. They half sat up, but Maffi smiled and nodded and said something I did not catch, and they stretched out again. We led our horses a short distance through the narrow, deserted streets, then mounted. Trying not to look as though we were running away, we moved through the streets, back in the direction from which we had first entered the city.

"They'll be expecting us to leave through the south city gates," said Ascelin, who was leading. "That's where they'll send guards when they find we're gone.

We can go out into the fields and groves on the north side of town and cut around."

The north city gates stood wide open, unguarded, unwatched. We rushed through, then paused to catch an easy breath for the first time since we had slipped out of our room.

"There are narrow tracks between the fields," said Ascelin. "I think if we start this way — "

"Look," said the king. "There's my friend the rose grower."

The enormous grower stood in our path, arms akimbo. King Haimeric rode directly up to him, ignoring Ascelin's warnings. "Thank you for taking us to the emir," he said. "We learned a number of useful things from him. And I'm glad to have a chance to see a fellow rose enthusiast again before we leave Bahdroc."

"And what sorts of things did you discover?" the grower asked. His manner toward the king seemed friendly, but he was still employed by the emir. I heard the quiet hiss of a sword being drawn by Ascelin behind me.

The king gave the grower a shrewd look. "Let me answer that question with another. Could you direct us to where the emir really grows his blue roses?"

The king seemed to have lost all sense, but there was nothing I could do about it.

To my surprise, the huge swarthy man put back his head and laughed. "You were very polite about it," he said after a moment, "but I could tell you were not fooled by my roses. Did you expect the emir to have the real blues in his palace?"

"It had been a thought," said King Haimeric. "Where are they in fact?"

The rose grower said nothing for a moment, instead making ruminative hums and grunts. "Go around to the south side of the city," he said at last, as though in sudden decision. "This track should take you much of the way. Ride south on the main highway for three days — the road that would eventually lead you to the pilgrimage sites. But on the fourth day, stop and look off to your right for two rocky peaks in the distance forming a gate, with a saddle of land between them. You will find a little path leading toward the peaks. The path will lead you up all the way up to the pass, and beyond the pass — well, if you do not find your blue rose, you will be closer than you are here."

"Thank you!" cried the king, pulled his mare around, and started along the track the grower had indicated. The huge man lifted a hand in solemn farewell.

Ascelin caught up with the king a quarter mile along and took hold of his saddle leather. "Don't you think we've followed this track far enough to put him off the scent?"

"Why put him off the scent?" asked the king in surprise. "It will be easiest to follow this way around the city."

"Because he's going to set the emir's guards on us!"

"And you think me a silly old fool?" said King Haimeric good-naturedly. "In fact, he has neither betrayed the emir's trust nor betrayed us. He told us the direction to take to the Wadi Harhammi but without ever mentioning its name. And did you notice he carefully didn't warn us against what we would find there?"

"But why do you think you can trust him, Haimeric?" Ascelin demanded.

"He loves roses," said the king. "Come on."

We found the path away from the main south road on the morning of the fourth day. It was well marked at the beginning, but it quickly became so faint we might never have been able to follow it for long without the sight of the gate in the line of mountains ahead of us. We needed the path, however, because it seemed the only way through a rough, dry land of crevices, bare eroded slopes that led down to exitless ravines, and tumbled boulders. Ascelin, bent low to the ground, led us as the path wound around and up, a way marked by little more than the occasional darker stone which an earlier foot had turned over, a different shade than the tawny color of stones exposed for centuries to the desert sun.

"No Ifriti have followed us, anyway," I commented, looking back north toward the emir's city.

"What *are* Ifriti?" Hugo asked me as we paused to rest our horses on a level part of the path. "You've been talking about them all trip and Arnulf's books mentioned them, but I'm still not sure."

"They're magical creatures," I answered, "created when the world was first formed. In fact, it is said that they were used for some of the more difficult parts, such as digging the rivers or pushing up the mountains. They're supposedly immortal, and over the millennia they've taken on something of a human shape, though they're far, far bigger."

"You think then, sire," said Dominic to the king, "that the Wadi my father wanted us to find lies beyond that line of mountains?"

"It certainly looks that way on the map," said the king.

"And there we'll find something wonderful and marvelous," said Dominic eagerly.

But there imagination failed us. "My father?" said Hugo without much hope.

"The Black Pearl?" said Ascelin. "But no. Even if it was once there, too many other people will have been there before us, from King Warin to the mage Kaz-alrhun."

"It might be Noah's Ark," put in the chaplain, "if the rumors Sir Hugo's party supposedly heard in the Holy Land last year were true. We know the Ark came to rest on a mountain, but Noah and his sons left it behind when they came back down to repopulate the land."

"The blue rose," said the king confidently.

Maffi and I had no suggestions.

Ascelin with his hunter's eyes and I with my far-seeing spells kept looking behind us, but the long day passed as had the three days before, with no sign of pursuit. Ascelin looked relieved, but I began to wonder if, on the contrary, the emir had not bothered to pursue us because he knew we would be captured by whatever lay ahead.

The path came in late afternoon to a last steep ascent up to the saddle between the peaks. "Shall we pass the night here," asked Ascelin, "or try to get through the 'gateway' before dark?"

"We can't stop now," said Dominic, his face alight. "We're so close! And look at my ring!"

The ruby was doing something I had never seen a precious stone do before. It was pulsing with an inner red light.

I pulled off my riding glove to look at the onyx ring Maffi had stolen from Kaz-alrhun. I never had been able to find the secret of the spell attached to it. It sat on my finger lifeless and dead.

"Follow me!" cried Dominic. He kicked his stallion who attacked the slope, rushing up the final half mile, hooves sure in spite of the loose stones underfoot. Maffi, riding behind him, held on desperately. "This is it!" called Dominic from the top as we hurried to catch him.

At the pass, we dismounted to rest our horses and look ahead. From here we looked down into a circular valley, five miles across. We stood on the rim, I realized, of an ancient volcano whose huge throat had partially filled through the millennia with rubble and earth. The floor was far below us and the walls so steep I could not tell how one was supposed to get down. The valley, which must catch any moisture from the sharp mountains ringing it, was just on the green side of brown. It appeared perfectly empty.

"I don't see any place for a rose garden," commented the king.

"Is this whole valley called the Wadi Harhammi," asked Ascelin, "or is that only one corner of it? How will we find the place where — "

He stopped and we all froze, following his pointing hand. A whirlwind rose from the valley floor, coming rapidly toward us. It grew bigger and bigger and, as I realized how far away it still was, bigger yet.

In the center of the whirlwind was a dark green, almost human figure, a heavily fleshed man like Kaz-alrhun but taller, five times, a dozen times taller.

"That — " gasped Maffi.

"That," I said, "is an Ifrit."

PART SEVEN

The Ifrit

1

There didn't seem much point in trying to escape, so we stood shoulder to shoulder and watched it come.

That is, all but Maffi. He had never left Whirlwind's back; he gave a shout, a tug on the reins, and was gone, scrambling wildly down the way we had just come. Dominic started to say something and changed his mind.

I heard Joachim murmuring, just at the edge of audibility. I turned toward his profile. He looked very calm, but I recognized what he was saying. It was the litany for the dying and the dead.

I took a deep breath, trying to rally what little magic I knew that might possibly help against an Ifrit, but I never got a chance to use it. The world rose, fell, and flipped around us.

It felt as though we were standing not on a rocky pass but on a tablecloth, and an unimaginably huge giant had seized the cloth's corners and shook. We were thrown into a void without light, with neither up nor down. I whirled blind, reaching out for Joachim and Hugo, who had been next to me until a second ago, and found nothing.

I opened my mouth to yell and it filled with sand. By the time I finished coughing and spitting, the world around me had settled down a little. It was now completely silent except for a tiny background noise of trickling sand. I rubbed grit from my eyelids and tried opening them. I could see a little now but still heard nothing.

"Joachim?" I said tentatively. "Sire?"

In answer I heard a deep, echoing chuckle somewhere far above me.

I grabbed for my spells and looked slowly up. My magic was gone, stripped away as though I had never known any. It would not have mattered anyway. I was sitting in the Ifrit's gigantic hand.

"And what are you?" he said, peering at me with an eyeball the size of my head. His deep voice vibrated, seeming to come from all around. Except for his size and color — he was a green the shade of the sea during a storm — he looked almost human, but his ears were pointed, and the nails on the hand that held me narrowed into sharp claws. His body blocked most of the view, but I thought he was standing in the bottom of the circular valley.

"I am a wizard," I said, though I had never felt less like a wizard since my first day at the school. "What have you done with my friends?"

"A mage?" inquired the Ifrit, his tone suggesting he was pleased and delighted something so small knew how to talk.

"A wizard," I said firmly. I felt I had had enough eastern magic to last me a long time. "What have you done with the others?"

He poked me delicately with the forefinger of the other hand; the thrust nearly knocked me backwards. "They're around," he said vaguely. "You seem remarkably bold, little man." In fact, I was so terrified that even struggling and shrieking seemed superfluous. "If you're a wizard, do a trick for me."

"I can't do a trick. Your magic has defeated mine. Let me have my spells back and I'll do some very charming tricks for you." I wondered desperately what an Ifrit might find charming.

"So you don't know magic after all," said the Ifrit in disgust. His hand started slowly to close around me. "I ought just to crush you."

I closed my eyes and muttered a scrap of the psalms between my teeth.

But then the hand opened again. "On the other hand, humans can be very amusing sometimes. Do you think you could be amusing if I kept you alive for a while?"

A second ago, death with dignity had seemed the best alternative. Abruptly, life without dignity seemed much more attractive. "What a good idea," I said.

The Ifrit turned his hand this way and that to get a look at me from different angles. His stubbly beard was very close. "I think it's because you humans always know you're going to die someday," he said after a minute. "That's what makes you so amusing — you act as though everything was important and had some sort of meaning."

"You could be amused a lot more," I suggested, "if you brought all my friends here." My voice sounded tiny and squeaky in comparison to his deep rumble. "By the way, here's an idea. I'll bet you were imprisoned in a bottle once, but it's hard to imagine how you managed to fit your entire body inside. Do you think you could show me?"

At least the Ifrit chuckled rather than crushing me at once. "Nice try, little man, but I won't be fooled that easily again. King Solomon, the son of David — may they both be revered! — bound me by the name of the Most High and imprisoned me in a bottle for over two thousand years. I'd still be in it if that mage hadn't let me out. But I'm certainly not going back in there *again*."

I had known all along it wouldn't work. But I would now never have a chance to tell Maffi, "I told you so."

"Did you know King Solomon?" inquired the Ifrit. "But that's right," he said before I could answer. "I keep forgetting what a short time you humans live. Even Solomon only lived for a few centuries. Maybe it would be a kindness just to kill you and get it over with."

"But then you'd be all by yourself again," I said, "with no one to talk to and no one to amuse you."

The Ifrit frowned, a creasing of his blue-green forehead like the violent erosion of a hillside. "I know what I can do," he said after a moment, his forehead clearing. "I can take all these friends of yours that you keep worrying about and set them tests. Humans talk about setting tasks for Ifriti, but it would be much more interesting to test humans."

"What kind of tests?" I asked cautiously.

"Tests of all the things humans worry about, honor, love, life itself. I already told you I've noticed how seriously you take things."

"And if we pass your tests — "

"Then I'll have had an amusing few days," said the Ifrit.

"And then you'll let us go?"

The Ifrit seemed more amused by this than anything else I'd said. "Of course not. You came here to my valley, and I'm under orders to guard it, so you'll all have to die."

Under orders. That meant, I thought, Kaz-alrhun, the only person I'd met in the east who could possibly master an Ifrit. "But none of them are dead yet?"

A few more days of life seemed a glorious reprieve — but then I didn't know yet what the Ifrit's tests might entail.

"I'm hungry and soon I'll be ready for a nap," he said, not answering my question. He lifted me up and put me on his shoulder. "Hold onto my hair." I took hold of three strands of greasy hair the size of cables and, as he rose from the ground, I grabbed onto his ear lobe as well. He flew swiftly, pausing once to swoop down and scoop up something from the sand.

I could see a little better now; we were indeed in the circular valley. Ahead was a group of palms, doubtless marking a spring, though I could not remember seeing them from the pass in the valley wall. The afternoon sun had dipped low. When we reached the far side of the valley, the Ifrit landed on the ground and reached up to pluck me from his shoulder. He placed me by his foot, then opened his other clawed hand to set something next to me. It was Joachim.

The chaplain sat up slowly, looking dazed. I staggered toward him.

The Ifrit bent to smile down on us, showing a row of enormous yellow teeth. "Do you want something to eat, too, little men?"

"There's plenty!" came a completely unexpected woman's voice.

Gripping each other by the arms, Joachim and I turned toward the voice. We saw the last thing I had expected, a slim, young, human woman wearing a big white apron and tending a fire. Three sheep carcasses were broiling over it.

She had black hair and eyes but very white skin, full breasts, and wore a gold necklace above the apron. Strung along the necklace were a number of rings.

She gave us a sharp, appraising glance. While we stared at her dumbfounded, she pulled one of the carcasses away from the fire and sliced off a large portion. "I'm having some myself," she said. "You'd better take some while you have a chance. The Ifrit doesn't need to eat very often and he sometimes forgets that humans do."

"Thank you," said Joachim gravely. I found I had nothing to say.

"You're a priest?" she asked, handing him a plate. "That should make it more interesting." For some reason she started to laugh.

"Have you seen the others?" Joachim asked me in a low voice.

"No one but you," I answered. "I don't even know if Maffi was able to get away while the Ifrit was distracted by the rest of us."

The mutton tasted surprisingly good. The nose and mouth could still appreciate fresh hot food, even if we were about to die.

The Ifrit crossed his legs and sat down, bringing him closer to our level but not by much. He tossed down a handful of melons as though they had been currents, then picked up a whole sheep carcass on its spit and bit into it. Greasy juice ran down his chin; he licked it off with a wide pink tongue.

"You didn't say thank you!" the woman shouted up at him, giving him a rap on the knee with a poker.

He bobbed his head. "Thank you, my dear." She smiled, satisfied, and he continued chewing.

"So, how do you like my wife?" he asked when he had finished the first batch of mutton and was reaching for the second. "Isn't she fine? Best cook I've ever had, and the sweetest body."

I was too horrified to answer.

"She's so delicate and graceful, and so pure," the Ifrit continued, pausing to wipe his jaw with an arm. "She keeps me amused. I like to call her my wife because she was going to be some human's wife when I captured her. She probably doesn't perform quite the services for me that she would for a man, but she keeps me happy!" Both the Ifrit and the woman laughed long and loud at this.

"I was a maiden pure, ready for my marriage to a prince," she said to us. "Not that I wanted to marry him! But this Ifrit came to the wedding like a hurricane. The prince had boasted that everyone who heard his voice must obey his command, that he could have ordered even Ifriti to attend the wedding if he had wanted. But I think he got more than he expected! The Ifrit scattered the decorations and killed half the guests — including the prince." From her tone, it had not bothered her very much. "Me, however, he treated very carefully, putting me onto his shoulder when he flew away. And I've been with him ever since."

The Ifrit finished the last of the mutton and stretched. "That was a good meal, my dear. Now I think I'll take my little nap. Come here and scratch my head while I fall asleep."

She took off the apron; she wore nothing else but her necklace and nearly transparent trousers. Joachim immediately offered her his goat's-hair robe, but she waved it away with a laugh.

The Ifrit lay down on the sand and she sat by him. He took a silver chain, heavy-linked though it was tiny in his hand, and clipped one end to her necklace. The other end he wrapped around one pointed ear.

"In case she gets some idea of trying to escape while I'm asleep," he explained with a wide smile. "When I'm asleep is the only time that I'm not fully aware of what my dear wife does, no matter where I am. Though you never *have* tried to escape, have you?" giving her what I hoped was an affectionate squeeze with his enormous hand.

She plunged her arms into his hair and started to scratch his scalp. "Here's the first test," the Ifrit said sleepily, closing his eyes. "I took her away from her wedding because I wanted to keep her pure and keep her for me. Isn't she lovely? A lot of men have desired her. While I nap, you may desire her yourself. But if you try to take her, I'll feel the tug on my ear, wake up and kill you."

He opened an eye and fixed me with it. "What sort of test is this supposed to be?" I asked, since some comment seemed called for.

"Just a first test, little mage," he said, closing his eyes again. "If the urgings of your body so overcome you that you don't worry about death, then I'll know you wouldn't be very amusing for my next tests." In a minute, he began to snore.

The young woman slowly stopped scratching and withdrew her hands. The snoring never ceased. Then she gave us a wink, reached up and unhooked the silver chain from her necklace. It drooped from the Ifrit's ear with nothing attached to it.

"There," she said, standing up and giving a sensuous stretch, as though showing off her body for us. "He'll be sound asleep for hours now. As long as I reattach the chain before he wakes, he never knows."

"Then you'll be able to escape with us," said Joachim. "Daimbert, do you think you could carry both of us and fly out of here?"

Before I had a chance to tell him that the Ifrit had taken all my magic, including the ability to fly, the young woman burst into laughter.

"Why should I want to escape, especially escape with you?" she said, in a voice I feared would be loud enough to wake the Ifrit, though he slept on contentedly.

"I *like* life with this Ifrit. He brings me whatever I want, even though he sometimes loses track of time. Why, when I told him last year I'd like some silk for new trousers, he brought me an entire silk caravan." This then explained the disappearing caravan Arnulf had tried to multiply in the telling — though not the sign of the cross left behind. "And where else would I find a 'husband' who let me order him around this way? Yet I can still get whatever I want from my own kind. . . ."

She gave us an appraising look again, then nodded abruptly. "Yes, you'll do. Both of you. Come and lie with me."

I had been having too many sudden shocks lately to be able to react at once. But Joachim spoke immediately and politely. "I'm sure this is a very generous offer, but I am a priest and sworn to chastity."

"And the Ifrit — " I stammered.

"That stupid Ifrit imagines I am a maiden still," she said scornfully. "Look at my necklace. I have here the rings of a hundred men who have lain with me while he slept and he's never thought to ask where the rings come from. As they say, 'Whatso woman willeth, the same she fulfilleth, however man nilleth.' I rather like that eagle ring of yours," to me. "I'll even let you keep the other one, the onyx ring. And what's yours," to Joachim, "a seal ring? Just a cross, not very interesting, but I have plainer rings than that."

"I'll give you my ring if you want it, my daughter," said Joachim. "But as I already told you — "

She tossed her head. "What's the matter, priest? Am I not attractive?" She strutted before us, her breasts thrust out. "I hope you can work up some enthusiasm in the next two minutes because, if you refuse to lie with me, I'll wake up the Ifrit and tell him you attacked me, and then he'll kill you."

11

The Ifrit grunted and rolled over. I held my breath, but his eyes never opened; in a moment he was snoring again.

"Listen, Joachim," I said in an undertone. "I'm sure the bishop would understand in a case like this, if — "

"I am, of course, sorry to die," said Joachim in a clear voice, "but I have no choice. I made an oath before God which I cannot broak."

She turned her full attention on him, ignoring me, though at the moment I was having trouble finding her attractive myself. "Your friend will die, too, in that case," she said. "I must have you both or I will scream and wake up the Ifrit."

"Are you working with him in this?" Joachim asked her. "Is he, in fact, fully aware of what you do while he feigns sleep?"

This startled her. "May God be merciful, I hope not," she said in an undertone, with a quick look toward the Ifrit's gigantic back.

"I think if he'd been spying on you he'd have said something before you'd worked your way up to a hundred men," said Joachim reassuringly. "I was merely wondering if the Ifrit's test of us was more subtle than it first appeared."

"Does he try this 'test' very often?" I asked.

"No," she said thoughtfully. "This is the first time he's ever dared a man to touch me. In fact — " She gave his monstrous shoulder a kick with a bare foot. The Ifrit's snore changed its note for a moment, but he did not waken. "God be praised," she said, looking back at us. "For a minute you had me worried he was actually testing *me*."

"Then where have the hundred men come from?" I asked. As long as we kept her talking, I thought, we might be able to keep her distracted from her purpose.

"I've been with the Ifrit for five years," she said, "since he snatched me away from my wedding. In that time we've traveled all around the East, though for this last year for some reason he's stayed close to this boring valley. But every few days he needs to eat, and after he's eaten he likes to take his nap, and there are often men who will hide in a garden's trees or sneak up for a closer look at a sleeping Ifrit. I've had my pick of kings and princes and even mages, and I don't know why you two should feel yourselves too fine for an Ifrit's bride!"

"I certainly can't deny your many charms," said Joachim, "but I am afraid I would give the same answer to the Queen of Sheba. It is not you I reject, but all sins of the flesh."

She sat down, and the chaplain sat next to her. "But I've had priests before," she said, thumbing through the rings on her necklace. "Are you trying to tell me that western priests are purer than eastern priests?"

"Not at all. I judge no man — only his conscience and God can do that. I simply know I must maintain what I am sworn to uphold."

"So you think the flesh is sinful?" she asked, twisting

to look at him coyly over her shoulder. "You do not think my body the gift of God?"

"Ever since the fall," Joachim replied, "mankind has been sinful, *both* body and spirit. We cannot make ourselves pure merely by foresaking the flesh, for the spirit can sin far worse in imagination. But as a priest I need to bring God's word to humanity, and therefore I cannot afford to be distracted by worldly concerns. It is not just the pleasures of the body I have given up, but the companionship of a wife and the joys of children."

"But in the East priests *do* marry. How about married people in the west who need a priest's guidance?" She turned back around and rested her chin on her hand while frowning at him. "Don't they feel you're missing something important?"

"This is an oft-stated concern," the chaplain said gravely. "In the first centuries of Christianity, its priests did frequently marry. Even in more recent years, some of the northern bishoprics have been rumored to allow married priests. But by far the majority of bishops favor a celibate priesthood."

"Here our priests are also our judges and our teachers," she said, looking both thoughtful and interested. "And we don't have women priests."

"I do not know about the priests of the Prophet, but Christianity has always had men as priests. After all, the priesthood established by Aaron was male, and Jesus and his first apostles were all men."

Of all the ways I had desperately tried to imagine to get us out of this, I had to admit that I had not considered discussing church governance and theology with the Ifrit's wife.

"So is it true," she asked, "that all of you in the west really do follow the Nazarene prophet rather than *the* Prophet?"

It had been night for several hours, though a half moon cast a thin blue light, and the fire had burned down to dull coals when the Ifrit's snores changed abruptly to a series of snorts. The woman jumped up from where she and Joachim were still talking and ran to reclip the silver chain to her necklace.

The Ifrit opened his eyes, squinted in the moonlight, and felt his ear. "Aha," he said, unwinding the end of the chain. "So you are still safe and pure, my dear."

"As pure as I've ever been," she agreed, planting a kiss on his stubbly chin.

"Then, little mage," said the Ifrit to me, "I think you'll be interesting enough for the rest of my tests. Are you sure you don't want to show me a magic trick first? No, that's right, I'm not supposed to let you."

I was afraid I knew who might — or might not — order the Ifrit to "let" someone practice magic. But I didn't dare ask about that. "Will your tests involve the rest of my friends?" I asked instead.

"They might, they might," said the Ifrit in a rumble. "I know you humans can't see in the dark very well, so you like to sleep at night. I think I'll leave you all here now, while I go find some more sheep. I believe we ate the last this evening. Maybe I'll get some melons as well. I'll be back in the very early morning, before it's light enough for your human eyes to see properly. I know my wife will be safe with you now that you've passed my test, especially since I can see all and know all when I'm awake."

Leaving us alone with her, if we had actually lusted for her, seemed quite different to me than the Ifrit falling asleep while she was — supposedly — chained to his ear. I rather doubted the Ifrit saw and knew quite as much as he thought. But I did not say so.

"In the morning, little mage," he continued, "while you try some of my tests, perhaps this other man can stay here and keep my wife company. She's been complaining there are too few people in the valley. Would you like that, my dear?"

"Yes," she said, as though surprised at her own answer. "We'll be able to talk. I would like that very much."

"Then sleep now, humans, and take your rest for tomorrow's adventures."

"Just as I was waking up last evening," said the Ifrit, "I heard you — or was it your friend? — talking about the role of sacrifice in your heretical western religion. I've heard you westerners have tried to alter the religion of Solomon, may God preserve his memory."

I again clung to his hair and ear as we flew across the valley floor, far faster than I could ever have flown myself.

"So perhaps one of the tests I should set you and your friends is to see how willing you are to sacrifice yourselves for each other."

After a night of exhausted and dreamless sleep, I had wakened feeling, quite irrationally, more hopeful about our chances of living beyond the next day. But the Ifrit's comment made my heart sink again.

"I'll test you alone first, however," he continued, "before I try to find the rest of your friends — I think I remember where I left them."

I didn't like the implications of "find" any better. Were they all buried beneath the sand?

"You claim to be a mage," said the Ifrit, "so we'll see how you deal with a magical situation I learned about not long ago!"

He began to fly even faster and I held on desperately, my eyes shut against the rushing wind. If he was going to give me a magical test, then he had to allow me access to magic again, but when I tried to reach out to the forces, I found an impermeable wall confining my mind. The words of the Hidden Language were as thoroughly gone as if I had never known them, and how one moved through magic's four dimensions was but the faintest of memories.

When I dared open my eyes again I saw white spires

and an arm of the ocean. Had we come back to the emir's city? Or were those spires some other city on the same estuary? If so, I wondered how I would ever find my way, on foot and without magic or even a map, back to the Wadi Harhammi.

As we dipped lower, I could see that the spires below were certainly not those of Bahdroc. It did indeed look like a city, but a city which had sunk abruptly into the bay. As the Ifrit flew over it, I could look down through clear water to city streets, to courtyards and fountains, to a market place and a princely palace. But all was silent, deep beneath the water. Only the tallest towers emerged, and a walled garden on a hill behind the palace.

The Ifrit set me down at the edge of the bay. "See what you can make of this ensorcelled city, little wizard!" he said with his deep chuckle and drew back, folding his arms and watching me with a grin.

Without magic I couldn't even check to see if the city really was under a spell or had sunk due to an earthquake. But I had no alternative than to try. I took off my shoes, went to the edge of the water and waded in.

The water was scarcely cooler than blood. Fish swam around my feet, the same brilliant blue, red, and gold I had seen in the fish pond in the emir's palace. I had certainly never seen fish like these in the west. The scales glittered and their protruding eyes were fixed on me, but I did not think they were automatons.

They seemed almost tame, swimming close to my feet, barely moving out of the way as I waded deeper. The red fish greatly outnumbered the other colors. I plunged in my hands and grabbed one.

I expected it to wiggle wildly as I drew it up for a closer look. Instead the eyes opened even farther, and the fish mouth gaped until it was as wide as a human mouth. "Beware, oh man, beware!"

I was so surprised that I dropped it, and it swam peacefully away. I bent down to the surface of the water for a better look. It again seemed to have an ordinary fish mouth.

The Ifrit sat a hundred yards back, grinning at me. I tried to ignore him and reached for a gold fish.

Again, as soon as I had it out of water it spoke with a human voice, "Beware, oh man, beware!" This time I managed to put it back in the water carefully, without dropping it. The blue fish was just the same.

"Ensorcelled city," I said to myself, wading back out. It was thoughtful of the fish to try to warn me, but I wished I knew what they were warning me against. Without magic I felt blind. Someone or something — perhaps the Ifrit himself — had turned the inhabitants of this city into fish. Apparently my test was to find out how, or why, and maybe even to turn them back into humans.

In that case, the Ifrit was quite unlikely to answer questions. A question might even be the sign I had failed the test. I turned instead toward the walled garden I had spotted, which stood on what had once been a high hill behind the sunken palace but was now on the shore of the bay. A staircase had descended from the garden to the back of the palace, but its steps now led down only into water.

The garden itself, however, was flourishing. Enormous bushes with purple blooms bent over half-concealed benches; paths led between arbors and fruit trees. I came in by a side gate and wandered for several minutes along the paths, among sweet-smelling flowers and highly decorative brick work. I saw no blue roses, or roses of any color, though I looked. I found myself constantly trying to probe with magic to find whatever malignant force might lurk behind the next bush, but all I could draw on was ordinary human senses.

In the center of the garden was a little round-topped pavilion. I was just starting cautiously toward it when a voice spoke by my elbow.

"Beware, oh man, beware!"

I jumped a foot and whirled, expecting to see a fish crawled up on dry land to warn me — against what I could not imagine. But instead I saw a rather pale young man, wrapped in a black cloak, sitting very still on a bench almost completely hidden under a flowering tree.

"Are you real or a fish?" I asked, then realized how idiotic I must sound.

But he took me quite seriously. "I am still a human," he said, "the only inhabitant of my sad city *not* to be a fish. Do not approach the pavilion if you value your life."

I sat down next to him. The Ifrit's test seemed to have begun. "I appreciate your warning. What is in it?"

"The dying or dead lover of my witch wife."

III

I passed a hand over my forehead. This really would have been much easier with functioning magical abilities. "I'm afraid I don't understand. I'd like to be able to help you and your fish people, but you'll have to tell me first what has happened."

He closed his eyes for a moment, as though gathering his memories or his strength, then looked at me fully. "Know then that I, thanks be to God, was once the prince of this city, and had married a wife, a princess beautiful as the full moon rising, whose eyes were the shadows of evening lamplight and mouth the sweetest of honeys. I married her knowing she was a witch and not caring, for I thought she loved me, too."

My blood went cold and I glanced involuntarily over my shoulder. Even in the west, wizards were suspicious of witches and their half-learned spells, always hovering on the edge of black magic. They tended to deal with the old magic of the earth, knowing little of the

Hidden Language, and were rumored to create monsters in their wombs. I didn't like to think what witches were like here in the east.

"But when we had been married a year, she began to come in the evening to this garden, to sit in the pavilion. At first I accompanied her, but then she said that she preferred to be alone, to feel the evening breezes and think her evening thoughts. I trusted her, for I loved her. I had not yet heard the saying, 'Whatso woman willeth, the same she fulfilleth, however man nilleth.'

"But after another year had passed, when it seemed she came here almost every night and often did not return to our sleeping mat until near the break of day, I became suspicious. When I tried to ask her to sleep by my side instead of in the garden, she first burst into tears and said that I was cruel, then darkened her forehead at me and said that I was a tyrant. She refused to listen to my entreaties but shut herself up with her handmaidens.

"And that night, as I watched in secret and followed her in silence, she went again into this garden. And in the pavilion, the worst of my fears and even worse than my fears were realized, for I found her lying in delight in the arms of my vilest slave!"

"So what did you do?" I asked quietly, when the horror of the memory seemed to have silenced him.

"They had left a lamp burning outside the pavilion; I could see their heads close together, their lips locked in kisses. And I thought that with a single stroke of my sword, I could cut off both their heads together. For I had feared something of this and brought my sword with me.

"But as I drew the blade, she must have heard the sound for she pulled sharply away and I, distracted by her motion, did not strike true. I missed her completely and I cut the slave's neck only halfway through."

Just because we in Yurt never hung anyone, I reminded myself, did not mean that the rest of the world did not assess the death penalty. But I still thought that he had been much too precipitate. I had started to feel sympathetic for this pale young prince, but now I felt sympathy only for the slave.

But the prince was not waiting for my sympathy. "When she saw what I had done, she cursed me with the deepest and blackest of witches' curses. Her hand she thrust straight into the lamp's flame, and she hurled fountains of fire and spells at me that would have destroyed me if they had touched my head. But instead — "

He paused and lifted his black cloak with his left elbow. From the waist up he was still human, but everything below the waist, including his left hand and right arm, which was stretched along his leg with the sword still in his grip, had turned to stone.

"And so you see me, traveler," he continued. "But even this was not enough for her. She turned with a cry of despair when she saw her slave lover almost dead and tried to revive him with her wicked spells and the potions she always carried with her, sobbing and calling him tender names she had never once called me. When she could not heal him immediately, she wrapped him most tenderly, both in blankets and in her perverted magic, and left him in the pavilion.

"Then she went down into the city like the force of vengeance and called on the dark powers that lurk beneath the waves. And in answer to her call, the nameless creatures of night rose up from the deep and swallowed the city. The breakers rolled across it and drowned it, even as you see it now."

"But the fish?" I asked.

"The people might have swum to safety even in the drowning of their city, for we are a sea people and used to swimming, but that would not have satisfied her. So she turned them all into different kinds of fish, red for those who follow the Prophet, gold for the Children of Abraham, and blue for those who follow the Nazarene.

When they are lifted from the water, they can still speak like men, at least a few phrases, but in the sea they are fish, and fish they must remain."

I wondered if they still knew who they really were. Someone transmogrified by western magic would still keep his original identity inside. The brightly colored fish I had seen in the emir's palace — doubtless brought there as a marvel — must think themselves in harsh captivity.

I realized the prince had been silent for several minutes and turned toward him. His deep eyes looked at me in entreaty. "Whoever you may be, traveler, you are the first to enter my garden in the two years since this happened. Are you perhaps sent in answer to my prayers to save me and avenge me upon my wife?"

"I might be," I said slowly. I couldn't see the Ifrit from where we were sitting, but he must still be only a short distance away. I knew it was useless to ask him again for my magic back, though I had no idea how I was going to dissolve a transformations spell without it. Even without the knowledge that he was testing me — and might keep my friends buried in the sand forever if I did not pass — I felt sorry for the fish.

"Does your wife ever come back to gloat over you?" I asked. Maybe I could somehow persuade her to break her own spell.

"Of course. She comes every evening, feeds me just enough to keep me alive, and then whips me until I sob with pain, to punish me again for what I did to her lover. I would have died from the blows many months ago — and often I wish I could — but she then salves my wounds with wicked magic so that I may heal by the next day and be beaten again. Then she crawls into the pavilion with the slave — that is why I warned you not to go in, for fear she would realize someone had been there. She calls on him tenderly and caresses him and begs him to be healed quickly. So far he has never answered her."

I put my head in my hands. The slave must be long

dead if he did not respond to magic which could heal the wounds from a whipping in a day. His body must only be kept from decay by some variation of the spell that held together the body of the wizard of the eastern kingdoms.

When I lifted my head again, the prince was almost smiling. "Are you perhaps a mage?"

"No." It was too complicated to explain. "But I think I have an idea."

I sat on the bench beside him all afternoon. He told me more about his city before all its people became fish. I was able to deflect his rather desultory questions about where I had come from — for him, the chief interesting thing about me was that I might save him. Late in the afternoon, somewhere in the distance, I began to hear singing.

"It is my people," said the young prince softly. "When they were still human, they used to sing as the sun set; even now that they are fish, they rise to the surface each day at this time to salute the day's passing."

The singing died away with the coming of twilight, and not long thereafter the prince whispered to me, "The witch usually comes at about this time, so make your preparations."

"Do not fear, for you will be a free man tonight." I stood up, hoping this was going to work.

I slipped quietly down to the little round pavilion and found my way in by feel. Slowly I groped my way across the floor until my hand found another hand, very cold.

I jerked back, just managing to stay quiet. If this was the slave, he seemed quite dead. I felt forward again and found his body, lying amid a heap of pillows and blankets on a sleeping mat. I lifted him up as well as I could, just as glad I could not see his slashed throat, and carefully carried him out the far side of the pavilion. There had already been too many slashed throats for me on this trip. I slid the slave under a bush and went back into the pavilion just as a bobbing light appeared at the garden gate.

I lay down on the mat where the dead slave had lain, but the light did not immediately approach. Instead, it was set down on the bench by the young prince. In the light of her lamp I could see the prince's witch wife. If eastern witches could touch someone's mind and tell who they were, she would know in a second that I was here. To the prince, she might have been as lovely as the full moon rising. To me she looked terrifying.

But she did not seem to have any immediate suspicions. First she fed the prince and gave him water to drink out of a skin, laughing mockingly at his inability to move more than his head and left elbow. Then she pulled out a whip and stepped back, her face dark with fury.

"For wishing to kill me," she shouted, "for almost killing my beloved, you deserve death and worse than death! As long as he hovers on the edge of life, you will pray to God each day that you might die!"

The young prince stood it for about five lashes, then started to whimper. When he began to cry out in pain, then to beg the witch by the love they had once shared, by her love for the slave, and by the love of God not to hit him again, her blows only intensified.

Lying where the slave had died, I put my hands over my ears. Without magic, there was no way I could oppose a witch with a whip in her hand and probably the supernatural forces of darkness in her spells. I had to wait for her to tire and to rub her salves into the prince's wounds. Even with magic, I certainly could not heal him overnight myself.

She seemed satisfied at last and put her whip away. The prince had slumped as much as he could being half stone and he no longer seemed conscious. But when she brought out little pots that glowed with a green light and rubbed the salve onto his back, he slowly revived and straightened again. "Until tomorrow night, husband?" she murmured in triumph.

But then her whole manner changed. She lifted up the lamp and approached the pavilion, slowly and almost shyly. I took a deep breath, tried to imagine how a slave might address a princess who was also his lover, and called out to her.

"Mistress, dear mistress, don't bring that light here, by the love we long shared!"

She was so startled she dropped the lamp and it smashed on the pavement by her feet.

Good. The spells of fire were no longer available to her. "It hurts my eyes, dearest daughter of the stars, and it has been so long since I've had my eyes open!"

She came toward me again with an indrawn breath of delight. "Is it then true, my darling, my pomegranate, my own? Are you alive again at last? You seem somehow — different!"

"Stay back, my precious one!" I said in a weak voice. If she crawled in here with me, even without the lamp, I wouldn't deceive her for long. And I was quite sure that after she had whipped me near or even to death, she would not put her magic salves on *me*. "I only seem different because it has been two years since we last lay together. But don't approach me yet. Even your delicate touch might set back my healing."

"But it's been so long since I heard your dear voice!"

And you won't hear it again until you meet your lover in hell, I thought. This was even harder than I'd expected. "My healing was slowed, my sweet," I gasped, "by all the noises I must endure."

"Noises?"

"The singing of the fish," I said. "The sounds of an ordinary city I could bear quite easily, but the sad wail of men and women made fish makes my heart break anew each evening."

She was silent for a moment, while I hoped she was thinking over my comment and feared she was beginning to suspect me. Her witch-magic, I thought, did not give her the ability to touch another mind or she would have long since realized the slave was dead, but if I already seemed "different" I would not be able to stall her much more.

"All right, then, my sweet," she said in abrupt decision. "Anything to make you more comfortable. I'll turn the fish back to themselves."

The moon was brightening and I could see the witch return to the materials she had brought with her to the garden. I wondered briefly if the dark powers she commanded through fire and potions might be playing with her, allowing her as a subtle and demonical form of torture to think her lover was still alive.

She poured some liquid into a dish, murmured low words over it until silver sparks cascaded upwards, then cried aloud and clapped her hands. The ground shifted below us, from the bottom of the hill came a massive roaring of water and, abruptly, the city rose from the bay.

I lay flat until the earth stopped moving. I didn't think anybody in the west had command of forces like this. When I lifted my head again it was to hear voices, human voices, babbling together in surprise and joy. Out the far side of the pavilion, I saw lights flicking on in the city below the garden. The emir would have quite a shock the next time he visited his fish pond. The prince's people were people once again.

The witch did not give me time to appreciate my success. "Are you satisfied now, dearest one?" she asked from just outside the pavilion.

"Thank you, my own, that is much better. But there is still another noise which has long hindered my healing."

"And what is that?"

I was tempted for a moment to leave the prince turned half to stone. But if Joachim didn't feel he could judge eastern priests, I shouldn't judge someone for murdering his wife's lover — especially since in the last two years he had been punished cruelly. "It is the prince, your husband," I said. "His moans and cries at night keep me from healing sleep. Even in the day I feel so much for his pain that I am almost mad."

"Then he shall be restored as well," she said comfortingly. Again she poured liquid in a dish and spoke words over it. This time, when the silver sparks rose and she clapped her hands, the stone of the prince's lower half split with a crack, and he slowly rose to his feet.

"But now I can bear it no longer, dearest slave!" she cried and rushed into the pavilion before I could stop her. She seized me wildly and pulled me toward her.

We both froze as the white moonlight fell on my face. The witch slowly pushed herself backwards. "You — you are not — " But before she could blast me with magic, she turned and saw the prince behind her.

I had forgotten he still, after two years, held the sword with which he had killed the slave. But he had not forgotten. He roared almost as loudly as the waters pouring from the streets of his city and rushed at his wife. She shrieked and fled, kicking over her magic bowls and potions as she went. As I crept, trembling, out of the pavilion, I could hear their cries retreating in the distance.

A shadow was between me and the moon. I looked up and saw the Ifrit descending into the garden. He broke several flower bushes with his gigantic feet as he landed.

"Not bad, little mage," he said with a chuckle. "You have freed the ensorcelled city. I think I have tested you enough to provide plenty of amusement and can start now on the rest of your friends."

"What about the prince of this city? Is he going to kill his wife?"

"As God wills, so it happens," said the Ifrit without

interest. "We could follow them, or would you rather have me find those other humans you were with when I first saw you?"

"My friends, of course." At this point, I no longer cared whether the prince killed his witch wife or she turned him to stone again — or even whether they made peace with each other. "But first, could you help me bury this body?"

The Ifrit scraped a deep hole under the bushes with a finger and I lowered the slave into it. "He *is* dead, isn't he?" I asked in sudden doubt.

"Of course," said the Ifrit in surprise. "He's been dead since the first day after the prince attacked him. I thought all you humans knew how easily you die. It must be strange," he added thoughtfully, pushing the dirt over the body.

IV

We flew back that night to the circular valley. Joachim and the Ifrit's wife seemed to be getting along very well. "The Ifrit's still testing me," I told him. "Today I managed to trick a witch into turning some fish she had ensorcelled back into people," but I said no more. The Ifrit still refused to tell us anything about the others.

But at dawn he snatched Joachim and me up and out of sleep, setting each of us on a shoulder, and flew straight upwards while we were still halfway between dream and a waking that seemed more desperately unreal than any dream.

"I think I remember now where I put your friends," he said in a low rumble and reached out his arm. I had just gotten my eyes properly open when the dawn sky around us snapped, flared, and turned over.

I clung wildly to the Ifrit's hair, my eyes clamped shut. Every angle felt upside down. But in a moment the world straightened out again. As we had flown straight up, we now descended until we hovered a short distance above the valley floor. Directly below us and immediately on the defensive was the rest of our party from Yurt.

"Put down your swords," Joachim called. "This Ifrit will not harm us."

I doubted this myself, but knew that the most Hugo could have accomplished by sticking his sword into the Ifrit's foot would have been all of our immediate deaths.

They were camped at a small date-palm oasis which I could have sworn was not in the valley a few minutes ago. Even the horses were there, except for Whirlwind.

"Where have you been?" I gasped to Ascelin and he to us, as the Ifrit set the chaplain and me down. They all looked weary but unharmed.

"Here in the valley," we all answered together. I glanced up at the Ifrit, who stood watching and smiling, his arms crossed. I knew perfectly well the others had not been here. But then there was now no sign of the Ifrit's wife, though we could not have flown a quarter mile of horizontal distance since we left her. It was as though the Ifrit's magic allowed more than one reality to exist simultaneously within this valley.

There was no time to explore the implications of this, to wonder if the Wadi Harhammi was here too somewhere, hidden by the Ifrit's magic. "The Ifrit's taken my magical abilities from me," I said. "I can't even tell what's real anymore."

"No magic?" said Dominic. "This is going to make it harder." He turned his ruby ring thoughtfully on his finger. It still pulsed slowly with light. "There's been no sign of the boy and my stallion. We hadn't even seen the Ifrit again since he first appeared and we were whirled through the air to this oasis. But we hoped that if we stayed here in the valley you'd be able to locate us again if you were still alive."

"Do you think your friends are ready for their tests, little wizard?" called the Ifrit to me.

"I'm ready to ask you if you know what happened to my father!" Hugo shouted back.

"He's probably dead, whoever he was," said the Ifrit with a shrug. "Most humans are dead, sooner or later."

Hugo whipped out his sword again. I could have stopped him if I still had my magic, but ordinary human reflexes were too slow. Before I could reach him he lunged forward and drove his sword into the spot where the Ifrit's leg had been a second before.

"None of that!" cried the Ifrit angrily, putting his foot back down and picking Hugo up by the back of the neck. "I may be immortal, but I bleed the same as any of God's creation!"

Hugo kicked and struggled and tried to swing around to stab at the hand that held him. The Ifrit frowned. "You seem to want to fight. Maybe that should be your test. But who should I have you fight? Not me, because I'd crush you at once and that would only be amusing for a few seconds."

This stopped Hugo's struggles for the moment.

"I know!" said the Ifrit happily. "You can fight another human. How about — hmmm. How about this one?" He seized Ascelin with the other hand.

The prince hung, dignified, from the Ifrit's grip on the back of his shirt. "We could give a demonstration of swordwork for your amusement if you like."

"No," said the Ifrit, peering at him with a frown. "That would not be amusing enough. I know! I'll have you fight to the death."

He set Hugo and Ascelin down. They stood uncertainly, their hands on their hilts. "Go ahead!" said the Ifrit impatiently. "This will be your chance to entertain me. I want to see what humans do when they are fighting for their lives."

They glanced questioningly at King Haimeric and at me. "Go ahead and fence," I said slowly, hoping desperately that a good sword fight would satisfy the Ifrit, that he was not serious about making them fight to the death.

They took off their goat's-hair robes and slid their shields onto their arms. Hugo removed his earring and they both tied back their hair before strapping on their helmets. Only their eyes showed as they exchanged the ritual taps of the sword that begin a tournament duel. They took a few moments to get the feel of the sandy surface, circling each other slowly, then Hugo suddenly lashed out and landed a blow on Ascelin's shield.

I had often seen Hugo practicing his swordwork, but could never remember having seen Ascelin in the tournament ring. He was extremely good. He had all the moves, the sudden thrusts, the ability to catch a sword either on his own sword or his shield, the quick turn to avoid a blow. When they had fought for ten minutes he was still not even breathing hard. Hugo didn't have anything like Ascelin's height or experience, but he was twenty years younger and even quicker.

I'd never been trained in swordwork myself, yet I could still appreciate how they managed to rain an impressive number of blows on each other, with sharp swords at that, without ever hurting the other. Their shields rang again and again; their armor flashed in the sun. Even tournament sword fighting was intended to make the other fighter drop his blade and yield, but these two could have been engaged in a dance, ready to keep on indefinitely.

"Stop!" shouted the Ifrit and thrust a fist into the sand between them. They stopped.

"You aren't really fighting," he said.

Hugo pulled off his helmet and mopped his brow. "I'll fight harder if you'll help me find my father, if he's still alive."

The Ifrit dismissed this. "I'm not interested in whatever relatives of yours might or might not be alive at the moment. I already said I want you to fight to the death."

"And what do you offer in return?" I called up to him, though I was afraid I already knew the answer.

"I don't 'offer' anything," said the Ifrit angrily. "I

don't know why you humans always seem to feel that Ifriti exist to grant your foolish wishes. Maybe I want you to grant *me* wishes for a change! I want to see an exciting fight where you know you're going to die."

Joachim tried to say something, but it was no use. The Ifrit snatched up the four of us who were not fighting, two in each hand. "Say you'll fight properly or I'll crush these friends of yours now."

Ascelin's eyes grew dark. "Of course I'll face death for them."

The Ifrit smiled and set us down on the far side of his foot from Hugo and Ascelin. The king coughed and clung to Dominic for support.

"So, you are ready to sacrifice yourself," said the Ifrit to Ascelin, sounding pleased. "But it won't be amusing if you just stand there and let this hot-headed little man kill you. You," to the king. "Order one to kill the other, and the other to defend himself."

King Haimeric bent his head. "I cannot order either one to do that. You can do what you like to me."

I had a nightmare feeling of paralysis, facing events moving far too fast, but if this was a nightmare I should have waked up long ago.

"I'm not going to kill you before you've had your turn to amuse me," said the Ifrit irritably to the king. "You two warriors! I want one of you to kill the other one, now! I don't care which one. But I do know how to make it more interesting. I'll give the winner the chance to live a little longer."

"And then?" said Hugo cautiously.

"And then I will kill him as punishment," said the Ifrit with satisfaction. "Slowly, maybe over a week or two. I think I will kill him both slowly and painfully."

They both looked at me. Just because I had once known western magic, they seemed to think I had some sort of insight into Ifriti. All I could do was shake my head. "He means it."

Hugo seemed to be working his way from misery over his father to indignation and anger. "So he's not going to let either of us go, no matter what we do? He wants to watch one of us die by the sword, and the other one by torture?"

"That's certainly what he says."

Ascelin turned sharply and pulled his helmet back on. "Defend yourself just enough to keep the Ifrit happy," he said to Hugo in a low voice. "We're both dead anyway. I'll kill you as quickly and painlessly as I can."

"But — " Hugo pulled his helmet back on as well and raised his sword. His voice was hollow from inside the helmet. "That means you'll let the Ifrit torture you!"

"Shut up and obey me," said Ascelin roughly. His first blow caught Hugo unprepared and sent him staggering.

But the young lord recovered quickly and swung up his shield. "You're not my prince!" he yelled. "I don't have to obey you!"

"Yes, you do," said Ascelin grimly, landing another blow. "That's right, appear to defend yourself. I'll try to make this quick."

"That's better," said the Ifrit with satisfaction, watching with his hands on his hips. "I don't know why you humans always raise so many objections to everything."

They were both really fighting now. All I had ever seen, close up, was tournament fighting, but even I could tell the difference. Their swords flashed faster than I could follow and their feet churned up the sandy soil. It would have been thrilling if it was not so terrible. Ascelin slowly backed Hugo toward a boulder, using his superior height and reach to full advantage. But the younger man ducked under what looked like a fatal thrust and landed a glancing blow on Ascelin's arm as he darted away.

Ascelin stopped and looked at him. Blood seeped

slowly onto his sleeve. "You aren't listening, Hugo."

"No, *you* aren't listening! If this Ifrit's already killed my father, I don't care what he does to me! I'll try to make this quick, Ascelin."

Without answering, Ascelin sprang forward. Their swords rebounded with great clangs from each other's helmets. Blood and sweat were dripping from them both now. I thought sickly that at least neither one of them would still be alive for the Ifrit to kill slowly. Joachim was murmuring under his breath again.

"Hugo!" said Ascelin, stepping back for a second. "Stop defending yourself! I know you don't like this, but it's for your own good."

Hugo didn't give him a chance to finish before he was on him, swinging his sword wildly. "I told you I'm not going to obey you! This is *my* quest, for my father, and you've been bossing me the entire trip, but you can't do it anymore!"

Ascelin caught Hugo's sword tip in his shield and gave a sharp jerk, wrenching it from the younger man's hand. But as he drove his own sword forward, Hugo dropped, rolled, grabbed his sword again, and bounced back to his feet behind Ascelin. The prince whirled just in time. I turned my head away, unable to watch.

"Ifrit!" came a bellow from beside me. "Ifrit! You must make them stop!"

It was a voice, loud and ringing, I could never recall hearing before. But when I turned I saw it was the king.

Hugo and Ascelin were both so surprised that they stopped, twenty feet apart, eyeing each other warily.

"Sire?" said Dominic cautiously.

King Haimeric, as slight and white-haired as ever, glared up at the Ifrit, trembling like a leaf in the wind but completely determined. "All I can offer you is myself, but I'm not going to let you make them kill each other!"

"And who do you think you are, little man?" said the amused Ifrit, lifting him on his palm to face level.

"I am King Haimeric of Yurt."

"Yurt," said the Ifrit softly, and the color drained from his dark cheeks. "I've heard of Yurt."

V

"If you've heard of Yurt," said the king determinedly, "then you know it is a kingdom where no one, not even criminals, is put to death."

"I was told," said the Ifrit, still very softly and as though he had not even heard this remark, "to watch for people from Yurt."

"And what were you supposed to do with us when we came?" demanded King Haimeric.

"I wasn't supposed to kill you," said the Ifrit unhappily. "Or at least not right away," he added, brightening.

"Then you can't make my warriors fight to the death," said the king firmly.

"I guess not," said the Ifrit glumly. "You, little warriors there! Stop killing each other."

Both Hugo and Ascelin collapsed where they stood, dropping their shields and swords and reaching up for their helmets with trembling fingers.

"How did the king do that?" I said to the chaplain as we rushed toward them. "I couldn't have changed the Ifrit's mind even if I had all my magical abilities. Maybe I've been using magic as a crutch all these years."

Joachim gave me what might have been a smile. "If so then I've been using religion the same way. Each of us has to use the abilities we are given, and Haimeric is a king and born to command."

Dominic and I helped the fighters remove their armor; Joachim found the bandages and Ascelin's salves. The two were bruised all over and nicked and bleeding on the parts of their bodies not protected by mail. None of the cuts were deep, but there were enough that I thought they both would have an impressive collection of scars — that is, if they lived long enough for the cuts to heal. Hugo fell asleep while we were still bandaging him.

"Christ," said Ascelin, his head between his knees. "That kid's good. Why wouldn't he let me kill him cleanly?"

"Be glad he wouldn't," said Dominic. "At least you're both still alive — for the moment. Stop twitching and let me get this bandage tight."

"I remember now," said the Ifrit slowly. "You people of Yurt have a secret. I'm supposed to make you tell me. Or maybe you're supposed to give something to me."

"What kind of secret?" the king asked.

"That's what I'm asking you!"

It was hard enough trying to deal with an unpredictable and enormously powerful magical being without dealing with a stupid one as well. "If you let me have my magical powers back," I called up, "I think I could tell you."

The Ifrit lowered the king abruptly to the ground, where Dominic caught him, and lifted me up instead. "Tell me first," he said avidly.

I looked into his terrifying huge eyes, weighing my words carefully. If the Ifrit wasn't supposed to kill us, it was certainly because Kaz-alrhun — or even some other powerful mage — thought we had a secret and wanted it. Once we gave up that secret, there would be no reason to keep us alive. My only hope was to satisfy the Ifrit for the moment. Then maybe we could find some way to escape — perhaps while he was asleep — before whoever had the power to master an Ifrit arrived to tell him he could kill us at his leisure.

In the meantime, it again seemed that everyone else knew something about Yurt that we did not.

"So what's the secret?" asked the Ifrit eagerly.

Since I had no idea what the real secret was, I had to stall him with something plausible. "It's this ring," I said, showing him the onyx. "See, it's even carved with the word Yurt."

"I can't read," said the Ifrit, frowning. "That other mage also wanted me to read."

"Your wife will read it for you," I suggested.

The Ifrit smiled at this, showing his enormous yellow teeth. "I'm sure she'd enjoy meeting you all."

Again the earth turned under us. What seemed a dozen suns raced across the valley's sky. When the whirling sand had again settled, the Ifrit's wife stood in the middle of our confused group.

"Do you think you have enough food for our guests, my dear?" asked the Ifrit.

It took a while to introduce everyone, to try to explain to the scandalized king exactly how this nearly naked woman could be called the Ifrit's wife. By the time that she had assured the Ifrit that the onyx ring was indeed carved with the name of the kingdom of Yurt, the noon sun had passed over, and I had been able to come up with a plan that might work. Maybe.

"Now, I can't perform the magic spell attached to this ring as long as you won't let me have my abilities back," I said, neglecting to mention I still had no idea what kind of spell it was. "But I can tell you what you can do with your own magical powers. Try a fairly generalized spell, one that will put any sort of nearly complete spell into action."

To my surprise, the Ifrit frowned. "I've never been very good at spells."

"But how do you work magic?" I demanded, shocked.

"I don't know, I guess I just do it," he said as though embarrassed.

I looked at his lowered green head and considered this. As a magical creature, perhaps even an immortal one, he did not need to learn the Hidden Language as did humans. Western magic had been channeled and rationalized by generations of wizards, but magic here, as I already knew, was far less focused. Magic for the Ifrit must be more like breathing than thinking.

"All right," I said. "Don't worry about doing any spells of your own if it seems too complicated. Just look at this ring" — I didn't dare give it to him for fear it would be so tiny in his hand that he would lose it — "and command it by whatever magic comes to you naturally to work its spell."

The Ifrit raised his eyes to me and gave me a terrible glance. He might be stupid, but I could not let myself forget for a second how dangerous he was. "You don't need to patronize me, little mage," he said coldly.

He grabbed my hand, ring and all, and pulled it up to eye level, the rest of me dangling painfully. He muttered syllables that might have been the Hidden Language — if I could still recognize it. The onyx ring trembled on my finger and buzzed.

His lips parted in a grin of triumph. "All right, ring of Yurt, let's see what your secret is."

The air around us began to tremble and glitter, as though again we were about to be shaken off a tablecloth, but this time the earth stayed still. As I looked around wildly, the empty valley near us began to fill up: first another oasis a short distance away, then a tangle of flowering bushes, then a rocky watercourse cutting across the valley floor, then a rider on an enormous black steed, then briefly a collection of baggage wagons; and suddenly, just for a few seconds, a small group of men in the middle distance.

The Ifrit gave a roar and shook me and the ring violently. The empty valley resumed its calm existence. But in those few seconds, I thought I saw that one of the group of men, beneath his desert headdress, had red hair.

"Mirage," I said aloud as the Ifrit dumped me

unceremoniously back on the ground. "It's a ring that creates mirages."

"Or lets you see things I do not want you to see," said the Ifrit grumpily. "I should kill you right now for seeing them."

I sat up, rubbing an elbow. Prince Vlad in the eastern kingdoms had told me he had put a special spell on the ruby ring, a spell we would need in the Wadi Harhammi. When Elerius set out to make a substitute magic ring for Arnulf, he must have chosen a spell that would reveal that which was magically hidden — as images reflected from the desert sky revealed cities and lakes far ahead in mirages. I could tell from its effects that it was a good spell, one I could not have duplicated even if I had my magic and my books. If the Wadi Harhammi still kept its secrets after fifty years and if Kaz-alrhun was trying to get in, it was exactly the sort of ring he would want.

This explained, then, why Kaz-alrhun had not pursued us from Xantium. He knew exactly where we were going and thought he might play with us by letting us think we had gotten away. But we, with his onyx ring, would arrive just as surely at the Wadi, where the Ifrit would watch over us until the mage arrived.

But was the red-haired man I had glimpsed really Evrard and, if so, who was the rider on the black horse? "Did you capture some other travelers in the valley recently?" I asked casually.

"I don't think this is a very interesting secret," said the Ifrit, scowling at the ring and not answering my question.

"Have you seen someone on a flying horse?" I tried again.

This got the Ifrit's attention. "The person on the flying horse was not very amusing," he said.

If the man on the black horse was real, then the other group was also real, which might mean that Sir

Hugo's party was right here in the valley with us, even though hidden by the Ifrit's magic.

I glanced toward Hugo. He was trying to sit up enough to eat. The Ifrit's wife seemed taken with him and bustled around, offering him choice tidbits of fruit. In the meantime, I didn't dare say anything to him about his father; he had had his hopes raised too often already.

It could have been either Arnulf or King Warin with the ebony horse, come to try to find the secret of the Wadi Harhammi but caught by the Ifrit before he could fly away again. If it was King Warin, I abruptly found myself hoping the Ifrit would protect us from him.

It was ironic, I thought wryly, to be seeking safety in an unpredictable creature who had planned to kill us — and still might.

"This is just the first part of the secret, Ifrit," I said. "So far I've proved to you that I'm not bluffing. But the man who commanded you to capture us might not want even you to know the rest, at least not yet, so I'd better wait until he comes. In the meantime, you promised to let me have my magical powers back."

He had in fact promised nothing of the sort, but he did not contradict me. "They're probably around here someplace," he muttered.

He said nothing more, only set me down on the ground again. But slowly at first, like the first trickle of water in a dry streambed, then more and more rapidly, I could feel knowledge of the Hidden Language coming back. It was as though blinders had been removed from my eyes and plugs from my ears. The world around me seemed much more real, much more visible and intense, when I could experience it with magic as well as normal human senses.

Even knowing we would all be dead shortly, I felt filled with unbounded delight. I was so grateful to the Ifrit for restoring my abilities, even though he had taken them away originally, that I could have kissed his stubbly cheek.

But I knew even more intensely than I had already guessed that my own knowledge of magic was trivial and indeed useless for combatting the Ifrit.

"Thank you!" I called up to him with my best smile. My mind seemed to be working much more clearly. "Could you tell me a little more about the man who commanded you to watch for us? I want to be ready when he comes."

The Ifrit frowned. "I am furious with him," he said after a moment. I didn't know if this was good or bad. "He was the mage who first freed me from Solomon's spell."

Kaz-alrhun, I thought. "And why are you furious with him?" I prompted.

"I granted his first wish, but he then betrayed me," said the Ifrit grumpily. "I let him have two wishes for letting me out of the bottle, of course, although he made me agree to come grant them whenever he called, wherever he might be. He finally called for his first wish last year, ordering me to guard this valley and keep my captives alive, especially people from Yurt."

Everyone in the East, except us, I was now convinced, knew something special about Yurt.

"But one of the people from Yurt put me back into the bottle," continued the Ifrit.

For a second I had a nightmare sense that either I had met this Ifrit before without remembering it or there was some other kingdom of Yurt somewhere that I ought to know about.

"The mage must have given him the bottle on purpose," added the Ifrit with wounded dignity. "Therefore I do not think I will answer when he summons me a second time."

I looked up at the Ifrit's furrowed brow. "In that case," I said craftily, "if the mage is not coming and you're supposed to keep us safe until he does, then you'll have to keep us alive forever." As long as we were still alive, I intended to escape well before forever came.

The Ifrit seated himself slowly on an enormous boulder and thought this over. "But the other man," he said, "the one who freed me the second time, said I should kill anyone who came to the valley, except for those other people from Yurt."

It looked as though the Ifrit had gotten himself into a moral dilemma by granting contradictory wishes to different people. I hoped to find out what had happened someday myself. "In the meantime you have to keep everyone from Yurt alive," I said firmly.

I left him trying to work through this and hurried back to the others. It sounded as though someone powerful might still appear at any minute, even if the Ifrit did refuse to grant the mage's second wish. I was in time to get some of the melon and settled myself again to look at the onyx ring. Now that I knew what kind of spell Elerius had put on it, I might have some chance of unraveling it.

"I keep thinking about that boy and my stallion," said Dominic, sitting down beside me. "Do you think he was simply trying to escape the Ifrit or was he going to alert someone after having led us into a trap?"

"It just looked like panicked flight to me," I said. "I don't know where he'd go. The emir's city wouldn't be safe for him and it took us many weeks of travel to get here from Xantium."

"It wouldn't take him nearly as long to get back, riding Whirlwind all out, especially if he didn't detour to the Holy City. I'm beginning to wonder, Wizard, if we should start expecting that mage."

"It would certainly take Maffi much longer than two days to reach Xantium," I said, "even on Whirlwind. And the Ifrit's just told me he's not answering any magical calls from the mage." I stopped speaking abruptly to concentrate more fully at the onyx ring.

While talking to Dominic, I had been teasing at it

delicately with little tendrils of magic. Suddenly I saw the whole spell as clearly as though it had been written out, step by step, in a book of wizardry. I could see exactly which words of the Hidden Language Elerius had used, the complicated and quite inventive way he had combined a spell of discovery with a spell of sight, his elegant means of attaching the spell to the onyx so that it was permanently latent in the stone yet would need someone with fairly powerful magic — or at least the right powerful spell — to put it into action.

I knew at once which words to say and, for a second, the valley again flickered with other mirage-like images, even if no one could see them but me.

But this was wrong. I had never been able to visualize a spell like this in my life, even my own. I knew I wasn't this good. In fact, I didn't think anyone was.

I looked up, startled, toward the Ifrit. Had he given me his magical abilities instead of my own?

No, because with this strange clarity I now had, it was quite plain that I had nothing more than the mix of school magic, herbal magic and improvisation I had always had, and the Ifrit had his own enormous fund of powerful though unfocused magic. But the difference now was my ability to recognize a spell and all its attributes.

"I think I see the difference at last," I said excitedly to Dominic, who didn't have the slightest idea what I was talking about. "Western magic is organized scientifically. There's very little scientific about eastern magic. That's why Melecherius had so much trouble explaining it, even if he understood it himself. Instead, it's an art."

"Do you and this scientific art know how to get us out of here?" asked Dominic.

"I'm working on it," I said. If this clarity only lasted, I should be able to discover the spell on Dominic's ruby ring as well. Maybe if the Ifrit wanted to take a nap and he took his wife off with him somewhere while he did so, then I could try to use the onyx to locate Sir Hugo's party and we could —

"What's that?" said Dominic sharply.

I looked up quickly, putting together far more easily than I ever had before a scientific far-seeing spell.

It was a flying carpet, soaring over the steep edge of the valley and approaching us rapidly. Seated on it were Maffi and the massive black bulk of Kaz-alrhun.

PART EIGHT

The Wadi Harhammi

1

I wrapped my magic firmly around me and stood up to meet Kaz-alrhun. He hopped off the carpet as soon as it had set down gracefully on the sandy soil. "If you are here to gloat over us," I said with dignity, "and to watch your Ifrit kill us, you might at least let us know first why everyone in the East seems to find the mention of Yurt so exciting."

But he ignored me. "Ifrit!" he shouted. "In the name of God, the all compassionate, I adjure you not to harm the tiniest hair on the heads of these people!"

My suppositions shifted wildly, but I had nothing with which to replace them. I had steeled myself to face a mage who was about to order the Ifrit to kill us, and instead he had just commanded the Ifrit to spare us.

An enormous bare foot was suddenly between Kaz-alrhun and me as the Ifrit stepped forward. He picked up the mage to peer at him. "They *do* have rather tiny hairs," he agreed, running a clawed hand through his own thick locks. His voice was about ten octaves lower than the mage's. "But I am guarding this valley and they came tumbling in. So did you, for that matter. Are you from Yurt?"

"Do you want me to bind you by the name of the Most High, as King Solomon once bound you?" Kaz-alrhun demanded. He was putting a paralysis spell together, one which I would never have been able to duplicate, full of eastern tricks and connections unlike anything I'd ever seen before but which I could observe as clearly now as though it were a picture before my eyes. I wasn't sure it really would bind an Ifrit, but it looked as though it had greater potential than anything of mine.

"All right," replied the Ifrit sulkily. He bent to put the mage back down on the ground. "I wasn't going to make them die an evil death anyway or, at least, not yet."

I expected Kaz-alrhun to accept this agreement, but he abruptly smiled, flashing a gold tooth, and threw his paralysis spell onto the Ifrit. With a stunned and rather puzzled look, the Ifrit subsided onto the sand, as majestically and inexorably as a piece of a mountain breaking free and tumbling toward the valley. His hand opened and the mage hopped out.

"Now!" cried Kaz-alrhun. "Onto the carpet! All of you, if you value the life God gave you!"

None of this made any sense. "But I thought you had set your Ifrit to capture us!"

His gold tooth flashed again as he smiled widely. "But this is not my Ifrit."

I had no time to create new assumptions, but my old ones were irretrievably gone. "We're never all going to fit on a little carpet like that," I said, the one thing I thought I could say with certainty.

"Watch and learn, Daimbert!" He said a few quick words, gave a great flourish and the carpet twitched, shivered, and grew until it was indeed big enough for all of us, even the horses. "Come!" he said when I hesitated. "Do you not wish to escape the Ifrit?"

I shook myself into action and herded the rest of our startled party onto the carpet with Maffi. The Ifrit, stretched out with his eyes shut, snorted as though he might soon awaken from the paralysis — and awaken furious. I had never flown on a magic carpet and had no reason to trust Kaz-alrhun's, but we didn't have much choice.

It lurched up from the ground, and we all clutched at each other. The horses neighed desperately as it seemed we must slide off the carpet's edge, but it straightened itself as it began to climb. We rotated twice, then sailed slowly up and over the rim of the valley.

From the air we could see for scores of miles across the sere desert landscape. I thought I could spot the glittering spires of Bahdroc in the distance and the uneven line of rocky hills beyond. I caught a flash of light reflected from the Dark Sea and, for one moment, saw what might have been the spires of the once ensorcelled city. The carpet turned around again, a quarter mile above the ground, then plunged downward to light on the steep hillside outside the circular valley.

I tumbled more than stepped off the carpet, glad to feel the solid ground beneath my feet again. For the brief moment we had been up in the air, the carpet's flight had seemed strong and smooth, but I could see it would take me a while to get used to the rough takeoffs and rapid landings.

"This is good fortune indeed," said Kaz-alrhun, straightening the odd-shaped pieces of silk that covered his enormous bulging body. "I have never before ventured to bind an Ifrit. Even you, Daimbert, were able to find a way out of one of my spells. I cannot be sure how long my magic will hold such a creature."

"But are we safe, this close?" asked Ascelin. He seemed to be rallying, though Hugo still looked too exhausted to care.

"Of course not," said Kaz-alrhun cheerfully.

"You wouldn't have come all the way from Xantium just to rescue us from the Ifrit," I said. "Why are you here?"

"My reason is the same as yours, Daimbert," said the mage. "I wish to enter the Wadi."

This entire trip I had had to keep adjusting my expectations, as everything turned out to be not quite what it seemed, as I looked for aid one moment to those whom at another point I considered my enemies. A very short time ago, I had feared Kaz-alrhun's arrival. Now, quite irrationally, I found myself thinking of him as an ally.

"You can have the onyx ring Maffi stole from you," I said, pulling it off. "Don't be too hard on him."

This set the mage into a paroxysm of laughter. "He told you he stole it?" He gave the boy a buffet on the side of the head, still laughing. "And you believed him?"

There were a number of things I needed to find out at once, but one took precedence. Maffi still stood on the carpet, carefully not meeting my eye. I took him firmly by the arm. "So Kaz-alrhun sent both you and this ring with us on purpose," I said, putting it back on my finger since the mage apparently didn't want it. "I should have realized, ever since you first offered to escort us to the Thieves' Market in Xantium, that you were working for him. Did you enjoy spying on us all the way from Xantium? Were you sending back messages from every oasis by means of the deep pools? And you made me believe that you wanted to 'learn' magic!"

Maffi looked as subdued as I had ever seen him, but he still managed a grin. "I do want to learn magic, my master! The communications spell was all Kaz-alrhun would teach me." He promptly created a large pink illusory spot on the front of my shirt, as though hoping this would placate me.

"First you need to learn to play chess," said Kaz-alrhun to the boy, "before I could begin to teach you magic."

"But don't forget," Maffi continued to me, "if it hadn't been for me, the mage wouldn't have known to come save you!"

Dominic stepped up at this point. "Where is my stallion, boy?" he demanded.

"At the first oasis north of the emir's city," said Maffi with another grin. "That really is a magnificent horse. I would never have been able to bring help so quickly if I'd been riding any other steed."

So when Maffi had escaped, he had ridden like the wind to the first place from which he could send a message to Xantium, and Kaz-alrhun had come swooping across the desert on his flying carpet. But if the mage had been using the boy to keep an eye on us and thought he had to come rescue us, then someone else had set the Ifrit here, someone who might himself appear at any moment.

"The Wadi's down there in the circular valley," I said to Kaz-alrhun, "but it's hidden — or only visible for a few seconds. The Ifrit isn't going to let us get to it if he can help it. Why did you let him out of the bottle in the first place?"

Kaz-alrhun smiled slowly. "It was not I."

"He said it was a mage — " But there must be many mages in the East, most of whom I hadn't met.

"That mage," said Kaz-alrhun enigmatically, "hoped that an Ifrit would help him find the Wadi's secret. He was mistaken."

"Then you and I and Prince Dominic need to get in before that mage gets here." I wondered briefly why a mage with the power to master an Ifrit couldn't find the Wadi's secret, but I pushed the issue aside. There were still too many other things I didn't understand. "But tell me first, Mage. What is in there?"

He looked at me thoughtfully. "You like a challenge, do you not?" I abruptly began to fear him as irrationally as I had felt a moment ago that I could trust him. "You are on a quest for something, but you do not know what it is. I, too, am on a quest, but its nature is such that I dare not hint to you what I hope to find. . . ."

"You don't know what's there, either," I said with much more confidence than I felt. "Good. We'll look for it together. We'd better get back to the valley immediately, before the Ifrit breaks your spell."

The mage unexpectedly put a massive hand on my

shoulder, making me shiver. "I can warn you and prepare you, even if I do not tell you." His black eyes met mine, completely serious for once. "I will not urge you to go. For if you proceed, you will be proceeding into dangers you cannot expect or even imagine."

"Prince Dominic," I called. "Are you ready to face unimaginable dangers to get into the Wadi?"

Dominic had been trying to get more details from Maffi about his stallion, what condition it was in, who was supposedly taking care of it now, and not getting answers he liked. But he turned toward me at once, the ruby of his ring still pulsing with light. "I have been ready since we reached my father's tomb."

I tried quickly to probe the spell attached to his ring and discovered that the clarity of vision I had had for a short time was gone. Either it was operative only within the valley or else it was just a short-term effect of having my magic restored by the Ifrit. Or I had imagined it, easily possible in this world of mirages and shifting expectations.

"I have never understood why you wizards of the west bind yourselves to kings and princes," Kaz-alrhun commented. I noticed him gazing fixedly at the ruby. "Your own magic should be strong enough that you do not need a prince with you."

"This is his quest and his is the ring from Yurt you actually wanted, Kaz-alrhun," I replied. "You didn't want the onyx ring at all."

"I have always known the onyx was not the ring I sought," said the mage good-naturedly.

"Then why were you willing to sell your flying horse for it?" I demanded.

"But it was not you who bought my horse."

I gave him up. At some point, the shadows and mirages might settle down again. "Let's get to the Wadi before the Ifrit gets loose."

We left the others sitting in the sparse shade some larger rocks afforded. Ascelin looked away to the north, searching for signs of the emir's troops. Kaz-alrhun, Dominic, and I again rose into the air on the flying carpet and swooped over the valley wall.

The Ifrit's enormous form still lay stretched out below us. His wife, sitting beside him, looked up at us and waved. Kaz-alrhun said a few words to the carpet and it descended slowly to hover near the Ifrit, who stared at us with unseeing eyes. "I have not done my spells amiss," said the mage complacently. "There are not many who can master an Ifrit, even for an hour's span."

"Watch," I said. "This onyx ring *is* good for one purpose."

I stretched out my hand and put the words of the Hidden Language together. The air of the valley shimmered with the magic that allowed people and objects to be hidden from each other. "Right *there*," I said, pointing to the dry watercourse. "That's where we're going." Suddenly, gloriously, I had the clarity of vision back, and I knew exactly what spell to say next. It was a spell I had never used, one which I was quite sure even Elerius had not known, but it came to me as easily as though another mind were guiding me. As the heavy syllables of the Language rolled from my tongue, the shimmering resolved itself and the watercourse became clearer and clearer while everything else faded.

The carpet dropped abruptly to the ground, tumbling us off. My spell, coupled with Elerius's spell on the onyx, had allowed us not only to see other layers of reality, but to pass into them as easily as the Ifrit apparently could. Dominic rubbed a bruised knee as he picked himself up but managed not to scowl; I was afraid he trusted me to know what I was doing. The Ifrit was gone.

Kaz-alrhun laughed. "Most excellent, Daimbert! How did you do that? I could never find any sensible spell on that ring — which is why I sent it with the boy. I realize I should have tested it more thoroughly before giving up a good automaton for it, but I had faith that you would be able to do something with it."

"It's western school magic," I said.

"Then your school may have something to offer after all," said the mage in pleased surprise. "When I last spoke to a master from your school, a great many years ago when it first opened, he seemed rather constrained and bookish. What was his name? Melecherius, I believe. I am glad there are also wizards like you there."

"I think we're going to need both eastern and western magic for this," I said.

But eastern spells could not get the flying carpet to rise again and I had nothing to offer. The sun beat down on the three of us as we hurried on foot across the valley floor toward where a deep rift now appeared. The Ifrit was able to create and change reality here, I thought, and armed with the onyx ring I could do nearly the same thing. I didn't like to think what long-term effects this kind of magic would have on the local physical structure of the earth; it was with good reason that Ifriti were considered highly dangerous. At least, I thought, when we left the reality where our friends were, where the flying carpet worked, we had also left the Ifrit behind.

He stopped us before we had crossed half the distance to the Wadi.

Kaz-alrhun opened his mouth, then froze. For the first time since I had met him he looked disconcerted. Sweat made rivulets in the dust on his dark skin.

"By what form of slaughter shall I slay you?" asked the Ifrit, glaring down with his arms folded. "I do not like little mages who try to tie me up. Solomon may have bound me, but you are not Solomon. And I do not even think you are from Yurt."

Kaz-alrhun's magic was gone, I realized, snatched from him as mine had been when I first reached the valley. Though I still had my magical abilities for the moment, I didn't dare use them against the Ifrit for fear of drawing attraction to them. I wondered wildly if this was the mage's unimaginable danger: probably not, because I could imagine quite vividly what the Ifrit was about to do to us.

"Listen, Ifrit," I said recklessly. "I have a proposition to make."

The Ifrit shifted his eyes from Kaz-alrhun and leaned down toward me. "What kind of proposition?"

"If you let us go, I can help you with your wife."

Kaz-alrhun recovered his equilibrium as soon as the Ifrit turned his attention away; he looked intrigued by this new development.

The Ifrit growled low in his throat. "And what are you trying to imply, little mage, about my beautiful, my pure young wife?"

"Just this," I plunged on. "In another ten years, her litheness and slenderness will begin to go. Twenty years after that, her white skin will be wrinkling and her black hair turning gray." I paused to let the Ifrit consider this. "But I can keep that from happening."

"But if I keep her with me, she will not have to die the way all you humans do," the Ifrit protested.

"No, it doesn't work like that. Even with my magic, she won't live longer than King Solomon did. And without my spells, she won't live longer than any ordinary human. But I can promise to keep her young a long, long time."

"Then you'd better do your spells right away," said the Ifrit, deeply concerned.

"No, because I don't trust you. First let us continue our explorations and then I'll cast my spells. We aren't trying to escape because we'll always be right here in the valley. This may take a day or two, but we'll never be far away. When we've found what we're looking for, then I shall cast the spells to give your wife long life."

"Maybe I do not trust *you*. If you play me false, then God shall play you false. If you don't come back and make my wife stay young and pure, then I'll crush all your friends."

If we didn't find a way to get away from the Ifrit

soon, before whoever had ordered him to watch for us appeared, we'd all be dead anyway. Rapid crushing would have to be better than undergoing any more of the Ifrit's fatal "tests."

"Of course," I said as firmly as I could.

I turned on my heel and started walking without giving him a chance to change his mind. Kaz-alrhun and Dominic were right behind me. As we hurried on, the mage commented with a small smile, "It has been two centuries since I was last without access to magic. This should be a novel experience." Then he added, as though in disapproval, "That was a noble display of generosity, Daimbert. I thought even wizards of the west knew better than to prolong life wantonly."

"We do. I would never artificially lengthen the lives of anyone at the royal court of Yurt." This was for Dominic's benefit. "But I think the Ifrit's own magical abilities could have prolonged her life anyway, even though he doesn't know it."

And then I realized the mage was smiling. He had not disapproved of my proposition after all. "I did not know that woman was the Ifrit's wife," was all he said.

We seemed to move at a snail's pace across the valley floor. The noon heat surrounded us so thoroughly that it felt it must be visible. The sun's glare made it hard to see. The mage was soon wheezing and I slowed my pace to his; he was twice my bulk as well as at least two hundred years older. Dominic would have been wheezing even worse at the beginning of our trip, though he now moved almost as easily as Ascelin.

When we finally reached the boulders that marked the head of the dry watercourse, my first thought was to sit down in their shadow. But I stood up again after a moment, while the mage was still panting, to look down into the Wadi Harhammi.

It had been our goal since the eastern kingdoms, but now that we were here it seemed almost an anticlimax.

For a place of unimaginable danger, it seemed very quiet. The watercourse appeared empty, although a curve hid most of its length. I still had no idea what Dominic's father had thought was in the Wadi fifty years ago or what might be here now — or even what Kaz-alrhun thought was here.

It was time to find out. I lifted the onyx ring and said the words to reveal what was hidden.

We scrambled backwards as the ground beneath our feet started to drop away, rocks rolling and sand sliding. In a few seconds, the narrow watercourse had grown to cover most of the center of the valley.

"Greetings," said King Warin. "I knew you'd be here sooner or later."

11

Dominic and I stopped dead, but Kaz-alrhun did not seem perturbed. "I wish to inquire of you about that onyx ring you gave me for my flying horse," he said. "It was not the ring I required."

King Warin fixed us with his dead cold eyes, making me shiver in spite of the desert sun. "And your flying horse is not the help you led me to believe it would be." The enormous black horse stood, completely still, beside him.

"You should always beware when bargaining in the Thieves' Market," said the mage. "Did I make any guarantee of my automaton's power against Ifriti?"

Dominic interrupted them. "King Warin," he said formally, "I accuse you before these witnesses of treating us falsely. When we return to the western kingdoms, I intend to assemble a court of our royal brothers to judge you for the crimes of theft and attempted murder."

"He obtained the onyx ring by stealing it from you?" said Kaz-alrhun with a smile of comprehension. "God's ways are secret ways; all of us and the ring are now here together."

"So is *this*," I asked the mage with a nod toward Warin, "the danger against which you didn't feel you could warn me?"

"Not at all," said the mage. "I did not expect him here, although I always knew his entry into the game at this point was possible."

"You've moved into a separate level of reality," I said to Warin with what I hoped was a wizardly scowl. All I had to oppose the king was my magic, and I wanted to make sure he respected it. "The ebony horse won't fly here."

"Do you not intend to answer my charge?" said Dominic, crossing his arms. From his manner, instead of being in a desert valley surrounded by rocks, sand, and treacherous magic, we could have been home in the west.

Warin hesitated, flicking his eyes back and forth between us. He might have no respect for the mage and me, but Dominic disturbed him. "I do not understand what you're talking about," he said brusquely. "I had nothing to do with that band of bandits."

"So you do know that we were set upon by bandits," said Dominic, as though making a point before a judge. "When the strange stories coming out of the east reached you, you learned there was a flying horse for sale in Xantium and its price a certain ring. . . ."

"The ring you tried unsuccessfully to find in Prince Dominic's tomb," I suggested.

Dominic scowled darkly. "No wonder the townspeople have become leery of the Church of the Holy Twins, if its sanctuary was violated by someone who would not hesitate to practice the black arts. I shall add desecration of a grave to my charges against you."

King Warin seemed momentarily caught off balance. "I know nothing of a desecration of a grave," he said with what appeared to be sincerity. But neither Dominic nor I were ready to believe him.

"So you stole the ring you had good reason to suspect Arnulf had sent with us," I continued. "How long did it take you to realize that the ring you gave for the horse, which you hoped would carry you safely to the Wadi and away again, was the same ring that the mage wanted in order to uncover the Wadi's secrets?"

Except that it wasn't. Now I was confusing myself. I caught an amused look from the mage.

King Warin pulled his lips back from his teeth in what might have been meant for a smile. "I told you I expected you sooner or later."

"We're here now," I said, not daring to lose whatever momentum I had. "We'll let you watch while we uncover the old secrets you hoped to obtain by deviousness and evil."

I rubbed the onyx with my thumb and wondered how many layers of magical reality there might still be before us. I again spoke the words of the Hidden Language, heedless of whatever permanent damage I might be doing. If this valley was indeed an ancient volcano, leading down into the heart of the earth, maybe it had an inherent, well-grounded stability, which was why the Ifrit could apparently manipulate reality here so easily. Either that, or he and I were disturbing the magma miles below, and molten rock was even now moving up toward us.

As the air's shimmering resolved itself, I thought I saw a group of people in the distance, from the corner of my eyes. But fifty yards ahead of us, and much more intriguing, something glittered in the sand of the rift.

I reached it first by flying, snatching it up before King Warin's hands could seize it. It was a bronze bottle made in the shape of a cucumber.

I hefted it cautiously. It felt empty. The mouth was closed with a lead stopper, but the stopper was loose. When I opened the bottle and shook, nothing came out.

Kaz-alrhun held out a hand and I gave it to him. If this was the secret of the Wadi Harhammi, I was not impressed.

But the mage lifted his eyebrows steeply. "This is a bottle wherein an Ifrit was imprisoned, Daimbert," he said. "Look at the seal on the stopper."

A seal had indeed been impressed in the lead, but I shook my head, not able to identify it.

"Do you not recognize the graven signet of Solomon, son of David?"

Dominic gave a low whistle.

"This is what Prince Vlad threatened me with," I said. "He warned me I'd find something dangerous in the Wadi, but he wouldn't tell me what it was unless I promised to return to his principality. It was an imprisoned Ifrit."

"Too late now to worry about releasing him accidentally," said Dominic.

"Someone *did* release him," I said slowly. "In fact, although the Ifrit's story seems a little unclear, he may have been released two separate times. He said at least one of the people who released him was a mage. What mage has already been here and what has he found?" I tried glaring at Kaz-alrhun, but he just smiled.

"This is *all* that is here," said King Warin darkly. "The secret of the Wadi was an imprisoned Ifrit from whom your friend Arnulf hoped to obtain wishes."

Dominic and I looked at each other in dismay. But I recovered quickly. "No, because the rumors concerning Yurt are much more recent than five years old and we know the Ifrit's been out at least that long. So the Ifrit himself can't be the whole secret." I frowned at King Warin in an attempt to match his own icy stare. "Why are you trying to mislead us?"

I looked at him from under my eyebrows, thinking rapidly. He didn't answer my question, but he didn't need to. He was trying to mislead us because he still hoped to find the Wadi's secret without us. But if King Warin had become trapped here in the valley, then he could not be behind all the strange events, and someone else, with powerful magic, was still at large and might arrive very soon.

I felt a sudden, completely irrational conviction that the mage who had freed the Ifrit, five years or more before, was not an eastern mage at all but a western wizard, King Warin's former royal wizard Elerius.

Warin interrupted my thoughts by turning his eyes on me and giving a completely unconvincing smile. These were real eyes, not the pebbles through which Prince Vlad could see in darkness, but they still were hard as stone. I tried to reassure myself that he knew no magic himself — unless he was working with a demon whose supernatural powers could mask his abilities from someone like me who used only natural magic.

"Well, perhaps you're right after all, Wizard," he said. "I know what is in the Wadi and you do not. You will be able to deal with its dangers much more easily if you know what to expect. I'll be happy to tell you."

I broke my glance away from his. While he looked at me, it felt as though we were linked by a bar of cold iron. "And in return?"

"You'll give it to me."

I managed a barking laugh. "I don't like your bargain. It's a good bargain only for you. I'm the only person here with functioning magical abilities." If he had had access to supernatural magic, I told myself, he wouldn't need me. But I surreptitiously checked my knowledge of the Hidden Language to make sure it hadn't evaporated in the last few minutes — so far, so good. "Of course it's always better to be forewarned, but I'm not afraid."

King Warin actually believed this patent lie. "Perhaps I misspoke. We shall share, although in light of my superior position I should have ultimate control. . . ." He looked thoughtful for a moment, then seemed to come to a decision.

"You'll like this proposal, Wizard. It's been a year since Elerius left and that school of yours hasn't been able to come up with anyone competent. How would you like to become my new Royal Wizard?"

I must have stared at him unbelievingly because he made another of his unconvincing attempts at a smile. "Elerius knew you at the school and always spoke very approvingly of your abilities."

I ignored this highly unlikely statement. "I'm Royal Wizard of Yurt."

I caught a glimpse of Kaz-alrhun rolling his black eyes at me, either in amusement at a western wizard feeling he needed an employer or else in warning. At the same time, Dominic cleared his throat.

"We would very much miss you, Wizard," he said gravely. "But when we decided to hire a school-trained wizard, we always knew there would be the possibility he would want to leave us for a bigger or wealthier kingdom. Warin's kingdom will have opportunities for you Yurt could never offer."

"You're quite right," said Warin in apparent good fellowship. "There is still wild magic in the mountains east of my royal castle, Wizard, and while most of the other lords in the kingdom keep their own magic workers, all of them need the firm hand of a senior wizard over them. You'll have the authority and respect you never had in Yurt. And you've seen my castle; I know Haimeric can offer you nothing so luxurious."

"I've been very happy in Yurt."

"And so you should." His eyes glinted at me in the desert sun. "I'm sure it has served you well as a first post. Isn't that what an ambitious young wizard does, take a first post at a small kingdom to carry him through until his abilities have matured and been demonstrated?"

Against my will, I found myself weighing the

proposal seriously. I would never be able to explain to anyone at the school why I refused it. Elerius had gotten the post in Warin's kingdom right out of school as a reward for his supremely good abilities. The three young wizards Warin had sent back to the City in disgrace had also doubtless been near the top of their classes. I, on the other hand, had at several points been in danger of not even graduating and had developed whatever skills I now possessed through a remarkable number of errors. For me to step into Elerius's former kingdom would be a tremendous honor. It was also, I hated to admit, exactly what I needed to overcome the ennui I had felt last winter.

For a second I tried to imagine myself constantly surrounded by liveried knights, who rose whenever I rose and arranged themselves around me whenever I was seated. I just couldn't see it. Maybe I could substitute some of the emir's dancing girls.

I could feel King Warin's eyes on me, though I assiduously did not meet them. After all, what reason was there not to take the position Warin was offering? Only the fact that I loved Yurt and did not want to be in the employ of someone who had sold his soul to the powers of darkness.

But that needn't mean my own soul was in danger, a voice in the back of my mind pointed out. King Warin was not the devil, only a human king, even if he did give every appearance of wanting supernatural knowledge not meant for humans. Elerius, after all, had served there for years without plunging into black magic. Maybe I could even function as a force for good within the kingdom.

Elerius had left, and I was no priest.

"You're wasting your time," I told King Warin. "If you don't want to tell me what you know about the Wadi — assuming you know anything — that's fine, but you must realize it would be a lot easier if we all worked together. I'd prefer in fact to be here without you, even if you did have some little piece of information we could use. I certainly have no intention of spending the rest of my life in your kingdom."

Dominic startled me by breaking into a broad smile and clapping me on the shoulder. It had never occurred to me he might miss me.

"If that is settled," said Kaz-alrhun, "let us see what else is in this watercourse."

But before we had walked more than a dozen yards, I caught distant voices brought faintly by the wind. I rose up from the rift in the earth to be able to see. The rest of the party from Yurt, Maffi with them, was coming across the valley on foot.

I flew to meet them. All of them were scratched and dusty. Ascelin looked exhausted, the king disoriented, and Hugo strangely pleased.

"It was the emir's men," said Ascelin, dropping to the ground as I reached them and wiping his forehead. "They must have been in hiding somewhere among the rocks and gullies, because they appeared almost as soon as you'd left."

And the mage had distracted me from probing for soldiers with his talk of unimaginable dangers. "But you all got away — " I said, looking from one to the other. Joachim tried to smile, but I noticed he was absently rubbing his scar with one thumb.

"Just barely. I had to carry Haimeric down the slope, while the chaplain and the boy managed on their own. Hugo held off the vanguard of the troops until we were all safely on our way. If the descent hadn't been so steep, I'm sure they would have followed us at once."

I glanced toward Hugo. For one moment he managed a triumphant grin. "Saying I held them off may go a little far," he said with quite unconvincing modesty. "I put my shield and sword arm between Ascelin and the troops. With a few lucky strokes, I intimidated them just long enough. Then, when they rushed me, I went down the valley wall on my belly!"

I looked up toward the edge of the valley with a far-seeing spell and could see the white turbans and glittering curved swords of the emir's soldiers. It was a large troop, at least a hundred men, and their swarthy faces looked angry and frustrated. Apparently sharing salt with us only meant that the emir would not kill us inside his palace — either that or he planned to capture us alive, which didn't sound much better.

But if they didn't want to come cascading down the nearly vertical descent after us, we were safe for the moment. As I watched, they settled themselves, apparently intending to wait us out. "What about the horses?"

Ascelin shook his head. He flicked his eyes toward the king, then back toward the sand. "At this point," he said in a low voice, "it would take the Ifrit to get them back. And all our supplies and food are gone with them. Even if we elude the emir's men and get out of this valley alive, I don't know how we'll ever get home."

I didn't answer. If we somehow escaped from the Ifrit and the emir, there were still hundreds of empty miles between us and Xantium, much less Yurt. Sir Hugo's party might have been in the same situation. They had never come home, either.

"Where's Dominic?" Ascelin asked then, looking up.

"Down in the Wadi. It *is* a dry watercourse. So far," I went on, remembering I had news of my own, "we've found the bottle the Ifrit was imprisoned in."

This took some of the despair from Ascelin's face. "Where is the Wadi?"

I looked around and could not see it. I had no idea what level of existence we were actually on, but at the moment it did not include the Ifrit, the Wadi, or Dominic.

Before I could try manipulating the spell again, King Haimeric stepped up beside me. Everything about him seemed old — his frail body, his wispy white hair, his wind-wrinkled cheeks — except for his eyes. They were bright and excited. "I'm not sure what you've been able to see, Wizard," he said, "but just before we got on that flying carpet, I saw the blue rose."

I turned my attention fully toward him. "You saw the blue rose?" I repeated idiotically.

"There wasn't time to say anything then, but it's here in the valley. I always knew it was. That's why the emir didn't want us to come here."

I hesitated only a second. If we had lost everything, even our waterskins, we wouldn't live long enough for a second chance to find the king's rose. Dominic and Kaz-alrhun between them could take care of Warin while I was gone. I didn't think King Haimeric had yet realized we would never get home, but he might as well die with his own quest fulfilled.

"Rest a little longer," I said to Ascelin and the others. "I'll take you to the Wadi shortly." Then I turned to the king. "Let's find your rose, sire."

III

King Haimeric and I walked across the valley floor, leaving the others behind. Even without any visible landmarks, the king seemed to know exactly where we were going. I murmured spells that made the air around us shimmer with a kaleidoscope of shifting images, including again the silk caravan. But I did not see the group of people who might have included a red-headed wizard — assuming I had ever seen them at all.

"There it is," said the king, stopping short.

We stepped into a flowering garden and out of the layer of reality in which we had been. The garden was surrounded by a low wall and was filled entirely with rosebushes.

We walked silently among them. The green, glossy leaves looked completely out of place in the barren desert; even the air around us was slightly damp. We passed enormous, showy red blooms, tiny pink buds no bigger than my littlest fingernail, and soft yellow blossoms whose scent threatened to overwhelm us. We saw no humans, but someone, I thought, must tend these bushes daily, for there were no insect borers, no faded blooms and no weeds.

The garden was much bigger than it at first looked. We walked half a mile, and the colors began to change. Here were maroons, rich violets, like what we had seen in the emir's garden outside Bahdroc but somehow brighter and more vivid. The king walked faster and faster until I was hard pressed to keep up with him.

But then he stopped so abruptly that I, following behind, almost knocked him over. Standing up from where he had been digging was the emir's swarthy rose grower.

I tried at once to shape a protective spell for King Haimeric, but I need not have bothered. After a surprised second, he sprang forward; he and the grower clasped hands in delight at their meeting.

"I had in truth hoped that even a western wizard might be able to find the magic to bring you here," said the grower, a smile splitting his face.

"Won't the emir be furious with you?" asked the king in concern.

"He gave me no specific instructions concerning you. I did most carefully obey his orders, and I never explicitly told you or any other man how to find this garden."

He smiled again and added, "The emir considers this *his* garden, of course, but while emirs rise and fall, the roses endure. All the attention, the rivalry and the weight of authority fall on the emir himself. As long as I am just his grower, I am free to do my crosses and to do what is most important in this life: to grow better roses."

"Are you working with the Ifrit?" I managed to ask.

"Of course. It was just last year, once stories of the blue rose began to spread, that the emir decided he must break part of my garden away from the rest and transport it entire to someplace no one else would find it. Nothing but an Ifrit would have the power to do that or to carry me quickly back and forth."

"A bronze bottle with an Ifrit in it was taken to the emir as something different and new," I said with sudden inspiration, "and the Ifrit agreed to help him in return for being released."

The grower smiled and nodded. For a second I even dared hope I was teaching him respect for western magic.

But the Ifrit himself had told me that a mage had freed him from Solomon's enchantment, and I was quite sure the grower didn't know any magic. Besides, the Ifrit had been freed for five years and the grower had just said this had only happened last year. But I didn't have a chance to work it out.

King Haimeric, showing no interest in Ifriti, had moved away, looking intently at the roses. The grower led us down the final pathway between the bushes. "Here," he said in a low voice.

The king drew in his breath but did not speak. This was it at last. A bush stood by itself, bearing a single blossom: an enormous, sapphire-blue rose. The three of us stood looking at it in silence. I probed quickly and surreptitiously with magic, but I already knew. At least where we were at the moment, this was no illusion but real.

It was as big across as a saucer, yet its stem easily held it upright. The petals were beaded with dew. From deep within the rose came a scent, both sweet and spicy, subtle yet unforgettable once caught. This was the blue rose the king had sought. Suddenly, I understood why it was worth it.

"You're the first and only outsider to find the blue rose," said the grower to the king after a minute. "Do you wish a root cutting?"

"I would like a root cutting beyond all things."

The grower produced his trowel. "I have started

several plants from seed in containers which the emir hopes to have in his palace in a few years, but you do not want a root-bound container plant for your garden. You need a piece from the adult far-spreading root."

We didn't need a piece of root but a way to get out of this valley, guarded against us by the Ifrit and by the emir's men. Even if we got out, a cutting would quickly dry up in the desert air and be worthless long before we died of thirst, trying to get back to Xantium on foot. But I said nothing.

The grower knelt down and began digging again. I looked out, away from the well-irrigated garden. The dry land beyond could have been seen through a pane of glass.

The grower packed the piece of root carefully in damp earth and paper. "It should last a few days," he said, frowning for the first time. "But it really should be planted as soon as possible."

King Haimeric frowned as well. For a few moments, his expression had been beyond joy or happiness, but the grower's comment brought him back to reality — or whatever one might call this. "I'll see what I can arrange."

He turned to me. "Thank you, Wizard. It's silly, I know, but I would not have wanted to die in this valley, having come this close to the blue rose, without first seeing it." Then he understood our situation after all. "Now we should try to find Dominic and the Wadi Harhammi, to see if he can find what *he* has been seeking."

"You want the dry watercourse?" asked the grower. "We are at this moment in it, although you might never know it. The Ifrit insisted that if he took my garden away from Bahdroc, this is where he would take it. If you leave the garden through that little gate over there, you shall find yourself in the Wadi."

I paused with my hand on the gate, wondering again if this rose garden could have been what the elder Prince Dominic had heard was in the Wadi. But the prince had been dead fifty years and, if we were to believe the grower, this garden had only been brought here very recently. With something so precious to him here, no wonder the emir's mood had changed when we mentioned we were seeking the Wadi and no wonder that part of the agreement he had extracted from the Ifrit had been to guard it closely.

This was the same sort of gate through which we had entered, with apparently nothing but the valley floor beyond. But I had given up assuming that what I thought I saw had any relation to what I would discover. We opened the gate and stepped through.

We were immediately sliding down the steep side of the Wadi, raining pebbles on those beneath. The garden where we had been a second before was gone.

Dominic jumped out of our way. Kaz-alrhun sat to one side, apparently enjoying the experience.

"Where's King Warin?" I asked at once.

"He left right after you did," said Dominic, "saying he would find the Wadi's secret by himself — though why he should be able to find it now when he hasn't before, I cannot say," he added in disdain. "I think he didn't want to have to answer my case against him."

King Haimeric was quite incurious about Warin. He turned eagerly to Dominic. "I've seen it," he said. "The blue rose. And I have a cutting."

Dominic managed to smile in spite of his own concentration on whatever might wait ahead. "That's excellent news, sire." He turned to me again. "We waited for you to go on."

I could understand Dominic waiting for me, but Kaz-alrhun was something of a surprise. He seemed remarkably deferential for someone who wanted to know the Wadi's secret himself, I thought as we continued. The ground underfoot was broken and patches of soft sand made walking difficult. Boulders were scattered in our path, none obstructing our passage, but placed such that it was hard to see more than fifty yards ahead.

As we walked, we started occasionally to notice something hard and white that was not stone, half-buried in the sand. I reached down to loosen a piece and realized it was human bone.

"What's here?" I said, dropping the bone abruptly and turning to the mage. "Is this the unimaginable danger you warned us against?"

"I know not whose bones these may be," said Kaz-alrhun in interest, "nor why they are here, though I would guess they are from earlier seekers after the Wadi's secrets."

As we continued, the king picking his way carefully so as not to step on any, the bones became more frequent. I kept probing with magic, finding nothing but scurrying desert creatures. Some of the bones were made into neat stacks. They all seemed fairly old, though I realized I was looking hopefully for fresh ones from Warin.

We came around a boulder and found a cave cut into the side of the dry watercourse. We were now at least thirty feet below ground level. The low cave entrance was blocked by a latticework gate of white marble, which looked as though it should be in the emir's palace rather than here in this sandy wash. But while the others clustered around it, I staggered and leaned against a stone for support because I felt a wave of magic pouring out of the cave toward me.

It was incredibly sweet, as though the waking revelation of the magical abilities I had sometimes dreamed I had. I checked quickly to see what new spells I might know, found none, but felt even more intensely before the strange clarity of vision. This cave was the source of that clarity and it made everything around us seem so vivid that I hardly dared probe for what might be hidden within it.

And it wasn't just magical clarity that poured out toward me. It was also quite irrational happiness.

Wizards are always more susceptible to magical influences than anyone else. We might be trapped here in the Wadi, with both the Ifrit and the emir determined that we not leave alive, and the desert determined that we not live even if we did escape, but at the moment it hardly seemed to matter.

"There are footprints in the sand," commented the king.

"If Warin was here, he did not win past this gate," said Dominic. "There is no obvious way to open it." He gave it an experimental tug with his right hand, then drew back quickly as though it burned his fingers.

But the moment his hand touched the latticework, it began to buzz, a high keen sound that made us look at each other with disquiet.

"What kind of magical defenses would the caliph — " I started to ask Kaz-alrhun, then stopped, for something was coming, something that clattered as it came.

We looked behind us in horror. Coming around the boulders, claws extended and venomous tail arched over its back, was a twenty-foot scorpion.

Dominic pushed the king behind him and whipped out his sword, though I feared many of the bones we had seen had been of men who had tried to fight a giant scorpion with steel. Kaz-alrhun scrambled out of the way while I desperately tried to put a binding spell together.

But the scorpion came straight on, too powerful and moving too fast for my magic to bind. The leg joints clattered as it scrambled over the stones toward us. The claws reached for me and I found myself staring into its enormous insect eyes.

With a wild facility born of fear and the strange clarity that still poured from the cave, I threw together a transformations spell and launched it at the scorpion. I had no time to put a proper spell together, not even time to find the words to turn the scorpion into a frog. Instead I grabbed at the spell I had discovered to transform something into itself, only larger, and I reversed it.

The clattering stopped. I opened the eyes I had involuntarily shut and looked down. There I saw a normal-sized scorpion racing across the sand, toward the shelter of the boulders. Dominic stepped forward and crushed it with the heel of its boot.

I took a rather shaky breath and wiped my forehead. The scorpion had torn a hole with its claw in the front of my goat's hair robe, just before I transformed it. "That shouldn't have worked," I said. "You can't put transformations spells on magical creatures — it would never work with the Ifrit."

"Perhaps this was not a magical creature," suggested Kaz-alrhun, "but a normal scorpion an earlier mage had transformed to a larger size, so you merely freed it from that mage's spell."

"I didn't notice you giving me much help," I said to him testily, "especially after you'd warned us against it."

"I do not think you needed my help," said the mage with a grin. "And it was not against this that I warned you."

Dominic put his sword away and peered again through the latticework across the cave. "The opening appears very small, if there is a true opening at all."

The very air at the cave entrance sparkled, like air in a mountain meadow after a storm. I was hit again by a wave of irrational happiness and forgot all about being irritated with the mage. "Dominic," I said, "here is where we need your father's ruby ring."

Vlad had told me he had attached a special opening spell to the ruby. But I now knew that the spell which had made the ring pulse with light since we first approached the valley was nothing that that wizard had created, but something far more powerful. The magic attached to Dominic's ring was as old as King Solomon if not older.

Dominic gritted his teeth and reached his left hand, with the ring, toward the marble latticework. I tried to find the words of the Hidden Language that would put the ring's spell into action.

But I didn't have a chance. A voice spoke from behind us, light and cheerful. "So there you are! By the way — don't touch the lattice."

IV

We all whirled around. I should have known. Standing there, looking lean and good-natured, was Sir Hugo's red-haired wizard, Evrard.

I embraced him so hard that all the breath went out of him with a "Whoof!" In the desert sun he had developed more freckles than ever. For a moment the strange, sweet happiness that poured from the cave made all of us giddy and we laughed and slapped each other on the back.

"I'd hoped all along that if we got in trouble on this trip you'd come find me, Daimbert," Evrard said with a grin, once he had his breath back. "It still seemed to take you long enough to get here!"

"And Sir Hugo?" asked Dominic. "Is he alive as well?"

"As well as any of us," said Evrard. "The Ifrit brings us food and water when he remembers. Mostly we're hungry and bored from hearing all of each others' life stories until we know them better than our own. Even touching the latticework and flying away from the giant scorpion lost its thrill for me after a while — and the others didn't even dare try."

"We killed the scorpion," I said modestly, then stopped. Something was not right. "But why are you here?" I asked. "It wasn't you who found a way to master the Ifrit?"

Evrard laughed. "I don't think anyone — except maybe Solomon — could master an Ifrit. I did manage to put this one back into his bottle temporarily, but at the moment we're at something of a standoff."

I rubbed my forehead, willing myself to understand at least something. "You didn't let it out of the bottle originally. But you tricked it into going back in by telling it you couldn't believe something so enormous could fit into a bottle that small."

"That's right," said Evrard cheerfully. "A traveler we met in the Holy City sold us the bottle — the same traveler who told us Noah's Ark was hidden here in the Wadi. Did you happen to meet him? No, I can't describe him. He never did let us get a good look at him. But I had the sense he was some sort of mage, even though he spoke like a westerner."

"Go on," I said. Maybe once I heard it all it might make sense.

"He suggested we present the bottle to the emir of Bahdroc as something new and marvellous, and at the same time ask his assistance in reaching the Wadi Harhammi. We'd already been trying to decide if we should go on south from the Holy Land, because the mage in Xantium — " He appeared to look at Kaz-alrhun properly for the first time. "But you've brought him with you!"

That was one way to look at it. "So two different people directed you here," I said. The traveler, with the same story of Noah's Ark that Elerius had once told me, I had to dismiss for the moment as beyond comprehension. But I turned sharply to Kaz-alrhun. "Why did you tell Evrard to come here to the Wadi? Was it as bait for us?"

"Of course," said the mage with his infuriating smile. "It is also good to note here the game the other player is playing."

And Kaz-alrhun would not have cared, I thought, whether Sir Hugo's party was alive or dead as long as we came looking for them. But the mage had already made it clear that it was not he who set the Ifrit watching for people from Yurt. "Why didn't you escape from the Wadi while you had the Ifrit imprisoned?" I asked Evrard.

"We weren't in the Wadi then," Evrard continued, clearly enjoying having a new audience after a year of only Sir Hugo and the same two knights. "We were still north of Bahdroc. Imagine our surprise when we came over a rise and found an Ifrit asleep in the sun, and a human woman with him who claimed to be his wife!"

I suddenly felt sure of where four of the Ifrit's wife's rings had come from, but I didn't say anything.

"Unfortunately, he woke up before we could get away," Evrard continued, then paused to prolong the suspense. "First he asked if we were from Yurt! I took a chance and said we were and it's a good thing I did, because otherwise he might have crushed us at once in his enormous hands. But he still threatened us and said that even Solomon had feared his power so much that he'd had to imprison him. That's when I thought of taunting him, of showing him the bronze bottle and telling him I didn't believe he'd ever fit inside. He went back into it to show me and I was able to slap the stopper in!"

"But the Ifrit is out now," said the king.

"I'm afraid my plan didn't work as well as I'd hoped," said Evrard ruefully. "When I first gave the emir the bottle, he treated us very hospitably and fed us bread and salt. I told him, too, that we were from Yurt. But his manner changed as soon as I asked directions to the Wadi Harhammi.

"We stayed in Bahdroc a week, but the atmosphere was tense the entire time, and we had gone only a few miles out of the city when the Ifrit captured us. We've decided that as soon as we left, the emir must have freed the Ifrit again in return for a promise to take us prisoner. For some reason the Ifrit still hasn't killed us." But with a wild Ifrit roaring after Sir Hugo's party, no wonder the slave girl had told us the desert had eaten them.

"Both the emir and the slave girls remembered you," I said.

Evrard smiled reminiscently. "One of the girls was really delightful — I wished we could have taken her along."

The emir's second wish in return for freeing the Ifrit, I thought, had been a request to transport the garden of the blue rose into hiding. Already constrained by a command to guard the Wadi against people from Yurt, it was no wonder the Ifrit had decided to bring the rose garden here. By promising to guard the valley, the Ifrit must have felt trapped here. It must have been extremely tiresome for a creature who could easily pass from the highest mountains to the uttermost depths of the sea in half an hour: little wonder he tried to make us amuse him.

"I've been expecting you for months," continued Evrard, ready to chat indefinitely. "Didn't you get my message that we were held prisoner by the Ifrit?"

"You mean the sign of the cross cut into the rock where the silk caravan disappeared?" I said as several things fell into place.

"The Ifrit's wife wanted a bolt of silk and, originally, I was going to make the Ifrit leave a message for people from Yurt — but then it turned out he didn't trust my messages and couldn't read or write himself! So I hoped that a sign of the cross would do as well, as an indication that an Ifrit had Christian captives."

Dominic had stopped listening and was peering again through the latticework into the cave. "We'll catch up on our stories later," he said. "This, I believe, is where what I seek is hidden."

"What is in there, Evrard?" I asked quietly.

He looked troubled for the first time. "I have no idea. All I know is that as long as I'm here, within about fifty yards of this cave — making sure not to touch the lattice, of course — I can work spells that will intimidate an Ifrit. Not make him *do* anything, apparently, but scare him into thinking I will in another minute. I've been able to use the power that's in there to make the Ifrit feed us and to promise not to kill anyone else from Yurt, but we haven't dared leave the Wadi. I've spent the last year not being able to learn anything more about it."

Could Evrard, with his combination of improvised spells and pure bluff, be the danger that the mage had warned me against? Kaz-alrhun had said almost nothing since Evrard had appeared, but all his attention, like Dominic's, seemed turned toward the cave.

"This is where we find out at last," I said. Dominic again reached out his hand so that the ruby, now flashing rapidly, was in contact with the marble gate over the cave entrance. With the strange clarity of vision whatever was in this cave had given me, I found the right spell to bring the magic in the ring to full potential. The words of the Hidden Language rumbled through the rift like the sound of rocks falling.

The latticework shivered, then slowly started to dissolve into vapor, losing its solidity even while it still held its shape. The sound of rocks falling continued even when I finished speaking, and as we watched the small opening beyond the gate grew larger. Dominic kept his hand extended until the cascade of stone had stopped, leaving an opening four feet high, and the white wisps of latticework vapor dissipated in the desert air.

We all shivered ourselves, then peered into the cave's dim interior, blinking in an attempt to see. "Can you make a light, Wizard?" the king asked quietly.

Dominic didn't wait for a light. He ducked his head to step within. But he stopped short almost immediately and backed out, rubbing his forehead. "There's another barrier," he said. "Is it glass?"

I probed quickly. "Not glass, but more magic."

The ground beneath us rose and fell, as sharply and smoothly as a wave under a dinghy. A faint rumbling came from deep within the earth. We paused to stare at each other, but a minute stretched out, two minutes, and the tremor did not come a second time.

Dominic reached out his hand to touch the invisible barrier again and went straight through it, almost losing his balance. His head reemerged. "What are you doing, Wizard?"

"I'm not doing anything. It's your ring." I could see the spell clearly now, spread out like a highly figured tapestry. "The latticework was just the first line of defense. The air itself is solid there, but your ruby ring is imbued with the power to pass through, apparently taking you with it."

"Then I'd better go through," said Dominic.

I glanced toward Kaz-alrhun, to see if he had any better ideas, but he stood a little way back, his thick arms folded, watching with interest.

I put a quick spell of light onto the ruby ring. Dominic stretched out his hand and from the mouth of the cave we could see the ring's firefly glow move down a dark tunnel and disappear.

Evrard pushed against the air turned glass and tried a few spells of his own, but it remained impervious. I found I could not sense Dominic beyond the glass barrier. If the ground shifted while he was in there, we would have no warning he was about to be crushed. In the distance I thought I could hear a low murmur, which could have been the emir's men, could have been the Ifrit, and could have been molten rock moving toward the earth's surface.

But in a moment, we heard Dominic's footsteps clearly again, and then the light of the ring reappeared. His head bent, he emerged from the cave carrying something awkwardly before him, and carefully put it down on the sandy floor of the Wadi.

It was a locked cabinet about a yard in height. The outside was enameled in geometric patterns and the elaborate lock was iron. The magical clarity and the strange happiness intensified to the point that for a moment it was difficult even to think.

"It should be possible to open this lock with magic," I said then. It would also have been possible to break the enameled cabinet, but I didn't like to do that.

When Kaz-alrhun showed no sign of helping, I knelt beside the cabinet and began to twist and turn delicately at the lock. The iron was free of rust in spite of long being underground. I felt I could see the mechanism through its casing, and in a moment the lock gave a great click and came off in my hand.

I stepped back to let Dominic kneel down and open the cabinet door. He reached inside and took out a ceramic amphora, big enough to hold a gallon of wine, and sealed with lead.

Dominic tried the stopper, but it was set in very firmly, and his hand trembled. The amphora dropped to the ground and exploded into shards of pottery.

Lying on the ground amid the shards was a golden box, the size of Dominic's two fists.

"No," whispered King Haimeric. "It cannot be. It was within a golden box, within a sealed amphora, within a locked cabinet, but the cabinet was inside a derelict ship sunk in the deepest rift of the Outer Sea."

There was no immediately obvious way to open the box, but when Dominic picked it up in his hand, the hand with the ring, a thin line appeared all the way around it. I tried the opening spell that had gotten us through the latticework without effect. But as Dominic held it, the thin line widened. With his other hand, he took hold of the top and carefully opened it.

Beyond expectation, beyond hope, lying in the box on a bed of black velvet was a black sphere. It was so dark that it appeared to absorb light, so smooth that when Dominic touched it with his finger it began slowly to spin: King Solomon's Pearl.

It took us several minutes to be able to speak again. Instead we stood in silence, looking at it.

I don't know about the others, but to me it seemed to have a voice, a low calling just beyond the edge of full intelligibility, speaking of magic before Solomon, before humans had made any attempts to channel magical forces into comprehensible or repeatable channels. And yet it was still magic, magic that I with my school training and my somewhat patchy knowledge of herbs could understand. This went beyond either ambition or happiness, but I knew that with the Pearl I could become the greatest wizard the world had ever known.

I looked toward Kaz-alrhun and Evrard and saw solemn expressions that I thought must match my own. The mage's magical abilities, I felt suddenly certain, had returned to him.

In a few swift seconds a complete vision passed through my mind, of myself returning to the wizards' school with the Pearl, demonstrating magical abilities beyond anything even the best and oldest of the masters had ever imagined. With my powers, I would immediately bring the eastern kingdoms and their wizards under the control of the west; I would stop all wars between aristocrats and wrangling between wizards; I would make the Ifriti into my agents; I would reconform both weather and geology to make the earth more comfortable; I would rewrite all the textbooks at the school to make them match my own magical vision; I would enrich the soil so that the crops never failed; I would regulate all trade closely so that all dealings were fair to everyone and goods were always available where needed; I would bring even the dragons of the wild northern land of magic under the control of organized wizardry. . . . Daimbert the Wise, they would call me, Daimbert the Just, Daimbert the God.

And the first thing that happened would be that I would have all the headaches and responsibilities of administration. The second would be that all the wizards and priests and aristocrats, as well as all the villagers and townsmen of the west, and probably even the dragons, would unite to overthrow me.

I closed my eyes, took a deep breath, then opened them again. And I had thought Warin's offer to be the Royal Wizard of a large and wealthy kingdom a temptation! Even with the Pearl, as I had always known and should always have remembered, no wizard can do more with magic than tug at the edges of the powers that had shaped the world. If this temptation to tug harder was what Kaz-alrhun had meant by unexpected and unimagined dangers, he had a point.

Dominic broke the silence at last. "This is what my father meant us to find," he said, then frowned, finding his remark somewhat inadequate. "It is indeed something wonderful and marvellous, something that makes those terms almost trite. . . . This Pearl," he continued, quoting Arnulf, "gives power to the people who hold it, so that they will always prosper, that their setbacks will be only temporary, and they will in the end find their hearts' desire. But I still don't know how my father learned it was here."

"I do," said Kaz-alrhun unexpectedly. "I told him about it."

We all turned to stare at him. "If you know the history of the Black Pearl," said the mage, "then you know that it was last seen a thousand years ago when the last of the caliphs, may God reward him, gave up both its powers and its perils by having an Ifrit hide it."

"In the Outer Sea," said King Haimeric again.

"No, although he let that story be generally known. Instead he hid it here in the Wadi Harhammi, protected by Ifrit magic. As an additional precaution, although he kept this very secret, he put the opening spell that would allow one to reach the Pearl onto a ruby ring. . . . Because the Ifriti have been controlled since the time of Solomon by the magic of his Black Pearl, not even all the Ifriti in the East together, and certainly no lesser power, could break through the combined magic of pearl and ruby to reveal its hiding place. A few true accounts were written and can still be found in the great library in Xantium, and doubtless also in the Holy City and in Bahdroc, and other accounts over the centuries hinted vaguely that there was something special in the Wadi.

"The caliph hoped to keep the Black Pearl hidden forever, even if he did hide it in a place from which he knew he could recover it again if he ever changed his mind. But he had ruled for over two hundred years and his whole region had come to depend on him personally. When he died there was no one with the power and authority to take his place. In the civil war that followed, the ruby ring was lost, its importance forgotten. When I first learned in Xantium's library that the Pearl was here, I knew I had to find that ring."

From the corner of my eye, I thought I saw Ascelin's blond head looking over the edge of the rift, but I was too absorbed in Kaz-alrhun's story to do more than glance toward him.

The mage turned to Dominic. "Tracing the ruby's movements over the past millennium took me — a certain interval. But by God's decree I came upon it at last. Fifty years ago, I met your father. You look like him; I would have recognized you when you approached my stall in the Thieves' Market even without the ruby snake ring on your finger.

"This was in the time of the emir's warlike youth. As he now controls this whole part of the east, he must have learned the secret of the Wadi, but he was in no position to uncover the Pearl himself. I was travelling in what you in the west call the eastern kingdoms — the governor of Xantium and I had had a disagreement of sorts and the climate of the city had become oppressive enough that it seemed better to leave town for a while. I thought that the combination of my magic and the force of a strong sword arm would carry us past both the emir's soldiers and the magery the emir would be able to command."

"And you gave him the ruby ring?" asked Dominic.

Kaz-alrhun's gold tooth flashed as he smiled. "That he had already found for himself, captured with a cache of other precious jewels whose origins were long forgotten. But he did not know its value until he met me. I told him the true story; I could not, of course, take the ring from him by force." I was surprised at this sudden fastidiousness in the mage, but he did not give me a chance to ask about it. "He agreed to accompany me to Bahdroc as soon as he had finished the campaign to which he was pledged. But what man wishes and God ordains often differ. The next thing I heard was that Prince Dominic was dead."

And the prince had died without daring to send open information to his family about the Black Pearl. Even his wizard, Vlad, had waited until recently to begin again his search for it, through his friend, King Warin's chancellor. This reminded me that we had not seen that king for a while. . . .

"But why," asked Dominic, "did you wait for nearly fifty years to try again for the Pearl? And why did you take the onyx ring in return for your flying horse when you knew it was not the right ring?" He still held the golden box open in his hands.

"When it became clear that I had lost that phase of the game," said the mage, "I returned to Xantium, to wait and see if Prince Dominic's mage — I never did trust him — or someone of the prince's family would make an attempt to find the Pearl. It seemed at first that time was on my side. But I am an old man now, even if I still am my city's greatest mage — fifty years was long enough to wait."

"But you still took the onyx ring from King Warin for your flying horse," Dominic persisted.

Kaz-alrhun smiled again. "When I saw the ruby on your hand in Xantium and realized that you and it were heading this way, it was, shall we say, easier to let you continue than to try to take it from you, especially once I found your father's letter on your wizard and knew for a certainty that you were making for the Wadi. The flying horse was no longer needed to draw you out of Yurt. Since I sensed that the second player had made the onyx magical, I thought I would give him a little room, see how he would play his game if he thought he had fooled me."

That was the second time he had mentioned another "player" in what he persisted in calling a game. I had to ask him about it once I had some guesses of my own. "I hope," I now said, "that we are not going to start a quarrel over who should control the Pearl's powers."

The mage rolled his pitch-black eyes at me. "Do not fear, Daimbert, that I shall do ill by one who has done well by me."

"If Solomon's Pearl will make the holder always prosper," said Dominic quietly, "I think it has enough power for all of us to share. By finding out for certain what happened to my father, by fulfilling his last wish, I have already found my heart's desire."

"In fact," I said, "I think we'll *have* to share. Don't you think that's why the caliph finally decided it was so dangerous he had to renounce it? It's not like any magic they taught us at school, but I know it has one important similarity." I paused, then gave them the condensed form of the lesson I had learned in my seconds of imagining the reign of Daimbert the Wise. "If one tried to use it jealously or with evil purpose, it would ultimately become one's destruction."

We had all been so intent on the Pearl, both with our normal senses and, for we three magic workers, with our magic, that we did not hear a step or sense a presence we should have heard and sensed.

There was suddenly a knife at Dominic's neck and a hand on the golden box. "Thank you for getting this out of the cave for me," said King Warin. "This is mine."

V

"Have you been taking tips from your bandits, Warin?" asked Dominic as the golden box was slowly taken from him. He did not stir a muscle, but his face turned dark red. "I shall add this to my bill of complaints against you once we're home again."

If we ever got home. I did not dare try a spell. If Warin took Dominic with him as a hostage, he would be able to get back to the ebony flying horse, threaten the Ifrit with the Pearl's power until the horse could fly again, and escape, leaving us to face the Ifrit and the emir's soldiers.

King Warin's hand closed around the Black Pearl as he backed slowly up the Wadi, Dominic necessarily backing with him as the edge of the king's knife pressed against his neck. "Stay where you are," he said warningly, but none of us had dared move.

"I tried to warn you to beware of him," Evrard muttered out of the corner of his mouth.

A hundred feet from us Warin lifted his left fist, the Pearl in it, and held his arm straight toward us. His face lit up with triumphant joy. From his lips came words of the Hidden Language.

It was a paralysis spell, short and awkward, with half the words mispronounced. But with the Pearl in his fist and the correct form of the words in our minds, Evrard, Kaz-alrhun, and I were frozen where we stood.

I would have gone stiff even if the spell had not worked. It was in the Hidden Language that controlled eastern as well as western magic, but its form was indubitably that of a school spell.

"You can't stop me without your wizard, Haimeric!" Warin shouted mockingly. "And your nephew's not going to be a lot of help against the Ifrit!" He gave Dominic an abrupt blow with the golden box on the back of the head, sending him sprawling on his face in the sand. Warin stood over him, the knife still in his hand. "Should I finish him now and save the Ifrit the trouble?"

Then he laughed a long and evil laugh. "But why should I waste my time with any of you? You'll never live anyway to challenge me. I shall rule all the western kingdoms, including the pitiful kingdom of Yurt, with the powers the Black Pearl will give me!" He gave Dominic a sharp kick and turned abruptly to run up the Wadi.

That is when Ascelin dropped on him.

Warin must have caught a glimpse of the prince coming over the rim of the watercourse from the corner of his eye, because he tried to whirl toward him, but it was too late. Ascelin landed on him with the full force of a thirty-foot drop. Warin's knife went flying in one direction, the Black Pearl in another.

I struggled desperately against the paralysis spell as Warin recovered from his surprise and fought back with what looked like inhuman strength. He yanked the prince from his feet and, when Ascelin rolled and recovered, Warin threw himself on top of him. He tried to hold the prince down with one arm, as with the other hand he reached out, groping closer and closer to where the Black Pearl lay in the sand. At the last moment he thrust Ascelin away from him, snatched the Pearl with both hands, and leaped back up.

Dominic, a dozen yards from them, pushed his face out of the dirt. "Don't let him get away alive!" he shouted hoarsely. "Don't let him escape with the Pearl!" In the middle of that shout, Ascelin made a dive for Warin's legs. As the king lost his balance the prince's long hunting knife slid smoothly upwards, between Warin's ribs and into his heart.

I broke the paralysis spell on me and on Kaz-alrhun. "School magic," I told him when he seemed surprised I could work any spell faster than he could. "It's easier to break than *your* spells if you know the trick." Evrard already had himself free.

Joachim's and Hugo's dark heads appeared over the rim of the Wadi, joined in a moment by Maffi and by the Ifrit's wife. "You'll have to go around to the top end of the watercourse and come down that way," Ascelin called up to them, then sat down abruptly, his breathing ragged. He pulled his knife out of Warin's body and slowly and mechanically started cleaning it, like the good hunter he was.

Dominic pulled himself shakily to his feet and went to retrieve the Black Pearl. It was spattered with Warin's blood, which he wiped off carefully on his tunic.

Kaz-alrhun stood motionless for a moment, almost as though still paralyzed. Then he shook himself and flashed his gold tooth at me again. "God gives and God takes away," he said with a shrug. It was a strange reaction, I thought, considering that he should be delighted that the Pearl was safe. But then something I did not have time to analyze began to nag at me as well.

King Haimeric sat down by Warin's head and tried to listen for his breathing, but it was quite clear that he was dead. The body began to age before our eyes. In life Warin had looked middle-aged, no older than Dominic, but as we watched in horror his iron-gray hair whitened, his cheeks wrinkled, and the veins of his hands became pronounced. Within two minutes his shriveled body looked older than King Haimeric, indeed far older.

From further down the Wadi, where we had not gone, I suddenly heard voices. I whirled toward this new threat and saw three armed men coming around a boulder toward us, two young knights and one middle-aged lord.

They stopped abruptly, seeing us. "Don't be concerned," Evrard called to them. "It's the forces of Yurt at last, come to rescue us!"

I had almost forgotten about Sir Hugo and his knights.

From up the Wadi came an abrupt cry of joy so intense it was almost pain. Young Hugo pounded past us, barely slowing down to avoid Warin's body, and threw himself into his father's arms. Sir Hugo fell flat from the force of the onrush and, for a moment, the two rolled together, laughing and shouting and crying all at once and pummeling each other.

The older man recovered first and eased himself to a sitting position. "Careful there, Hugo, I'm not as young as you are! But what's this? Who have you been fighting to get wounded like this?"

"I held off the emir's men while our party escaped," said Hugo proudly. I noticed he did not mention his fight with Ascelin.

"Then you did better than we ever did!"

Joachim came up to stand by Warin's shriveled body. "I'd better say the rites for him."

"I'm not absolutely certain," I said, "but I think he'd sold his soul to the devil."

Joachim fixed me with his enormous dark eyes. "Only God can judge him. The church's rituals are to help us all, living and dead, saved and damned, in a fallen world where all of our salvations are uncertain."

The Ifrit's wife met the two knights who had accompanied Evrard and Sir Hugo and greeted them like very old friends.

Dominic had recovered the golden box and brushed the sand off the velvet before putting the Pearl carefully back into it. He sat down next to Ascelin. "You saved the Pearl and you probably saved my life," he said. "Yurt owes you more than I know how to repay. Ask whatever you will from me."

Ascelin had been sitting with his face resting on his arms. Now he looked up, a slight smile crinkling the tanned skin around his eyes. "I thank you, Dominic, but the kingdom of Yurt has already given me more than I could ever have asked. You yourself might not be able to give me what I desire above all, but the Pearl may be able to do so. My heart's desire is to see the duchess and our daughters again before I die."

I stood to one side, listening to the faint, not quite intelligible voice of the Black Pearl. For reasons I could not define, the voice sounded different.

Joachim finished the litany for the dead and went over to Ascelin. The tall prince glanced up, then nodded without speaking. He pushed himself to his feet and walked slowly away down the Wadi with the chaplain, listening to him with his head bowed.

While they were gone, I told Evrard the highlights of our quest to the east to find him. "I'm flattered, Daimbert," he said with a grin. "So finding me was your heart's desire?"

I shook my head and smiled. "What you seek and what you find, will ofttimes be of different kind. I wouldn't go so far as to say you're my heart's desire, but I am delighted to have found you."

But even as I spoke I realized that the sense of boundless happiness, along with the Pearl's voice at the back of my brain, had altered, become less intense, or perhaps taken on a more somber hue.

Evrard looked thoughtful for a moment and I wondered if he had been briefly contemplating the triumphs of the reign of Evrard the All-Merciful. "The school's going to want the Pearl."

"I know. When I first heard the rumors it had been found, I told Zahlfast about it. He said an object that powerful and dangerous would have to be controlled by highly skilled wizards — which I presume excludes you and me. We know it has enormous power, but Zahlfast is right that if that power is going to be channeled we'll first have to find out how it works. I hope the masters of the school have the wisdom to realize how quickly it could become accursed if someone tried to appropriate all its powers to himself." Evrard met my eyes. He knew exactly what I meant.

"But it's Dominic's Pearl now," I added, looking toward where he sat by himself, fifty yards away. "Neither we nor the school can take it from him."

"I almost forgot to tell you," said Hugo from where he was sitting with his father. "The reason we came over to the watercourse after you was that the emir's men had finally gone around to the far side of the valley, where the wall's not as steep, and come down into it. They were still several miles off, but I think they're headed this way."

With two school-trained wizards and a mage, I thought, we should be able to resist — or at least avoid — armed soldiers, even without yet mastering the Pearl. I flew up to the rim of the Wadi but couldn't see them. I tried the onyx ring and saw the emir's rose garden again but not his soldiers. I came back down feeling less complacent. A warning would help, as would any reassurance that the Ifrit was not about to reappear and take our magical powers away again.

"Now that Warin's dead," asked Hugo, "who's going to rule his kingdom?"

"I don't think he had any children," I said without interest, "but he's probably got a cousin or a nephew somewhere. If not, the aristocrats of the region will elect one of their number king. A wealthy kingdom like that won't lack a king for long, once they realize Warin won't be back." I didn't like to think how close I had been to becoming the Royal Wizard of a kingdom now without a king, or what I might have had to do to protect my new lord.

"If I'm not your heart's desire," Evrard asked me, "what is?"

"Magic," I said slowly. "After all these years I think I've finally gotten passable at western magic and now I've learned a great deal of eastern magic as well. Maybe not even particular spells, but an orientation, a knowledge, that there are other ways than school ways to contact the universe's forces." I held Evrard's light blue eyes with my own. "And I know this will sound strange from someone who's been practicing magic his entire adult life, but I think I've also realized that there are important powers and abilities in this world that have nothing to do with magic."

Ascelin and Joachim came back at this point, interrupting our conversation, although neither said anything but sat down on either side of Warin's body.

The tall prince, I thought, might be the only one who

had not found his heart's desire on this quest, as well as the only one with a death on his soul. I had discovered eastern magic, Hugo his father, the elder Sir Hugo and his party had found the rescue they had long awaited, King Haimeric the blue rose, Joachim the Holy Land, and Dominic his father's unfulfilled quest for the Black Pearl. Even Kaz-alrhun had won his game by locating the Pearl at last.

Trying to understand the not quite clear and definitely darker voice of the Pearl at the edge of my mind, I thought that even my new understanding of magic might not be the "heart's desire" of the old stories, because there were still plenty of gaps and room for improvement — but then even Joachim had not found all his spiritual yearnings fulfilled in the Holy Land.

The Ifrit's huge green face appeared abruptly above us, blocking out the sky. "So I see that another one of you has died," he said conversationally. "I keep trying to remind you how easily and senselessly humans die, but you never seem to understand."

"Please help us bury him," said Evrard imperiously. I wasn't at all sure the Ifrit would continue to obey him or if Dominic would have to threaten him with the Pearl. But maybe it had become a habit. The Ifrit shrugged and nodded, then reached down a hairy arm and picked up King Warin. For a few minutes the Ifrit disappeared, then he put his head back over the head of the Wadi.

"Did you know, by the way," he said to Evrard, "that there are a whole troop of soldiers coming this way? They are only about a hundred yards off." This brought me abruptly to my feet. "Do you think they are from Yurt, or should I kill them?"

"No," said Joachim before Evrard could answer. "Let's not have any more killing."

"This is the one you found amusing, isn't it, my dear?" said the Ifrit to his wife. "Well, I won't kill them yet, anyway. But I'd better get all of you away from the soldiers. For one thing, little mage," to me, "you still haven't worked your magic on my wife."

Before she could ask what he meant, the Ifrit stretched out his hand, and the quiet air shimmered and whirled. We were caught up in a wind that swept us, and a great deal of rock and sand, into the air. I caught a brief glimpse of startled faces beneath white turbans, then somersaulting and gasping we were carried across the valley and set down in the oasis where we had first met the Ifrit's wife.

The air around us immediately became still and hot as we tried to recover our equilibrium. Kaz-alrhun's flying carpet and ebony flying horse waited under the palm trees. Dominic still held the gold box with the Pearl inside, and the enameled cabinet he had found in the cave rested at an angle by his foot.

Maffi had spoken very little, but he suddenly took the Ifrit around the ankle. "I know what I want to be," he called up. "I want to become an Ifrit."

The Ifrit picked him up, a smile splitting his bristly face. "And what makes you think you could become one?"

"I wanted to apprentice myself to a mage," said Maffi, matching the Ifrit's grin with one of his own, "or even a western wizard, though none of them seemed to want me. But I realize now that to apprentice myself to you would be much more rewarding."

The Ifrit put him back down with a chuckle. "Ifriti are very old," he said, "and you are very young. Come talk to me again when you have lived longer than Solomon."

Maffi picked himself up and dusted himself off. "I never said you could not be my apprentice, boy," said Kaz-alrhun. "But you must realize it is possible to be too young for a mage, as well as too young for an Ifrit. The experiences of this trip may teach you something, however. Ask me again when we have returned to Xantium."

The boy's assumed dignity vanished at once and he turned to the mage with shining eyes. "I already know one spell," he said eagerly, "one out of western school magic. Let me show you — would you like some illusory color on your chest? I figured out on my own how to do both pink and purple at the same time. Will this make magery easier?"

So even Maffi, I thought, might have his heart's desire.

"What's this spell the wizard is supposed to put on me?" demanded the Ifrit's wife.

I had promised this and now had to carry it out. "I can slow down natural aging," I told her. "It won't make you any younger than you now are, but it will keep you youthful much longer. The Ifrit couldn't bear the idea of his beautiful wife becoming old."

She whirled away from me and smacked the Ifrit on the foot. "So just because I'm your wife, you think you can make my decisions for me?" The Ifrit frowned, puzzled, but she didn't give him time to answer. "I like being human! I don't want to live for centuries like some mage! And what makes you think I'd want to live longer than normal if I had to spend all the extra time with you?"

"But I thought you liked me, my dear," the Ifrit protested in a small voice — or what would have been a small voice in anything but such a large being.

She relented and smiled up at him, her hands on her hips. "Of course I like you. I'm sorry I scolded. But don't make arrangements about me without consulting me!"

The Ifrit nodded. "But now that I've consulted you — "

She laughed. "Thanks, but no thanks. I don't need anyone's spells but yours, my dear."

Pleased, the Ifrit picked her up and planted a kiss on top of her head that left her wiping saliva off her hair.

"All of you probably want some food," said the Ifrit, frowning and trying to count us. "How many of you are there, thirteen? It's hard to keep track of such little beings." I myself counted and, with Sir Hugo's party, our party from Yurt, plus Kaz-alrhun, Maffi, and the Ifrit's wife, got the same answer. "Well, get the fires started, my dear, and I'll bring you a few more of the emir's sheep."

As the desert evening came on, cooling the clear air, I licked meat juices from my lips and looked across a valley that now had no sign of the emir's soldiers in it. The Ifrit and his wife sat off to one side, apparently trading funny stories with each other, but the rest of us were gathered around the dying embers of the cooking fires.

"I guess all there is to do now is to get safely home," said Hugo. He and his father sat together, their shoulders touching. "It's strange because the whole trip was painful and dangerous and frustrating, but now that it's almost over I find myself wishing we could go on forever."

I pictured the original six of us as we had set out in early spring, all the equipment which was now in the hands of the emir's soldiers carefully packed on our horses, when our worst danger was the lord of the red sandstone castle and when I had not yet discovered school magic in the spells of an evil king. I agreed with Hugo; I wished our trip was not ending but would continue forever.

But the thought of Yurt and the king's garden, where he would soon be planting his new rose, was also abruptly sweet. The forested hills of Yurt would be turning yellow and red; the air would have the tang of fresh apples.

"It's going to be a long trip, even with a flying carpet," commented Ascelin.

"Do you think you can get all of us onto your carpet?" Dominic asked Kaz-alrhun. "With it we'll be able to cross the desert even without our horses and supplies. Let's stop at that oasis, however, and see if my stallion is still where the boy left him! If we leave the two of you in Xantium, we can then fly on to the western kingdoms. I'm certain our wizard will be able to work the carpet's spells."

"If the carpet can get us over the mountains," continued Ascelin, "we can go straight from Xantium to the great City and drop off Sir Hugo's party there and then the rest of us can continue on to Yurt. We'll send the carpet back to you once we're home."

The chaplain nodded slowly. "Yes, it will make more sense for me to come to Yurt with all of you at first. From there I'll go on to the cathedral city of Caelrhon after a few days."

I turned my head to stare at him. Joachim was wrapped up in his desert robes and his dark eyes were shadowed, but he must have caught my expression. "Didn't I tell you, Daimbert, before we left Yurt this spring? The bishop agreed that I should indeed make the pilgrimage to the Holy Land with the king. But as soon as we're back, I shall have to resign as Royal Chaplain and go to join the priests of the cathedral chapter."

Then the home we were returning to would not be the home we had left. The Yurt I had always known was a kingdom with Joachim as Royal Chaplain. I reminded myself that I, too, was different, both in my knowledge and in my magic. It didn't help.

"So will you allow us to borrow your carpet," Dominic said to Kaz-alrhun, "to get ourselves and King Solomon's Pearl back to Yurt?"

Kaz-alrhun rolled his black eyes at him. "Are you certain it is as easy as that?"

"Why, are you worried about how we'll share the Pearl's powers if you stay in Xantium and we take it to Yurt?" Dominic frowned and looked toward the king. "I'm sure if you wanted to come to Yurt with us, then . . ."

Kaz-alrhun shook his head and looked briefly amused. "I mean that it will not be as easy to take the Pearl home with you as you seem to think. It is the way of God to raise up nothing of this world, except He cast it down again. For a while yet, the Pearl may continue to bring you your heart's desire. But if you take it to Yurt now, spattered with the blood of a man killed for it, it will soon cease to make you prosper, and instead will put you under a curse that will blight your entire kingdom."

VI

We met each other's eyes in dismay. "Then take it to Xantium," said Dominic.

Kaz-alrhun shook his head, still looking amused. "I want Xantium to continue to prosper and I am already the greatest mage the city has ever known, even without the Pearl. It would have been an even greater triumph to be able to learn how to control its magic, but I did find it. I deliberately did not tell you to search the Wadi, did not touch the ruby with its opening spells, and stood back when you took the Pearl out of the cave. I knew its potential perils, and its curse should not touch me. I will not take it."

"But what was I supposed to do?" Ascelin burst out. "Should I have stood by while King Warin tried to kill Dominic?"

"And should I have just told Ascelin to let Warin go, so that he would be accursed instead?" demanded Dominic.

"There was, after all, an excellent reason," Kaz-alrhun replied, "why the caliph renounced the Pearl and all its powers a thousand years ago."

Dominic took a deep breath and placed the Black Pearl on the sand in front of him. The smooth dark surface winked in the firelight. "Then I shall renounce it also," he said after only the shortest pause. "Let it remain here with the Ifrit or back within the Wadi where we found it."

We were all silent for a moment, then Joachim said quietly, "In this fallen world, *no* man, even the wisest, could consistently do good if he could wield this much power. To lock it away may have been the wisest decision Solomon ever made."

Dominic shrugged, as though trying to reestablish normalcy. "If there isn't enough room on your carpet for all of us when we leave here, Mage, maybe we could put the overflow on your flying horse. Or *is* it your horse anymore?" he added with a forced chuckle. "Someone certainly has bought it from you by now, maybe the chaplain's sister-in-law."

We waited for Kaz-alrhun to answer, then I realized he was slowly shaking its head. "It is much too late to renounce the Black Pearl that easily. It was taken from its hiding place by a prince of Yurt. After Warin stole it a duke of Yurt killed him to recover it. Its curse will affect Yurt whether it is with you or back in the Wadi."

For a moment we sat in silence, trying to imagine a curse on Yurt: the green hills becoming parched, fires ravaging the fields, blizzards killing the livestock, the bandits who almost never bothered us appearing on the highways, fatal disease spreading and infecting the children, both the children of villagers and the children of kings and princes.

"There has to be a way," said Dominic abruptly. "This is a flawless pearl, beyond all price. It was a gift to King Solomon from the Queen of Sheba, a gift to be treasured. If, as the mage says, blood and evil desires can pervert its magic, then there has to be a way to purify it again."

I stared at the Pearl until its winking in the firelight set up a pattern within my brain, a pattern that suddenly made sense of that voice I had not quite been able to hear.

"There is a way," I heard myself saying. "One of us will have to die."

Kaz-alrhun's eyes met mine. "You surprise me, Daimbert. I did not think a western wizard would understand that."

"The Pearl itself told me."

This startled him again.

"The Pearl must again be hidden," I said as though someone else were speaking. "Inside its golden box, inside the locked cabinet, sunk in a derelict ship in the deepest rift of the Outer Sea. The Ifrit can take it there and with it shall go someone of Yurt. Then the curse will be lifted. Yurt will not prosper so thoroughly as it would have, by the Pearl's grace, if no one had been killed, but the free giving of a life will break the curse brought about by violent death. And if the Pearl is found again, in five years or five thousand, the finder may, if he keeps free of evil, find his heart's desire."

My voice rose and I spoke now for myself, not the Pearl. "The Ifrit says that all humans die senselessly and even you, Kaz-alrhun, sometimes speak as though you feel we have no ultimate control over our fate, that life has no more meaning than a game. But living and dying *can* have a purpose. King Warin, his soul given to evil, sought the Pearl even before we knew that was what we sought. He and his bandits almost killed several of us to bring the Pearl's powers into his own hands. He's dead now, gone to the supernatural realm where his soul will be surely judged. But even in the natural world, good can be brought out of evil and our heart's desire need not turn to a curse. A life that Warin couldn't take by force will be freely given and thus repair the evil he left behind."

I added, before I could realize what I was saying, "I myself shall accompany the Pearl to the deepest rift of the sea."

There were immediate protests and questions in eleven other voices. I put my hand over my eyes and wondered if I meant it and was afraid that I did.

Ascelin stood up, somewhat stiffly, and faced everyone else down. "I killed Warin and brought the curse on all of you." He met the chaplain's eyes and gave a humorless smile. "The wizard is right that that evil must be repaired and I shall give myself to do so. Let's get that Ifrit over here and do it *now*. When you're home again, tell Diana I always loved her."

This brought immediately renewed protests. The Ifrit heard our raised voices and came over. Dominic was trying to outshout Ascelin, telling him, "You only killed him because I told you to!" I kept silent, still thinking it ought to be me and unable to say so a second time.

"So you're competing for which one of you will die?" the Ifrit asked me. "This is even more amusing than having those two little warriors fight each other."

The Ifrit's wife came over, too, graceful and bare-breasted. The Ifrit perched her on his knee while continuing to follow the discussion as though watching a play.

"Ifrit," I said suddenly, "this is really a private conversation. I don't think you should be listening. I know you find it amusing," I went on quickly before he could object, "so I'll offer you a deal. Very shortly, one of us is going to accompany the Black Pearl to the deepest rift in the Outer Sea." I took a deep breath, thinking it was still most likely to be me, and pushed ahead. "If you'll agree to take him there, then you can listen while we decide which one of us it will be."

The Ifrit nodded but then frowned. "The last deal you made with me, you never upheld your end. I know my wife didn't want your spells, but . . ." His grumbling trailed off in his interest in the scene before him.

King Haimeric had risen to his feet, the only person who could have made everyone else fall silent. "I know you're not my liege man, Ascelin," he said, "so I cannot order you against your will. But do not offer yourself to save Yurt. I thank you deeply, I know what you're offering and I cannot let you do it. The penance for killing Warin to save another's life cannot be the loss of your own life."

Ascelin, who towered over him, tried fairly convincingly to shake his head, but the king was not finished. "Of all of us, you're the only one who has not found his heart's desire on this trip because, for you, the goal was the quest itself, to travel, find adventure and come safely home again. And besides," with a smile, "I wouldn't want to have to explain to the duchess that I'd let you die. No, Ascelin, if Yurt is to be freed from a curse, it must be freed by the king of Yurt."

Dominic jumped up again. "Or the royal prince!"

King Haimeric reached up to put his hand on his nephew's shoulder. "I'm an old man anyway. Even if we manage to find a way to escape from this valley and make our way thousands of miles home again, I will not live very much longer." Yurt seemed to be changing every moment before my eyes, even if we did somehow reach it again. "Why do I need to live any more? I've gotten everything I ever wanted. I didn't tell the queen when we left, but I never expected to see Yurt again."

Dominic tried to interrupt, but the king waved him to silence. "Would not sacrificing myself for my kingdom make a fitting end for a delightful life?" finished King Haimeric, smiling at his stunned audience.

"Sire," said Dominic again, "listen to me." We all listened. Ascelin took a step back, looking both miserable and relieved. "I agree, sire," said Dominic, very seriously, "that Yurt must be saved by a member of the royal family. And I know you're growing old. But you have a wife who loves you and a little son who should be guided by you. I have *nothing*.

"No, let me speak!" as the king started to interrupt. "I've spent my entire life preparing and waiting for a future that never came. You may now have everything you've ever wanted, but I've never had *anything* of my own. I have no wife, no child, and no crown. I had to find what my father wanted us to find, but I've done that now. And I've done it wrong: in finding the Pearl, I put a curse on the kindom I love. This is my last chance to do something truly significant. If you won't let me die to take the curse from Yurt, to give it whatever prosperity the Pearl may still grant, then my life will finally end with no meaning at all."

There was a few seconds' silence, broken by the sound of the chaplain clearing his throat.

"And don't try to tell me how sinful suicide is, Father!" Dominic cried. "This isn't suicide because I'm not throwing away God's gift of life from despair. Doesn't it say in the Bible, 'Greater love hath no man than this, that a man lay down his life for his friends' ? I would have cheerfully died for Yurt in battle and this is no different. Now is my only chance to get the rest of you home alive, to a kingdom that will always prosper."

He looked from side to side in the twilight, appearing absolutely determined, and I knew we could not resist him in this.

But it didn't keep us from trying. All of us, from the king to Maffi, immediately began talking and shouting at once. Dominic ignored everyone except for Joachim, but he didn't seem to agree with him, either.

The Ifrit spoke beside me. "This is getting boring again," he said, absently stroking his wife's hair. "But I have an idea how to liven it up." He stretched out a hand. "I can get those soldiers back again."

The air shimmered all the way to the sky. A quarter mile away, uneasy but grim-faced, were the emir's soldiers, their curved swords in their hands. In the dim and dusky landscape, the steel of their weapons and their white turbans seemed almost to glow.

"Evrard!" I said to him urgently and directly, mind to mind. "We need a magic shield!" But Evrard didn't seem to know the spells I needed, and the shield I desperately tried to create just wasn't working.

Dominic did not give me any further chance to put one together. "Ifrit!" he shouted, slamming the Pearl into its gold box and throwing it inside the cabinet. "Lift me up! The Black Pearl can make do without an amphora this time. It and I are headed for the Outer Sea!" The cabinet's lock clicked shut.

But when he hoisted it to his shoulder and sprinted toward the Ifrit, Ascelin tackled him around the legs. They rolled together for a moment, grunting and trying to pin the other, while the Ifrit watched in interest.

Normally Ascelin, a foot taller than Dominic and muscled from a long journey on foot, would have been able to outwrestle him easily. But he had in close succession fought Hugo, carried King Haimeric down the vertical side of the valley, and killed King Warin.

Dominic jerked away just before Ascelin pinned him to the ground and got an arm around the tall prince's neck long enough to squeeze the breath out of him. Then he jumped up and scrambled onto the hand the Ifrit held out for him.

"I am ready to obey, Master," said the Ifrit in his deep bellow.

That stopped all of us. "Am I your master?" asked Dominic, held at the Ifrit's face level, trying to maintain his balance with one arm and clutching the cabinet with the other.

"You control the Black Pearl and the Pearl controls all Ifriti. If you command me, I must obey you."

"Then stop those soldiers!"

The Ifrit bared his yellow teeth in a grin. He reached out his other hand, the one not holding Dominic, and fire shot from his fingers. The emir's soldiers, a hundred yards away, were suddenly blocked by a wall of flames that stretched the entire width of the valley.

"Is that what you wanted, Master?" asked the Ifrit.

"Exactly what I wanted," said Dominic. This was, I thought appreciatively, *much* better than Prince Vlad's wall of fire. The soldiers scattered backwards in panic.

"And get all my friends' horses and supplies again!" commanded Dominic.

The Ifrit sprang upwards into the air and disappeared, Dominic still in his fist. The soldiers, seeing them go, shouted and tried to shoot at them, but the arrows fell harmlessly.

"Is he gone?" said King Haimeric into the abrupt silence.

"He is not gone yet," said Kaz-alrhun gravely.

First to appear again was a tumbling whirlwind of

sand, which settled down to reveal our confused horses, their packs still on their backs. And five minutes later the Ifrit was back with Dominic and, this time, Whirlwind.

The chestnut stallion landed unceremoniously on his side. But he scrambled to his feet at once and reared and kicked wildly until Dominic, still sitting in the Ifrit's hand, reached down to grab a handful of mane and slap his neck. "Easy, boy, easy," he said as though the horse could understand. "They'll take you home." The stallion stopped kicking and seemed to be listening. "Let someone else ride you besides me, all right?"

"Don't forget that horse and I saved your life!" piped up Maffi.

Dominic frowned. "If I asked, Ifrit, could you turn this boy into a worm?"

"Or anything you liked, Master!"

Maffi sprang behind Kaz-alrhun's legs, but Dominic showed no sign of requesting an immediate transformation. His face was sober and he seemed all at once to have lost the momentum that carried him out of Ascelin's grip.

"I realize something, little warrior," the Ifrit said to him. "You and this western mage say you want to go to the Outer Sea, but while we're gone all these people from Yurt are going to try to escape. I promised the first mage who freed me that I wouldn't let them."

"Then don't go!" cried the king.

"Wizard?" said Dominic to me.

I glanced toward the wall of fire, wondering how long it would hold the emir's soldiers before someone volunteered to charge through it. I didn't want to answer Dominic because I felt that in doing so I was sending him to his death. But it was, I reminded myself grimly, his decision.

"Listen, Ifrit!" I said. "The power of King Solomon's Pearl surpasses all other authority over an Ifrit — including wishes the Ifrit himself may have granted.

Additionally, the mage to whom you promised to guard the Wadi betrayed you, by arranging for you to be imprisoned in your bottle again. His wishes have lost all validity." I left out the emir, not wanting to confuse the issue further — besides, his wishes still had validity. "Remember, you promised to keep the people from Yurt safe — their safety may, in fact, lie in escape!"

The Ifrit's dark green brow furrowed as he tried to work it out, but he nodded slowly, seeming to agree.

I expected Dominic to give the order for final departure at once, but he too frowned again, looking down at us from twenty feet in the air. "You seem to know all about this Pearl, Mage," he called to Kaz-alrhun. "What's the limit on what I can make the Ifrit do?"

"There is very little limit," said Kaz-alrhun, "on the powers of a man who commands the Black Pearl and has an Ifrit to obey him. Even without a working knowledge of magic, you could do much. But — " He paused for a long moment. "But you could do nothing to counter the Pearl's curse when it began to work."

Dominic bit his lip. "And the first workings of the curse would be that I would be tempted to make myself King Dominic of Yurt, of all the western kingdoms, of the world, and would still think I was acting for good." He wrapped an arm firmly around the Ifrit's thumb. "Good-bye, sire! To the Outer Sea, Ifrit! We're going *now*!

"Don't worry!" Dominic added in a joyous shout as the Ifrit sprang up into the air. "You'll be safe from the soldiers because the curse is being ended before it has a chance to work!" He waved and the red of his ruby ring flashed in the evening light. "I have found the purpose of my life at the end of it!"

When the Ifrit rose from the valley floor, the wall of flames disappeared and the emir's soldiers almost immediately regrouped.

"Do not concern yourself with that!" said Kaz-alrhun as I desperately started over again creating some sort of magical shield. "Everyone, onto the carpet!" He had increased its size.

King Haimeric didn't want to go. "He was still so young," he said, the tears streaming unchecked down his cheeks as he stared into the empty sky. "My own life is nearly at an end, but there was so much Dominic could still have done! Now we won't even be able to visit his grave."

"He fulfilled both his life and his quest," I said, helping the king onto the carpet. I had to pick up and give him his carefully wrapped rootstock or he would have left it behind.

"I never had a chance!" cried Hugo in genuine distress, sounding more like a boy than a blooded warrior. "I never asked him to forgive me for putting ribbons in his stallion's mane!"

"Come!" called Kaz-alrhun impatiently. "In pouring forth tears, there is little profit."

The Ifrit's wife wouldn't go. "I'll be fine," she said. "The soldiers won't find my oasis." She thumbed the rings on her necklace and smiled at Sir Hugo's party and, somewhat less jauntily, at Joachim, as she stepped back under the palms.

We lifted into the evening sky on the carpet, piled as closely together in the center as we could, only twenty yards ahead of the turbaned soldiers. A few arrows hit the bottom of the carpet but bounced away harmlessly. I leaned cautiously over the edge and watched the Ifrit's oasis wink away into safety, to another level of reality or to non-existence.

EPILOGUE

Fountains sparkled in the glow of the magic lamps in the courtyard of Kaz-alrhun's house in Xantium. The evening air was still warm and, even here in the middle of the city, little stray breezes found us, scented with the tang of the sea and with desert sage. Automata, simple self-propelled serving carts on wheels, rattled over the flagstones to bring us a variety of hot and cold dishes.

"So you do not grow eggplants in Yurt?" the mage asked King Haimeric. "Take some from Xantium for your queen. The market will also have every kind of cotton fabric you might desire. And certainly buy coffee beans as well, but remember you will first have to grind them to a sandy consistency to brew the beverage." When the king did not seem as pleased at this suggestion as Kaz-alrhun apparently expected him to be, he added, "You can buy all the presents for your queen in the government-regulated market if you prefer, rather than the Thieves' Market."

The king tried to smile. "She'll be happy with anything I bring her, but none of it will make up for coming home without Dominic."

The mage laughed, startling one of his automata, though it was able to recover without dumping its load of spiced lamb. "Is that it?" he asked, looking around the table at the rest of us. "Is this the reason you have all had long faces since we left the Wadi?" None of us answered. "I would expect at least you, Daimbert, to know better."

"We shouldn't have let him do it," said Ascelin.

"I would not say you 'let' him do it," replied the

mage with a chuckle. "If so, what do you do when you do *not* wish someone to go? I saw you try to hold him back. Or do you regret not wrestling the Ifrit as well? Your Prince Dominic played his game brilliantly at the end. He lifted the Pearl's curse and sent the rest of you home safely on my flying carpet."

"We have just enough money left to book sea passage from here back to the western kingdoms," said the king. "Whirlwind should be able to carry Ascelin for the rest of our trip, so we'll make good time."

"Nonsense," replied the mage. "I already told you I would let your wizard borrow my carpet. It is late in the season for as long a journey as you still have before you, especially for an old man. And you know you shall need to plant your rootstock very soon if you wish to grow a blue rose yourself."

When King Haimeric did not look cheered by this thought either, the mage leaned back and spread out his hands on the table. "I spent much of my career searching for King Solomon's Pearl, first trying to find the secret of its location and then attempting to maneuver others into uncovering it in a way that would not bring its potential curse down on me. I found it at last, but I lost it almost in the moment of finding, and never even held it in my hands. Life is a game and you play as well as you can as long as you can, yet you must be prepared not to win every time. Dominic fared much better on his quest than I on mine and yet you do not see me bewailing my fate."

None of us tried to answer. I was seated next to Joachim, who paid no attention to the rest of us or even to his dinner, as though his mind was already on his duties in the cathedral.

When the automata began clearing the plates from the lamb course, Kaz-alrhun rose to his feet. "Come with me, Daimbert. I want to show you something."

I followed him up narrow, dark stairs to a balcony at the very top of the house. The last light was fading from the sky above us. We looked out across the city where fairy lights gleamed and out across Xantium harbor. Voices and snatches of song rose faintly toward us.

The mage leaned on the railing for a moment, then shifted his massive bulk to look at me in the dim light. "This is what I wanted to show you," he said, "Xantium, my city, where there are many religions and many conflicting forms of political organization, but only one supreme mage, myself. Are you not the supreme wizard in your own kingdom of Yurt?"

"I'm the only one," I said. I wasn't sure what point the mage was trying to make, but if he was saying that it was good to have one's own home even without the Pearl, well, the Pearl had never been my goal anyway.

"I want to ask you something," I said. "During the long flight here I was trying to make sense of what happened. Was it indeed you who started the rumors that King Solomon's Pearl had been found again?"

"That indeed was I," he said, "as you know well. When I decided to try again for the Pearl, I hoped that widespread — though false — stories of its discovery would bring you to the East if you ever planned to seek it yourselves. But I could not be sure what, if anything, the elder Prince Dominic had told you in Yurt of his quest. It had after all been fifty years since his death. It was even possible, I thought, that you knew neither the ruby ring's powers nor of the very existence of the Black Pearl. So while broadcasting the general rumors of the Pearl, I also arranged for a separate rumor, one that might bring the ruby ring to me even if those of Yurt knew not its powers.

"I made sure that two separate stories followed the trade routes to your western kingdoms, separate because I did not wish that anyone should realize I was the author of both. The second was sent very secretly, that my ebony horse was on sale in exchange for a magical ring from Yurt. This news I sent only to a few, those whom I already knew were sometimes unscrupulous."

That, I thought, certainly described Arnulf and Warin. "One of them, I hoped, would bring the ruby ring to me in Xantium without necessarily knowing its true value."

He cocked his head at me. "When you first approached my stall in the Thieves' Market, flaunting the ruby ring on your prince's finger but attempting an elaborate charade of buying my horse with some other ring from Yurt, I realized you knew full well that I was the author of both rumors, and that in mocking me you sought to establish yourself as a worthy opponent."

If he had thought me a worthy opponent, I didn't plan to tell him how little I had understood when we first reached Xantium.

"I would also ask *you* something, Daimbert," he continued. "Ever since I renewed my search for the Black Pearl, I have sensed another player in the game, but I have never been able to see him. He is a wizard or mage, of a certainty, but he has kept himself well back from events, as though knowing the danger of the Pearl's curse, and as though playing a long-term game where he felt no urgency to win at once. At first I thought it had to be you."

"Not me," I said, startled. "I knew nothing of the Pearl until this year."

"I realized it was not you when I met you, unless you had erected a highly skillful façade." I was afraid this wasn't a compliment.

"He and I seemed to be working in parallel," the mage continued. "He traced the ruby ring from the caliph's court as I had fifty years ago and he found the trail less thoroughly cold than it had been for me because of my own earlier search. Like me, he initially reached a dead end at the elder Prince Dominic's tomb. And like me, when he finally learned the ring was in Yurt, he knew better, because of the threat of the curse, than to use violence to obtain it."

"Or he recalled," I said in a low voice, "the oaths all

western wizards take on magic itself, to help and not injure mankind. It was Dominic's ring. Another western wizard couldn't have taken it from him by force any more than I could." It was now full night and the mage was only a silhouette against the slightly lighter sky.

"Do you know then who this wizard might be?"

I shook my head, reluctant to voice my suspicions, although I didn't think he could see the gesture.

"Have you turned your thoughts, for example, to who might have freed the Ifrit from his bottle in the first place?"

I was silent for several moments before answering. Down in the harbor a ship was coming in, lamps hung from its mast and along the rails.

"I have thought," I said at last, "that the 'mage' who the Ifrit said originally freed him must have been Elerius, a western wizard, the best wizard the school has ever produced. The chief reason I think so is that King Warin was his employer, and Warin seemed remarkably well informed about the East. I also think it must have been Elerius who appeared, in disguise, to Sir Hugo's party in the Holy City, urging them to go the Wadi. The only two people from whom I have heard the highly unlikely story of Noah's Ark being found are Evrard, who said a 'traveler' told it to them at the same time as he sold them the Ifrit's bottle, and Elerius, who said he thought they must have heard such a story."

"Why would this wizard have freed an Ifrit?" When the mage shifted, the balcony made somewhat alarming creaking sounds, but it held firm under our weight.

"I think he freed the Ifrit originally in the hope of using him to break through the Pearl's magical defenses, and when he discovered that wouldn't work, he reserved the two wishes he had earned until he might need them for something else."

"An excellent strategy," said Kaz-alrhun approvingly. "Do not waste anything; if a move does not profit when you take it, reserve it until it may."

"Last year," I said, "he used his first wish to order the Ifrit to guard the Wadi against anyone from Yurt. But he may have outmaneuvered himself in giving Evrard the Ifrit's bottle." Some of this I was still working out as I spoke. "It was an excellent ploy. He had the Ifrit waiting to capture people from Yurt, then sent Sir Hugo's party to the emir with a bottle that would most certainly gain them admittance to his presence, as well as a request to guide them to the Wadi that would result in their being imprisoned — where they would serve as bait for those of us from Yurt. By the way, I expect he told them specifically to eat the emir's salt before asking about the Wadi because he intended to keep them alive." Unlike you, I thought, who didn't care. "But because Evrard met the Ifrit *before* they reached Bahdroc and was able to trick him temporarily back into his bottle, Elerius's link with the Ifrit was broken."

"In any game," said Kaz-alrhun, "one should prepare for *all* contingencies, even the most unexpected. Do you think, then, that Elerius is also the wizard who made the onyx ring? He must have persuaded Arnulf and King Warin it would do to buy my horse — though he knew well it would not — with the intention of making me reveal my hand, just as I played along with King Warin in the hope of making your Elerius reveal *his* hand."

"He guessed your plans just as you sensed his," I said in agreement, "and wanted to precipitate them. I've wondered for a long time what payment Arnulf could have offered him in return for making a substitute 'magic ring from Yurt,' and I realize now that it was to be informed when we reached Arnulf's house. Arnulf said something about the school checking up on us, which I should have realized was highly unlikely — it could only have been Elerius. And then, at Elerius's urging, Arnulf directed us along the road to the mountain passes that went through Warin's kingdom. In case Arnulf couldn't persuade us to bring the onyx ring to you in Xantium,

Elerius wanted to be sure Warin had it instead."

"A fine strategist, your Elerius. He knows the most subtle and effective form of maneuver is to allow others to think they are acting in their own self-interest."

"He is not 'my' Elerius," I replied, mostly under my breath. I thought, but did not like to say, that he seemed willing to use even the self-interest of a man who had given himself to the powers of darkness — to the point of teaching him a little school magic. He had, also, almost certainly been in contact with Warin's chancellor's friend, Prince Vlad, who was now doubtless absorbed in rebuilding his body with the magic of blood and bone. "The most discouraging aspect of it is, Elerius surely thought of himself as acting from the purest of motives."

"And he is the best of your school-trained wizards," said Kaz-alrhun in satisfaction. "A worthy opponent, then. When both he and I directed you toward the Wadi, both of us even using your friends as bait, you never had a choice. Was he trying to obtain the Black Pearl for himself or so that your school could use its powers?"

"I don't know," I said slowly. "But I suspect he never hinted to the school about any of his plans, intending to keep them entirely secret unless he succeeded."

"If a western wizard could resist boasting even about mastering an Ifrit," said Kaz-alrhun, "then he must indeed keep his own counsel."

"If he wanted the Pearl for the school, he would have had to betray his employer, who certainly wanted it for himself." But Elerius had left Warin's kingdom. *Had* he intended to get the Black Pearl for his own use, telling Warin just enough about it to send the king on the hunt for it, shielding himself from the Pearl's curse but knowing he could always obtain it from Warin later — or obtain it after the king died of whatever curse he was bound to bring down on himself?

"Once your school learns what has happened," commented Kaz-alrhun, "they may not be pleased with you, Daimbert, for sinking the Pearl beyond recovery in the Outer Sea."

I had thought about that at some length. Evrard and I would have to make sure our stories matched as we tried to explain delicately to Zahlfast what had happened to the most powerful manmade object out of the old magic.

"I'll have to tell the school about the Pearl," I said, "but I don't intend bringing any accusations against Elerius. I have no proof of any of this, only guesses, and if he denied it they'd certainly believe the best graduate they ever had rather than me."

"I would say he has maneuvered you as well," said the mage thoughtfully. "Even if you did wish to accuse him, what accusations could you bring? It comes to mind, Daimbert, that he may at some point seek to use your abilities — or even seek your friendship. You will need to sharpen your own strategies for when you and he meet again in the future."

"And had *you* prepared all your strategies," I asked, "for the Pearl being cursed almost as soon as we found it and for it now lying at the bottom of the Outer Sea?"

A low chuckle came out of the darkness. "You have outmaneuvered both the East's greatest mage and your own western school's best graduate. Find satisfaction in this! It seems to me, Daimbert, that you have played the game better than any of us."

THE END

BUILDING A NEW FANTASY TRADITION

The Unlikely Ones by Mary Brown
Anne McCaffrey raved over *The Unlikely Ones*: "What a splendid, unusual and intriguing fantasy quest! You've got a winner here. . . ." Marion Zimmer Bradley called it "Really wonderful . . . I shall read and re-read this one." A traditional quest fantasy with quite an unconventional twist, we think you'll like it just as much as Anne McCaffrey and Marion Zimmer Bradley did.

Knight of Ghosts and Shadows
by Mercedes Lackey & Ellen Guon
Elves in L.A.? It would explain a lot, wouldn't it? In fact, half a millennium ago, when the elves were driven from Europe they came to—where else? —Southern California. Happy at first, they fell on hard times after one of their number tried to force the rest to be his vassals. Now it's up to one poor human to save them if he can. A knight in shining armor he's not, but he's one hell of a bard!

The Interior Life by Katherine Blake
Sue had three kids, one husband, a lovely home and a boring life. Sometimes, she just wanted to escape, to get out of her mundane world and *live* a little. So she did. And discovered that an active fantasy life can be a very dangerous thing—and very real. . . . Poul Anderson thought *The Interior Life* was "a breath of fresh air, bearing originality, exciting narrative, vividly realized characters—everything we have been waiting for for too long."

The Shadow Gate by Margaret Ball
The only good elf is a dead elf—or so the militant order of Durandine monks thought. And they planned on making sure that all the elves in their world (where an elvish Eleanor of Aquitaine ruled in Southern France) were very, very good. The elves of Three Realms have one last spell to bring help . . . and received it: in the form of the staff of the New Age Psychic Research Center of Austin, Texas. . . .

way of formal training. So one night she goes up to play for the Ghost of Skull Hill. She'll either fiddle till dawn to prove her skill as a bard—or die trying. . . .

Paksenarrion, a simple sheepfarmer's daughter, yearns for a life of adventure and glory, such as the heroes in songs and story. At age seventeen she runs away from home to join a mercenary company, and begins her epic life . . .

ELIZABETH MOON

"This is the first work of high heroic fantasy I've seen, that has taken the work of Tolkien, assimilated it totally and deeply and absolutely, and produced something altogether new and yet incontestably based on the master. . . . This is the real thing. Worldbuilding in the grand tradition, background thought out to the last detail, by someone who knows absolutely whereof she speaks. . . . Her military knowledge is impressive, her picture of life in a mercenary company most convincing."—**Judith Tarr**

About the author: Elizabeth Moon joined the U.S. Marine Corps in 1968 and completed both Officers Candidate School and Basic School, reaching the rank of 1st Lieutenant during active duty. Her background in military training and discipline imbue The Deed of Paksenarrion *with a gritty realism that is all too rare in most current fantasy.*